Paul Mendelson has written for the theatre and television and is the author of eleven non-fiction titles concerning mind-sports such as bridge and poker, as well as being a crime novelist whose first novel, *The First Rule of Survival*, was short-listed for the CWA Golden Dagger Crime Novel of the Year in 2014. His second novel, *The Serpentine Road*, was long-listed for the same prize in 2015. Both have been translated into several languages.

Also by Paul Mendelson

The History of Blood
The Serpentine Road
The First Rule of Survival

PAUL MENDELSON

APOSTLE LODGE

Constable • London

CONSTABLE

First published in Great Britain in 2017 by Constable

This paperback edition published in Great Britain in 2018 by Constable

Copyright © Paul Mendelson, 2017

1 3 5 7 9 10 8 6 4 2

The moral right of the author has been asserted.

A CIP catalogue record for this book
is available from the British Library.

ISBN: 978-1-47212-187-5

Typeset in Bembo by Photoprint, Torquay
Printed and bound in Great Britain by
CPI Group (UK) Ltd, Croydon CR0 4YY

Papers used by Constable are from well-managed forests and other
responsible sources.

Constable
An imprint of
Little, Brown Book Group
Carmelite House
50 Victoria Embankment
London EC4Y 0DZ

An Hachette UK Company
www.hachette.co.uk

www.littlebrown.co.uk

PROLOGUE

She descends the steep Bo Kaap cobbled street cautiously, glancing to her left between terraced cottages at the sparkling silver water beyond the glass skyscrapers, dazzled by the intensity of the light. She pauses in a pool of shade, pushes her veil a little forward so that it is low over her eyebrows, wishes that she had water. Even now, before nine in the morning, the heat is settling heavily in the City Bowl, buildings and pavements still exuding warmth from months of unrelenting, unprecedented heat. Even the wind, the theoretically cooling Cape Doctor, is hot and breath-stealing. She leans against a white-painted wall under bright scarlet bougainvillaea, looks at the topographical arms embracing the city: Devil's Peak ahead of her, Signal Hill behind, Table Mountain itself, sharply defined, free from cloud, augmented only by the revolving cable car, refracting the sun like a jewel as it approaches the summit.

She adjusts her backpack, her shoulders stiff, wipes sticky hands on the coarse black material, steps out down the hill.

She crosses Buitengracht Street, congested with cars, engines turning over fast to power air-conditioning, pumping fumes into the low smog, which forms earlier as each week goes by. She finds little respite in the shady narrow confines of Shortmarket Street: a line of cars is backed up, hawkers and porters weaving between them with carts and trolleys. She studies each of them as they

1

approach her, registers their fatigue, the narrowing of eyes as they take in her veil and heavy black robes. She is panting now, the exertion wearing on tired limbs. She looks up to find that she is almost at Long Street, one of Cape Town's central avenues, a Mecca for tourists and locals alike, fronted by bars and restaurants, hotels and backpackers' lodges, African artefact emporia and independent clothing stores. Commuters and visitors jam the pavements. She turns at the sensation of ice-cold air seeping from the opening door of a fluorescent-tube-lit tattoo parlour. Ahead, she sees the building that was described to her. She stops, composes herself, checks her backpack.

The small white truck drifts up the right-hand side of Long Street, pulling out around double-parked cars without warning, ahead of the slow-moving traffic. It accelerates past two youngsters on scooters, picking up speed. The driver sees the traffic lights ahead change to red, registers the Metro police car to his right, brakes hard.

From two hundred metres up the hill, she hears the brakes squeal, turns into a thunderous blast, glimpses the first second of the vast explosion, tongues of fire, like the arms of an anemone, human mouths wide, screaming silently, arms raised, lifted from their feet away from the invisible core of the detonation. She finds herself jolted backwards, head hitting the pavement hard, eyes scalded, vision gone, a siren in her ears, consciousness seeping away, her last coherent thought for what would be forty hours: her long-sought, hard-fought interview appointment missed.

PART 1

The hall at the Inns of Court in the centre of Cape Town is grandly proportioned, ceiling high and elaborate, tall leaded windows running its length overlooking dusk descending on the Company's gardens. On the opposite wall hang huge oils, dark portraits of white men who carry their gravitas heavily.

At the lectern, Dr Grace Bellingham says:

'The belief in Manichaeism is that the battle between good and evil – God and Satan – was not external to the human race, but intrinsically located within us. The human was the battleground in which these powers fought: the soul defined the person. Nothing about us was assumed good or evil, but rather that we possessed both light and dark, that the battle was ongoing and never-ending through the reign of humanity.'

Colonel Vaughn de Vries of the South African Police Service opens one of the heavy wooden doors, slides inside, glances down at his cheap, tarnished shoes against the shiny parquet floor, eases his way to the back row of seats, slips into a chair on the centre aisle. He glances around, sees the sides and backs of heads he senses belong to the distinguished – a larger gathering than he had expected – inclined slightly upwards to face, in the dusty funnel of light, the raised lectern at the far end of the room.

5

'If it is true, as many studies suggest, that every one of us has, at some point, considered an act of extreme violence, including murder, what but our own brain can possibly be considered in our search for the source of an evil that allows us to commit such a crime? And whether our actions induce remorse or we remain unmoved is surely only determined by our own moral barometer, and how it might have been set.'

De Vries ducks his head, clears his throat, looks back up. Only the monotonous insistence of SAPS bureaucracy has made him late. He is embarrassed, though he has little interest in the subject matter, dreads the socializing with his fellow audience members.

Her voice is clear and deep. He stares at her face, smiles, remembering their late-night conferences, their faces close, lips almost touching. The intensity between them not from the dead-lines of a murder investigation but their own physical attraction, her smell, her touch. In three years of working together, he can remember every expression that crossed her face, but not one word that was discussed.

'There is, naturally, one other consideration: influence, and the hypothesis of learned or inherited behaviour. Can our innate, inbred control mechanisms be manipulated, or are they truly set within us?' She looks out across her audience as if applying her question to each member. 'We might, I suppose, be grateful to Charles Whitman. In 1966, at the age of twenty-five, the former marine killed seventeen and wounded thirty-two in a mass shoot-ing at the University of Texas. That morning, he had murdered his wife and mother. At this first crime scene, he left a suicide note.' She looks down at the lectern and reads, '"I do not really under-stand myself these days. I am supposed to be an average, reasonable and intelligent young man. However, lately (I cannot recall when it started) I have been a victim of many unusual and irrational thoughts. Pay off my debts and donate the rest anonymously to a mental-health foundation. Maybe research can prevent further tragedies of this type."'

She looks up at her audience. De Vries is suddenly aware that there is silence. He has been meditating on how their life together might have been and how, now, both have two children, both have left their spouse, both are alone in the city they call home.

'Did Whitman sense that evil had infested his brain, disoriented his previously balanced moral compass? Is the concept of evil nothing more than a distortion of our brain function? And, if that is so, can evil – as a human concept – actually be said to exist at all?'

She bows minutely, takes a step back from the lectern. The applause sounds strident in the cavernous room. The audience begin to shuffle and chatter, rise from their seats, greeting one another with noncommittal smiles, firm handshakes. Double doors between portraits open and slowly people move towards the tables laid with glasses of Champagne, sweating canapés, sad tumblers of orange juice.

'Vaughn . . .'

De Vries turns to see the director of his Special Crimes Unit, Henrik du Toit, in full uniform.

'Sir.'

'I had no idea you were attending this evening.'

'I have some interest in the cerebral, sir. When time allows . . .'

'After the events in Long Street last week, to contemplate such questions must be considered timely . . .'

'Is it just the quantity, do you think?'

'Quantity?'

'Of victims,' De Vries says, 'that make it headline news. That many die every day around Cape Town. Every newsman loves a bomb, or a plane crash.'

Du Toit leans towards him. 'They were tourists and professionals.'

De Vries snorts. 'Does the differentiation of victims lack humanity?'

He feels Du Toit's hand in the small of his back, permits the gentle pressure to rotate him, finds a photographer, knees bent, lens pointing. The man snaps, turns away.

'Now I see why you're here, sir.'

Du Toit is media friendly. At least he protects De Vries from them, allows him to work.

'The entire city is afraid. Eleven dead. What is it? Forty-something injured?' He lowers his voice. 'Nobody knows who these people were, what they hope to achieve. We can't even identify the driver. No one's claimed responsibility.'

Another photographer attracts their attention. Du Toit stands to attention. De Vries turns away, walks towards alcohol, takes a glass, moves to a corner by the doors. In his pocket, his cellphone vibrates. He reads the message, smiles. He drains his glass, takes a final glance at the self-congratulatory gathering, slips out between the doors into the cool of the stone stairwell, descends, strides into the street.

Mlungisi Solarin walks through the tall bronzed doors of the anonymous SAPS building into the hot Pretoria air, across the pavement, into the waiting people-carrier. His small bag is loaded into the boot. The driver slams the door, gets into his seat, starts the engine. Solarin glances back at the austere, castle-like structure, still in awe that this is his workplace. He turns to the man beside him.

'Good to be getting out of the city.'

'Hot down south too, my friend.'

The vehicle sets off; the air-conditioning accelerates. He sits back, digesting the three-hour briefing they have just been given on the explosion in Long Street, Cape Town. In the seats ahead of him, two officers speak quietly; the man next to him rests his head against the frame of the vehicle, his eyes closed. This is his first assignment outside Gauteng, his opportunity to be part of a taskforce, to travel his country. This is why he studied, worked weekends through university, excelled in the ranks of the SAPS, aced his promotion exams. So that he could be sitting here, en route to Wonderboom National Airport, Pretoria, on the flight down to Cape Town, no longer to be merely the child of an illegal Nigerian immigrant and a South African mother. No longer Mlungisi. He is, he reflects, as he sees his face in the copper-hued window, Lieutenant Mike Solarin of the Major Crimes Unit Taskforce.

De Vries stands as she reaches the table.

'You won't be missed?'

Grace Bellingham embraces him, kisses both cheeks, allows the waiter to place her to De Vries's left.

'The speeches I can give, the glad-handing defeats me.' Her voice is husky from years of smoking; her posture is confident; her eyes are wary – perhaps, he thinks, afraid.

She surveys the ornate dining room, part of a grand former banking hall now the Taj Hotel at the top of Wale Street.

'I can't imagine this is your local?'

'You said you wanted Indian food. This is, I'm told, the best. And, no, I have never been here before.' He looks curiously at the waiter who is spreading his napkin across his lap. 'There's a good takeaway just around the corner from my house.'

'We could have gone there.'

9

'This place has air-con.'

They order drinks, balance heavy menus on their laps.

She says: 'Did you hate everything I said? I can almost imagine you rolling your eyes . . .'

'I was late, as you know.'

'Were you?'

'You saw me slip in.'

'Did I?'

'I know you, so I know you did. Why are you trying to trap me?'

She smiles at him. 'Because this is the game we play.'

He nods. 'I've missed it.'

They eat ornate, refined Indian food, converse happily. De Vries stares at her, hair untied, eyes no longer occluded by dark spectacles, still wearing barely any make-up. He thinks that she still exudes the beauty of the precociously intelligent woman he met over twenty years ago, after he had joined the SAPS. Over those years, their paths have crossed sporadically, including 2003 to 2005 when she worked with his previous Major Crimes Department, building profiles of rapists and murderers. A six-month placement with the FBI in Quantico, Virginia, has propelled her to the forefront of criminal profilers in South Africa, an author and private consultant in the States.

He watches her eat, lay down her cutlery, speak; there is a delicacy to her hand movements, her posture, a style that he, and his circle of friends, wholly lack. She always had control over him: his awe made him her puppet, his lust juvenilized him. He wonders why she has contacted him now.

'I'm coming home. For good this time, I think.'

'To do what?'

She sits back, sighs. 'Little, I hope. Write, probably teach. Maybe sit on a sunny stoep. Semi-retirement.'

'Brace yourself. It's been the hottest summer on record. The dams are dry. No sign of respite.'

'You're as bad as the Brits. I couldn't believe them. Obsessed by the weather.'

'In case you've forgotten, we have much more weather than the Brits.'

'As if you care . . .'

'You've been away from Cape Town for too long.'

She picks up her glass, toasts him. 'And now I'm back.'

'Leading a discourse on the nature of evil. You've picked an apposite moment. Everyone is jittery.'

'No word on the bombing, who, or why?'

'The powers that be are characteristically tight-lipped.'

'They don't know?'

'So I'm told.'

'Terrorists like to claim responsibility, so I'm surprised.' She eats a couple of mouthfuls, lays down her cutlery. 'And the lecture, it's just publicity for the book, a way to announce my return, to the select few.'

'You'll be in demand.'

'A demand I may not meet. I'm tired, Vaughn. You should know: dealing with the people we do, you can rationalize all you like, but there's a tangible cost. It reroutes your brain. They have destroyed all joy in me.'

'They're welcome to whatever I have left. Go to waste otherwise.'

'Those who use us think that we study them to learn and that we remain untouched, but the truth is that they eat away at us, they feed on us.'

He pats his stomach. 'I have flesh to spare.'

11

She doesn't smile. 'Be careful,' she says. 'Before you know it – before I knew it – you live only in their world. You lose yourself entirely.'

'My wife lives happily in Jo'burg with some media type, my girls have finished university, starting work. It's just me and my house. I live for the work. Nothing else does it for me.'

'Nothing?'

He smiles, remembering their history, a meal together in more modest surroundings than this, a flirtation that nearly evolved. 'That was then. I was just married, faithful. You were taken. I used to see you with your kids, your husband, wonder what it was we had . . .'

'Or didn't have . . .'

'We had something, Grace. I was never sure what.'

'We're both older, Vaughn.' She looks up at him. 'Just because a girl loves a puppy doesn't mean she wants a dog.'

He shunts piles of rice with the back of his fork, pushes them into thick, sweet sauce. He senses she is watching him.

'What do you want, Grace?'

She shrugs; a half-smile creates a dimple in her right cheek.

'I don't know . . . Company, a familiar face, something to ground me back into my life here . . . Love, sex, friendship.'

'Apparently I was only ever good at one of those.'

'And have you considered,' she says, head tilted, 'perhaps, now, you aren't my type?'

He does not raise his eyes. 'Women often say that before they sleep with me.'

She does not laugh, even smile. 'You're very sure of yourself, aren't you?'

He looks up. 'I don't care any more. When I was young, being rejected was the end of everything, so I was nervous, but now . . .'

'Now you're used to it?'

They stare at one another, each keeping a straight face, until he laughs first. 'It never happens.'

The bright dark sky reveals the stars blurred through the almost viscous warm wind. They battle uphill, tired and intoxicated. No one sits outside. Smokers press themselves against the walls of restaurants and bars, watch sparks fly as they flick tips. They climb the stairs to 15 On Orange Hotel, amid up-lit white right-angled pillars, the lobby level illuminated brightly beneath a hazy glow from the upper storeys of the tinted-glass rectangle.

Arm in arm, they cross the lobby to the lifts.

'Three nights,' she says, 'courtesy of my publisher. I need to find an apartment.'

The lift doors part. She steps in ahead of him. His cellphone rings. He snatches it from his pocket, squints at the screen.

'I have to take this.'

She cups the edge of the lift door, preventing its closure, watches him listen, his eyes close.

'I have to go.'

She sighs. A philosophical smile forms beneath fallen eyes.

'You know there are some things I can't ignore. I'm really, really sorry, Grace.'

She lets the doors close, says: 'So am I.'

Sweat forms over his entire body. He feels feverish and disoriented from the downhill jog back to his car. His back hurts, neck aches. He battles the car aggressively across town, honking and flashing at the slow and weaving populace, crawling on wheels or foot. He joins Kloof Nek Road, runs through the gears of his under-powered car to climb the steep gradient towards the cable-car station, crests the humpback mountain pass, follows the main road down above Camps Bay.

Twenty-five years ago, this area was still considered wretchedly windblown and sun-bleached; properties were ramshackle, the vertiginous land cheap. Now, the view down to the blue bay, the white-sand beach fringed with palm trees, overcomes concerns about inhospitable terrain and the blistering wind. Every portion of land that can be built on has been. The seafront has morphed from traditional town thoroughfare to neon-lit strip of high-priced cafés and restaurants, boutique hotels and a promenade for the rich to cruise in their imported supercars, to lunch and dine and club the night away. He rarely comes here now.

From high above, the crescent of beach is dimly lit by the multicoloured beams of light projecting from the bars and cafés, the sky and sea battleship grey, the water crowned by the start-lingly white crests of the waves being blown back on themselves into sheets of spray. To his left, the Twelve Apostles – the peaks at the back of Table Mountain, running almost as far as Hout Bay – are deep purple, fringed with translucent, elongated wisps of cloud.

He brakes hard at the first sharp corner in the road, fighting the adverse camber, strains to see the black on white signposts indicating side-streets. He free-wheels down the hill, tapping the foot-brake, finds Plumbago Lane, notices that it runs on both sides of Camps Bay Drive. He instinctively turns left, sees flashing lights at the end of the narrow street, his choice vindicated. He slows before he reaches them, takes out a cigarette, lights it, inhales deeply. Within the chaos, the tragedy and fear, he must focus only on what he can see and feel about the crime scene. To him, the politics, the regimen, are unimportant. He drifts down the slight incline, noting that the substantial properties at either side of the road are built on wide plots. There are no cars parked on the street, save for the SAPS vehicles.

As he draws up behind a marked patrol car, he sees a small group who are residents, he assumes, craning their necks past a uniformed officer. He takes a final drag on his cigarette, pushes it hard into the ashtray, one among a hundred *stompies*, opens his door.

The wind, driven up the side of the Mountain, funnelled up ravines, squeezed between buildings, hits him. He holds his door as he stands straight, steps away, lets the wind slam it shut.

He looks behind him. The lane is dark, the small streetlights off. Gnarled trees, mostly leafless, lean back like limbo dancers; spiky hedges in front of electric fences mark boundaries. Lights glow dimly behind drawn curtains. As he turns back, he sees his warrant officer, Don February, walking towards him, his arms wrapping his oversized suit jacket around his small, slender frame.

'Be careful, sir. I was almost blown over.'

De Vries smiles. 'That's because there's nothing to you.' De Vries pats his stomach. 'Alcohol anchors me.'

'Yes, sir.'

'We have one body?'

'Yes, one.'

'Old?'

'The victim is not old. Nor is her body. But, sir, I do not know what you will think.'

'Think of what?'

'What you are about to see.'

They start to walk, past the gathering of neighbours, as far as what appear to be the final houses on each side of the lane. The sandy tarmac road opens up to form a turning circle, beyond which there is a thicket of contorted trees and long grasses leading to a rocky escarpment.

Don gestures ahead and to his right.

'Down here, there is one further property. It is called Apostle Lodge.'

He walks ahead of De Vries, produces his torch, illuminates a turn down a steep incline, leading to large garage doors at the base of a cast-concrete structure, featureless and dark. To its right, the entrance hidden by an overgrown evergreen shrub, Don indicates a narrow raised walkway, which runs around and over the driveway. He gestures for De Vries to take the lead.

A coarse metallic screech startles him.

'What the fuck's that?'

Don points to the roof of the house. Against the dimly glowing sky, De Vries can just make out the angular form of the bird-shaped chimney cowl. It turns again in the wind, squealing mournfully.

De Vries exhales, looks down at the narrow walkway above the deep caldera of the garage area.

'What is this place?'

'All I could discover is that it was built by a young female architect in the 1970s, one of the first houses on the street. The windows are all black from the outside. You will see, sir. It is a very odd house.'

'Who lives here?'

'Nobody. It is for sale. I have contacted the real-estate agent, but I have received no reply. According to the neighbour, it has been on the market for many years.'

At the end of the walkway, a uniformed officer stands at the door under an opaque glass globe, its light grey and dim. Within, De Vries sees a whiter, colder glow. He steps into a hallway panelled in dark bare wood, lit by recessed fluorescent tubes above each wall. The light is cold and sickly. He is immediately aware of a minute rapid flickering, which makes him feel nauseous, of the pervasive chill, many degrees cooler than the hot night air from which he has come. He lets Don overtake him, lead the way through a Spartan kitchen – more concrete, dark wood – into a wide living room, floor-to-ceiling windows overlooking a garden and, in the distance, far below, the bay and the vast expanse of shadowy sea beyond. The angle to the ocean means that he can see no moon, no horizon.

The back of the room is also clad in wood, the same flickering lighting. There is an oversized silver free-standing lamp, with a wide, curving arm, ending in a chromed globe. It is not illuminated, hanging over nothing but the highly polished grey and black terrazzo floor. There is no furniture but for a narrow, almost Z-shaped, chrome and black leather chaise longue, facing out to the view, and a single dining chair. As he approaches, the smell of excrement and urea begins to intensify. He sees the back of Harry Kleinman, the department's senior pathologist, bent over the couch.

'Harry?'

Kleinman does not move. 'Give me a moment.'

De Vries rarely sees Kleinman outside his lab, let alone the building itself. He turns to Don. 'Why is Dr Kleinman here?'

'I asked him to attend.'

'Why?'

Don opens his mouth, closes it again. 'I want you to see, sir.'

De Vries steps forward.

'Sir, wait.'

He freezes. 'What?'

'Look down at your feet.'

On the floor, De Vries discerns movement. He squats, sees Don offering his torch, takes it, points it. A wavering line of ants, dark orange-brown against the almost black floor, meanders between his shoes.

'Ants.' He shrugs his shoulders. 'So what?'

'There are two other trails. One heading towards the corner of

17

the building there.' He points towards the far right-hand corner. 'The other leads towards the door in the wall to the left.'

'There's a body. There are always bugs.'

A deeper, more certain voice says: 'They're not interested in the body.' De Vries turns towards Kleinman, who stands straight, arching his back slightly. 'Flies, maggots, cockroaches, many other what you call bugs, but the ants, they have a different destination.'

'Can we talk insects later? Let me see the victim.'

Kleinman smiles grimly, glances at Don. 'Of course.'

He steps aside. De Vries finds himself staring into the black, bloody, empty eye sockets of a woman's face, her mouth wide open, distorted, screaming. Dry rust-coloured blood stains her face, like tears. He feels a cold shiver pass down his back, a feeling like static electricity reacting with his damp skin. He takes a breath, tries to retain his dignity.

'Shit.'

He forces himself to study the body. She is probably in her late thirties or early forties, dark hair curling around her face, bound to the chaise longue by her wrists and ankles. Her blouse is raised over her breasts, her bra still in place; her skirt is pushed high to her thighs. De Vries ascertains that she is wearing no underwear, looks away again, wishes she was covered, knows that this cannot happen until he has borne witness.

'Where are her eyes?'

'Follow the ants, Vaughn.'

De Vries looks up at Kleinman, back at the floor, sees the two trails converge on the dining chair. On the black leather seat cushion, two eyeballs sit apart, smothered in crawling ants, moving tentacles of insects stretched out behind them. One is nearly at the edge of the chair.

'I imagine that they were placed next to one another,' Kleinman says, 'possibly lined up to give the impression that they are looking back at her. The ants are attempting to move this one.' He points with a pencil at the eyeball near the edge of the chair.

De Vries exhales, wipes his face, feels both chilled and suffocated; wonders how Kleinman and Don February can seem so calm.

'Her eyes: before or after she died?'

'Afterwards.' Kleinman studies him. 'Are you all right, Vaughn?'

'No. Why are you?' He looks accusingly at both of them.

'I should have warned you, sir.'

De Vries examines the room. The low ceiling, exposed concrete and dark panelling make the space seem barren and hard. He turns back to the scene, determined to study it dispassionately.

He works his way up from her bare feet, past the light summer dress. Her skin is lightly tanned, smooth, healthy.

'Sexually assaulted?'

'You don't like speculating and neither do I,' Kleinman says, 'but, from a cursory examination, I would say yes. I've taken swabs already but, once you're done, we're going to transport her and the chair back to the lab – still attached.'

'Time of death?'

Kleinman folds his arms. 'There are so many factors at work here, I'm guessing. With that understood, I'll say that life probably became extinct between twenty-four and forty-eight hours ago. When I examine her and calculate exactly, based on the readings provided, I can be more accurate . . . No obvious cause. Something frightening, agonizing – but that's your department, isn't it, Vaughn?'

'Then why are you here?'

'Because,' Kleinman says firmly, 'I was intrigued by Warrant February's call to me, his description of, and his initial reaction to, the scene. It's good that I've seen her *in situ*. I can tell you now: she is dehydrated, the wounds beneath her bindings old. I think she has been here a while. She was bound to this chair,

19

raped, terrified and, over a period of perhaps several days, she was left to die.'

De Vries stands still, his back to Don February. It is his ritual to absorb the atmosphere of the scene, to study details, to commune with the victim, to devote himself to them. He wishes that he could be more objective, more disinterested, but that is not how he operates. The victim, helpless and unknowing, naked and exposed, has taken him into her confidence, and he vows never to betray it, never to give in.

He turns from the interior to the dark garden, the rising moon beginning to backlight the bent branches of the surrounding trees. After a couple of minutes, Don squats with his torch, produces an evidence bag and a folded piece of white paper. He scoops up several ants, tips the paper into the top of the evidence bag, seals it. He stands, puts the bag in his jacket pocket.

'What do we know?'

'We have not even begun house-to-house yet,' Don says. 'There are neighbours outside, but I have not spoken officially with any of them. We have a team ready.'

'Who found her?'

'All I have been told is that the neighbours' children discovered the body and their father raised the alarm.'

'They saw her from outside?'

'No, sir. We can see out of the windows but, from the outside, you cannot see in. On the outside, the glass is black. There is a side door from the garden into a utility room, and another door into the house. Both these doors were open when officers arrived.'

'They touch anything? The kids or the officers?'

'The Camps Bay guys say no. I have not spoken to the children yet.'

'No ID?'

'Nothing apparently belonging to the victim. Caucasian. No jewellery, but maybe she wore a wedding ring, and an engagement or eternity ring. I have not touched her fingers but, if you look, you can see a wide, pale band on the fourth finger of her left hand.'

'We need to find out who she is. Who called us?'

'The Camps Bay guys said that they called in what they found to their captain and he called our unit immediately. Everywhere is short of men because of the bomb in Long Street. As you know, everyone has been called in.'

'Because we must be seen.' De Vries rolls his eyes, finds his gaze upon the woman's eyes on the chair, stops, swallows hard. He nods in its direction. 'Look at the chair. It's facing the chaise longue.' He walks gingerly over to stand behind it. 'Did he place it there after he killed her, took her eyes?' He turns on the spot, scrutinizes the room from the far end and back again. 'No one can see in . . . No one nearby to hear anything . . . Or was he sitting there?' He looks up at Don February. 'Watching her die.'

The forensic technicians assume control of the scene. De Vries observes them, head tilted back on his neck, studying their scrutiny, follows what they retrieve, from tweezer prongs to evidence bag. In his mind's eye, he divides the room and stares at each section.

The chaise longue – with the victim's body still attached – is wrapped and carried through the hallway, down the narrow walkway to waiting transport. De Vries follows it outside, thankful to be out of the room, of the dwelling itself, for the wind in his clothes, drying his face. When Don February is at his side, De Vries says:

'Talk to the neighbours out here, then start house-to-house. Wake people up if necessary. Anyone not at home, come back

21

tomorrow and check again. Try to find out who everybody in the street is, even on the other side of Camps Bay Drive. A complete layout of Plumbago Lane.' Don moves away. 'And the kids: are they next door?' He points at the house along from Apostle Lodge. Don nods, waits, then turns towards the small group still waiting behind a non-existent line.

Before De Vries reaches the gate at the boundary of the house next door from, and above, Apostle Lodge, it buzzes open. He walks to the front door. A broad, middle-aged man stands in the frame. He is wearing nothing but shorts.

'You in charge?'

'I need to speak to you and to your children, sir.' De Vries holds out his ID.

'Who was she?'

'We don't know yet. Can I come in?'

The man does not relinquish his position. 'They were playing with another boy, Thomas Vermeulen, from number thirty-four, across the way there.' He points. 'It's not the first time that boy has got my sons into trouble.'

'They're not in trouble.'

His voice is deep and harsh. 'They broke into that house. Far as I'm concerned, that's trouble.'

De Vries shrugs. 'I need to talk with them now, sir.' He steps forward, still finds the man unmoving.

'You should talk to the Vermeulen boy first. He's behind this. My boys wouldn't do that. Not without being influenced.'

'Influenced?'

'His parents. They're no good. Especially the wife. She can't control the boy.'

'What is your name, sir?'

'Marten Cloete.'

22

'Right, Mr Cloete. I want to speak to your children now. Then I'll speak to Thomas Vermeulen.'

The man stretches his shoulders, pushing out his hairy stomach. De Vries smells body odour and beer. It is not a combination unfamiliar to a policeman.

Cloete says: 'Why not the other way around?'

'This is the deal, Mr Cloete. You want me to talk to your children in their own home,' De Vries says quietly, 'or will you make me take them down to Camps Bay police station and interview them there?'

'What's your name?'

'Colonel Vaughn de Vries.'

'So, Colonel, this is how it should be – if you are being fair. You can talk to my boys after you have interviewed Tony Vermeulen and his *kak* son. He's responsible.'

De Vries grits his teeth, speaks quietly but firmly: 'Don't tell me my job. I'll speak to whoever I want, when I want. I'm not interested in what your children, or this Thomas Vermeulen, did. Let me in now, or I will make trouble for you. Next door to you, a woman died a very painful death. You are interfering with my inquiry.'

Cloete stares at De Vries, takes a step back inside his house. De Vries moves forward.

'I've brought up these boys myself. Mother left years ago. They're good boys. This is nothing to do with them.'

De Vries opens his mouth, about to turn and call for officers to back him up. Cloete turns, walks into his home. De Vries sighs, shakes his head, yawns, follows him.

In the centre of town, Long Street bustles but for the taped-off area three-quarters of the way up the street, guarded by uniformed

23

Metro officers, a void in the melee of tourists and locals, like a knot in a piece of wood.

The scene is a hundred hours old. Plastic hoardings have been erected so that the passing public cannot see the mangled vehicles, broken glass, bloodied tarmac. Even so, Mike Solarin observes the morbidly curious staring from distant office windows, even from the balconies of restaurants and bars lower down the street. Reporters and photographers have finessed their way into the nearest vantage points, although most have tired of the mundane routines. Their every move will be scrutinized, analysed and judged. Whether Cape Town can quickly regain the confidence of tourists, both domestic and international, will rest on their ability to solve the case and apprehend the perpetrators. The Christmas season is already upon them; most will visit anyway, but the Easter season might be decimated by the attack. All the taskforce agents have been warned that politicians, media and public await results: they are not to fail.

Most of the taskforce gather in the shade from a cast-iron balcony that has defied the destruction. The death toll stands at eleven, the critically injured number sixteen, the remainder are out of danger or have already been discharged. As he has done on the two previous visits, he walks slowly around the scene, observing the forensic technicians still at work, imagining the build-up to the explosion and the effect it would have had on human flesh and man-made structures. The question that has been posed, yet to be answered, is: was the explosion intended at that moment, at this point on Long Street, and, if so, why?

He approaches Gugu KwaDukuza, a forensic technician he has worked with before, with whom, he believes, there is the beginning of a connection.

'Howzit, Gugu?'

24

She looks up, smiles broadly. Her face is flushed, wet with sweat. 'Hey, Mike. *Ja*, tough, man.'

'You find out what these marks are?' He points with his toe to a patch of gooey, blackened gel. 'I see more and more of them each time I'm here.'

'Look more carefully, Agent Solarin.'

He gets to his knees in front of a patch, studies it; puts his head over it, sniffs. 'I don't get any smell. It fruit?'

'*Ja.*' She squats next to him, points with a narrow metal scraper. 'See there. Grape pips.'

'There were grapes in the vehicle?'

'Maybe. It's not where I'm working. We're all taking quadrants. Everything gets fed into the system but we don't know much about what anyone else is finding.'

'Anything else I should know?'

She stands, stretching her back, looks around her, says quietly, 'They tell you about the explosive?'

He shrugs. 'There was a lot . . .'

'*Ja*, that's true too.' She turns again as part of a renewed stretch, covers her mouth casually with her hand as she speaks. 'It's old. Forty, fifty years old. You can see the residue everywhere. Modern explosives don't leave this shit around.'

'Mining explosive?'

'Good call, but no. More like military. The explosives team are working on it.' She faces him. 'You have to be careful, man. You heard the boss. We're not supposed to be talking . . .'

'*Ja.* What is that?'

'The paparazzi out there have their cameras aimed. They film us, get in lip-readers, find out what we're saying, quote us in the press.'

'Shit.'

'And the politicians want it all locked down, like yesterday.

25

So, keep your head down and your mouth shut. That's what they told me.'

'You gonna be here longer?'

'Long as they want us,' she says. She unscrews a litre bottle of water, downs half of it. 'Not offering you any. You guys probably going out to lunch, eh?'

'I get to see you one evening?' Solarin says. 'Early dinner?'

She smiles at him. 'You not working?'

'Being given nothing. They tell us you guys haven't turned up anything.'

'Do they? Maybe we have dinner and I give you something.'

He raises his eyebrows. 'I was hoping you might say that.'

Brigadier Henrik du Toit pushes his hand between the closing doors, enters the lift sideways, waits until the doors close.

'Sorry you got the call so quickly last night. Shortage of personnel generally.'

'So I heard.'

'Didn't disturb any plans, I hope?'

'I never have any.'

Du Toit studies him; sees nothing. 'I gather it was coming our way anyway.'

De Vries nods. 'Anything difficult ends up here. Better it comes immediately.'

'It's difficult?'

'We'll see this morning. Maybe there are fingerprints from a guilty husband, a spurned lover, incriminating DNA all over her. Then we sign it off and move on. That would be easy, good for business, wouldn't it, sir?'

'But you don't think so?'

The lift slows at their floor.

'You don't want to know what I think.'

'Why?'

'Why not enjoy the next hour? I may be wrong.'

Du Toit holds his gaze.

De Vries shrugs. 'Empty house, two pieces of furniture, one ago-nized body with her eyes gouged out. Prolonged torture, murder. Doc Kleinman thought she hadn't died quickly.'

The doors part, their paths diverge.

'Nine a.m.,' Du Toit says.

The Special Crimes Unit is divided into four teams. De Vries is the most senior team leader, the others a lieutenant colonel and two lieutenants. Most officers of the rank of colonel and above are administrators. De Vries insisted otherwise. Here, he has his own fiefdom; regular colleagues whom he has chosen, form his core team.

Shortly before nine a.m., they gather in the squad-room. As well as Don February, there is Sergeant Sally Frazer, the collator who co-ordinates and disseminates information received; Constable Ben Thwala, who leads house-to-house enquiries and backs up Don February. There are four other junior officers and a civilian office manager. Also present is Dr Steve Ulton, De Vries's favoured in-house forensic supervisor, and Dr Harry Kleinman, one of the three unit pathologists. Every department on these three floors of the building has priority access to the in-house forensic, ballistic, technical and pathological information. This is what, in theory, gives them their edge; outside here everything moves slowly, inefficiently, requiring layers of bureaucracy, which serve only to hinder the pursuit of justice. The standard waiting time for SAPS detectives to receive forensic results is eight months. Limited budgets prevent more than a select few of those samples being fast-tracked to private laboratories. Henrik du Toit fought to create and retain his Special Crimes Unit but, in the new SAPS, in the new South Africa, the number of old white officers in these elite units, many having served during apartheid, has caused resentment and animosity within the hierarchy.

Du Toit arrives astride a wave of silence, stands straight, arms behind his back.

'As you all know, events in Long Street last Thursday have changed everything. Remain aware that the public are in a state of shock. That will make your jobs harder. We will attempt to withhold the more gruesome details of this new crime from the press, but do not be surprised if word spreads quickly. Everyone is nervous, everyone is watching us. They are looking to us to be guardians of the city. Expect the pressure to grow and, when the opportunity presents itself, reassure the people you interact with that we are in control and that they are safe.'

De Vries waits for a moment, says quietly, 'Because Drs Kleinman and Ulton and their colleagues have worked through the night for us, we will hear the key elements of their reports now, act on this evidence and get moving immediately. As you know, these first few hours are our time. Do we have an ID for our victim?'

Sally Frazer raises her hand.

'A woman named Bethany Miles was abducted on Friday last week from the car park of Rose's nursery and garden centre in Constantia. The description given matches our victim. As soon as you tell me, I'll visit the husband, ask him to come in for a formal identification.'

De Vries writes, 'Bethany Miles?' on the whiteboard.

'Did we know about this abduction?'

'Constantia SAPS distributed a description and alert to every station. The Camps Bay officers should have been briefed to be aware.'

'Aware?' De Vries echoes.

Frazer says: 'It was the day after the bomb, sir.'

De Vries turns to Kleinman. 'Doctor, can you précis the relevant findings of your post-mortem?'

The pathologist stands. '*Ja.* As we suspected yesterday, the victim was seriously dehydrated. Taking into account all the elements, including excretions, I estimate that she had no access to food or water for a period exceeding ninety-six hours.'

'That would match up with an abduction on Friday last week,' De Vries says, counting days on his fingers.

'The building, as officers who attended will recall, was extremely hot and dry. I am estimating time of death as between six p.m. Tuesday and ten a.m. Wednesday. It is not as narrow as I would like, but there are reasons for doubt.'

'Cause of death?'

Kleinman says slowly, 'I make no apologies for prevaricating. The provisional cause of death is asphyxiation. This conclusion is not without problems. I have examined her body extensively and can find no evidence of pressure applied to it other than, obviously, where she was tied to the reclining chair, and possibly where she was leaned upon while she was being raped. There is little to suggest that her windpipe was obstructed or constricted. Nor is there any evidence of smothering in her nostrils, sinuses or oesophagus.'

'So?'

'So something caused her to stop breathing . . .'

'The dehydration?'

'Possibly. There is evidence of damage to her organs but not to such a degree that I would expect them to fail. Certainly not her lungs.'

'So what, then?'

Kleinman takes a deep breath, staring at De Vries. 'I know you want answers. Sometimes there aren't any. Further evidence may point to a more certain conclusion.'

'What details on her rape?'

'She was raped, probably on two or three occasions. There is damage to her internal organs, which leads me to believe that the rape was rough, but beyond the act itself, not violent. There was no ejaculate, no foreign pubic hair, but there is evidence of a slight secretion of spermicide, which would suggest that he wore a condom.'

'The removal of her eyes?'

'. . . Was post–mortem, immediately or very soon after.'

'Anything else that might help us at this point?'

'Dr Ulton will tell you more about how you found the body. Gruesome as it may seem in the pictures, her mouth has been posed post-mortem to suggest a scream. There is no reason to suggest that her death would have been especially terrifying . . . no more terrifying than for anyone facing death, raped, bound, and at the mercy of a sadistic killer.' He looks around the room. 'I don't mean that in a flippant way, just that when you see the pictures you may be shocked.'

In the silence, De Vries says: 'I have attended many scenes. This one . . . I tell you, it was fucking horrible – the house, the room, the state of the victim.'

'I will say one more thing,' Kleinman says, 'so that you do not underestimate what this victim suffered. Beneath the blood that flowed from her eye sockets, I found a build-up, probably from many days, of saline evaporate – salt from tears. Bethany Miles cried many times while she was held in that house, and her tears poured down her face, covered only after death by her own blood.'

De Vries looks out numbly at the gathered officers, the heat and silence suddenly suffocating him. He nods at Steve Ulton, the scene-of-crime supervisor.

Ulton rises, calm, controlled. 'We have many prints and DNA markers from around the scene, but none on the chaise – or whatever you want to call it – apart from those of the victim, who is not in the system. There are none on the single dining chair. These surfaces have been cleaned recently.'

'The house was for sale, apparently for some time,' De Vries says. 'We'll have to track down the agents, find out who was shown around the property, and anyone else who had access.' He observes each member of the team writing notes. Don February will divide up the workload and second other officers to assist. 'Access to the building?'

'The back door leads into an anteroom and a second door onto the living area. Both these doors can be opened by the keys the children used to gain access to the building. According to the report, they found them in a terracotta pot by the back door. These were generally used by the gardener.'

'The three boys,' De Vries states, 'the two Cloete boys and the Vermeulen boy, claim that only Thomas Vermeulen entered the room, glimpsed what he thought was a body but, more importantly, retreated because of the smell and the flies.'

'There's no evidence to contradict those statements,' Ulton says. 'However, neither is there much to indicate who else might have used that means of entry. We checked the doors, walls of the anteroom, surrounds to the door and the keys themselves, but there isn't anything we can use. Unless the killer had access to a full set of keys, it seems unlikely that he used the front door, and the garage, while empty, would be risky to use due to the noise of the automatic doors and the narrowness of the staircase leading from the garage to the entrance hall of the house.'

'So we conclude,' De Vries says, 'that the killer used the same entrance as the boys?'

'We can't be certain. It seems the most likely scenario.'

'Don, who has keys? The estate agents?'

'I left two messages last night with the estate agent on the land-line number. I called the cellphone number of the manager, but there was no answer. The cellphone was not switching to voice-mail. I have called again this morning and there is still no voicemail. The phone just rings.'

'Someone needs to get down to the office after this meeting,' De Vries says. 'Is it a Camps Bay business?'

'The company have four offices,' Don says, 'with head office registered in Camps Bay.'

'Until we speak to the agents, we're in the dark over keys and access, even what was in the house. Was there an alarm?'

'There's no working alarm system,' Ulton says. 'The one in the house is old and was disconnected.'

'Right. I spoke to the three children last night. The two younger boys . . .' De Vries looks at his report '. . . Robert and Patrick Cloete – they're eleven and twelve – were following the older boy, Thomas Vermeulen, aged fifteen. They climbed under the fence from the Cloete house, which shares a boundary with the garden of Apostle Lodge, to snoop. It was an adventure. If you haven't seen it already, I can tell you, the place is weird. Not surprising no one wants to buy it. The children independ-ently assert that they found the keys in a terracotta pot by the back gate, tried the side door, opened it and went inside. The other key opened the inner door. The Vermeulen boy entered the main body of the house, smelt something bad, saw the woman on the chaise longue and got the hell out of there. The younger boys told their father and he called Camps Bay. They had officers there within fifteen minutes.' He pauses. 'Be aware, Marten Cloete, the father of the two younger boys, at number thirty-four, is very defensive, to the point of being obstructive. He's a single dad, big chip on his shoulder. He doesn't like the Vermeulen boy or his parents.' He looks at both Kleinman and Ulton, but neither volunteers any further information. 'Sergeant Thwala, Ben, what have you got from the neighbours?'

Thwala towers above everyone else, speaks in a clear, deep voice.

'We have two officers still in Plumbago Lane following up residents who were not at home last night. All those who we talked to have stated that they have not seen anything suspicious in the last few days. No strange cars, no one on foot. No one reported having seen lights on at Apostle Lodge, or having seen anyone enter or leave the building. The Vermeulen household say that the house has been on the market for over four years and that they cannot remember when they last saw anyone viewing the property. In other words,' Thwala looks up, 'no information.'

Don February says, 'Would you see lights through those windows, even if they were on?'

De Vries glances at Steve Ulton.

'We haven't done a specific analysis, but there was no obvious light showing at any of the windows when we were inside last night. My previous experience of this tinting process is that, if you put your face right up to them, cup your eyes, you can see a faint lightness, a glow, but it wouldn't be observable from afar.'

'So anyone could have operated in the house without being seen.' De Vries turns to Sally Frazer. 'I want a layout plan of all the properties on Plumbago Lane. It continues over the main road too, *ja*?'

'Yes. Just seven houses on the other side.'

'All right, I'm going to ask Warrant February to bring in Bethany Miles's husband. I'll keep you here, Sally. We need to speak to him on the record, so keep it silent or, at worst, neutral in the car. I'll come down to Camps Bay once I've spoken to the husband, assuming the victim is Bethany Miles. Warrant February will assign as required . . .' He turns away, then back again. 'Team four are signing off on their last case and have personnel free. I've already cleared it with Lieutenant van Zyl, so we'll get the extra bodies.' He looks at them. 'We break this now or it gets sticky, as you know . . .'

The officers disperse quickly. De Vries returns to his office at the back of the squad-room, glass walls fitted with cheap blinds providing little privacy. He sits down, adrenalin pumping, running through what he will have to accomplish in the coming hours. The air-conditioning has been programmed to a low setting throughout the building and the office is already hot, even before the afternoon sun hits the thin windows. Who takes a woman, starves her, perhaps watches her, rapes her and takes her eyes out? His fear rises; he swallows it back down.

Jaw locked, Luke Miles identifies the victim's body as his wife, Bethany. He shuffles from the mortuary to the lift, leans against the wall of the tiny car as it rises slowly, stumbles into an interview room. Fighting for breath, he gulps a large glass of water, sways in his chair, vomits across the table, head thumping down into his excretion, neck limp. Every last muscle in his body has crumpled. He stays there for a full minute, before he hauls his head up above the table-top and howls with grief.

De Vries watches from the other side of the long mirror in the interview room. The display of grief is ostentatious. He thinks of Oscar Pistorius in the courtroom, puking into the wastebin. He observes Luke Miles, unmoved; has long ago accepted that, professionally, it is impossible to empathize with others' grief. His sorrow is always for the victim; it is she whom he represents now.

He instructs Don to move the man to the second interview room, call a medical officer, ensure that he remains supervised. He walks slowly back to his office, ruminating on Luke Miles, on what he must have been shown of his wife to complete the identification, of his own reaction.

The report from the Constantia officers – operating out of the Rondebosch hub – on the abduction of Bethany Miles is brief, investigation thorough but fruitless. All investigations in the days after the Long Street explosion will have been foreshortened.

Rose's nursery is less than a kilometre from Constantia village shopping centre, widely known and used by Constantia residents. A long-established, popular garden centre with a large gravelled car park, it sits amid old London plane trees, surrounded by lush hedges. Other than the one above the cashier's till inside the low building, there are no CCTV cameras. No witnesses among the staff or customers have been discovered or have volunteered information. At eleven forty a.m. last Friday, a female customer discovered the tailgate to Bethany Miles's SUV open and a young child crying and screaming. When a parent or nanny could not be located, staff called the police, who attended the scene, traced the vehicle registration and contacted Luke Miles. From that moment on, no evidence had been found of Bethany Miles's whereabouts, how or by whom she had been taken. A cursory interview with Luke Miles noted some marital stresses, probably due to bringing up two energetic toddlers, and a vague suggestion that Bethany was depressed, could have suffered a breakdown of some kind, and just walked away. The child, aged three, was unable to recall what had happened, just that her mother had put her into the child seat in the back of the car and then disappeared.

After twenty-four hours, Bethany Miles's picture and details were circulated by the Missing Persons team, notices were displayed at Rose's car park and also at Constantia village shopping centre. No pertinent calls had been received.

The voice is more angry than sad. 'I've been asked this already, more than once.'

Luke Miles's demeanour has changed from shock to nervous belligerence. De Vries sits casually, to the side of the table in the interview room, observing the widower.

'I want to be with my children. They're only young, Josh has his leg in plaster. Lucy hasn't stopped crying all weekend.' He makes a cursory attempt to stand, sits back the moment De Vries speaks.

'Mr Miles, you spoke to local officers about your wife's disappearance. This is now a murder inquiry. Two different things. So, I ask you the questions, you answer them, I watch you answering them, and then you go home. It's just the way it has to be.'

'You watch me?'

De Vries nods.

'You're going to ask me if I killed my wife?' Miles meets his eye. 'No, I didn't. Of course I didn't. I was at work on Friday. All day, like every day. You can ask anyone at my offices.'

'I will.'

'Nothing was different that day, nothing was different in the days and weeks leading up to it. We've been married for nine years. We occasionally argued, mostly about the kids. All our friends argue, fight. Bethany hadn't told me about anybody or anything that was worrying her. She said she might go to the nursery because the heat had killed some bedding plants outside our stoep. What else? We always went to Rose's nursery, in the same car. Jesus, I don't know.'

'In your statement about her disappearance, you mentioned the possibility that she had been kidnapped, for extortion. There was no contact with anyone?'

'Of course not. I would have been on to you guys immediately.' He shakes his head. 'I've been successful, but I'm not super-rich or anything. We have a couple of staff, Beth looks after . . .' He sighs. 'She brought up the children herself. There are no nannies, no child-minders. She devoted herself to them, to the family.'

His face crumples. He covers his mouth, eyes squeezed shut. De Vries studies him silently. Miles has a high forehead, curly dark hair, slightly greying, long, neatly shaped sideburns running down to well below his ears. He is lightly tanned, dressed in casual but expensive clothes. He wears a simple broad gold wedding band, with no watch, no other jewellery. When he raises his head, sniffs, De Vries says, 'Did Bethany wear a wedding ring? Other rings?'

'*Ja*. A wedding band, like this.' He holds up his left hand. 'Her engagement ring. Big stone. They're gone?'

'Can you provide a description of the engagement ring?'

'I have photos. The insurance guys have photos. I'll get them sent to you.'

'What is your business, Mr Miles?'

'It's a software company called UnityAveco. I started it a few years after leaving uni, still own seventy per cent of it. It rationalizes warehouse to wholesaler to retailer orders, deliveries and payments.'

'Doing well?'

'*Ja*. I have two hundred and fifty staff.'

'Have you or your company received any threats?'

'No. Listen to me. It's not possible whoever took Bethany knew her. Anyone who knew her would know that she was beautiful and loving and strong . . .' His composure fails once more. 'People who do business with me know how I do it. I'm tough and

37

ambitious and fair, and if I piss anyone off, they take it up with me. They know that.'

'Happen often?'

'What?'

'You piss people off?'

'No. Look, business is business.'

'Piss anyone off badly? Piss anyone off who didn't know the rules – about taking it up with you?'

'No.'

De Vries waits. Luke Miles meets his gaze.

'You mentioned before that Bethany might have been depressed . . .'

'Nothing that would make her abandon the kids. Her mum got sick in the summer, probably won't live much longer. Jesus . . . She was upset.'

'Was there anyone your wife mentioned from her past? An old boyfriend?'

'No one long term. That's what she told me. I never met any previous guys.'

'A lover, an affair?'

'No. She had everything she wanted.'

'We don't always know that . . .'

'I do.'

'Sometimes couples have secrets. Do you have any suspicions at all? Any behaviour that seemed odd, out of character?'

Luke Miles seems to regard himself. 'Think what she had. Why would she want anything else?'

On the Camps Bay side of the Mountain, a bleak, blinding sun refracts from a billion grains of sand, windblown up hundreds of metres of slope, across the dark, matt tarmac. That wind is now a breeze, the sea black. At Plumbago Lane, De Vries slows, makes the turn, pulls in immediately. He walks back to the junction, studies a bent metal stump in the cracked tarmac pavement, then looks up across the road, sees a cul-de-sac sign with a bullet hole in it. He ambles back to the idling car, glancing up each side of the street, then, with just one pump of the accelerator, drifts down the gently sloping road almost to the end. He pulls up behind two other unmarked vehicles he recognizes as belonging to members of his team.

'Did the husband confess?'

He turns, sees Don February behind him.

He snorts. 'Not yet. Ostentatious show of grief, immediate recovery, looked positively excited when I asked him about his business. Commented on the size of the diamond in his wife's engagement ring, the value of his company, his financial status. Got the feeling he only has eyes for one mistress – his job.'

'Their house is grand. One of the best roads in Bishopscourt.'

'An "ambassadorial-level residence" . . . Isn't that what the estate agents call them?'

Don shrugs. 'I have called the estate agent for Apostle Lodge again, but there is still no reply. I will go and visit the office just now.'

'Good.'

'And I have been thinking, sir . . .' He begins to walk towards the end of the road, De Vries following. 'Anybody could drive along here, drive down into the garage area and, even without actually entering the garage, their car would be hidden from view.' He gestures down into the hollow, overhung by trees. 'There are steps up the left-hand side to the level of the garden and the back door. Dr Ulton's team have examined them. I do not know what they found.'

'If they haven't told us anything, they have nothing. You know how it is: either a great big fingerprint, a pool of DNA, or nothing at all. The moment we saw the scene, we knew what this would be.' He turns away from the steeply dropping driveway, stares down the narrow street, jumps at the metallic screech. He turns, stares up at the metal bird-cowl on the top of the chimney, silhouetted now against the clear blue sky. The bird turns again, faces him.

He swallows, swivels back to the street. 'Any of the neighbours have anything to say?'

'Nothing. A few extra cars drive along here since the sign at the end of the road was knocked over. The cul-de-sac sign.'

'The one on the other side has been used for target practice.'

'They say people turn off thinking it is a short cut towards Clifton, turn around at the end here. It's been down since the winter.'

'Anyone see the estate agent or people viewing the property?'

'Not that I have heard. No one comes to see the house. There is no board, no open-house afternoons. None of the neighbours like it.'

'Who lived here before?'

'A German family. They left about four years ago. They are asking twenty million for it.'

De Vries shakes his head. 'Why?'

Don knows how many of his superior's questions are rhetorical. He waits and usually De Vries starts talking again.

'We still have guys in there?'

'Yes. There are forensic technicians, and a uniform at the gate to the walkway.'

'I'm going to take a look. What are you doing? The estate agent?'

'I must speak to the neighbour almost opposite, Mrs Vermeulen, then I will go.'

'Good luck. Ben Thwala said she was pissed. Didn't care what her son was doing, didn't know where her husband was. Have fun.'

De Vries moves towards the officer standing by the gate to the concrete walkway over the driveway, up to the front door. Apostle Lodge looks no less bleak this morning than it did the previous night. The cast concrete is patchy and water-stained, the windows black and hollow. He thinks of Bethany Miles's eyes, reflects that the windows are like them: blank, unseeing sockets. He walks on, stops, remembers that he cannot see in but the windows can see out; what Bethany Miles could see is now the subject of the investigation.

At the end of the walkway, he turns right, edges past the blank front wall of the house into the garden to the side. Between Apostle Lodge and the neighbouring property there is a tall, thick hedgerow of windblown trees and spiky shrubs. A lush lawn runs down to the far boundary, maybe thirty metres away. From here, De Vries can barely see the horizon on the ocean. He walks the boundary, sees broken branches and light from the next garden, squats and observes that ground and lawn both reveal faint scuffing. This is where the children entered the property. He stands, follows the light depressions in the grass across the garden, towards the opposite side of the plot where, again, trees and shrubs form a high but less dense hedge, beyond which there is a shallow ravine, overgrown with leafier trees. He realizes that this is one of the run-offs that carry water down the Mountain in winter. Now all he can hear is the rustle of dry leaves, whistling grasses, the distant sound of cars decelerating on Camps Bay Drive.

He turns back to the house, walks the gentle incline to the side door, examines the pot in which the boys claim they found the keys, looks around. The back door is invisible from the street or any other property. The moment the killer brought Bethany Miles

41

to Apostle Lodge, he would have been safe from observation. De Vries stands still, imagines the man carrying the woman from his car, hidden in the dip from the lane, up the stairs on the left of the house, to the narrow paved path at its side. Here, he could enter the building, lock himself in, be certain that he could neither be seen, nor likely be disturbed . . . The killer knew the house was empty, that there would be no viewings, no visits. This means that he surveyed the property over a period of time, or had contact with the estate agents, even the owners. He walks up to the rear windows, peers into them, sees nothing but a darkened reflection of himself. He cups his hands against the glass, still sees nothing. Suddenly, there is a thump on the glass. The pane vibrates. He jumps back. From inside, he faintly hears a voice.

'You want to come in, sir?'

He gulps, barks: 'No. You gave me a fucking shock.'

'Sorry, sir.'

He hears laughter from the crime-scene technicians. It evaporates in a gust of wind. Something about this cold, empty house consistently unnerves him.

He returns to the side door, glances back once at the garden, follows the path to the stairs, which take him back down to the parking area and garage doors.

He calls up to the uniformed officer, who is staring at his cell-phone, probably sending an SMS.

'Hey! Have these garage doors been opened?'

The officer leans over the railings. 'I don't know, sir.'

'When you see Warrant Officer February, ask him to come here.'

Before he looks back down, a tall, broad silhouette appears at the top of the driveway.

'I have the remote for the garage door, sir. It was on the side-board in the hall area.' Ben Thwala jogs down the steep drive until he is standing next to De Vries.

'You've checked what's in here?'

Thwala presses a button and the double-width metal door begins to rise.

'There is nothing, sir. An old foot-pump, but otherwise it is empty.'

The door rises slowly, accompanied by a cacophonous metallic grating. De Vries recoils. When it is fully risen, slotting into place on the ceiling of the garage, the screeching ended, De Vries says: 'I'm guessing our killer didn't garage his car.'

Thwala turns to him. 'I asked all the neighbours if they had heard anything. None mentioned the garage doors.'

They walk into the dusty, dark space. De Vries scrutinizes each of the three walls. At the back, there is a bare metal door, fitted with two heavy bolts and a lock.

'Is there a key for this?'

'Not that we have found. There are stairs down to the other side of it. There are bolts on that side too.'

'Any other keys to anything?'

'No, sir.'

'How did we get the front door open last night?'

'The locks on the front door can be opened from the inside without a key. There is no mortise lock. The officers who answered the call were directed to the side door. When the scene was secured and we arrived, I suppose they opened the front door.'

De Vries pauses. 'Go back up there and look down. I want to know what you can see from the street.'

He watches Thwala bound back up the stairs to street level, step away from the railing. De Vries waits until he reappears.

'Nothing until you are right here, on the walkway. Even then, you have to lean over.'

De Vries gives him a thumbs-up, slowly follows his constable's steps up the concrete staircase back to the street.

'If you wanted to abduct someone, tie up, rape and starve them to death,' De Vries says to Thwala, 'this seems a really good choice.'

The serpentine Camps Bay Drive down the side of the Mountain into Camps Bay is the one stretch of road that makes De Vries feel sick. The adverse camber, sharp turns, jolting gear changes all conspire to make him ill. Don February drives carefully and slowly, allowing more aggressive drivers to overtake him on the bends. Below him, De Vries sees the white-sand beach deserted; even the bergies – the homeless and drunk – and hawkers are absent from the grass between the palm trees. Once the season is over, the town will become normal again, the preening city folk and tightly costumed lobster-pink tourists gone for the duration of the winter. But now it is too hot for tourists on the beach; sand blows inland onto the roads; locals stay indoors, windows open, curtains drawn.

The offices for Nobuhle Estates are located on the first floor of a weather-beaten white courtyard development, one row back from the seafront, above a tired sushi restaurant. A display of properties for sale takes up the far left window of the restaurant, next to which is the door that leads to the upper floor. De Vries scans the properties, does not see Apostle Lodge, pushes open the door and leads Don upstairs. In the upper hallway, there is another display of real estate, which, on the bottom row, advertises Apostle Lodge. The paper and photograph are faded, but the price is shown on a white label, which has obviously been added more recently.

The office itself appears open plan, and when they enter the air-conditioned space, three heads look up eagerly. One white, one Cape coloured, one black: the Rainbow Nation. Within seconds, they have been assessed as unlikely purchasers and all three heads drop back to their desks. Reluctantly, the Cape coloured woman closest to them hauls herself up, greets them.

'I want to speak with Miss . . .' De Vries frowns, turns to Don.

'Miss Dlomo Nobuhle.'

'Miss Nobuhle is out of the office today.'

De Vries produces his warrant card, pushes it up close to the woman.

'We have been trying to contact Miss Nobuhle since yesterday evening. Call her and tell her that we need to speak with her.'

The woman sits, slides her cellphone towards her, presses a key, holds the phone to her ear. After a few moments, she says: 'There are police here, Miss Nobuhle. They want to speak with you. Please return this call as soon as possible. Thank you.' She looks up at them.

'Where is she?'

'I don't know, sir.'

The white man at the far desk stands up, strides over to them, his voice loud, assertive. 'Is this about Apostle Lodge?'

De Vries stares at him. 'You are?'

'Greg Harrisson.'

'What do you know about Apostle Lodge, Mr Harrisson?'

'What happened, *ja*? Everyone around here is talking about it.'

'Are you involved with its sale?'

The man laughs, glances at the two women in the office.

'The company is, *ja*. Sure. We've been trying to shift that place for the last . . . I don't know, three, four years. We're all involved, I guess.'

'Mainly you, Greg.'

De Vries looks at the black woman. 'Mainly Mr Harrisson?'

Harrisson blushes, smiles. '*Ja*, I guess, mainly me.'

'When did you last show a client around the property?'

He looks to involve the women again, then says, 'In the

spring. September, October? It was before the vendor put the price up again.'

'And who is the vendor?'

'I'm not allowed to tell you that.'

'I think you are, sir.'

Harrisson glances at the women yet again, says: 'You'd better come to my desk.'

He leads them to the back of the office, invites them to sit in front of his immaculate, almost empty desk. As he sits, he smooths the collar of his jacket, which is hung on the back of the chair, ensuring that he does not crush it as he leans back.

'Some clients are easy, some not. The vendor for Apostle Lodge moved his family to Germany, won't sell for any less than his asking price, and that keeps rising every six months. We keep advising him: lower the headline price, get potential purchasers through the door, but he has his figure, and each time I speak to him, it's the same thing. No negotiation.'

He smiles at De Vries, glances at Don. 'It was a dead woman, *ja*?'

De Vries ignores him. 'How many other agents work from this office?'

'This is it. The four of us, including the queen bee, Miss Nobuhle.'

'Where do you keep the keys for the properties?'

'Sometimes we don't have keys. Some clients always want to be there when we show purchasers around, but when we do . . .' he stands up, twists on the spot, swings open a key safe mounted on the wall behind his desk '. . . they're kept in here.'

'Who has access to those?'

He shrugs. 'Just us.'

'Nobody else?'

'No. The safe is locked at night. We change the combination monthly.'

'What about the keys to the side door?'

Harrisson frowns. 'Side door?'

'To Apostle Lodge.'

'I don't know.' He opens the safe again, scans the paper index on the inside of the door, retrieves a heavy set of keys from the hook marked '13', examines them. He holds out individual keys to De Vries. 'These open the front door. This is the remote for the garage. I don't know what these two are for. Maybe these?'

De Vries looks at Don, who says: 'They are similar to the keys used to open the side door.'

'Does anyone else have a set of these keys?'

'No. I mean, possibly the vendor, but we haven't seen him.'

'What about a gardener or domestic worker?'

'There is a guy who comes in to look after the garden, mow the lawn, sure.'

'Does he have these keys?'

'I don't know.'

'You have his contact details?'

'No. We don't employ him. He worked for the vendor. As far as I know, still does.'

'I need the vendor's details.'

'I need to talk to Miss Nobuhle first.'

De Vries dislikes the self-assuredness of Harrisson, his creaseless fitted shirt, tight suit trousers.

'Where is Miss Nobuhle now?'

'I don't know.'

'She doesn't contact me within two hours, I want those details from you or you'll find yourself in court. You clear? Give me a card.' He takes the card Harrisson proffers. 'She open up the office this morning?'

Harrisson plucks a set of keys from his desk.

'I have keys. If Miss Nobuhle isn't here, I open and close up the office. If I'm out on call or on vacation, one of the girls does it.'

De Vries turns to the two women, their heads bowed over their desks. 'So, you all have access to this office and the clients' keys.'

The black woman says, 'Only Greg holds the keys. If he is off sick, and Miss Nobuhle is not available, one of us must collect the keys from his home.'

'Unless I'm away,' Harrisson says, 'then I leave them with Mary,' he nods at the black woman, 'or Anita.' The coloured woman by the door raises her head, but does not turn it towards them.

'So you and Miss Nobuhle have access to the office and the keys at all times. You have an alarm here?'

'Ja . . . Just a basic one. We have no valuables here overnight. We take our own laptops and tablets with us.'

'You've had any break-ins this last year?'

'No.'

'Any enquiries about Apostle Lodge? Anyone who asked about it, but didn't want a viewing?'

Again, Greg Harrisson looks over to the two women before answering.

'No. You can see for yourself, it's an odd property. It's over-priced. It's the kind of place you either fall in love with or you don't. And no one has.'

De Vries says: 'I think someone did.'

The briefing room is full. Mike Solarin estimates that there must be in excess of thirty officers sitting, perhaps another forty on their feet at the sides of the space.

The next speaker stands before them, a computer display projected onto the screen.

'The vehicle containing the explosive material has been

identified as a 1999 Nissan Cabstar 3.2 diesel, manual, four by two, grey engine unit, fitted with a white load box body. This was reported stolen five nights ago from a warehouse yard located in Farm Valley industrial estate, Oudtshoorn . . .' He peers behind him. 'The picture on the screen now is the actual vehicle, photograph taken approximately two years ago. We're sending officers to interview the owner, check for possible CCTV or witness reports, but the local SAPS sergeant who took the report says he's known the guy eight years. Owner's been there since the units opened in the 1980s. Never reported a theft before, no criminal record.'

Mike Solarin raises his hand. The speaker points at him.

'What is the business of the vehicle keeper?'

'Business is called . . .' he looks down at his notes '. . . Build It For You. Sells, delivers and assembles low-cost kit furniture for small offices, clubs and residential.'

He looks out across the room, continues: 'We're looking for any sign of this vehicle on the N1, N2 freeways or the R62. It's anonymous — probably cannot travel fast anyway — and speed cameras have not picked it up in any of the usual places. We'll be sending guys out to every garage between Cape Town and Oudtshoorn. Some have auto-plate recognition but we expect records to have been expunged.'

He nods at the room, stands to the side.

Colonel Brent Juiles walks to the front.

'We will focus our primary search for the perpetrators between Oudtshoorn and Cape Town, a distance of some four hundred and sixty kilometres, with a breadth of a hundred kilometres, but we cannot discount the possibility that the ordnance was transferred at Oudtshoorn because another vehicle was failing, or for security, en route from another location. Taskforce officers will report to me immediately following this meeting, as accorded in the schedule you have before you. Time is against us. Those above want results, answers, explanations, above all reassurance. It's our job to give them that. Let's go.'

De Vries drives back up to Plumbago Lane, in control of his stomach contents.

'Any of them could have lent keys to be copied, but if the gardener just leaves them in the pot by the back door, then it doesn't really matter, does it?'

'The owner could have extra sets of keys also.' Don says.

De Vries nods. His stomach rumbles. No dinner, no breakfast. 'I don't like Greg Harrisson,' he says. 'I think he's been questioned by the police before. Look him up, *ja*?'

'You think that?'

'I think *ja*. Just by his manner. Find out.'

As they turn left into the opposite end of Plumbago Lane, De Vries says, 'You been along here yet?'

'No. Ben Thwala has taken names and talked to owners, but there are only seven houses there.'

'Anyone show any interest in Apostle Lodge?'

'I do not think so.'

The narrow lane is almost identical in feeling and architecture to the longer section on the other side of the main road, a mixture of sleek modern buildings and old-fashioned, often single-storey dwellings with tiled roofs. Three houses face one another across the narrow lane, with a two-storey Victorian-style villa on the right-hand side overlooking another shallow ravine, umbrella pines and tall grasses disguising the topography. Only the occasional whine of a car decelerating down the mountain road disturbs the almost silent breeze, the rustling branches of dried and dying shrubs and trees.

De Vries pulls up, exits and stands next to the car, facing towards what little breeze there is. After a while, he sits back inside the cabin of the car, angles the air-conditioning vents towards himself. Don stays silent.

De Vries says, 'I'm thinking . . . a crime like this . . . No evidence, no witnesses. This is planned, and I'm telling you, it doesn't feel like his first.'

'You need to see this,' Sally Frazer says, as De Vries ambles across the squad-room. She indicates the plan she has prepared of Plumbago Lane. 'I've transcribed and cross-checked all the names Ben Thwala and his team have provided from the house-to-house and there's an interesting one. Leigh Finnemore, at number one. It's on the other side, but look . . .' She gestures De Vries to a computer on the desk nearby. 'He has a section-eighteen mark against his name.'

De Vries frowns. 'Restricted to the highest level. You don't see those every day.'

'I've only ever seen a handful in all my time,' Frazer says. 'What is it? A mental illness warning? Potentially dangerous suspects not arrested? Can we see what it is?'

'I don't know what the definition is, but it's serious. I'll have to talk to Brigadier du Toit. It'll need a joint approach from both of us. I'll call him just now.' He looks back up at the plan of the lane. 'No one else of interest?'

'Just the usual selection of minor stuff. The family on the opposite side from Apostle Lodge, in number thirty-four, Tony Vermeulen – his son, Thomas, was one of the boys who found the body – he's been arrested for punching a neighbour, another guy called . . .' she runs her finger along the line of houses on her plan '. . . Mackenzie. Something to do with him reprimanding Thomas for skateboarding. Went all the way to a hearing, and

51

Vermeulen was fined and warned. Two or three neighbours didn't seem to like the Vermeulen family very much at all.'

'I thought the father was a shit,' De Vries says, 'but that's my default impression of the public. He's done well, but the whole dysfunctional family seem out of place in surburbia, probably gets loud when he's pissed. The wife's clueless and the son's a little shit version of Dad, a bored teenager with too few friends.'

He glances over the squad-room. Everybody present is looking busy but, he senses, busy to no end, stalled. 'I'm going to find out about this Leigh . . .'

'Finnemore.'

'*Ja*, him. Right now, a section eighteen looks the closest thing we have to a clue.'

'We will be called upon this afternoon.' De Vries follows the line of Du Toit's finger to the chair opposite his desk, and sits. 'That is what I've been told. A closed meeting. I got the impression it may be someone from the medical profession, but they're telling me as little as possible.'

'It seems a section eighteen enquiry does, at least, produce a reaction.'

'A resented one, yes. What else is happening?'

'Everything and nothing. Legwork's done already. Nothing, but you only have to look at the scene to know that. It was planned. Unless the killer was focusing solely on Bethany Miles . . .' he runs the heels of his palms from his forehead across his hair '. . . I have a feeling that it may not be a unique event.'

'Don't say that out loud, for God's sake.'

'You haven't seen that house. Something about it that reeks of misery. You read the report? There was a chair facing the chaise longue, like he was watching her die.'

'You don't even know COD yet.'

'We have a provisional cause of death. Kleinman said there was nothing wrong with her heart, that dehydration would have been unlikely to weaken it sufficiently. He takes her eyes, displays them, poses them, distorts her body post-mortem. That is someone taking a lot of care. Then he steals her rings. That's something different.'

'A memento?'

'Perhaps . . . But you know what it suggests . . .'

Du Toit holds up his palms. 'Don't even mention it, Vaughn. We all have enough to worry about.'

De Vries sighs deeply, shuts his eyes.

'You all right?'

'I was in the army. I've seen bomb victims, torture victims, mashed-up corpses, but yesterday, Jesus, when I saw her there, in that place . . . Not good. Couldn't sleep last night, lay awake. All I could see were Bethany Miles's black eye sockets and that gaping, screaming mouth.'

'I saw the pictures.'

'You know me, Henrik. I get up in the morning to find evidence, but this . . . There's something about it I especially don't like. I hope I'm wrong, and maybe in a few hours' time I'll know I am, but whatever reason this man had to kill Bethany Miles, he took his time. He made it just what he wanted it to be. I'm telling you, I think he did it for fun.'

Henrik du Toit's office door is closed, blinds lowered. The air-conditioning trickles tepid air onto the sweaty crowns of heads, each man in shirt sleeves. Around his desk sit De Vries and the Special Crimes Unit's advising attorney, Norman Classon. The fourth man, Stephen Jessel, represents the Department of Section Designation, responsible for the issuing and monitoring of vulnerable and dangerous people in society. He sits upright in his chair, angled towards them, neat moustache above a creased tartan tie.

'Leigh Finnemore,' Jessel begins, 'is thirty-one years old, lives alone at number one Plumbago Lane, Camps Bay, Cape Town. The house belonged to his paternal grandfather and was passed on to Finnemore in 2009, since when he has resided there following supervised relocation regulations under the section-eighteen mandate.'

'As we explained,' Du Toit says, 'a murder investigation is under way following the discovery of a body at the opposite end of Plumbago Lane to Mr Finnemore's house. As with all residents, we have tried to make contact with him, without success, although we believe that he is at home. We need to know why Mr Finnemore has a section-eighteen flag in his record.'

'As you are aware, Brigadier,' Jessel says, 'those covered by a section-eighteen order are being supervised and, on some occasions, their movements are restricted to protect the public.' Jessel folds his arms, cosseting the file on his lap.

De Vries shuffles.

Du Toit says: 'We require the terms of the section eighteen.'

'I understand, but those are not available unless the department deems the reason essential.'

De Vries feels his fists clench. Jessel's stillness, his guarding of the file, his stilted delivery: all these things annoy him.

Du Toit speaks calmly: 'How can we judge that without knowing anything about this man?'

Norman Classon leans forward, his voice booming in the small room: 'The correct procedure has been followed to obtain the contents of the report by suitably ranking officers. It is not, I believe, Mr Jessel, in your gift to grant or withhold it.'

'As the senior case officer in charge of this man, I retain the right to withhold the information if I deem that it is not safe either for Mr Finnemore or for the general public. I will require guarantees that the information does not leave this room, and that, if Leigh Finnemore is to be interviewed, we are given advance notice so that someone qualified, ideally myself, is present when this occurs.'

'Brigadier du Toit is the director and Colonel de Vries the senior officer of the Special Crimes Unit,' Classon booms. 'There is no reason whatsoever to withhold such information from them. They are advised that, unless the information is directly relevant to their investigation, it will remain within this room and it is further understood that Mr Finnemore requires accompaniment if he is to be interviewed at his home.'

Jessel balks, straightens himself. 'Leigh Finnemore is an exception to the usual criteria for such a classification. You must understand that he remains a patient, under scrutiny, both for the scientific understanding we might gain from him, but also for the protection of those around him. We are still uncertain if particular stimuli might lead to an adverse reaction. We are not being obstructive. We have legal and moral responsibilities.'

'We have,' Classon says patiently, 'dealt with those. There is no reason to prolong this process.'

Jessel opens the file, withdraws a sheaf of papers, shuffles them until he has found what he requires. He speaks quietly, in a gentle monotone, showing no emotion:

'In 1996, at the age of ten, Leigh Finnemore killed his four-year-old sister, Susie, by drowning her. Her mother answered the telephone and asked Leigh to supervise Susie in her bath. Julie Finnemore was, according to testimony, tired and angry, deeply frustrated with her daughter, who had been boisterous and noisy all day and in the preceding weeks. Susie continued to scream and shout when she was in the bath and her mother called repeatedly from the living room for her to be quiet. During the inquiry, it was agreed that she may have used phrases such as "You are driving me mad", "I can't cope any more", "I can't go on with you". Leigh Finnemore took it upon himself to quieten her by ducking her head under the water and keeping it there until all movement had ceased.' Jessel looks up at them. 'In the minutes afterwards, it has been established that Leigh had no idea that he had killed his sister, but his mother attacked him, breaking one of his arms and beating his face. In his testimony, Leigh Finnemore recounts his mother saying, "Why Susie? Why my darling, beloved Susie?" and telling him, "I always knew you were the devil."

'Following the incident, Leigh and Susie Finnemore's father, Jonathan, died, also by drowning, in a deliberate act of suicide. Julie Finnemore blamed her son for her husband's death, and refused to see him or speak to him. Within eighteen months of the incident, she had sold her house and moved elsewhere, relinquishing all responsibility for Leigh. It was previously thought she had gone to another province of South Africa, but there is now reason to believe that she left the country and started a new life and career abroad.

'Leigh Finnemore, at the time on the borderline of legal responsibility, was counselled, supervised and accommodated by a specially trained foster family. In this case, he will never be fully free. He will remain under some form of assessment and supervision for the duration of his life.'

'Why is he living in Plumbago Lane?'

Jessel looks at Du Toit. 'His grandfather, on his father's side of the family, was, it appears, appalled by his grandson's treatment by his mother. The home, which would have been left to his only son and his family, was transferred into Leigh Finnemore's name on the condition that he might reside there at a time when it was deemed safe for him to do so. There is also a trust, which finances his living expenses.'

'What do his neighbours know?'

'Nothing,' Jessel says firmly. 'And that situation must remain. When Leigh was moved there, his neighbours were informed that he was an agoraphobic artist who wished to be left in peace. This they have largely done.'

'Is he an artist?'

'Of sorts, yes.'

'Does he work?'

'Not in a traditional sense, no.'

'So, what does he do?'

'He reads. He sculpts. Much of the time, he – the medical term escapes me – meditates or trances, locked in his own thoughts and memories of his life before the incident.'

Du Toit says quietly: 'Is he considered a threat?'

Jessel hesitates. 'I am told not.' He flicks pages, reads from one. 'The most recent psychological report – three months ago – indicates that he remains agoraphobic, afraid that his mother will return to harm him, and locked in a mental prison of guilt and remorse.'

'You are the officer assigned to him?' De Vries asks.

'I am a supervising officer, yes. We try to keep regular weekly appointments as well as unscheduled visits, but it is not always possible. I have been involved in writing a paper on his case and reporting to the Justice Department. For that reason, I see more of him than I might other subjects of cases we handle.'

'Does he leave the house?'

Jessel turns back to Du Toit. 'As far as I am aware, rarely. He has been driven by friends, on the first occasion with me present, to Newlands Forest, to look for wood. The outing was not entirely successful – Leigh's agoraphobia seemed worse – although he did express satisfaction at leaving his house and hoped that he might return to the forest. I am not sure that he has.'

'But he is free to leave his property?'

'Yes. He is certainly able to drive to go shopping or walk down the street. Leigh understands that there are places where his presence . . . could lead to unfortunate or embarrassing situations.'

'Dangerous situations?'

Jessel looks up at De Vries; his mouth twitches minutely.

'For Leigh, yes.'

'I meant for others.'

'No, I don't think so.'

De Vries shakes his head, frowns.

Du Toit says: 'Who are his friends? How did he make friends?'

'For some years, Leigh lived in a supervised hostel for young people where friends were permitted to visit. If you meet him – although I hope you will not – you will find he is an agreeable man, intelligent and, when well, good company. He was befriended by other residents and their friends, as well as his adoptive brothers in his long-term foster home. As far as I am aware, he socializes only rarely and always at his own home.'

'How do you know that he doesn't leave his home?'

'I ask him, and he tells me.'

'But,' De Vries says, 'can he be trusted?'

Jessel says: 'Leigh Finnemore was a child when he did something with a fatal outcome. It is extremely unlikely that he had any awareness of the consequences of his actions, less still what might happen as a result of such actions. But this does not interest me – indeed, *must* not interest me. I am required to supervise his rehabilitation, report to those who study him, ensure that he attends psychological sessions, and help him to lead as normal a life as possible. I have no reason to believe that Leigh lies to me.'

'Ever?'

Jessel frowns at De Vries, looks first at Du Toit, then Classon. He shrugs his shoulders. 'Do any of us always tell the truth?'

De Vries smiles sourly. 'I'm not interested in any of us, Mr Jessel, just Leigh Finnemore, and whether there is any chance he could have committed the crime I am investigating.'

'I am not a medical practitioner,' Jessel says, the calmness leaving his voice. 'I have neither been told nor read any suggestion of a violent element to this man's mental state.'

'But earlier you said that you were uncertain if particular stimuli . . .' he emphasizes the word '. . . might lead to . . . What did you say? "An adverse reaction".'

'He remains under scrutiny. There is no evidence that would occur.'

'But there is evidence, isn't there? When he was ten, he murdered his sister.'

Jessel turns to Classon. 'This man knows nothing about the matter other than what he has just heard. It is irresponsible even for him to express his opinions.'

Classon says: 'We don't censor opinions. This is an unusual situation. Children who have offended like this are either released after rehabilitation or, if they are considered a serious risk, detained. It is Colonel de Vries's duty to examine all possibilities.'

'He knows nothing about Leigh. If there is blame to be attached, it is to Julie Finnemore. She failed to supervise her children and she abandoned her son.'

De Vries stares at Jessel until he faces him. 'I know one thing. When I was ten years old, I knew the difference between right and wrong. I think almost all children would . . . And if I had committed murder, I would expect the consequences.'

'Colonel.'

De Vries turns back, leaving Classon to escort Jessel to the lifts. He waits for the door to click closed.

'Why do you do it?' Du Toit says. 'Why can't you leave these people alone?'

'He annoyed me.'

Du Toit shakes his head. 'He's a glorified social worker, probably with an unsustainable workload. He has a certain power and he wanted to brag about it. So what?'

'I thought we didn't censor opinion.'

Du Toit smiles thinly at De Vries. 'We may not censor it, but we might counsel its withholding – when it serves no purpose. If you want to talk to Leigh Finnemore, you may have to work with this Jessel.'

De Vries sits down in his chair. '*If* I want to talk to him?'

'When, then?'

'Doesn't it annoy you, Henrik? A ten-year-old boy murders his sister, probably because she is the parents' favourite, causes the destruction of the family, and it's him receiving all the help, the money, the attention. What happens to the innocent?'

'He was a child.'

De Vries shrugs. 'Ten? Maybe. Anyway, you know me. I'm interested in the victim. Seems to be a rather unfashionable view.'

'If you're interested in the victim, Vaughn, go away and find who murdered Bethany Miles. If anything points to Finnemore, you can demand anything you want.' De Vries stands. 'And, for God's sake, no mention of patterns. You have nothing. There's enough panic on the streets as it is.'

'The owner of Apostle Lodge,' Sally Frazer says, 'is a Hubert Swartz. His family were originally from Germany and he left Cape Town, with his wife and two children, four years ago.'

'The owner of the estate agency contacted Don?'

'No. A guy you spoke to, Harrisson, asked for you. You were in a meeting so I took the call. He said you expected the details.'

'I did.'

'I called Swartz in Germany, got his wife. She said they hadn't been back to South Africa since leaving, were much happier gone. She sounded frustrated about the house but her husband had appointed Nobuhle Estates, and she had left it to him. Apparently, the architect has made a name for herself in Germany and he bought it from her there. It had cost him a lot of money. Husband calls every three months, still follows the property market out here.'

'And the gardener?' De Vries asks.

'She didn't know about that, but said they had used a Malawian guy and she assumed it was him. He had a bank account so she suggested that her husband probably paid him by transfer.'

'You get a name?'

'*Ja*. Blessings Silumbu.'

'We can find him?'

'Already doing it. He stays out in Mitchells Plain.'

De Vries turns away, then back. 'Did Harrisson say he'd spoken to his boss, this Nobuhle woman?'

'Just that he wanted to give you the information.'

'Sensible man.'

Colonel Brent Juiles has a complexion like worn tan leather in an old car, his hair thin, eyes red. Mike Solarin and a white officer in his fifties, Ray Black, sit in front of him. They have been placed almost at the back of the queue of briefings.

'You two are going west to east along the R62.' He holds up his hands. 'Before you say anything, I know it's unlikely these guys took this road. But our mechanical team said that those vans run for half a million kilometres, no problem. The owner said it was a daily runabout, always reliable. So, we know the R62 has mountain passes and some tough going, but this vehicle could have taken it. And, if they wanted to keep off the radar, it's the quickest route out of Oudtshoorn and they're unlikely to see much traffic, even this time of year.'

'If they did stop,' Solarin says, 'they're more likely to be remembered.'

'I agree. Unless they brought their own fuel, they stopped somewhere. We don't know yet what time the van was stolen, but if it was before midnight they could drive the best part of the way to Cape Town in darkness.'

Ray Black shakes his head.

'Not happy, Warrant Black?'

'They're not driving that truck down the R62 at night. Be crazy.'

'It's just one theory. More likely, the vehicle was stolen, taken to a rendezvous and the bomb was fitted. Then – could have been two, three days later – it's driven to the detonation point.'

'Do we know if it was a suicide run? Remote detonation?'

Juiles turns back to Solarin. 'No, we don't. Guys sifting through the debris say no detonator has yet been identified.'

'No identification on the men in the truck?'

'Again, no. We'll find teeth, maybe DNA, some way to ID them, but they were at the epicentre. They're all over that scene in a billion pieces.'

'Witnesses said two men?'

'Yes. We have agreement from multiple witnesses. Two men. No positive ID on race. Sun was low, windscreen was lightly tinted, may have been dirty. The cab could hold three, pushing it four, sitting across. There were only two. Whether there were more in the back, in the transport box – the trailer – we don't know, but there's no immediate evidence to support that idea.'

'So, two men driving this truck into Cape Town. Why detonate at eight fifty a.m.? Why not wait until more tourists are on the street?'

Juiles stares at Solarin. 'Great you're using your head, Lieutenant, but those aren't questions for you. We have analysts for that. You have your job. You leave first light tomorrow morning. Any sightings of the Nissan lorry, anything suspicious at garages, service stations. It's tedious, but it needs doing. Full reports logged constantly. You can't find the server, you call them in manually. Everything is being fed to us here. We'll tell you if we want you to divert. Otherwise it's a straight line along that road. You detour to anywhere the perpetrators could have stopped. You clear?'

The two men nod.

By the end of the day De Vries has nothing. Each avenue of standard investigation has been exhausted. Sally Frazer has checked Silumbu, found him to be honest and capable, confirmed with him that he had kept the keys in the pot by the side door since the house became empty and he had left them behind at his house one day. The journey in from the township and home again was arduous enough without making it no end. He was emotional and apologetic, confirmed that he had neither seen nor heard anything. He also stated that, although both keys had been left for him, he never entered the main building, only the anteroom, to collect his tools, turn on the water supply to the outside tap, to wash and change. He had been inside the house once, coming up from the garage, helping Hubert Swartz to carry something. He said he did not like it. Did not like it inside, or looking at it from the exterior, with its blank grey walls and black windows.

De Vries's office is tepid, air stale, but when he puts his hand against a window, he can feel the heat in the glass. He looks down to the street, sees the weary gait of tourists looking for cool bars and air-conditioned restaurants. His own two-storey Victorian house is cool downstairs, but hot in his bedroom. He has been sleeping, sporadically, on the sofa in the back room overlooking the garden. He feels deflated and disappointed that no single lead has emerged, knows that his team must be re-energized and encouraged.

Don February appears at his open door, knocks softly, walks in. 'I'm going.'

'Ja.'

'You want anything tomorrow?'

'Don't know . . . Don, this morning, why were you talking to Mrs Vermeulen?'

'She had told Ben Thwala that her fifteen-year-old son, Thomas, has been going out at night and she did not know where. I wanted to ask her again what she thought he was doing.'

'And?'

'She did not know. Said he was always back at home in the morning and went to school.'

'That was it?'

'Yes, sir. I did ask her if any of his clothing had gone missing, or if she had seen blood on any items, but she said no.' Don frowns. 'She did not even seem surprised that I asked her.'

'Ben talked with the father, Tony?'

'Last night. Yes. He did not like his opposite neighbour much, the Cloete man. He said that he had never been inside Apostle Lodge, often forgot it was even there.'

'All right, we get Thomas Vermeulen in here – bring his father too, if you can – find out what he has to say. It doesn't seem likely that he'd foul so close to the nest, but you never know. Did Thwala say anything about the boy?'

'He is a teenager, with all the anger and confusion you would expect.'

64

'But not anything else?'
'Not that Ben said, no.'
De Vries nods slowly. 'We'd better see ourselves.'

De Vries stands in shorts and sandals, one palm flat above the coals, waiting for heat, the other cooled by the side of an icy beer bottle. He has flirted with craft beers, but this is a lager summer. He flips his raw steak in its marinade in the metal tray next to him, drains the bottle, wanders inside for another, returns to the braai. Above him, behind the boundary wall of his garden, the topmost branches of the tall gum trees scarcely move. He feels sweat from the crown of his head occasionally drip on his shoulders, run down the small of his back. His pool is green, despite the chemicals he has thrown in; his skin smelt stagnant as he lay rigid earlier, trying to imagine that he was not so hot.

He arches his back: the pain at its base is intensifying. Finally, he picks up the meat and throws it on the grill, hears the marinade sizzle. He takes two cooked *mealies* and places them carefully at the edge, watches the food cook, tries to dodge the invisible currents of even hotter air, which seep towards him on an imperceptible breeze.

He is agitated by the lack of response from Dlomo Nobuhle, presumably the owner of the estate agency, realizes that she, or any other of her employees at the Camps Bay office, could visit the property at any time and have the perfect excuse for doing so. He recalls the face of Greg Harrisson, his expression both solicitous and dismissive, recollects an impression of aggression beneath a gaudy veil of camaraderie.

The meat sits heavily on him, but he falls asleep in the garden in a white plastic chair, bottle in loose fingers hovering over the hot pink bricks of the pool terrace until it drops, almost silently, rolls away to the base of a bougainvillaea.

At dawn, they meet in the car park of the motel where they are billeted. Ray Black offers to drive first, but Solarin retains the keys, takes the wheel. He wants to be the passenger once they reach Route 62, so that he can scrutinize the surroundings, not for the first hour or ninety minutes as they speed out of Cape Town towards Paarl. He does not tell Ray Black this and the warrant officer does not comment.

The route takes them onto the busy N1 freeway where, despite it being early and approaching the Christmas break, traffic is heavy travelling into town. They pass through the four-kilometre-long Huguenot Tunnel onto De Toitskloof Pass, heading towards the agricultural and industrial town of Worcester, then drop onto the R60, through faded, dusty farmland, as far as the junction with the R62. Despite the air-conditioning in the Toyota hire car, the glass is hot to the touch. Ray Black sweats, filling the small cabin with stale cigarette breath and body odour. Solarin finds that the inadequate engine whines whenever tested; the brakes squeal when he brings the car to a halt. It frustrates him, but he reasons that if the Nissan truck came this route, it too would have been hot, underpowered and with brakes that struggled.

'You want breakfast?'

Ray Black turns. '*Ja.*'

It is their first interaction since the hotel.

De Vries leaves early, but still catches the rush hour into town. Even taking the high road around the Mountain, he is caught in queues into the business district. The weather has created a new schedule for many workers: arrive almost at first light, leave mid-afternoon.

He is first in the squad-room. He throws his jacket over the back of his chair, strolls into the main area to study Sally Frazer's information board. There are brief mentions of negative information received from neighbours, the location of the two known sets of keys, basic outlines of the children's testimony, and the lay-out plan of Plumbago Lane. No witness names or photographs; no evidence.

He must recheck Blessings Silumbu, whether the man could have sent another in his place at any time, whether others knew from him where the keys to the property were. He is all too aware that his department is decried as the 'White Crimes Unit' by many high up in the SAPS, but that is what he knows. It is the reason for his unit's existence. It is a generalization, but the perpetrators of psychopathic crime against white victims are overwhelmingly white themselves; the statistics tell him this.

At seven thirty a.m., a coloured officer he recognizes by sight knocks at his open door. De Vries beckons him in, observes that he is distressed, invites him to sit down.

'I don't know your name.'

'Constable Apolles, sir.'

'What do you want?'

He takes a deep breath, sits up straight on the edge of the chair. 'I stay in Strand, sir. Last night, I met with two friends who are based at Strand SAPS. We have a braai outside. We are talking generally. I mention – without disclosing any details, sir – that we are investigating a woman who has been tied to a reclining chair. That the room is empty. That she has been held for many days. This is the point, sir. They say there is a case like this in Strand. A woman was found tied up in an abandoned block of flats. She was dehydrated and she died after being there many days.'

De Vries sits forward. 'Raped?'

'I think, yes.'

'Her eyes?'

'I did not mention her eyes. Your instruction, but they did not say. I thought you should know, sir. I could not decide whether I should try to contact you last night. My friends said no, that maybe this is not the same . . .'

'When was she found?'

'Maybe five weeks ago.'

'You know who's leading the investigation?'

'My friends say it is an officer called Malgas.'

'I know Captain Malgas.'

De Vries looks up at the squad-room. Two officers are talking with Sally Frazer at the other end from his office. He lowers his voice, fixes Apolles with his stare. 'Never talk about our operations here, not with friends or even colleagues unless they are part of our group. We work in a different field, and you don't know who they will tell. Don't discuss anything where it might be overheard. Do you understand?'

Apolles nods.

'You did well telling me. If it's linked, it could be a break-through. Don't discuss it with anyone here yet. Not anyone at all. If they ask what you were doing in my office, tell them I wanted a coffee.'

'Sir?'

'Get me a coffee.'

Apolles stands, still nervous, relieved, exhilarated. De Vries registers all his emotions in a moment, recognizes himself in the young officer.

They cut through the mountains, turn into the Klein Karoo town of Montagu, find the main street slowly coming to life. They drift slowly down the road towards the sharply angled Dutch Reformed Church at its top. Solarin pulls in on the left, outside a café called Tracy's, window boxes flourishing, flags scarcely moving in the still, clear air. He switches off the engine.

'You want to eat or work first?'

Ray Black shrugs. 'Whatever. No way they stopped here. Not so close to town.'

'Everywhere checked. Pictures shown, witnesses noted. We're ticking boxes, but we're ticking them right. *Ja?*'

Even after forty-five seconds, the cabin is heating up. Solarin wants to be out of this space. He checks his mirror, swings open the door. The heat slaps his face, leaving it wet with sweat. He opens the boot, pulls out his jacket, swings it over his shoulder. 'We'll eat. Get some liquid inside us too.'

He looks over at the café. One pale family of tourists sits outside on the sweltering terrace. Inside, there is a cooler dark dining room, ceiling fans turned up full, beyond that a small courtyard with four tables under umbrellas.

They choose the dining room. Solarin sits with his back to the courtyard, directly under a fan, lets the strong breeze cool his neck. The paper napkins on the table flutter, the menus bow in the draught as they hold them. He watches Ray Black study the laminated card.

'One plate, Ray. Then we go to work.'

The N2 out of Cape Town passes the airport, crosses the Cape Flats, then rises up Sir Lowry's Pass to track the southern coast of Africa for some seven hundred kilometres as far as Port Elizabeth. Fifty kilometres from the centre of Cape Town, the road narrows and hits a series of traffic lights between Somerset West and

Strand. De Vries turns right towards the sea, heading for the ever-expanding conurbation of Strand, meaning literally 'beach'.

De Vries has few colleagues with whom he has worked whom he sees now; fewer still who seem pleased to see him. The elite units are, by definition, exclusive, taking him away from the every-day reality of many police stations, especially in the tougher areas where motives for murder can be as prosaic as one man drinking from another man's glass at a bar, picking up the wrong bottle in a shebeen, teasing the wrong guy, on the wrong drug, at the wrong moment. He has no idea how officers live their lives among such mindless carnage.

Danie Malgas is an exception: a coloured officer close to thirty years on the job, his ethics unimpeachable, his energy if not undimmed then still present, whom De Vries has commanded and, subsequently, worked with casually through the years. He is stationed now at Strand, the town where he was born and has always lived; De Vries sees Malgas as a constant in a sea of change within the SAPS. Some see him, and De Vries, as nothing more than old and tainted by the past.

'Not "captain",' he tells De Vries, when he meets him in the main car park for the Strand SAPS. 'Not since April. Don't you know anything up there in your ivory tower? Captains and majors are phased out, lieutenants and lieutenant colonels expanded. So, the same old Danie is now lieutenant, and don't you forget it.'

De Vries smiles, counts the teeth left in Malgas's mouth when he grins. 'Nothing changes, though, does it?'

'Nothing changes. Only the names and the colours . . . and the numbers. Jesus, did you see the stats?'

De Vries shakes his head.

'You don't want to. Colleague down in Philippi – something like thirty murders a week now. Even coming and going from work is an ordeal. Officers shot at, Molotov cocktails thrown at you. Jesus, it's out of control. You think we close a case down there? You people solve the crimes that reach the press. That's what the middle classes want to know – and I'm talking whites and blacks now. We'll just keep the dockets filled with victims and no chance of finding who or why. And, mind you, Colonel de Vries, that's just the bodies we find.' He opens the doors to his car. 'You going to tell me what we doing, or you going to keep me in suspense?'

De Vries gets into the car, says: 'You've got the docket?' Malgas squeezes into the driver's seat, nods. 'Get out of here and I'll tell you.'

They drive in the slow traffic along Beach Road, past the restaurants and bars, new apartment blocks and old-fashioned, almost Art Deco, low-rise flats, painted pinks and yellows. The traffic is rerouted into narrow lanes as workmen sweat in the sun building a paved promenade, the suburb gentrifying. On their left, beyond the building, the narrow yellow beach is busy, the shallows full of paddlers all the way along from Melkbaai as far as the dunes in the distance. The sky and sea and sand seem never to end, a sandwich of defined colours all the way to Muizenberg and the mountains beyond.

'Eish, man, it is getting hotter than the Mother City out here.' Malgas twists the air-conditioning knob hard to little effect. 'All the money my people have now, they come build these fucking great skyscrapers, drive around in Mercedes Benz cars, flash their toys, and wonder why they're getting treated like you whiteys. All the boys from the gangs are coming in now from Nomzamo, Khayelitsha and Macassar. Robbery rate's up God knows how many per cent, and now they're getting careless and the knives are flying and the guns aren't just being waved, you know? Bad enough being pistol-whipped, but when the trigger's pulled . . . Pulled for fun.'

'It's everywhere – maybe not the tourist areas – and it'll only

71

get worse as the population explodes,' De Vries says. 'One suburb bleeding into the next. Won't be long before everything's joined up between here and Cape Town.' He turns to Malgas. 'You been given more people?'

'Oh, *ja*, more people, *ja*. Quantity, not quality. All I do is train them and watch them pass me by, but none of them know the first thing. Not *fokkol*. I'm telling you, we're breeding a whole generation of slackers and morons.'

'What about you, Danie? You going to get booted upstairs sometime? You going to sit behind a desk?'

'Never gonna happen, man. They want me doing what I know. Donkey work. I can't make a fuss, can't put a line in the sand . . .' He brakes suddenly as a woman pulls out of a parking space in front of him. '*Jeeez*, look at her. Cell in one hand, coffee in another, cigarette on the go. Lucky she's got her fat thighs for steering, eh?' He turns and laughs at De Vries.

'When you got the call,' De Vries says blankly, 'what did you make of the Marie Garsten scene?'

'I knew the moment you said you wanted to talk about a case you thought I'd caught it would be Marie Garsten. That one's branded me, you know. We moved on, but she's still bothering me. Something really bad.'

'Just tell me, Danie.'

'All business today, eh, Vaughn? You haven't even told me why all this interest. You got another?'

'What do you mean, another?'

'I felt all along it wasn't a one-off. Had nothing to back it up, so I kept my big mouth shut. You'll see when you read my report. There's no evidence – maybe a receipt that seemed out of place, maybe a couple of little pubic hairs our guys reckon aren't from her. Like Velcro down there. Good chance something stuck when he pulled out. Might have a follicle to analyse, but we'll get nothing back from the labs for maybe five months. Tried to get it prioritized, but they said no.'

'He wear a condom?'

'They think. And there was nothing else. Not a print, not a smudge, not a smear.' Malgas turns from the road to look at De Vries, turns back. 'I felt from the moment I saw her that this was part of something. Jesus, you can tell me . . .'

'It's possible.'

'Shit, man. I knew it.' Malgas bangs the top of the steering wheel impotently. 'He bound Marie Garsten up with ties and raped her. Our pathologist reckoned she'd been there maybe six days. No food, no water. Won't get DNA from her now, but sometimes you get other stuff. Disappeared from Somerset West, and no one saw anything. You'd think something, anything . . .'

'COD?'

'Complications from dehydration?' Malgas says. 'Respiratory? Pathology open to opinion.'

He prods the indicator stalk to turn right off the main drag, takes a side road inland for a hundred metres, past a half-finished tower block, turns left, brakes hard in front of two scruffy gates. He pulls himself out of the cabin, his stomach catching on the steering wheel, grips the door frame for support. De Vries gets out on the other side. The heat engulfs him.

Malgas squints at the padlock. '*Ja*, it's the same one. They've just left it, like I thought.' He reaches forward, pulls down on the padlock, is left with just the barrel in his hand. 'The foreman admitted it was like this when they set up the gates in the first place. Spend tens of millions building but can't afford one padlock.'

He pushes the gates apart, toes a brick against each to keep them open. They get back into the car and drive into the dusty building site. Above them, the grey untreated concrete skeleton of a tower fifteen storeys high looms dark against the deep blue sky.

At least it throws shade. The structure is windowless, without scaffolding, seemingly deserted.

They get out, sweat forming on their brows even in the darker light.

'They stopped building after Marie Garsten was found?'

'They stopped six months back,' Malgas says. 'Ran out of money. Tried to sell the flats off-plan to raise the cash but, you know, we're just a bit far along out here. Most can't see sea because of that block there – so you're paying to look at your neighbour's washing – and you've got the squatter camps starting just over there. They say they'll be cleared, but you know what happens once they become established. Then there's talk they'll be developing along the dunes there. Could be decades of building. Dust and noise and traffic. Doesn't look like luxury to me.'

They walk towards a pair of doors to the right-hand side of the building.

'Who was handling the sale?' De Vries asks.

'What? You mean the estate agents? I don't know.'

'Not Nobulhe Estates?'

Malgas shakes his head. 'Never heard of them. It was one of the big boys. Some bust-up between them and the developers.'

They reach the doors. Malgas pulls hard at the handle and one opens. On the ground-floor level, the interior is completely bare, the only light leaking from slashes of sun through gaps in the concrete slabs. Malgas takes out his torch, shines it around a large, empty foyer. From above, there is a pitiful scream, which reverberates on the concrete around them.

De Vries has one hand on his weapon, the other clenched tight. 'Shit.'

Malgas shines the torch at his face, making himself look ghoulish.

'It's fucking kids, or druggies. We've tried to clear them but they come back. You go up there, you need protective suits. Even then if they're high they come for you with syringes.'

'Jesus.'

De Vries smells the remnants of bitter, acidic smoke, sees polythene bags and greasy newspaper balled up in the corner opposite the entrance. The howl sounds again. He cannot tell whether it is male or female: it is animal-like, as if something is trapped in a snare. 'This place is a death trap.'

'These people, that's why they come here,' Malgas says. 'They're half dead already.' He turns, pointing his torch at ground level towards an open door, leading to a set of concrete steps down. There is police crime-scene tape over the frame at waist level. Malgas pulls it away, takes the lead down the stairs.

Above them, there is staccato laughter, but it is not happy: choking, coughing, maniacal. The sound follows them down the bare staircase, reverberating from wall to wall as it tumbles ahead into the subterranean space.

'You carrying?'

De Vries nods, takes the final step down, eyes straining in the gloom, heart pumping hard. He follows the beam of light from the torch, jumps when Malgas speaks.

'This would have been the plant room, electrical controls, air-con, security. Watch yourself on the ceiling where you step up. It's low.'

A few steps further, the windowless room opens out on both sides, the ceiling low, the air thick and warm. Within moments De Vries feels claustrophobic; his nostrils itch and burn.

Malgas sweeps his torch beam to the left, then turns right, walks as far as he can go, stops, illuminates a patch of concrete floor, scratches and stains still showing through the dust. 'Right here.'

'What was there?'

Malgas points the torch at him. 'You'll see in the pictures.'

De Vries shakes his head, protecting his eyes with his palms against the glare of the beam. Malgas lowers it.

'What did *you* see? Tell me, Danie. I want it in your words.'

'Okay. It was like some kind of modern art – sculpture.' He moves the torch beam jaggedly along a patch of ground. 'Paving blocks, about half a metre square, laid out, nine, ten blocks high, like a bench, but at an angle, like a reclining chair, a couch . . . but hard, you know? Her arms are tied behind her around the back of the blocks, her thighs around the entire mass of the thing, ankles, spreading her legs, to each corner. You should have seen the marks on her. He tied her so hard the blood can't pass. Her thighs were blown up like purple balloons . . . He leaves her skirt, bra, no knickers.' Malgas hesitates. 'Shit, piss, blood – the angle she was lying in, man. It was fucking horrible.'

'Black cable ties?'

'Black cable ties, linked together.' He points his torch to the foot of where he has indicated the stone couch to have been. 'And then there was a second pile, about a metre high, kind of a stool, like he was sitting on it, looking at her.'

De Vries feels cold in his palms. The pads of his fingers swim in sweat as he rubs them against one another, pressure growing.

They stand silently, side by side, staring at the bare ground.

De Vries asks quietly, 'What made you think he'd done it before?'

'You know how it is? You don't say so. You don't say out loud. But, Jesus . . . You want to rape a girl, maybe you bring her down here, you shove her up against the wall, maybe tie her up, screw her, leave her, kill her, I don't know. But this? He'd had to have planned it out, taken his time, stacked up the concrete slabs, made this place. Some kind of torture chamber. He knew the site was empty, no one around for months. Even if anyone came in, he'd hear them on the stairs.'

'The kids, squatters?'

'Upstairs where it's light, kind of rooms on the lower floors, views from the top, sure, but down here? Why?' De Vries nods. 'Anyway, Crime Scene said the swing lock on the door back there in the hallway could have had a padlock on it. There are scratches. If anyone got curious, they couldn't get in.'

'What about her face?'

Malgas shrugs. 'Tape over her mouth. Not there when we found her, but glue on her lips, on her cheeks.'

'Her expression?'

''Bout how you look when you've been raped and starved.'

'Nothing happened to her eyes?'

'No.'

'No posing post-mortem?'

'Not that was noted. Your vic the same? Different?'

De Vries gestures for the torch, takes it, shines it around the space. Blank, grey, air thick. He swallows, feeling grit in his throat. He wipes his other hand down his face. 'Let's get a drink, Danie.'

They take a table at the back of Ben's Diner, near the padded bar, away from the other customers sitting in the window overlooking Beach Road and the ocean beyond. The waitress moves a fan so that it blows directly across them, brings them two light beers. Malgas seems to know the staff. They leave menus and stay away from the policemen.

'Of course, we're still working it,' Malgas says, 'but you know how it is.'

'A dozen other cases . . .'

'Two dozen, three. Take this copy of the docket. I keep 'em close by in case anything suddenly strikes me but, these days, that doesn't happen so much.' He glances around, sees no one within earshot. 'I know you can't say, but just tell me. You seen this before?'

De Vries nods, jaw locked, voice quiet and tight: 'Bindings, rape, length of time, the facing chair. We need to get the pubic-hair samples back, processed by my guys now. If they find anything on my vic and it's a match, we'll know what we've got.'

'You want me to retrieve it from the lab?' Malgas says. 'And get it to you?'

'*Ja*. My boys can do it overnight.'

'That's just unfair, man. We're up to close on ten months now for standard analysis unless we pay to go private.' Malgas gulps down his beer. 'What were you asking about eyes?'

'He took them out of her. My girl, Bethany Miles. Her eyeballs. Put them on the chair facing.'

'Shit.'

'And her facial expression was posed post-mortem.'

'You going to take this on? Marie Garsten?'

'Looks like it. Who else has been involved your end?'

'Just the team.'

'If you tell them to keep quiet, will they do it?'

Malgas tilts his head. 'I don't know, man. The ones who didn't see her, maybe, *ja*. But you take over the case, there'll be questions. I can try.'

'The press'll get it soon enough. We need time without them. You understand what's happening, Danie? If this is the same guy from before Bethany Miles, he's escalating. The posing of the scene, taking the eyes, adjusting the mouth, it indicates growing confidence. If the books are right, then if it was five, six weeks between attacks just now, it'll be less before the next one.'

Malgas holds up his hands. 'This isn't my playground, Vaughn. That's why we have you guys, in your smart suits,' he looks De Vries up and down, smirks, 'and I know you probably get a whole shitload of hassle when you turn up and take away a case, but you aren't going to get any from me.'

'Just get me the sample, *ja*? Today. Now.'

'Sure.'

De Vries looks down at the docket. 'I'd better go.'

'No lunch? The Greek lamb Athena here . . .'

'Not hungry now.'

'Another beer?'

'Nothing, Danie,' De Vries says quietly, as he gets up. 'I feel like nothing.'

Cape Route 62 used to be the major route from Cape Town into the Klein Karoo, linking farming towns for four hundred kilometres east. The communities on the route became wealthy from the traffic but, in 1958, when the South Coast Highway, the N2, was opened, traffic decreased dramatically on the winding inland road, with its mountain passes and long, flat, narrow plains. As a result, many of the towns are still well preserved, unchanged for almost a century, and although the townspeople may not be as wealthy as they used to be, the farmers largely are.

In Montagu, the photographs of the white truck meet with blank expressions and outright denials. Most townsfolk seem to be in bed by nine p.m. Agricultural lorries are the norm here, but it is still too early in the season for anyone to notice them.

Mike Solarin has sent the results of their visits to petrol stations and businesses back to the Greenpoint HQ, via a secure electronic link, and now, Solarin still at the wheel, they drive the sixty-five or so kilometres past yellowing fields, half-empty dams, dried-out riverbeds. On the other side of the mountain range, in the distance to their right, lies Swellendam, an old and always hot early Cape settlement. The temperature rises to forty-three degrees on the little LCD readout in the car. As they approach Barrydale, Solarin realizes that he has read about this country town, how it is an oasis in the crook of the low mountains that bound the route on each side. Now, late in the morning, he sees a low-lying community just off the main road, largely brown and yellow, with just the odd patch of green grass, and a line of healthy-looking trees banking an active stream or river.

He turns the car off the R62 and drops down into the town. Here, scarcely anyone is on the streets. Black farm workers huddle under tall eucalyptus trees, presumably hoping for some casual work later in the day. Visits to the Caltex service station, and other small automotive-based businesses, yield nothing.

'Why would these guys turn off the highway to come here?'

Solarin turns to Ray Black. 'Because they're running low on fuel – they're maybe three hundred kilometres from Oudtshoorn. The owner thinks the tank of the stolen truck was only half full.'

'They not turning off. No way.'

Solarin is hot, claustrophobic, bored by the repetition of questions, the only variation being language. Here, Afrikaans predominates; the words themselves seem spoken in reluctant, dry, disparaging tones.

'We're just doing our job. You heard Colonel Juiles: we're not paid to think.'

Black snorts. 'This your first taskforce?' Solarin nods. 'Each one you're part of, you'll enjoy it less. Trust me.'

'What is it?' Du Toit says. 'Why are you shutting the door?'

'Bad news.'

'Where have you been anyway?'

'I've been in Strand talking with Danie Malgas.' De Vries sits. 'You remember him? Six weeks ago, he investigated a scene where a woman . . .' he looks down at the report in his lap '. . . Marie Garsten, was found bound to paving blocks, clothes the same, raped, a chair facing her.'

Du Toit's eyes widen. 'How did you find this out? The JOC – Joint Operational Committee – meeting isn't until next week.'

'One of my team was, tangentially, discussing cases with officer friends from Strand. They realized that something similar was on the books there. He kept it quiet, but reported it to me. Captain – Lieutenant Malgas was the assigned detective. I met him, looked over the scene, have a copy of the docket.'

'Her eyes?'

'Not removed, but he raped her and their guys think he may have left pubic hairs. We might get lucky. I'm having Malgas intercept the samples at the lab – if he can find them – and bring them here today. I've asked for a re-examination: maybe our guys will find something more on Bethany Miles.'

'At least we'll know for certain, but, Vaughn, if it is . . . My God . . . This changes everything.'

'Until the press get it, it changes nothing. We link the crimes, we compare. If we can find links, we can find him.'

'It's not that simple,' Du Toit says, already anxious. 'If the press find out we have, let's say, a multiple killer, and we didn't tell them about it, didn't warn the public . . . You see where this goes?'

Du Toit and De Vries's loyalty to one another has been constant, but De Vries resents how his boss always reduces his work to how it will be seen, how it will be judged. To him, this deviates from their only task – to find the killer – but Du Toit has adapted to the new media-friendly SAPS, to the corporate world, and that is how he sees his role.

'Until we have a sample comparison, we know nothing, so nothing need be said. My team will start work assuming linkage, but it'll be kept solely within our group. If and when we know, you or the big boss himself, General Thulani, can make the call on what you tell everyone. Is that fair enough, Henrik?'

Du Toit nods.

'Our esteemed general cannot make his office cold enough right now. Passed over for the Provincial Command in the re-shuffle, the bomb, and now, possibly, this.' Du Toit looks up. 'You'll get in more personnel?'

'Already in hand. I have a contact who might be able to assist with a psychological profile too. I'll talk to her this evening.'

Du Toit smiles. 'The charming Dr Bellingham? Apparently you were seen dining *à deux*.'

'If that's supposed to mean together, then yes. Grace Bellingham and I go back, as you remember, sir.'

'Try to keep it on a professional level, Vaughn. You mix it up with personal stuff, it compromises her position and yours and, far more importantly, the case.' He fiddles with items on his desk. De Vries can see his restless leg twitching, the foot bouncing rapidly on the floor. Du Toit continues: 'I'm going to have to tell General Thulani. I can't let you brief your team on this and keep him in the dark. Just do me a favour: if he asks to see you, behave. I don't know why, but he and David Wertner, the Internal Investigation Unit, are leaving us alone right now. Ever since we started this Special Crimes Unit, they've been on our backs . . . Significantly, they're even leaving you alone. So, if they're not on your case, try to keep it that way.'

'I must be a terrible weight on your shoulders, sir.'

Du Toit smiles wanly. 'Without your results you'd be dead weight. Remember that.'

He is intercepted by Don February even before he reaches the squad-room.

'Thomas Vermeulen in the interview room for you, sir. Neither parent would attend, so as he is only fifteen years old, I have a duty social worker on standby.'

De Vries nods. 'I'll talk to him just now. Get the social worker in there, will you? And then, Don, have everyone in here for a meeting at . . .' He glances at his watch. 'Let's say two thirty, *ja*? Everyone.'

'A breakthrough from your meeting?'

'Yes and no. I'll tell you when I'm done with this Vermeulen boy.'

The signs to Ronnie's Sex Shop always startle, even if you know they're coming. The road is featureless in either direction, the mind wanders: people have been known to drive off the road into the Little Karoo until their car hits a tree or rock.

The small, rectangular building is plain and white. To one side there is a dirty concrete foundation on which a deck and pergola in orange wood sit, with a plethora of parasols, providing the merest protection from the blasting sun. Wind, so hot it sucks the moisture from your mouth, gusts across the car park. Inside, curious visitors discover a tiny bar, overhung with autographed brassières, graffitied walls, and Ronnie himself, white beard so long it drags over the cluttered counter. When he first opened here, fifty kilometres from anywhere, no one came until his friends added the word 'sex' to the painted name.

When Mike Solarin and Ray Black park outside, before they have time to open their doors a party of, maybe, thirty bikers arrives, engines revving, dust flying. One parks close to the driver's door of the Toyota.

'I'll take these guys,' Black says. 'You happy with that?'

'Biker at heart?'

'Have a Goldwing.'

Solarin raises his eyebrows, watches the warrant officer get out, greet the men as they take off their helmets. Solarin edges over the gearstick onto the passenger seat, then out into the car park. The side deck is full, buzzing with tourists. He moves indoors, speaks to Ronnie and a few taciturn locals, nursing beers disconsolately. The tourists on the deck seem a waste of time, even to him, but he undertakes the task, asking questions and showing the pictures of the Nissan truck. When he has finished, he looks over at the bikers. Ray Black is laughing with them. He does not appear to be questioning them, or showing them the pictures of the truck. When the first group of men start to walk towards the bar, Black goes with them.

'Ray.' The man turns. 'We're going.'

Black's shoulders slump. He breaks away from the group, strolls towards him. 'Thought we could grab a beer, maybe talk to these guys casually . . .'

'No. We have to go.' He tosses the keys at him. 'And you're driving.'

Thomas Vermeulen sits in the interview room looking so relaxed, so self-confident, that the sullen female social worker with him seems the more apprehensive. De Vries sits opposite him.

'You remember me from two nights back?'

Vermeulen shrugs.

'You described how you and your friends entered Apostle Lodge. Have you anything you want to add to what you said?'

'No.' The boy pouts.

'You been in that house before?'

'No.'

'Never been in there? In the garden?'

'Told you. Patrick said he'd seen the gardener with the keys put them in the pot. Never been near that place.'

'Patrick Cloete, from across the road?'

'Yeah.'

'When my warrant officer spoke to your mother, she said you'd been out at night a lot. Is that right?'

Thomas Vermeulen laughs stridently. 'She say that?'

'She did.'

He shakes his head, smile cocky. 'Dunno how she'd know. She's always pissed way before dinner. Usually drops a plate on the kitchen floor. Stays there till the maid comes. I need my food, so I go out.'

De Vries studies him. Behind the swagger, there is something empty in his eyes. De Vries does not know whether it is an escape from a domestic nightmare, or something else, something more defined and premeditated. 'Your parents at work?'

'Dad is,' he says, 'but, you know . . . Mum, some bar with her friends.'

'Do you spend time out of your house at night?'

He shrugs. 'Yes. Course.'

'Where do you go?'

'Places. Down the beach, over the Mountain: Long Street, Green Point.'

'On your own?'

'Sometimes. Sometimes with mates.'

Vermeulen's face is narrow, nose sharp, eyes squinting to focus. His skin is pale and spotty. When he is speaking, he seems relaxed but, when De Vries stops, remains silent. De Vries sees the unease, senses discomfort almost emanate from him.

'When you go out, when you come back, you see anyone around Apostle Lodge?'

He shakes his head.

'Neighbours? A car?'

'No.'

'Where were you? At night, when your mother says you weren't at home.'

Vermeulen says nothing.

De Vries can see the pulse in his neck beating fast.

'I'll make it easy, Thomas. Generally, I don't care what people are doing, where they are. I'm interested in only one thing. A woman was held, raped and murdered in Apostle Lodge, almost opposite your house. I need to know where you were, who you were with, and exactly when, for the last week. You give me that, I leave you alone.'

The boy swallows. 'What if I don't want to say?'

'You can talk to the lady next to you. She's a social worker here to check we're treating you right. She'll tell you that we never repeat what we're told in here unless it links to our investigation. She and I guarantee that we won't repeat what you tell me to anyone. Not your parents, not anyone else.'

Vermeulen's eyes swivel towards the woman, back again to De Vries's neck. Eye contact, scarce before, has now transmuted to none. The boy's demeanour has changed entirely, the brittle confidence cracking. 'What if it's something else?'

'What? What is it?'

'What if it's something that might get someone into trouble?'

'If it's not serious, it won't matter. There's no statement here, no record. We're just talking . . .'

Vermeulen shakes his head, his lips closed tightly.

'The point is, if you don't tell me, I have to consider you a suspect. That means I, or other officers, will have to investigate where you were, what you were doing, officially. Then we involve your folks, your friends, the law. Or you can tell me and, if it's nothing, I can get on with catching the man who did this.'

De Vries sees blood rising to the boy's face, his lips suddenly dry. He has seen these physical reactions so many times, knows now that it is sex or drugs, probably sex. He wishes he did not have to make the boy speak.

'I meet someone. We hang out together. I always come home.'

'I need to know who it is.'

He shakes his head. 'I can't tell you.'

'Why not?'

'Just can't.'

De Vries's way would have been to bang the table, jolt the information out of the boy, but he has watched Don February quietly and gently coax information from witnesses and he has pledged to try this method first. It is an effort to remain calm, keep his voice even.

'Whoever it is, whatever you're doing, it doesn't matter. You have to account for your whereabouts.'

'If I say, he'll get into trouble.'

De Vries hears the male pronoun, knows this makes it harder still, remembers that Vermeulen is only fifteen, fears that this now opens new avenues of investigation, reports to other agencies. All his life, sex has brought him pleasure and pain, the former out-weighing the latter, but, professionally, it is nothing but trouble. It seals people's lips, ferments lies and distortion, results seemingly only in recrimination and misery.

'All right, listen to me. I don't care what you and this guy do together. If you have a problem with it, you're being forced into something you don't want, tell me now. I'll deal with him, and that will be it. But if you're happy with what goes on, just tell me who it is. I'll speak to him myself. Just me. I give you my guarantee, he will be in no trouble. You understand?'

De Vries feels the social worker's stare, ignores her, remains focused on the boy.

87

'It's about priorities and trust,' De Vries says. 'I have to stop a man who has raped and killed. Who could do again what he's done. That is more important than embarrassment and discomfort on your part. What we do, who we do it with, it's up to you. I don't care. Anyway, you're nearly an adult and you can do whatever you want.'

'You tell my parents?'

'No.'

'You promise?'

'I promise.'

Vermeulen looks at the woman. De Vries looks at her. She shakes her head.

'He's called . . . He's called . . . Tom Stoker.'

'That's good. Where does he live?'

'Flats top of Long Street, across from the baths. The block with the giant ad all over the windows.'

De Vries pushes paper and pen across the table. 'Write down the address for me.'

Vermeulen starts writing. De Vries sees his hand shake, eyes redden. The boy pushes the paper back to him.

'When were you here, at this address, in the last week?'

The boy's eyes widen, his teeth grit. He speaks from beneath the flap of blond hair in front of his eyes, the sides of his head shaven. 'Most evenings. Not Wednesday, not Sunday. That's when we went into the garden, went into the house. Flies everywhere, disgusting. Saw the woman's arm . . .'

'One more time: you've never been inside Apostle Lodge before?'

'Never.'

'Okay.' De Vries stands, thanks him. He thanks the social worker, ushers her out of the room, turns to Vermeulen, who is still sitting, eyes down, says quietly, 'No one's judging you. There's nothing to be ashamed of. But you're young, and there are laws to protect you, whether you think you need protecting or not.' He produces one of his cards. 'Be careful. You want help. Call my number.'

Vermeulen takes the card, meets De Vries's eye.

'I don't need help.'

De Vries knows that his investigation has done what it always does: opens sores, overturns rocks, disrupts and disorients. Every secret in every life with which he comes into contact is laid bare and then – almost always – man, woman and secret discarded.

They stand facing one another, Vermeulen leaning on the table with his fingertips, swaying. De Vries watches as the boy's face reddens, tears form, his body shakes, he begins to cry. De Vries pushes the door closed with his shoe, lets him sit back down, arms curled around his head, face on the table; sits opposite him, waits.

The road from Ronnie's Sex Shop is relatively featureless. Ray Black drives fast, but well. The air-conditioning seems to be faltering, the cabin heating steadily.

'You show your friends the Nissan pictures?'

'Ja.'

'And?'

'And nothing. Few of them said maybe, but they pass a hundred trucks, even along here.'

'You note their IDs?'

Black turns momentarily to face him. 'No one said yes. "Maybe". That was it. That's nothing.' He turns back to the road.

'Next time anyone says "maybe", I want their ID and their statement. When, where, how many drivers? It may not mean anything on its own, but it can build up to form a picture and then we may get a break. You clear, Ray?'

'You're in charge.'

'*Ja*. Slow down to a hundred k.p.h. I want to be able to see where we're going, what we're passing. You may think this is shit, but we'll do it right.'

The report of the investigation into the murder of Marie Garsten mirrors his own team's work on Bethany Miles. Marie Garsten was thirty-eight, married for eleven years, three children, a house in Somerset West not ten kilometres from where she was found. Her car discovered unlocked, abandoned around the back of a small retail cluster on the outskirts of town. No cameras, no witnesses. The search for her began immediately, without recourse to the twenty-four-hour period for missing persons, and continued in earnest for five days, overseen by a sergeant from Stellenbosch SAPS, a friend of the victim's husband, who ensured that extra officers were drafted in to look for her. Their reports show extensive questioning, a roadblock on the main drag from which the mini-mall car park was accessed, flat-to-flat enquiries in the nearby residential area. Just as De Vries's own team had discovered, her abductor had left no trace. A man presumably, unnoticed.

De Vries looks up from the copy of the docket, knows that there must have been a car, a period of time when, even if he is parked right next to his victim's vehicle, he must assault her and then get her into his own vehicle. This involves a high level of risk. That both known attacks have taken place in daylight displays a knowledge of the areas involved and the confidence to carry out the assaults. A plan of the parking area shows that the victim's car was parked to the side of the shops, under trees, presumably to provide shade. They had also provided cover for the abduction.

The post-mortem examination on Marie Garsten indicated severe bruising on the back of her head, consistent with her being struck by a heavy object, probably rendering her unconscious. When she came to, she would have found herself held captive, either in a car or van, or already in the basement of the apartment block. From there, if she were able to cry out, either no one would hear her or she would have been assumed to be just another homeless addict.

The whiteboard is now divided into two sections. One for Marie Garsten, one for Bethany Miles.

'This afternoon,' De Vries tells the meeting, 'Sergeant Frazer and Warrant February will co-ordinate you to build profiles for these two victims, to search for connections between them and, importantly, whether they ever met. Within that search, we hope to find locations, perhaps even people, in common. Until we find forensic evidence on Bethany Miles that can be compared to the pubic hairs taken from Marie Garsten, we won't know for certain that these two murders are the work of the same man, but we will work on that assumption for the rest of today. No word of the possible connection between these crimes is to be discussed outside this room. If these crimes are connected, if they are the developing work of one killer, then we face the possibility that this is just the beginning of a sequence of crimes. We cannot afford to let that information leak to the public and risk starting a panic.'

He looks to the back of the room, sees both Henrik du Toit and Norman Classon observing him.

'No one goes home until after we meet here at six p.m. If you're out on enquiries, Sergeant Frazer must be updated with your information before five forty-five.'

He steps away from the board, walks slowly towards the back of the room. He can hear Don February and Sally Frazer putting his orders into action. The sensation tangibly pleases him.

PAUL MENDELSON

'What did our great leader have to say?'

Brigadier Du Toit speaks quietly, keeping De Vries between him and the rest of the room: 'General Thulani said what we would expect: we wait until we hear about DNA. If we do. Obviously, anything we turn up between now and that point will influence what we tell the public.'

'The bloody public.'

Classon laughs.

'We are but servants,' Du Toit says.

'I hate the fucking public.'

'And, doubtless,' Du Toit says calmly, 'the feeling is mutual.' He seems unwilling, perhaps unable, to rise to the bait. 'Just get on with it, and report to me before you leave, *ja*?'

De Vries bows. 'Yes, sir.'

'We're running everyone through the system as fast as we can,' Sally Frazer tells him, standing at the corner of his desk. 'Only one hit that may be significant. Gregory Harrisson, works for Nobuhle Estates, was arrested for attempted rape in 2013. The case was moving to court, but the victim changed her mind and refused to testify so the case was dropped.'

'Who was the victim?'

'You'll have to find that out.' She speed-reads a print-out. 'She was a thirty-year-old Caucasian woman, resident in Blouberg. I only have a precis of the statement. She claimed stalking and, after she'd attempted to reason with him, he tried to overpower her in her apartment.'

'Nothing else?'

'That's it. I have the docket code if you want to see the detail.'

'I'll follow that up. Don and I spoke to him. Guy's too smooth for his own good.' De Vries hesitates. 'Does it say what he was doing in 2013 in Blouberg?'

'He was working in real estate there too. AE Estates was the company. He was laid off when he was charged.'

'Good. Do me a favour. Call Nobuhle Estates – Don's got the details – see if you can locate Dlomo Nobuhle. Don and I have tried, but she's keeping well out of the way. I want her at her office or in here today. Maybe a woman's voice will appeal to her more – and, if you do get to her, don't mention Greg Harrisson.'

Frazer tilts her head. 'I'll put on my best woman's voice, sir.'

They cross the Touws river and, after half an hour, come to Ladismith. Every parked car they pass is covered with a thin layer of orange dust; even the palms and jacaranda trees are heavy with it. They take the right-angled turn to stay on the R62 by the Little Karoo Co-op, drive through the quiet Karoo town, its farm shops and cafés largely empty, traffic light, pull into Hicks garage on South Street.

Mike Solarin asks the black attendant to fill the tank with unleaded to the top, walks across the forecourt to the kiosk, feels the cool air from the fans blow across him, drying his sweat. He pulls four cans of cold drink from the fridge cabinets and approaches the cash desk. In broken Afrikaans, he asks if there is anywhere in the town that might be able to recharge air-con. '*Is daar 'n winkel in die stad wat lugversorging kan herlaai?*'

The answer comes back gruffly in English. 'At Larry's.' She looks at her watch. 'But he sleeps afternoons.'

Solarin laughs, pays for the cool drinks, asks about the Nissan truck, showing the photograph. The cashier stares blankly at it. He shows it to her colleague, who shakes her head, returns to checking social media on her phone. He turns, pauses under the fans, exits the little shop and walks briskly back to the car. At the side of the building, next to the entrance to the toilets, he sees Ray

Black talking on his cellphone. Solarin squints at him, studies his body language, until the attendant re-holsters the fuel pump, announces the cost. Solarin pays, asks him to clean the front and rear screens, tips him three rand. Ray Black saunters back to the car.

'Important call?'

He looks up at Solarin, meets his eye. 'Girlfriend. Not happy I'm away.'

'I got cool drinks anyway.'

'Okay. We have something to eat here? There's a coffee shop just back there. Give the car a chance to cool, *ja*?'

Solarin wants to drive on, knows there are more towns and villages in closer proximity to one another, that Calitzdorp and even Oudtshoorn itself are within striking distance. It is after four p.m. They have made good progress.

'*Ja*. Let's eat.'

By six p.m., it becomes apparent that there are few connections between Bethany Miles and Marie Garsten. They are both white, in their thirties, married with children. They live fifty kilometres apart, children go to different schools, with no apparent overlap, husbands work in different professions. Marie Garsten had qualified as an accountant, but had never practised, preferring instead to bring up her children. Bethany Miles had worked part-time before she married. If they ever met, no one has so far discovered where; if they have friends in common, no connection has yet been found. De Vries has failed to speak with Mark Garsten, the first victim's widower, as he has moved his children to Durban to be with his parents. He expects to reach him, by telephone, in Durban the following morning at eight thirty a.m. He dismisses his officers by six thirty, tells them to arrive early for work tomorrow and prepare for a long day.

He returns to his office, frustrated, the energy ebbing from him. Sally Frazer appears at his door, waits for him to look up.

'I spoke to a woman at the Camps Bay office of Nobuhle Estates. She said that Miss Nobuhle is not answering her cell and that her answer machine is switched off . . . but, with a bit of persuasion, I did get her to admit that the reason might be because she has been attending a big pan-African real-estate conference from Monday to today, trying to do some big deal for the company.'

De Vries nods. 'Can't let anything get in the way of business. Where is this conference?'

'Up till,' she twists her wrist and glances down, 'just now, it's been at the International Conference Centre, but at eight tonight, there's a reception for delegates at the Grand Africa Café & Beach.'

De Vries raises his eyebrows. 'All right for some.'

Sally Frazer smiles. 'I'll be here until later anyway.'

'You were here early. Get home.'

'Nothing is more important than this.'

'That what I always used to say – and look at me now. Get some rest. I'll see you first thing.'

She backs out of the doorway, moves to her desk, sits down.

Lacy's Coffee Shop is styled like an American diner: light blue leatherette semicircular banquettes, stools up at the counter, two elderly waitresses smelling of nicotine, wearing pale blue paper hats at a jaunty angle, desultorily waiting tables. It is cool, rather than cold, largely quiet, but for a couple both wearing dungarees, sitting in silence opposite one another. The girl has a black eye the colour of her boyfriend's intensely tattooed arms. Solarin stares at her until she sees him and scowls.

They order steak, eggs and fries, sit to wait with coffees and cool drinks. Ray Black's cellphone rings. He glances at the display and stands. 'Be back just now.'

He ambles out of the restaurant onto the forecourt. Solarin studies him, wonders what is so private that he would endure the dry afternoon heat to avoid being overheard. The plates of food arrive, eggs speckled with black burned flecks. Solarin waits momentarily, then begins to eat. Ray Black looks frustrated and angry. They appear to make eye contact momentarily, although, through the dusty glass, Solarin is not certain that Black sees him. Black turns his back to him, continues to talk.

When he has eaten half his food, Black comes back in, sits, sighs heavily. Solarin looks at him. Black says: 'Food good?'

'Ja. Okay.' He studies his fork going into the food, to his mouth and back again; does not look up.

The law of the land is that alcohol may not be consumed on a public beach. It is, at least on the fashionable beaches of Cape Town, a rule to which everyone quite strictly adheres. The Grand Africa Café & Beach, behind an unassuming broken-tarmac car park, is a warehouse of a restaurant, also containing a couple of boutiques, which spills out onto a man-made sandy beach, with tables, chairs, umbrellas and modern art, leading down to a geo-metrical concrete breakwater, permitting little, if any, access to the icy seas just beyond the Waterfront. For New Year's Eve and many balmy summer evenings, it is one of the places for the wealthy of Cape Town and myriad tourists to wile away an evening, with alcohol, right next to the roiling ocean.

De Vries parks several hundred metres down Beach Road, which joins the Waterfront to the newly fashionable Mouille Point, around the dramatic and beautiful Cape Town stadium, a much underused legacy of the 2010 World Cup finals. Even now, after dark, the sea air moves slowly over the land, salt and pollution mingling to form a syrupy breeze, which seems to heat, not cool, all who stand within it.

He ambles down through the rough car park, arrives at the outer entrance to the venue, prepares to joust with the imported security guards to gain access. At the sight of his ID, the guard ushers him inside immediately, along the boardwalk and towards the glowing cavern of the main building. On his right, there are photographers taking no notice of him; to his left, the yellow beach is awash with the well-dressed, violently groomed glitterati of Cape Town, along with, he assumes, estate agents. The sun has set beneath the horizon, but the sky still glows a pinky-yellow above dark water.

He takes a glass of Champagne from the tray held aloft by an aloof waiter at the doorway, strolls into the middle of the warehouse space, its vaulted ceiling providing an escape for the hot air forming around him. By the steps down to the beach, people are posing for yet another photo shoot, watched over by others. A few faces seem familiar, if more lined than he remembers. He assumes he recognizes them not professionally but from the cover of some magazine. He pities these people. The celebrities all look hungry, their clothes too tight, faces shiny, hair metallic. He glances around, loses himself in the cacophony of dialogue. They face one another, listeners with a rictus grin, eyes staring past their interlocutor. He imagines they hear nothing but the slow trickling away of their fragile fame.

He walks towards the beach, sees a group of black African women, heads towards them. When he reaches them, they seem to close in around one another, excluding him. He smiles to himself, quite used to the reaction of those who see themselves as above him.

'Dlomo Nobuhle. I'm here to meet her.'

They turn to study him; one seems embarrassed, an almost imperceptible shudder.

'Miss Nobuhle?'

She detaches herself from the group, smile beaming, gestures for him to follow her away from the group, down the beach towards the breakwater where there are few guests. She turns in the sand to face him. 'What do you want? Who are you?'

'You know who I am, Miss Nobuhle. I am the policeman who has been leaving you messages for two days – until you turned off your voicemail – because a murder occurred in one of the properties your company is marketing.'

Her eyes flare. He sees her lips purse, anger rising.

'How dare you come here! This is a private occasion. I am at work.'

De Vries now has his back to the sea, looks past her to the party up the beach, the coloured lights in strings above the tables, the jazz band on the tiny stage built out over the sand, platters of canapés held above waiters' heads. On the surface, it is a glamorous and beautiful scene on such an evening.

'You think that a party is more important than the life of a woman, bound and raped, perhaps tortured and left for dead?'

'It is not my house and, besides, she is dead now. Nothing I do will bring her back.'

De Vries listens to the harsh voice, each word enunciated individually. Her hair is beautifully plaited into two horns, which are pushed back from her temples, like those of an oryx, her make-up is exotic and immaculate, but her mouth is small and, he thinks, ugly.

'When I have completed my business here, then I will return my calls. That will be on Monday. Now, go away. I have deals to be completed and contracts to sign.'

She turns away from him, begins to stride up the sand.

'Dlomo Nobuhle.' His voice is loud now, his hand stretched out displaying his ID. She stops, turns again. 'You speak with me now, or I will arrest you right here, cuff you, and lead you out across this charming party to my car. And then you will spend the weekend in my cells before you talk to me on Monday.'

She hurries back towards him, ankle turning in the sand as she stumbles, gesturing for him to lower his voice. Already, behind her, he can see groups twisting to look down towards the sea.

'You can't do this.'

'I can, and I will.' She opens her painted mouth again, but he continues. 'If you talk with me now, maybe for ten minutes, then you can return to your party and complete your business. This is your last chance.'

She shudders, overcome with frustration. 'You will show me your ID again and you will hear from my attorney.' She turns. 'Come with me. We will talk in my car.'

She strides towards the entrance across the beach, ignoring the enquiring glances from guests as she passes. De Vries follows at a saunter, out along the fairy light-lit boardwalk into the car park. Ahead, he sees her throw open the door to a black BMW Z4, slam it shut. He ambles to the car, opens the passenger door, gets in.

'If my deals are interrupted because of you, I will sue the police.'

De Vries waits until she turns to him.

'As the owner of the sole agency representing the sale of Apostle Lodge, you are responsible for its security. When I investigate a murder, I expect the co-operation of everyone. If you receive a message from a member of the SAPS again, answer it immediately.'

'Do not lecture me. You think I do not know about our history?'

De Vries stay calm, feels unaffected by her constant threats and barbs. 'There is no history here, Miss Nobuhle. If you want co-operation, threats will not ease your path. Are you ready to answer my questions?'

'Show me your ID.'

He produces it again.

She takes her cellphone, pushes it close up to the pass, photographs it twice. 'You ask what you want now, hope that you still have your job in the morning.'

He smiles again. 'When did you, personally, last enter Apostle Lodge?'

She angles her head down towards her lap, her jaw tight.

'I do not conduct tours. I am the owner of an important business. My job is to supervise and control.'

'So, have you never been inside Apostle Lodge?'

'Of course. High-worth properties receive my personal appraisal.'

'So, when were you last there?'

'I met with the owner maybe four years ago. Since then once, last year, to check that the open house was set up how I had specified. Maybe April. I am not in charge of the disposal of that property. That is the responsibility of Gregory Harrisson, one of my sales representatives.'

'Has anyone contacted you personally concerning Apostle Lodge in the last eighteen months?'

'No. There has been no interest in that property. It is unrealistically priced.'

'Why have you kept it on your books?'

'I told the vendor that I would sell his property, and when he is realistic about the price, that is what I shall do.'

'And it looks good to have a premium property on your books?'

'I have many such properties.'

'There are no other eight-figure properties in your window.'

She opens her mouth, hesitates, flicks away the question with her left hand. 'I have many.'

'Apart from the three members of staff in your Camps Bay office and yourself, who has access to the key safe at that office?'

'No one. Apart from me, only Gregory Harrisson has a key. He acts as the day manager for that office.'

'But the safe is left open during the day?'

'That is not procedure. The safe is to be locked at all times.'

'It was open when I visited.'

'Then procedure has been violated. I am not responsible for the failings of my staff.'

'Have you lost or mislaid your keys in the last four years?'

'No.'

'No?'

'I tell you. No.'

'Are you aware of the owner of Apostle Lodge returning to Cape Town since he left?'

'No. He emails me every three months to hear what viewings have been conducted, and tells me at what price I should advertise his property.'

'How many viewings have your colleagues conducted in the last eighteen months?'

'I have conducted none, but my staff have shown the house maybe six times.'

'Six times? You have the details of those you showed around?'

'The details will be in the office.'

'Before you employed Greg Harrisson, did you check his criminal record?'

She smiles, twists to face him, tone sarcastic. 'Oh, yes. I know about Gregory's past. He told me when I interviewed him, but he was not convicted. The woman who accused him was unreliable and weak. Besides, what do I care? This is business and Gregory is my number-one sales representative.'

'You are not worried about him showing houses to women alone?'

'No. Why should I be?'

'Because of his past.'

'His past, as you say, was made up by one woman and you, the SAPS. It is nothing.'

'Have you ever met or had business dealings with Luke or Bethany Miles?'

'I do not know these people.'

'Bethany Miles was found dead in Apostle Lodge.'

She shrugs. 'Okay.'

'Have any of your staff ever lent keys to or used properties that you were selling?'

'No. They would be fired if they did.'

De Vries thinks about further questions, realizes that, however much he may dislike Dlomo Nobuhle, she has told him what he wanted to know, the relevant boxes ticked.

'When will that property be available for my people to clean and prepare it for showing?'

'Very soon, Miss Nobuhle.' He opens the door and steps out.

Before he closes it, he hears her say, 'Policeman.'

He ducks down to see into the cabin.

'You are not even saying my name right. It is Nobuhle. Nobuhle, you understand?'

De Vries drives from the stadium back into town, up Long Street, onto Orange Street, stops in a lay-by close to the 15 On Orange Hotel. He dials Grace Bellingham's cellphone number.

'I can't talk now.'

'I wanted to see you.' He can hear that he sounds too casual, too desperate. 'To say sorry for the other night.' In the background, he can hear conversation, music.

'I'm busy tonight. Call me tomorrow.'

'Later?'

'Tomorrow.' She disconnects the call.

De Vries is tired and hungry, does not know whether to eat or sleep. He turns up the air-conditioning, wipes sweaty hands on his shirt, drives through the night towards a bar, towards beer.

The road twists around the low mountains, the sun blinding him in his rear-view mirror when the car faces due west. There are hints of dusk in the sky to the south. Ray Black guides him off the R62, down Hoof Street towards Zoar, then double-backing to the settlement of Amalienstein down Suikerbos Avenue. The roads are dirt tracks here; behind them, they leave a thick dusty trail, which hangs in the air.

'Why here, Ray?'

'Cos this is the kind of place they might come, stop off.'

Mike Solarin looks at the low shacks, each with its own burned-out backyard. There are a few stalls but no shops, no garage. He pulls over. 'There's nothing here.'

'You wanted everywhere checked. Thought we should tick this one off too.'

Solarin points to a tiny superette under a corrugated-iron roof on the corner of the street ahead. 'You go ask in there, Ray.'

Black collects pictures, clambers out of the car, walks along the road.

Mike Solarin gets out also, stretches. They have been driving for only half an hour, forty minutes since eating, and already he feels stiff and sticky. His cellphone rings; a number he does not recognize. 'Mike Solarin.'

'Lieutenant, Colonel Juiles. Where are you?'

'Between Ladismith and Calitzdorp, sir.'

'Good progress. There've been developments here. We're recalling everyone to HQ.'

'Suspects?'

'We've made identifications. I'm not discussing it now. We need you and Warrant Black back. Turn round, retrace your steps, drop down to the N2, whatever you want. Get you back tonight, ready for work tomorrow.'

'You want us back tonight?'

'That is correct, Lieutenant.'

'Yes, sir.'

'Tomorrow, eight a.m., both of you. We have a debriefing and new assignments.'

He disconnects. Solarin stares at the home-screen of his cell-phone.

'Nothing.'

Solarin turns. Ray Black stands on the other side of the vehicle.

'We're going back.'

'What?'

'Back to Cape Town now.'

'Why?'

'Orders.'

Black gets into the driver's seat, slams his door. Solarin waits a moment. No complaint, no argument, no curiosity; Black's phone taken out of his left trouser pocket as he got in when, as he left the car, he put it in his right. He looks down at the roof of the car to where Ray Black is sitting. Then he climbs into the cabin.

The telephone call between De Vries and Mark Garsten is fruit-less and depressing. The man's life has been torn apart. Five weeks on from the discovery of his wife's body, he seems utterly unable to cope, to work, to care for his children. At the end of the call, his father comes onto the line, begs De Vries to find who murdered his daughter-in-law, to make some progress so that his son has some closure to mark the end of one life and the beginning of a new one. De Vries tries not to promise results; has fallen into doing so before now through weakness, left himself with unsustainable pacts and a deeper guilt when failure and the pressure of the next case overcome him.

No sample considered to be from a second party has been discovered on Bethany Miles. De Vries reflects that this, too, may be an escalation. The attacker has realized that he must be more careful, that he must plan more intricately. To his surprise, Brigadier du Toit has concluded that the evidence from the two crime scenes is compelling. As a result, he has met with Assistant Deputy Provisional Commissioner Thulani, and the wheels of the SAPS public-relations machine have begun slowly to turn. De Vries has enjoyed his last few cases, each without interest from the press or requiring interaction with the hierarchy of the elite units. Each quietly resolved, reports complete, charges laid, trials forthcoming.

Work continues on connections between the two known victims. De Vries calls Stephen Jessel, the case-worker who supervises Leigh Finnemore, arranges to meet at his charge's property after lunch. His office is so hot, he longs simply to leave it, and the entire airless, claustrophobic building, to find cool air somewhere. He decides to drive back over Kloof Nek, down into Camps Bay, to talk to Greg Harrisson in the cool of his effectively air-conditioned office.

Before ten at the weekend, traffic is light in Cape Town. He reaches the crest of the pass, waiting only a few moments as the queue of vehicles heading for the cable-car station make their way along Tafelberg Road searching for the already elusive parking spaces. He decides against taking Camps Bay Drive and turns right instead, down the serpentine Kloof Road, between the tall pines and huge boulders, slowing as he takes the sharp turns to enjoy the framed vistas of the bay beneath, the iridescent turquoise sea, the blank, perfectly unblemished blue sky. At the bottom, he turns left to join the strip, already busy with tourists and locals enjoying late breakfasts or cool drinks at the many cafés and restaurants. Stallholders and hawkers block pavements, taxi-vans and minicabs double-park on the street. Everything moves slowly, but, to his delight, when he opens the front windows of his car, a cooler breeze sweeps across him, the air chilled by thousands of kilometres of travel over freezing ocean rooted in Antarctica. On the beach, sunbathers have laid out towels, ice-cream sellers prowl, children run towards the sea and retreat screaming as the ankle-achingly cold water rushes towards them. At some point, probably even earlier this morning, a small group of elderly sun-tanned swimmers will appear with bathing caps, in some cases wetsuits, and wade into the sea for ten minutes. Precious few others will be seen submerged today.

He finds a vacated parking space directly outside Nobuhle Estates, steps out, takes a few paces to the door of the block, climbs the stairs and enters the office. Inside, the cool saturates his clothes. Only Greg Harrisson sits at his desk; otherwise the space is deserted. He sees De Vries, his face struggling to form a smile. He stands up, proffers his hand. 'I'm alone this morning, Colonel.'

'I just have a few questions, Mr Harrisson.'

'Yeah, that's what I'm saying. I can't speak now. I have to keep an eye on everything.'

De Vries's smile contains no more humour than Harrisson's. 'When the phone rings, or a client walks through the door, you can look after them.'

Harrisson sighs, gestures to the chairs in front of his desk. 'You're going to ask me about the girl in Blouberg, aren't you?'

'Why do you think that?'

106

'I received a late-night call from my boss.'

'Did you now? That was nice of her.'

'Not nice. She doesn't do nice.'

'So, what should I know about the girl in Blouberg?'

'It was nothing. A misunderstanding. I admit I liked her, fancied her. We talked in a bar, I got her number. I called her a few times, she didn't seem keen. I saw her at another bar and went over to her. She was a bit drunk, seemed up for it, so I walked her home. She invited me in, lay on the couch with her legs apart – you know how women can be? I took it as an invitation, but apparently it wasn't. Nothing happened. The charges were dropped.'

'What nothing happened?'

'Nothing. I stopped when she told me to get off her.'

'Just like that?'

Harrisson meets his eye. 'Nobody says different.'

'Well, your victim did, didn't she, at first?'

'She wasn't a victim and she changed her mind, okay?'

'Why was that?'

'She realized I hadn't meant any harm. I'm a red-blooded male. I haven't seen her since. I was happy to move away. It's like another world out there, so far from the Mountain.'

'And Miss Nobuhle grabbed you, did she?'

'I'm good at my job.'

De Vries sees the confidence seep back into Harrisson's demeanour; wonders if he has missed the line of questioning the man had, at first, undoubtedly feared. 'Where do you stay now?'

'Seapoint.'

'Own a place? Renting?'

'Renting just now. Like to feel free.'

'Never know when you're going to be moving on?'

De Vries watches Harrisson's reaction, then sees a shadow in the mirror behind him. Harrisson sits up, expecting the door to the office to open, but the figure moves away again.

'Ever lived in Strand?'

'Strand? *Ja*, for a while. Got one of my first jobs in the industry there . . . 2007. Why?'

'I like to know things. Have you got a girlfriend now?'

Harrisson frowns. 'I don't think I have to discuss my private life with you.'

'You'll find with me, sir, no topic of conversation is out of bounds.'

'Look, I'm twenty-eight. I play the field, go to bars, clubs. Sometimes I meet a girl and I think maybe she could be the one. We bond, you know. Talk into the early hours. But I'm a free agent. I like it that way.'

'What car do you drive?'

'Am I a suspect? Is that what you're telling me here?'

'Yes.'

He answers quietly: 'I have a Sirocco. New model, last year. White. It's around the back in the bay for the office.'

'Have it cleaned?'

'Yes. I expect you have your car cleaned too.'

'When last?'

Harrisson shrugs. 'I don't know. Two weeks?'

'I might just take a look at your car, sir.'

Harrisson snatches up a bunch of keys from his desk, throws them at De Vries. 'Help yourself. Go through the back door. It's right there. I leave the office and the boss sees, shit hits the fan.'

'Tough cookie, is she?'

'You met her.'

'Still have the bruises.'

Harrisson smiles, genuinely this time, stands up as the door from the street opens.

De Vries takes the short corridor to the back of the shop, passing a locked office door, a toilet and a small kitchen area. He unbolts the back door, steps out into the tiny courtyard. The heat slaps his face, the reflection off the white paint of the car stinging his eyes. It stands in one of the two parking spaces beyond a metal sliding gate. De Vries finds the Volkswagen-branded key-fob, de-presses the unlocking button and the boot release and pokes inside the sweltering cabin. The back seats are small, the roofline low; access from the door would be difficult even if you were conscious and able-bodied. One back seat is folded forward and the front half of a surfboard is visible. He backs out, slams the door, peers into the boot. Apart from the board, there are flip-flops, a towel, a wet-suit, damp board shorts and half a dozen plastic carrier bags. The carpet is sandy. He studies the gas-struts, trim protectors, cubby-holes, sees nothing suspicious. He closes the hatchback, locks the car, re-enters the back door of the office. Inside, he can hear the agent describing a property to a potential client. He places the keys back on his desk, glances across the surface, walks towards the front.

'That's all in order, Greg,' he says, as he passes him and a young couple. He smiles at them, raises a palm to Harrisson, winks.

'See you soon.'

He drives back up the Camps Bay side of the Mountain. Harrisson's car seems an unlikely vehicle for an abduction, his knowledge of Strand probably no more than coincidental if, at least, marginally significant. He wonders what, on first seeing him enter the office, had so concerned the man, yet, moments later, questions under way, allowed him once again to relax.

The briefing room contains fewer than twenty officers. The lights are on full, the atmosphere flat. Mike Solarin thinks that the ceiling seems lower, that energy has seeped from the space. He sits in the second row of chairs, looks around for Ray Black, but cannot find him.

PAUL MENDELSON

Colonel Brent Juiles sits on the edge of the table in front of them, casual, as if he is addressing friends.

'Gentlemen . . .' He scans the room, nods to himself, smiles. '*Ja*, just gentlemen. At sixteen hundred hours yesterday, we received positive identification from our labs of the two suspects in the Nissan truck in Long Street. They were Akram Ibrahim Jabouri, twenty-eight, originally from Iraq but from 2013 identified as being in Niger, and known associate Abdu-Allah Baravan, twenty-six. These guys are known to our security services as being loosely associated with al-Mourabitoun, as you should know, also known as al-Qaeda West Africa. They may or may not have had dealings with Abubakar Shekau but, as yet, we have not received a claim for the incident.

'What happens now is that our analysts get to work and try to piece together why these guys should mount an operation in South Africa, Cape Town in particular, and whether their actions were sanctioned or rogue. We're betting on the latter.' He stands, paces from one side of the room to the other.

'No country with corrupt governance has been able to tackle extremists effectively. Resources get diverted before they can be channelled effectively. Bribery is widespread. This is why these people are flourishing in eastern and central Africa and they are moving south. Make no mistake. Authorized or not, this will not be the last we see from these guys.'

He turns to them. 'I want to congratulate all of you. Job well done. I'm standing you down from Cape Town and you'll return to Pretoria in the coming days. You'll be assigned new duties.'

General Thulani's office, so often an icy cave of misery, is today, at least, gloriously cold and refreshing.

'These are dark times,' Thulani intones, looking down from his huge chair at his long-time colleague David Wertner, head of the Internal Investigation Bureau, Henrik du Toit and De Vries. 'Every unmarked van that stops is suspect. The shops in town have reported falls in sales and foot traffic. The bomb has been news in every country in the world, and everyone is concerned about next summer. And now,' he stares at De Vries, 'you bring us this.'

'The two crimes are not centred on Cape Town City Bowl, the tourist area,' Du Toit says.

'They are centred on Cape Town. My city. When we release this to the press, however careful we may be, there will be renewed fear, panic even. And remember this, gentlemen. When there is crime unstopped, we are to blame. No one else. Our new leader has made that quite clear. We cannot blame crime on the criminals, we must bear the responsibility ourselves. That is what the public think.'

'The public . . .'

Thulani stares at De Vries. 'What did you say, Colonel?'

De Vries checks himself. 'Hard to please, the public, sir.'

'Impossible but, nonetheless, it is your job to try.' He draws himself up. 'Let us be candid here. What do we have? A spree killer, a serial killer?'

Du Toit looks at De Vries, who says, 'We have two killings linked only by the modus operandi, what might be considered the natural development of a killer who is escalating his actions. We do not know whether these women are linked in any way. At present, it seems not. If that is the case, there is danger that we have a serial killer and that his timetable will escalate until he is caught.'

'So, we don't know?'

'No. To call two linked crimes by pejorative titles is counter-productive. It will not help us, and the press will frighten people.'

Thulani raises his shoulders in a demonstrative shrug.

111

'Who knows what the press will do?' He turns his attention to Du Toit. 'Knowing how little Colonel de Vries cares for the press, you should be responsible, Henrik. You,' he continues, turning to De Vries, 'stay on the case, to the book, and impress us once more with your abilities, Colonel. And I am going to say this once again, with Colonel Wertner here in front of you: the press will be watching. Pretoria will be watching. Cases such as these reflect not only on you and your unit but on me also. I want only to bask in your success. You understand?'

'He is stealing jewellery,' Don February says. 'According to the docket on Marie Garsten, she only wore a gold wedding ring. Nothing else. Bethany Miles wore a gold wedding band and an engagement ring with a five-star, four-carat tanzanite stone surrounded by diamonds. Her husband emailed the photographs, asked us to sign off on the insurance.'

'After three days?'

Don looks at Sally Frazer. 'Either he is a very efficient man, or the insurance payout has great value to him.'

'Sorry to be the one asking this,' Ben Thwala suddenly says, 'but what about the ladies' knickers?'

'According to the docket,' De Vries says, 'in the Strand killing, Marie Garsten's underwear was discovered at the side of the room. That item was sent to be analysed so it's not missing.'

'But the underwear from the Camps Bay scene?'

'Not found, as far as we know.' De Vries stands up. 'This man isn't leaving messages. If he's staging scenes to tell us something, we don't yet know what. The jewellery could be mementoes, it could be robbery. It could even be to give the perception of robbery. Just check with the husbands where the jewellery was

112

purchased, will you? You've checked dentists, doctors,' he lists these on fingertips, 'obstetricians, gynaecologists, hairdressers, beauty salons, all of that, have you?'

'I don't know about obstetricians and gynaecologists,' Sally Frazer says, taking a note. 'We checked salons, clubs, gyms. I'll get it covered.'

'We need a connection,' De Vries says. 'If there's nothing, we have a man picking victims seemingly randomly. In terms of catching him, or not catching him, I think we all understand the significance of that.'

Mike Solarin enters, sits when Colonel Juiles gestures towards the chair, waits in silence as the CO writes on the desk in front of him. Juiles signs a paper hard, looks up.

'This has been good experience for you,' Juiles says. 'You pick up how we work here?'

'Yes, sir.'

'This is just the start. We are going to be on the front line from now on. You want to be involved in anti-terror?'

Solarin nods.

'There's a problem, Lieutenant?'

'No, sir. Just questions.'

'Ask away.'

'Isn't it unusual that there has been no claim?'

Juiles sits back, surveys Solarin. '*Ja*. But, as I said at the debriefing, we think that this may have been unauthorized. Two young guys frustrated by a lack of action, yet radicalized. Perhaps there is an imam, a religious leader, who inspired these guys. We don't know. That's what our analysts will want to discover in the coming days and weeks.'

'Do we know whether they self-detonated or whether it was remotely detonated?'

'We don't know that. The blast was, as you saw, as you've read, enormous. We've brought in the best people, but resources aren't unlimited, even for us. We'll find the detonator soon. We'll piece together what happened. I know what you're asking: is there another guy out there? A man who pushed the button, dialled the number, sent the signal. We don't know, but, in these cases, that would be unusual.'

'And the explosive. I was told that it was old.'

'Who told you?'

The three words warn Solarin. The forced casualness of the question, jarring with the speed at which it was asked.

'No one. The guys were saying it wasn't modern explosive. The residue seemed to suggest old ordnance, although my recollection of the exact science is sketchy . . .'

'These guys aren't state-of-the-art. They utilize what they can get their hands on. It might have been smuggled in but, more likely, it's old stolen material, sold on the black market, perhaps even in the Eastern Cape.'

Solarin nods. 'Yes, sir.'

'As a senior officer, you have the choice of staying here a day or two over the weekend or flying back this evening. Up to you. Chill out on the beach?'

Solarin had been told. Solarin affects casual better than Juiles. '*Ja*. Meeting friends at Fourth Beach, Clifton, tonight. Going to enjoy the Mother City.'

'Good man.'

Juiles studies him. Solarin sits, unblinking. Juiles nods. Solarin gets up from his chair, leaves the office. He books an Uber cab to pick him up, stands in the car park, in the full sun, the heat on the back of his neck causing drops of sweat to fall down the marked ridge between his shoulder blades. He does not feel it. He dials another number.

'Hey, Gugu. You still in town? I need to see you.'

When De Vries arrives at the short end of Plumbago Lane, he sees Stephen Jessel getting out of his white Toyota Prius, waving him down. He pulls up next to him.

'Before we go in, Colonel, I'd like to speak to you. Perhaps in my car?'

De Vries parks, locks his own car, walks over to Jessel's vehicle, gets into the air-conditioned cabin.

'Nicer here than on the street.' Jessel fumbles in the centre console, offers De Vries a sweet from a tin. 'No?'

'What do you need to speak to me about, Mr Jessel?'

'Leigh does not see many guests. As I have explained to you, he does have friends and they do occasionally visit him. The strangers who come to the house are usually there to study or evaluate him and, naturally, he is suspicious. No one likes to be watched, their home life scrutinized. So, I'm asking you to be gentle with him, show him respect, and understand that this will be a difficult encounter for him.'

'It should be a simple matter.'

'But it will not be simple. Leigh's mind is such that he will assume you suspect him for this murder because of his past. That he will always be suspect because of it. It is for this reason he is unable to lead a normal life.'

'Is that it?'

'There is one more thing,' Jessel says. 'While medical professionals are reluctant to categorize it as such, Leigh suffers from a form of dual-personality complex. I have spoken to him twice already today and he seems stable. If that is his mood when you speak to him, you will find him a polite and calm man. However, he can become intensely depressed, surly, difficult. It is not surprising. If this is the case, I would suggest suspending your questioning until another time.'

'All your points are noted.'

'Good.' Jessel lets himself out of the car, waits until De Vries has closed the passenger door, then locks it. They walk slowly along the road, looking down on the mirage that blurs the view of the bay.

'Thank you for coming in an unmarked car.'

'I never drive a marked police vehicle. I prefer anonymity.'

'I'm sure we all prefer that. Although I imagine most people recognize you pretty quickly for who you are.'

They reach the front door. Jessel rings the bell three times.

'You don't have a key?'

'I do, but I prefer to show Leigh respect. It breeds a healthier relationship.'

The door opens on Leigh Finnemore, and De Vries is taken aback by the imposing, slim man who stands before them. He is close on two metres tall, with red hair swept back over his forehead, a light beard, very pale blue eyes and freckled white skin. His wrists are adorned with hundreds of pieces of coloured thread. Around his neck, there are more small objects. He wears a T-shirt, rust-red shorts, and his feet are bare.

'Leigh, this is Vaughn. I was telling you about him.'

Leigh Finnemore stares at De Vries. His eyes narrow, his brow furrows, then his mouth breaks into a wide smile. He holds out his hand.

'Hello, Vaughn.' He looks at Jessel. 'Hello, Stephen. Why don't you come in and have some tea?'

The living room is at the back of the house, doors open to a small, burned-out lawn, which slopes steeply upwards towards a line of bent trees. Over the doorway a cast-iron balcony is supported by iron columns. The room itself is cool, an oversized ceiling fan rotating on the high, ornately plastered ceiling. The room also contains a selection of antique South African furniture made from yellow-wood, stinkwood and mahogany. Underfoot, a light Persian-style carpet lies over aged blond parquet flooring. Books are stacked untidily on shelves, tables are covered with magazines and books, and there is a pile of vinyl records by an old-fashioned music centre. On the walls are three large, brightly coloured naive paintings of the view of Camps Bay from above. The room is elegant and calm.

Finnemore seats them, exits, and then returns, only a few moments later, with a tray holding a teapot, three cups and saucers, milk, sugar and a plate of biscuits. He pours each of them a cup, hands it to them, then offers sugar and biscuits. Everything is formal, his actions precise, mannered, silent. When they all have tea, he sits back in an upholstered armchair, affects a strained smile.

De Vries looks at Jessel, who nods to him.

'Did Stephen tell you that I need to ask you some questions?'

'Yes. About Apostle Lodge.' His voice is quiet and controlled.

'That's correct. These are questions which I and my colleagues have asked every one of your neighbours. Everyone on the street.'

'I understand,' Finnemore says, facing De Vries in his chair, his body language open and unrestricted.

'Have you been inside Apostle Lodge since you moved here?'

'No.'

'Have you walked up to it to see it from the outside?'

'Stephen drove me to the end of the road. The other side. He told me that I should see my neighbours' houses and what the rest of my street looked like. I've lived here all this time and never walked the length of it.'

'You don't go out on your own?'

Finnemore glances at Jessel. 'Not often.'

'Have you ever met a lady called Bethany Miles?'

'No.'

'Are you sure?'

'I don't think so. Unless she was in a hospital I was in.'

'Did you know that a lady had been killed in the house at the other end of this road, in Apostle Lodge?'

Leigh Finnemore's face falls. He nods. 'And I know why you're here. Because when I was a child I killed my sister. I drowned her, and everyone knows why except me, and everyone remembers it except me, and that's why you're here.' He stares at De Vries, challenging him to deny his motives.

'But you didn't kill the lady, Bethany Miles, at Apostle Lodge?'

'Is that a rhetorical question?'

'No.'

Finnemore smiles indulgently at him. 'Then no.'

'Thank you.'

'I try to never hurt anyone or anything.'

De Vries sits back, picks up his cup, sips. It is a fragrant Indian tea in delicate china. He looks at Leigh Finnemore, who has sat back straight in his chair. His long fingers hold his cup awkwardly, but he sips his tea, replaces the cup on the table to his side. Everything is calm, under control.

'Are these paintings yours?' De Vries says, indicating the canvases on the walls.

'Is that it? You ask me whether I killed the woman, I say no, and then you ask me about art?'

'My interests are surprisingly broad.'

Finnemore turns to Jessel, shrugs his shoulders. Jessel just smiles. 'All right,' he says, returning to De Vries, indulgent again. 'Yes. I am an artist, a hermit, an outsider. The world outside my window does not welcome me. So I have a house full of paint and canvas. My grandfather liked to paint too. This has always been an artist's house.'

118

'It's a lovely view.'

'It is what I see from my bedroom at the top of the house. I paint there. I only paint landscapes.'

'Not abstracts or portraits?'

'Never portraits,' Finnemore says. 'I can't paint people.'

'But you've painted your cat, haven't you, Leigh?' Jessel says.

Finnemore glances at Jessel, lips pouting. 'It didn't look like him. I destroyed the canvas.'

'Why do you think you are not welcome outside?'

Jessel sits up, says, 'Vaughn.' He laughs. 'We leave Leigh to make his own decisions, to decide what he wants to do.'

De Vries looks at Finnemore, sees no reaction on his face, just a slightly blank, happy smile. 'I'm just curious. Do you ever go to the beach?'

Finnemore's eyes widen. 'No.'

'You see it every day. You paint it. Would you like to go to the beach?'

'No.'

'Why not?'

'All right, Vaughn,' Jessel says, with a pronounced firmness, despite keeping his voice light. 'No one likes friends to ask personal questions.'

'Because I can't be trusted,' Finnemore says. 'Because I might harm someone.'

'Is that what people tell you?'

'No, Colonel,' Finnemore says, more loudly now. 'It is because I am, and always will be, a killer. I killed my sister and I don't even remember it. So, how will I know if I go to the beach? I might kill again, and still not know anything about it.'

'It's all right, Leigh.' Jessel says.

'So, that is why I stay here, away from people, children especially, because I can't be trusted ... I can't be certain I can trust myself. Can you imagine what that might be like?'

'I don't know.'

'Look outside at my garden. There used to be a pool there. They filled it in. They even took out the baths and put in showers, because imagine what it would be like to be with me in a pool – or in the sea – knowing what you know about me. Imagine when you're out of your depth and you don't want to be seen moving away from me or swimming back to shallow water, when you check that I'm not coming towards you, when I raise my arms and you think, Maybe, maybe Leigh will put his hand on my head and push me under and not let go until I have no breath.'

'I wouldn't think that,' De Vries says.

Leigh Finnemore smiles, his breathing fast, face red. His hand reaches for the cup and saucer. The china rattles in his quivering hand. He puts it back on the side table. 'That's what people say, but I know what they think. And I know what you think too. You would watch me, Colonel. You would watch me very carefully.'

De Vries speaks to her in his office.

'Number One Plumbago Lane, a Mr Finnemore – the section eighteen – I've spoken to him and I don't think he has anything to contribute. Something of a recluse.'

'I know you can't say,' Sally Frazer says, 'but the section eighteen. It was all right?'

'*Ja*. I'm sworn to secrecy. If anyone wants to talk with him, I need to know, okay?'

She nods.

'You get my note about Greg Harrisson?'

'*Ja*. I've put in requests elsewhere, including Strand, for any information or record on him. So much gets lost even now, and that's if it's even entered in the first place.'

'He's hiding something. So far, he's pretty much all we've got.

Connections to both Camps Bay and Strand, suspicious past, probably pretty insensitive to women, but there's a difference between insensitivity and murder. If it's him, he's very good.'

'Good?'

'He's slick and smooth, and I don't like him. But Cape Town's full of them.'

'You rate our killer as young?'

De Vries raises his eyebrows. 'You're right. I think he's older. We need a profile.'

'Your lady friend?'

'One dinner. I eat one meal with a woman and now she's my "lady friend"?'

'Nothing stays private for very long, sir.'

'No.'

'Whoever he is, he's killed twice already and left nothing. He's clever.'

'He left pubic hair at the Strand scene . . . if it's his. We can't take anything at face value.'

'Why don't we get the idiot criminals?' Frazer says. 'The ones you see on TV robbing a bank disguised as a tree, or who leave their cell-phones behind after a burglary?'

'Because they go to the rest of the SAPS and, if they don't fuck it up, they strike one for the good guys. We just get the clever bastards.'

Don February sees a shadow pass behind the peephole in the door to 35 Plumbago Lane. He can hear breathing. He stands patiently, holding out his ID.

'*Ja*?'

'Police, Mr Cloete. I am Warrant Officer February.'

Marten Cloete opens the door, sweating, his knees dirty, shorts stained.

'I need to ask you some more questions about the incident next door to you.'

'Not a great time now. My sons will be home from their day camp soon.'

'I am required to ask you questions, sir. And I must do this now.'

Cloete seems to look over and past Don, across and down the street. 'What's this about?'

'It is very hot here, sir. Please may I come in?'

'Why don't you talk to the other householders first? Leave me till later?'

'I must talk to you, sir. I can ask my questions here if you will not let me into your home.'

Marten Cloete backs up, watches Don cross the threshold to his house. 'Go on through to the kitchen at the back.'

Cloete leaves Don standing by the table, takes a can of Grapetiser from the fridge, gulps most of it.

'You know, I'm sick of always being the one you guys talk to. I'm a working man, and I come home early so I'm here for my sons when they get back from school. Now you're here again.'

Don opens his notebook, pencil poised over the page, voice quiet and calm. 'What do you do for a living, sir?'

'I'm a builder. I own a building company. Why do you need to know that?'

'And the name of the company?'

'Why?'

'Because it is my job, sir. I am told to ask questions, I report the answers and the murder inquiry continues. That is all I do, sir.'

'Cloete. It's my name. My business.' He drains the can, flicks open a sliding drawer and tosses it inside, then kicks it closed with his toe. The drawer speeds back, halts a few centimetres from its position, glides slowly into place.

'Have you ever been inside the property next door, Apostle Lodge?'

'You could have asked me this when that other guy was here. What are you guys doing? You have any idea who killed that woman? I've got kids. We want to know you're doing your jobs, keeping us safe.'

'Colonel de Vries questioned your sons, sir, but not you. It is procedure.'

Cloete sits at the head of the table, his back to the garden, spreads his legs and places his elbows on the surface. 'Get on with it, then.'

'Apostle Lodge, sir. Have you ever been inside?'

'*Ja.* I saw it when they had an open house about two years ago. It had been for sale for years already. I wanted to see what it looked like inside.'

'Why?'

'I build houses. It's an ugly building, but it's interesting, you know? The vendor is asking a lot of money. I wanted to know why.'

'Was that the last time you were inside?'

'I went into the living room through the back door when the gardener was there. Maybe a year ago.'

'Why was that, sir?'

'Why? My boys flew their remote-controlled plane, helicopter, or whatever it was, into the garden, so I retrieved it. The gardener guy turned up, said he had found a cricket ball on the grass. I said it was ours and he went inside to find it. I followed him in and the door to the living area was open, so I walked in.'

'What was in the room?'

'I don't know. Nothing. It was empty.'

'A chair, or a chaise longue?'

'*Ja*, a bed thing, zigzag, like a couch, black leather, chrome.'

'A chair too?'

He shrugs. 'I don't know. Who cares?'

'You walked around the room?'

'I looked in. Maybe took a few steps. I told you this.'

'You haven't been in since?'

'No . . . the garden, *ja*, because footballs, cricket balls, you name it, boys kick it over there. But not in the house.'

'It is just you and your two sons, Patrick and Robert Cloete. Is that right, sir?'

'*Ja*, that's right. Just us, last six years.'

'Anybody else stay here, or go next door to Apostle Lodge?'

'No one goes next door. A girlfriend stayed for a while, but she's gone back to Gauteng now.'

'You didn't hear anything, notice anything strange last week at any time?'

Cloete stands up. 'Okay, that's enough. Another of your guys, big bloke, already asked me this shit, did I see anything, hear anything? Of course I didn't or I would have said, *ja*? I'm trying to bring my boys up well, Officer, and I don't want the police here when they get home.'

Don breathes gently, waits a few beats until Cloete has stopped. He looks at Cloete's knees. 'Have you been next door to the garden since Thursday, Mr Cloete?'

'Why do I want to go anywhere near that place? Fucking death house now, isn't it?'

Don closes his notebook, scans the kitchen, slowly walks towards the front door. On the table in the hallway, he glances at a small pile of mail, sees on top a letter addressed to Apostle Lodge. He stops, picks it up, scrutinizes it.

'These letters, sir. They are from next door?'

Cloete recoils, grabs the envelope out of Don's hand.

'I take them in. They're left out there in the mailbox, sticking out, for weeks. The agents are supposed to collect them. It's like shouting out the place is deserted.'

'You are not allowed to tamper with the post, sir. I will take the letters.'

'Help yourself. I drop all of them in to that estate agent down there every month.'

At the door, Don turns back to him. 'When did you last take the letters out of the mailbox?'

Cloete shrugs. 'Last week. Monday, Tuesday maybe?'

'The victim was inside the house then. You are sure you did not see a car, anybody near the house?'

'*Ja.*'

'If you think of a car, you will let us know, won't you, sir?'

'*Ja.*'

Marten Cloete stands at his threshold, watches Don walk slowly away, turn right towards Apostle Lodge. He observes him study the mailbox, open the unfastened tin hatch at the back, replace it gently. He watches him walk back to his car, wearing his thick suit, tie fastened, not a bead of sweat on his face.

The restaurant spills out onto the wide pavement, smokers sitting on the outside at the double-sided bar, facing inwards. They have both lit cigarettes. The ashtray, unemptied and smouldering, has ensured that no one sits opposite them.

'You remember when we did this at that place in Seapoint all summer?' De Vries says. 'Talked about cases, got drunk?'

She nods. 'That was twenty years ago. Forensic science is transformed — even the way we assess suspects psychologically is completely different.' She looks up at him. 'And we had other things on our minds . . .'

'Did we?'

'You did.'

He sits back, hands behind his head. 'You were distracting.'

'But we got the work done. I learned from you too, Vaughn. I won't forget that.'

'This city seemed a lot smaller then,' De Vries says. 'Policing seemed simpler. Not in the townships. Not on the Flats but, here, in town.'

'Everyone had been concentrating on the Struggle,' she says. 'Whichever side you were on, whether you said you cared or didn't. When we all became one, that's when we started noticing the trouble.'

'Our kind of trouble.'

Grace Bellingham smiles at him. 'We're not the people we were then, Vaughn. We're older and wiser, jaded and cynical and, frankly, I for one am damaged. I think you are too, if only you could see it. That's what happens to people who do what we do. We live in another world, and it is not a happy place.'

'It's my place.'

She smiles wanly. 'I was so happy to see you the other night but, afterwards, I realized it was a mistake.'

'Why?'

'Because you're everything I'm trying to escape. I left California, I ran away from London, and I came back here, came home. I can't keep going with my old life here. Here has to be sanctuary . . .' She draws hard on the cigarette, sighing her exhalation. 'It was a good evening. My talk went well. I escaped like a naughty school girl to my rendezvous with you. Even that blustery walk through town made me smile. But then, when you got called just as we were about to go upstairs, I remembered who you are.'

'A bad man?'

'A policeman. A policeman chasing the same men I've faced

126

across the table in the cell that could be anywhere in the world for the last twenty-five years. When I flew in, I looked down on the Mountain, and I saw what the tourists see – a beautiful, sunny city, surrounded by turquoise sea, deep blue sky. That's what I want it to be, need it to be, now. You see another city – and I know it's there – but I have had enough of the darkness, the shadows, the evil men do.'

'And you can't look at me without seeing all of that?'

'No, man. You know it's not that. I always knew what you were thinking, and I know now. You told me the other night. You've been a husband, a father, and now it's just you. I know what drives you – and that excited me then, when we were young, but not now. Not any more.'

De Vries waves at a waiter. 'Have another drink. Maybe you'll feel differently.'

She smiles again. 'Sorry. I've spoilt the evening.'

'No. You've just warned me it's not going to end the way I want it to.' He looks up at the waiter. 'Another bottle.'

The man nods.

'You don't know how I felt about you. It's not black and white. I just have to protect myself now. I've been hurt, and I'm not strong enough yet to be hurt again.' She puts her hand on his. 'Be a friend for me, Vaughn. Maybe I'll heal. Maybe things will be different but, just now, be here.'

He drives home along an empty freeway, windows open, the syrupy night air swirling around him, his car taking the slip road to Liesbeek Parkway as if on tracks. He heaves the wheel left at the traffic lights and ambles up his road to the gates of the family home, an old Victorian villa surrounded by pepper trees. He fumbles with the remote control, edges into the driveway, extinguishes the engine, slumps forward, his head on the wheel. He pulls himself up and out of the car, clumsily jams his thumb against the button which closes the gates again. He is drunk, wretched.

He undresses, splashes cold water against his face, opens the windows in the bedroom. He hears a television, loud and tinny. On the side of the neighbouring house, the small rectangular balcony is illuminated – a small screen in a vast dark cinema. He squints through branches, sees a thin black woman with an Afro haircut sitting propped up on a mattress, a dog at her feet. He adjusts his position, cups his hands around his eyes. She sits surrounded by a fridge, microwave, two-ring cooker, a pile of clothes atop an old tan suitcase. She seems relaxed, but not sleepy, as if she is preparing to sit up the whole night.

Inside the house a bare bulb illuminates the gutted interior. He sees a short black man, bald on top but with dreadlocks, cupping a mug, aimlessly checking doors and windows. De Vries looks back at the woman, sees her light a cigarette, her face occluded by a cloud of smoke, the television flickering in the haze, like distant lightning in a night sky. A car accelerates up the road to his side; the dog raises its head, opens its mouth to yawn and yowl, eyes squeezed tight shut.

De Vries turns, yawns, lies on his bed, curls up.

He wakes, head heavy and aching, pulse beating in his temples, turns to the empty side of the bed, closes his eyes and listens to himself breathing. An angle-grinder sends a spasm of pain to the apex of his head. He swings himself upright, showers, dresses, is out of the house within a few minutes. He strides past his car, out of his gates, to the house next door, its own gateway open.

'Hey!'

A coloured guy in blue overalls turns.

'It's seven thirty, man. What the fuck is going on?'

'When we start.' Saws buzz, hammers hammer.

'It's Sunday.'

'We're behind. Only the morning.'

'It's not allowed. It's the law. No building on Sunday. It happens again, you'll find yourself at the police station. Turn off the machines. If you want to work this morning, it's hand tools only. You understand?'

The man nods.

'The girl on the balcony in the night. Who's she?'

'Site guards. A lot of expensive equipment and supplies here. My boss always has them.'

'What's happening anyway?'

'You can come see.'

De Vries doesn't move. 'Just tell me.'

'Clients refurbing everything.'

'Who bought it?'

'The property? Don't know, man. We just do as we're told.'

'Well, just do it quietly. I know the law, so tell your boss he won't catch up if he fucking wakes me up. *Ja*?' De Vries turns away, mutters under his breath, rubs his eyes.

They gather in the same formation as on previous days, each in their place.

'Marten Cloete,' Don February says, 'told me that he had been in Apostle Lodge at least twice. Once when the estate agents had an open day, another time when the gardener went to retrieve a cricket ball he had put inside the anteroom. And, yesterday, he acted strangely. His knees were muddy, his shorts were dirty. I think he had been back to the garden, crawling through that gap in the hedge.'

De Vries says: 'The gardener told me that he never opened the inner door to the house, just the anteroom.' He tilts his head. 'Someone is lying.'

'There is one more thing,' Don says. 'Cloete was taking the mail from the letterbox and keeping it in his house. He told me that he took it to the estate agents' office in Camps Bay, but I do not think this is true. Two of the envelopes had been opened.'

'Could Marten Cloete have carried the body through his house, through the hedge?' They turn to Sally Frazer. 'Or maybe he took the body to Apostle Lodge at night, but visited the victim through the hedge. No one would see or hear that, and there would be no risk. It might explain his hostility, how angry you said he was about his sons being in the garden and in Apostle Lodge.'

'And,' Don says, 'if we had found his DNA, he has already admitted that he has been in the house on occasions. That could protect him.'

They turn to De Vries.

'He certainly knew Apostle Lodge was empty. If he kept in touch with the agents, he might know if or when they would have a showing. I was going to say that it doesn't feel right, keeping the victim so close to where he lives, but we don't know what happened to his wife. He's there alone with his kids. Doesn't like letting people into his house.'

'Self-employed. He can come and go and no one takes much notice,' Frazer says. 'We pay him more attention?'

'We do.' De Vries turns to the room. The officers are focused. 'I want you, Ben,' he indicates Thwala, 'to follow up on Greg Harrisson. Talk to the estate agents in Strand, find the woman who accused him of rape, then dropped the charges. Find out if he tried to tie her up, bind her to a chair. Don't worry if you get in Harrisson's face. He doesn't like it and that means I do.' He turns to Frazer. 'We're looking backwards here. The attack in Strand was almost six weeks ago. Look for unsolved attacks on women involving bindings, plastic ties, eyes, peeping Toms. I'm guessing that we're talking about more than maybe two months prior to the Marie Garsten attack. Anywhere in Cape Town, Somerset West, Gordon's Bay areas, maybe Stellenbosch too. The two victims we know about show that he's mobile. If we find a third victim from earlier, we may be able to triangulate a home position.' He looks up. 'Let's be clear. Unless something is really off here, this is the same guy and, if we don't find him, there'll be another victim, and another . . .'

He trails off, waves them away, stands by the whiteboard. He watches his team work; knows too little is happening.

Henrik du Toit's office is shaded until the afternoon, the air warm but not stifling. His desk is piled high with folders and reports, the stacks moving but seemingly never diminishing. De Vries wonders how he can fill his days with administration, have turned his back on policing, on investigation. Now he seems only to fight for the continued existence of his cherished Special Crimes Unit, solid in his belief that it makes a difference, stoical against the claims that it investigates too many crimes against white victims, that its arrest rate does not justify its budget. Yet both men know that those they pursue are criminals who cannot be allowed to remain free, men – and occasionally women – whom the under-funded, undermanned, inefficient and sometimes corrupt standard SAPS stations, even the Hawks, might not catch without the determination of many older, more experienced officers. That they may be tainted by their time serving the old apartheid regime is a public-relations price that must be paid. Each of the senior officers knows that, within the general pool of officers in the new SAPS, they would be drowned out, eased to desks in central offices, persuaded to retire in favour of the young, up-and-coming, poorly trained, naive.

'You've seen the press?' Du Toit asks. De Vries shakes his head. 'They've taken what we gave them and woven it into a story. We're not quite at serial or spree killer yet, but they've taken the connection and run with it. I know you don't care,' Du Toit says, 'but, for my sake, give me something each day I can pass on to them, even if it's nothing. They are beasts which must be fed.'

'I thought we were here to slay beasts.'

Du Toit sighs. 'I'm not playing that game with you, Vaughn. Just do as I say. You may not like being in the public eye, but you are, so get yourself together.' He moves a pile of papers left and right, then back to its original position. 'If this is a series of crimes, are you obtaining a profile?'

'Cyril Fenner is in Jo'burg. We got hold of him and he's busy.'

'Fenner isn't our only profiler, surely.'

'He's the best we have. There's some new guys, but we get a profile from some kid who's read a few books, passed a few multiple-choice exams, it can do more harm than good.'

'I thought that you and Grace Bellingham . . .'

'Dr Bellingham and I are old friends. The whole team know we had dinner together, and that must be fascinating for everyone, but she's not working right now, and she certainly doesn't want to work for us.'

'What about working for you?'

'Maybe . . .'

'How did your interview with our section-eighteen man go?'

'If he's telling the truth, he stays at home pretty much permanently. Utterly paranoid that everyone will think he's responsible for anything bad that happens. I can't see how either he or any-one else is sheltered by having him living there, but Stephen Jessel is very protective of him.'

'That's not what I meant.'

'He's a murderer living a couple of hundred metres from a mur-der scene.'

'Vaughn. I'm not interested in your opinion of the treatment of this man. Is he involved?'

'I doubt it, but beyond the veneer of charm, there's a knowing-ness about him I don't like.'

'You don't like anyone knowing anything.'

'Maybe I'm just not convinced that he's a victim. Everyone else is.'

'If he's not involved, he's not your problem. What are you doing now?'

'What we do. Rechecking neighbours' statements, looking backwards to see if there are earlier crimes, maybe get a descrip-tion, some idea where he operates.'

'Nothing concrete?'

'No, sir. Nothing concrete. Nothing that would make good copy.'

'The press are here at six. I want something.'

De Vries gets up, his smile fixed. 'There'll be something.'

De Vries leaves the office, walks to Long Street and the crossroads with Shortmarket Street, where he enters the cool, sweet-smelling interior of one of his many regular coffee shops. He orders two double espressos and asks the so-called barista to heat a cheese and bacon sandwich in the microwave oven. He drinks one of the coffees watching the digital countdown, takes the second to have with his brunch. Whenever he is absorbed in a case, his meal routine becomes disrupted or non-existent and, as he grows older, he finds that he begins to tire more easily. The first coffee fuels him to walk quickly back to the office, hugging the shaded side of the street. The still, stagnant air hits him the moment he passes through the revolving door into the lobby of his building. The lift car is warmer still, the interior dim, mechanism buzzing. By the time he reaches the squad-room, his entire body is sweating.

He slams the door of his office, throws his jacket over the back of his chair, sits at his desk, shoes on top of a pile of dockets. He realizes that the blinds over the internal windows onto the squad-room are raised, but he does not move to lower them. He unwraps the tepid sandwich, chews with his eyes closed.

When he has finished his coffee, Don knocks at his door, enters. 'I gave you ten minutes. Did you enjoy your sandwich?'

'No.'

'Marten Cloete is not answering his cellphone or his home number. Apparently, the house appears empty and his car is not there. Maybe he has taken his sons away.'

A loud knocking startles them.

'Sir,' Sally Frazer says, 'you should see this.' She beckons them out into the squad-room. Don waits while De Vries struggles to lift his feet from his desk and back to the floor. As they approach, Frazer says: 'We're just starting to look for any possible linked earlier crimes, and one sticks out.' She points to a sheet on her desk. 'It's an attack on a woman in Claremont, back in September. It's in her own home, but she's blindfolded, and the binding of wrists and ankles to a chair with black cable ties is the same. He demonstrates an intention to rape her, and the only reason he didn't is that her son returned home and disturbed him.'

'Either of them see anything?'

'Nothing that's mentioned in the report.'

'Anyone else? Neighbours?'

'No, but I know the road. It's behind Cavendish shopping centre, parallel to Main Road. All the cottages are behind high walls, tall gates. No one can see the street from their house, and there are always people trying to park there to avoid paying – like me.'

De Vries squints at the report. 'You think it's our guy?'

'It feels right, and the timing fits your theory, but you know how it is, we're guessing, hunting for a break.'

'You and me, we'll go now. Can you check she's there?'

'Done, and she is.'

'Good work.'

Frazer smiles. 'Thank you, sir. And I need to warn you. Hazel Calder and her son, they're little people.'

De Vries is already walking. 'Aren't we all?'

De Vries looks right over her into the tiny cottage, then bows his head to her and the smell engulfs him. Her voice is assertive, demanding.

'It's my sauce.'

De Vries stares down at Hazel Calder, broad but barely 1.2 metres tall. 'Excuse me?'

'I make sauces. That's what I do. Little Sauces, that's what they're called. We sell them at markets and food fairs, in cafés and pop-up cafés. Pick and Pay wanted them. They wanted Little Sauces, and I said no. You cannot have it. Today is the last day of cooking for Christmas. I sell three-quarters of everything in December. Makes an original present, uses up turkey, stimulates the taste buds after all that rich food.'

De Vries finds himself staring at her small, puckered mouth, the stream of words delivered in a high-pitched yet husky voice. He is aware that she has stopped.

She stands aside with a flourish, beckons them in, leads them

135

to a lounge overlooking a tiny patio. She walks bow-legged, limping. Over dark floral wallpaper, framed photographs are displayed, each of a tiny man in heavy make-up, engaging in circus acts, performing in what De Vries assumes are pantomimes.

'That's Ricki, my son. He's an actor. We keep a record of everything he's been in.' She points to a picture of Ricki in a sequined jacket and bow tie on top of a grand piano, apparently tap-dancing. 'That's his current show. It's in town. In the orange tent, like Cirque du Soleil.'

She lowers herself into a small upholstered armchair, De Vries takes a full-size dining chair, and Sally Frazer squats awkwardly on a low, curved sofa facing an enormous flat-screen television.

Hazel Calder picks up what appears to be an oversized plastic tumbler and sips enthusiastically from a tall straw. She faces De Vries. 'Why do you want to talk about September the fifteenth?'

He indicates Sally Frazer, who says: 'We're investigating two further rapes, which sound like they could have been committed by the same man who attacked you.'

'So you didn't catch him?'

'We're a different department.'

'Is that what happens? One lot can't get him so it moves to a different department?'

'No.'

'When we met them – when we spoke to the officers, we knew they wouldn't catch him, wouldn't do anything. They weren't interested.'

Frazer talks over her: 'We've only just heard about your case, and we will catch whoever attacked you, but we wanted to check that you hadn't remembered anything new since the original report. Something that could help us find this man.'

'Something new? I'll tell you what I remember. I came home and found the gates weren't working so I got out of my car, found

136

the handle that disengages the motor and pulled them open myself. It was almost dark. I drove in. I didn't close the gates again because I knew that Harold and Ricki were due back and I thought it was easier to leave them.'

'Harold?'

'My husband. He had the day off and he was picking Ricki up from town and bringing him home. I know that's how the man got in. I know it was my fault for being careless . . .' She trances momentarily. 'I carried the shopping, one bag at a time, into the kitchen, and when I closed the front door, he hit me. I didn't see or hear him, I just felt pain in my neck and the back of my head and I think I must have passed out. When I woke up, I was in this chair – my chair. He'd put something over my head, like a carrier bag, but thicker, bundled up, and I couldn't breathe. He gagged me.'

She sits up, brings arthritic hands to her mouth. 'I was tied up, to the chair, with those plastic ties . . .' She pulls up her skirt and opens her legs, pushes each thigh apart as far as she can manage. 'Ankles to the chair legs here, wrists to the arms, like this.' She poses silently, her body contorted and stretched to reach even to the corners of such a tiny piece of furniture. De Vries lowers his gaze, shields his eyes from her. 'I couldn't call out, couldn't find a voice, but I'm trying to talk to him, trying to make him realize that I'm a human being. I can't breathe through my nose and I want to moan or cry but I can't. I can't move and I can't struggle and I can't call out. He had a knife. I didn't see it, but I felt the tip of it against my body because he started to cut my clothes, down here.' She points between her legs. 'He was breathing hard, and it was strange, but I glimpsed his hands at the very bottom of my field of vision, under the bag. I think he was shaking, that he was afraid. And he whispered to me, almost under his breath, but I heard it . . .'

She pauses, eyes wet, voice breaking, her body still spatchcocked across the chair. 'He said: "You should never have been a mother."'

She freezes. They hear the sound of taxi-vans honking on Main Road, a siren, perhaps at the crossroads.

De Vries jumps when Sally Frazer says: 'What happened then?'

'I heard a car outside, an engine. Heard voices, Ricki's. He'd forgotten his father was fetching him. He'd taken an Uber and he was outside.'

'What did the attacker do?'

'He didn't do anything. He just wasn't there.'

'Where did he go?'

She shrugs. 'I don't know. Maybe into the garage. There's a connecting door from the kitchen. Ricki started opening the front door, calling out. I was trying to make a noise and the next thing I know, he's taken the bag off my head and he's screaming.'

She reaches down for her drink, relaxing her limbs, wriggling back into a more normal sitting position.

De Vries looks up, sees Sally Frazer still listening to her, watching her intently.

'And neither of you saw him?'

'No. Ricki just wanted to hold me, untie me. He went to the kitchen and got scissors and cut me down. Then he called his father and then the police.'

'Did you get any impression,' De Vries says quietly, 'of the man, the attacker? Race or age?'

She puts down her glass.

'I didn't see him, but I felt he was white and not young. Not a child. He didn't speak, just whispered that one thing. "You shouldn't have been a mother." I don't know. I assumed he was white, but he could have been coloured.' She looks up at them. 'He sounded white, as much as you can sound anything when you're whispering. He didn't smell. I suppose I can't say that, can I? He didn't smell black.'

De Vries says: 'You can say whatever you like if it helps us find this man and put him in prison.'

'My mother was Indian,' Hazel Calder says conversationally. 'I grew up there and smell was very important. It's part of my DNA – and a very important facet of a good palate, you know. In India, you could tell how smart someone was by their smell. My mother used to say you could smell a person's caste.'

'I'm sorry to ask this,' Sally Frazer says, 'but can you think of a reason why he should say what he said to you?'

'You can ask, dear. It's not the first time I've been asked. Harold and I – Harold is your size – we thought a long time before deciding to have children. We underwent genetic testing and they told us they did not know whether Harold's or mine would predominate. We knew there'd be a chance that our offspring would inherit my health problems too. Boys, especially, have a shorter life expectancy, but the doctors felt there was a good chance that a child would grow normally. We had three sons, but now we only have Ricki.'

'Your other sons passed away?'

'Jerry was only six and Jack was seventeen. People judged us for bringing our boys into the world. Maybe that's what he meant. Or maybe he just didn't like how I looked. Maybe he was afraid of me . . .'

The squad-room is quiet. No phones ring, no one talks. The people alone do not make it seem busy.

'What is the *New Cape Gazette*?'

Sally Frazer sits in a neighbouring chair, pushes away from the desk, rolls herself next to Don February.

139

'It's a new tabloid. Someone called it "Berliner-style". I think it's trying to be an independent voice in journalism. No political affiliations.'

'The myth of objectivity.'

They both turn to De Vries.

'Sir?'

'Nothing is objective in this world if it's reported by another person. Think about witnesses: what they see, what they think they see, what they say they've seen. It's all subjective.'

Don and Frazer exchange a glance.

'Sir,' Don says, 'there is this journalist. She works for the *New Cape Gazette*. Her name is Ali Jelani. Look at what she has written.'

He indicates four A4 pages displayed neatly on the adjoining desk. He points at the first.

'This is from November the eighth. The woman you have just been interviewing, Hazel Calder. There is an article about her, about the attack.' He moves his finger to the sheet below. 'She wrote this piece on November the eleventh, about a woman called Michelle Ricquarts. She was kidnapped by a man who blindfolded her and drove her out towards Milnerton Beach. The shacks on the other side of the railway line, he took her to one of those and bound her to a wooden bench inside. He went away, and she escaped because the wood was rotten. In the article it claims that she saw nothing.'

His finger moves up and to the right. 'The articles start as just paragraphs, but they get longer. Look who is here next. Marie Garsten. This article was published on November the fourteenth. That's only two days after she was found. But notice, sir: one every three days. No interview, obviously, but a biography of the victim and, at the end, she states that she was bound with black plastic ties. She actually ends the piece . . . Look.' He reads: '"This is the third attack on a mother involving the victim being bound with

140

black cable ties. An empty chair faced the body of the victim. Did the attacker of Marie Garsten sit there and speak to her? Did he whisper his warning?"'

Don can feel De Vries's hands on the back of his chair as he leans over to read the enlarged newsprint.

'Last. Yesterday. Bethany Miles. It points out that, like the other women, she was bound with black cable ties, raped. She once again describes the crime scene, that she was laid out on the chaise longue, that there was a chair facing her where her attacker may have watched her suffer. She describes that the eyes were removed.' Unable to swivel because of De Vries's hold on his chair, he twists around to face him. 'I do not understand, sir. The crime scene, the detail about the victim's eyes. You were clear that this must not be released. Where does she get this information?'

'A leak,' De Vries says.

'She does not say it clearly but she is making a connection between these crimes.'

'And faster than us,' Sally Frazer says.

'Who is this second woman?' De Vries asks.

'I have been looking into the case,' Don tells them. 'The docket is still open, but no one knows who is leading the inquiry. She was taken from outside the back of Ruby's Lounge.'

'The strip club, off Loop Street,' Sally Frazer says. 'You know it, sir?'

De Vries glances at her. 'I knew Ruby,' he says blankly. 'Until he or she was shot in his or her car at the traffic lights at the top of Orange Street.'

They stand in silence momentarily.

'So we have the Central guys and also Milnerton hub. Something has gone wrong.'

De Vries shakes his head rapidly, runs sweaty hands through

damp hair, his balding crown stinging from sunburn as he passes his palms over it.

'Sally. You need to find out everything about Michelle Ricquarts. We need to know if she's connected, what happened to her and what she remembers. You, Don, and me. We're going to this *New Cape Gazette*. I want to talk to the editor and I want to talk to this Ali Jelani. We need to know how she knows what she knows.'

The offices of the *New Cape Gazette* are located in a former factory at the city end of Albert Road. The raised freeway snakes into town, partly encircling the small, formerly industrial area in a horseshoe bend of smoke and noise.

The office conversion itself is smart, a façade of tall and broad multi-paned iron panels of windows, heavy steel doors and utilitarian fittings. Inside the enormous main double doors, from behind a bare aluminium reception desk, a young coloured man calls the editor's office and, a few moments later, leads them to the ground-floor office housing the *New Cape Gazette*.

De Vries and Don stand in the doorway, unimpressed by sparsely populated, well-spaced desks and the unadorned bare brick walls.

'We've been here seven months and we still don't know how to make it seem more . . . I was going to say homely, but I mean like a newsroom.'

A very tall white woman, perhaps in her late fifties, immaculately dressed in a well-cut navy pin-striped trouser-suit, stretches out a long arm at De Vries, then Don.

'Penelope van Reidel.' She studies each of them. 'I suppose it is good that the police are angry at what we have printed.' She speaks in a low voice, each word enunciated, intonation and emphasis very deliberate. 'It demonstrates our determination to remain independent of the government, the political pressures of globalization, the establishment.'

She seems to study their reactions from above, haughty.

'Why would you think we were angry with you?'

'One of your officers contacted me, discussed your need to speak to me and to Ali Jelani.'

'Yes,' De Vries says. 'But what made you think you were in trouble?'

'Ali warned me that you might come.'

De Vries frowns. 'She will be available to speak to?'

'I've spoken to her on her cell. I think she was expecting it.'

'Then,' De Vries says, 'while we have you, we should talk immediately.'

She turns away from them, walks through the middle of the quiet newsroom, towards glossy blood-red metal double doors. She throws them both open and continues into a large office. Don only just catches the second door before it slowly clicks shut. De Vries enters the room, waits for Don to join him.

Already, she is sitting behind an oversized wooden desk, her head lower than the tall scarlet-upholstered chair back. Behind her, there is a floor-to-ceiling Gothic arch of stained glass, lit from behind. Between towers of papers, the table is highly polished. They stand in front of it.

De Vries says: 'Who is Ali Jelani?'

'Don't you trust Wikipedia?'

'I'm asking you.'

She smiles. 'Exactly. You go directly to the source, if necessary by a trusted third party. This is what we do here.' She points to the two chairs in front of her desk.

'I'm not interested in a sales pitch.'

'Ali Jelani is not employed full-time by the *New Cape Gazette*. She is a contributor. An increasingly interesting one, but a free-lance none the less. What do you want to know? Kenyan descent, attended UCT's first new journalism degree course in 2009, and graduated top of her year. She made contributions to some local and provincial titles here, before spending a year in New Orleans, USA, writing about the plight of those widowed by Katrina, made homeless, unemployed and forgotten. Then she came back here.'

'There are four stories that interest us, Ms van Reidel.'

She watches Don February gently lay the four printed sheets in front of her in a two-by-two pattern. Her hooded eyes study each momentarily; she shrugs.

'This is Ali Jelani's latest project. She may have discovered a sequence of crimes against women, escalating as you can see. I sent a reporter to the press briefings, but there was no mention of a connection. It made me wonder even more. Do the SAPS – what do you call your department? Special Crimes? – have no idea what is happening, or is there some reason you are withholding information from the public?'

'We withhold it so that when secret information comes to light we can judge whether it suggests suspicious behaviour on the part of the person who is aware of it.' She seems to sneer at De Vries. 'Or to confirm that someone who confesses is truly who he claims to be.'

'Is that game-playing with the lives of women?'

'No, it is an attempt to protect them.'

'It seems you haven't succeeded so far.'

'Well, unlike a glib headline, or a half-story, a multiple homi-cide investigation requires great attention to detail.'

She raises her eyebrows. 'A multiple homicide investigation. Is that what it is? You haven't told us that before.'

De Vries feels the soft pads of his palms itch like prickly heat. He grits his teeth. 'Does Miss Jelani claim to have a source within the SAPS?'

'She has a source certainly. I can't confirm or deny from where it emanates.'

'Whoever it is,' De Vries says, 'is compromising my investigation.'

Van Reidel smiles broadly. 'I would say that it seems to be aiding your investigation. Did you know already about Hazel Calder and Michelle Ricquarts?'

'We've interviewed them, yes.'

She gently scratches the right-hand side of her nose, meets De Vries's gaze. He looks away, looks down.

'I spoke to Michelle Ricquarts yesterday. She told me that she had not been contacted since the original investigation into her abduction stalled and subsequently evaporated.'

De Vries bites the insides of his cheeks. 'She is being interviewed this morning, perhaps now, as we speak.'

'After viewing our coverage?'

'I'm not here to play one-upmanship games with you. Several pieces of classified information have appeared in these articles. I need to ask you: do you know your freelance's source?'

'If I did, I wouldn't tell you but, as it happens, I do not. If Ali Jelani were a staffer, I would insist upon it, as a matter of due diligence, but in this case all the information in her reports seems to be accurate.' She locks her dark eyes on him again. 'Doesn't it?'

De Vries stands, stumbles backwards a few centimetres. He feels disoriented.

'If I find that you're withholding information from me, there will be repercussions.'

She holds up slender fingers in a stunted gesture of surrender, gemstones sparkling under the spotlights that illuminate her desk.

'We withhold nothing and, as a token of good will, I am happy to show you what we will be running on the front page tomorrow.'

She opens a drawer, extracts a tabloid-sized sheet, pushes it across the desk, facing De Vries.

THE CAPE TOWN COP AND THE MISSED CONNECTION

Beneath, there is a photograph of Grace Bellingham and himself sitting at the bar on Bree Street, smoking and drinking. He scans the text beneath.

Renowned profiler Dr Grace Bellingham has returned to her home city just in time. Bombs explode, a series of attacks has escalated to torture and murder, but the officer leading the SAPS investigation, Colonel Vaughn de Vries, seems more interested in socializing than finding the culprit. These are the people who should be working to protect us, yet instead relax at a fashionable city-centre watering hole.

De Vries looks up at her. 'This is outrageous. This was taken at eight p.m. on a public street. You want to call yourself a highbrow paper, but you print this rubbish?'

She withdraws the paper, floats it back into the open drawer. 'When you read the entire article, you will see that what we and Ali Jelani have to say is a great deal more interesting than rubbish.'

De Vries bridles. 'Print whatever you like about me, but leave Dr Bellingham out of it. She is not involved in this case.'

'Perhaps she should be. It seems you need help.'

'Grace Bellingham has retired. When you have to deal with the kind of people she has battled to understand throughout her professional career, there is a price to pay. She deserves some respect.'

'She is yet to earn that from me. Have you actually felt the atmosphere on the streets?'

'I understand "the streets" very well.'

She smiles. 'You're almost invented, aren't you? Street-smart heavy-drinking cop, struggling in the new world. Can't quite cope with women, authority, the rules.'

Don February clears his throat.

She ignores him. 'We could interview you personally about this investigation. Would you agree to that? An exclusive? I'm sure that you – and your colleague – could benefit, in more ways than one.'

'I strongly advise you to consider not printing that front page tomorrow.'

'Shall I include that threat in the article?'

'It was not a threat, Ms van Reidel. It was a request to aid the investigation and, possibly, to protect you from charges of hampering my inquiry.'

'I can assure you, I am quite protected.'

De Vries feels his jaw locked. He presses his tongue into the roof of his mouth; the tension reduces minutely. He keeps his voice even, aping her.

'When did Ali Jelani file that copy?'

'For what it's worth, around lunchtime yesterday. It's her picture – she has declined my offer of a photographer – and, although we contributed to your background and reputation, the story is hers.'

'Thorough in her character assassination, isn't she?'

'She claims that a photographer would draw attention to her,' she says, disregarding De Vries. 'Might warn the subject that they were the focus.'

'Where is Jelani?'

'She's not here.'

'Why not?'

'I told her that I would speak to you first. I fear that if you met her now, your attitude would prove most counter-productive.'

'When a SAPS officer asks that someone make themselves available for interview, that is what I expect.'

'Ali Jelani has no legal duty to submit to your interview. If you wish to arrest her and take her to your headquarters, you surely better have due cause.'

De Vries opens his mouth, but Don says quietly:

'Please would you provide Miss Jelani's contact details so that we may request such an interview directly?'

'And I am not required to do that. However, I will supply you with her email address, which is her preferred method of contact.' She writes it on a small piece of heavy card, passes it to Don. She stands up. Behind her, the glowing stained glass partly silhouettes her, making her tall, contained features seem darker still. 'Don't make an enemy of me, Colonel de Vries. We've already advanced your investigation once. It may be that we can assist you again.'

'You haven't assisted me at all.'

She smiles, removes her black-rimmed spectacles.

'Perhaps we are wrong about the contribution Dr Bellingham might make . . .' she says lightly.

'You are.'

'Perhaps it is *you* who requires profiling.'

The car seats burn the underside of their thighs even through the fabric of their suits. Every window is misted and damp – the air-conditioning has little effect. De Vries yanks the control to off, winds down his window, elbows Don to do the same on his side.

'Email that Jelani woman now. Tell her that if she doesn't agree to a meeting immediately, the full force of the law will descend on her.'

'I am allowed to phrase that in my own words?'

'You sound like Penelope van Reidel.'

'She is a lady who works hard to create an effect.'

'I'd say that she was a rich wife with a passing fancy to dabble in journalism, but I'm afraid that she is much more than that.' De Vries brakes suddenly as the car in front stops in the middle of the road for seemingly no reason. The car edges forward; there is still nothing obvious to have caused such a manoeuvre. He struggles to retrieve his cellphone from the shiny material of his inside jacket pocket on the back seat. He speed-dials Sally Frazer's phone, which goes straight to voicemail. He drops the phone into the centre cubby-hole, toots his horn as the car in front fails to move forward with the queue of traffic ahead.

'Sir.'

'What?'

'The traffic is merely the lights ahead . . .'

De Vries squints through his windscreen.

'It's a woman, Don. She's on her phone, she's doing her hair. I saw a woman a couple of days ago who had tongs plugged into the lighter socket. Tongs. This is what women mean when they say they can multi-task. Doing lots of things except the most important one.' He turns to the passenger seat. 'And I'll tell you, I'm just about done with women already today.'

Don turns to his window, stares intently at the summit of the Mountain.

It is almost five p.m. before they gather in the squad-room. The air-conditioning does no more than push hot air around the space. The sticky, dusty windows overlooking town reveal a low bronze smog descending below the tops of skyscrapers. It is both beautiful and claustrophobic.

Sally Frazer says: 'Michelle Ricquarts is thirty-four, lives in the Disa Towers. She's divorced, looking after her two daughters, who are eleven and fifteen. The ex-husband has ceased all maintenance payments and gone off radar. She started working at Ruby's

Lounge in January last year and says that she makes sufficient earnings to cover all her costs, but that she fears her time working in that environment is limited.

'On October the fourth, she left Ruby's at eleven thirty p.m. and walked no more than thirty metres down the street to the corner where she usually picks up her cab. A car stopped behind her. She says she glanced back, glimpsed the driver but cannot imagine what his face looked like, other than she is almost certain that he had a pale complexion. The next thing she knew, she was hit around the back of the neck and woke up in the back of a car, her wrists bound together, her right ankle bound to the seatbelt holder. She was blindfolded and gagged. She estimates that she was driven for half an hour to forty minutes and the driver took the freeway towards the Southern Suburbs. She was untied and marched over what she felt was uneven sandy ground. The man was wearing what she felt were leather gloves. Still blindfolded, she was made to sit on a wooden bench and bound by wrists and ankles to it. She says that the man whispered to her: "You left your children alone."'

'She's certain about that?'

Frazer looks at De Vries. 'So she says. She estimated that the accent was white South African, not, she felt, Afrikaner, but it is only five words whispered. She said that the attacker left almost immediately, padlocking the door. She waited a few minutes, then started pulling at her bindings. Her right wrist came free when the backrest to the bench snapped. She removed the gagging and blindfold, and managed to break the wood holding her left wrist. Then she was able to pull the bench from the wall, turn it at an angle and stamp on it until her ankle bindings could be slipped off. She showed me her wrists. They are still deeply scarred. Black cable ties. The Milnerton boys entered them in evidence. From there, she found more rotten wood in a back corner, split it open with

150

another piece of wood, and made her escape.' Frazer regards each of the officers present. 'My view is that Michelle Ricquarts is a very strong, resilient woman and that her testimony is accurate.'

'Any intent to rape?' De Vries says.

'She states that she is not certain if it was his hand but that she was being touched between her legs. She admits that her mind was racing and that rape was the most likely thought.'

'What about this shack by Milnerton Beach?'

Ben Thwala says: 'I've got a copy of the docket now. Forensic officers found nothing to identify the abductor, or any witnesses who saw the car or Michelle Ricquarts. The cabin was scheduled for demolition, to be replaced with more modern warehousing, and had been empty all year. The area is not well lit and there are many cars parked around it at all times. There is very little residential building nearby.'

Frazer nods, continues: 'She waved down a car driven by a woman, who took her to the station. There was no sign of her handbag or cellphone, which has been off since the attack.'

'What's interesting,' De Vries says, 'are the whispered comments to Hazel Calder and Michelle Ricquarts. Without that, it would be difficult to be certain of the connection. And we don't know what, if anything, he said to the two murder victims, although the placement of the chair suggests he was watching them and, possibly, speaking to them.'

Sally Frazer says: 'We have one crime in Claremont, one in town, ending in Milnerton, one in Somerset West, Strand area, and most recently Constantia, ending up in Camps Bay. This is a really wide catchment area.'

'The perp is travelling. He's driving around the peninsula,' Ben Thwala says.

'Yes, he has local knowledge of the movements of the victims, but, if all four crimes are connected, as we believe, notice the way that, apart from the first victim, Hazel Calder, he takes his victim away from where she lives by some kilometres.' Sally Frazer turns to De Vries. 'I know that Dr Fenner is not available, sir, but right now what we really need is a detailed profile.'

De Vries stands still, expression blank, the knowledge of the next day's newspaper front page suddenly flooding back.

'I'll talk to Grace Bellingham.'

Don February follows De Vries silently, enters the lift after him. De Vries jumps.

'What I am thinking, sir,' Don says, 'is that the connection between Hazel Calder and Michelle Ricquarts could only have been made by someone who had access to the dockets. The attack on Hazel Calder did not receive any press coverage, and from what I have found, there have been only two very small mentions of the Michelle Ricquarts crime. Neither contained any details which could possibly link them.'

De Vries nods slowly. 'But it doesn't make sense. Even if someone from the SAPS was leaking this information, how would he or she have had access to both dockets?'

'Notice that Ali Jelani did not write her articles about the first two crimes until well after the events,' Don tells him. 'Perhaps she, or her source, did not make the link until the third crime, the Marie Garsten abduction and murder in Somerset West and Strand.'

The lift doors open onto the gloomy, stifling lobby. De Vries steps out, walks slowly towards the exit, says nothing.

Don waits, then says: 'I wonder, sir, whether you should speak to your friend, Captain Malgas. It was after that crime that the coverage started, that someone made the connection.'

De Vries's mind is racing. There is a gap in the logic some-where, but he cannot see it yet.

'Where are you going now, Don?'

'Home. Tomorrow is not going to start well, is it? With that front page. I think I will need all the sleep I can get.'

'Yes.'

'Where are you going, sir?'

De Vries turns to him. Every piece of clothing he wears is damp; his chest aches from inhaled humidity; his pulse throbs at his temples.

'I'm going to where beer is, Don. Perhaps wine, but probably beer.'

The tree-lined roads in Greenpoint are busy with evening traffic, lit lengthwise by deep golden sun, pavements filled with tourists and locals heading to bars and restaurants, walking into town. The World Cup football stadium seems to hover, almost as if preparing to rise from a mesmeric shimmering heat haze. The sky-scrapers of the Central Business District are divided in two by the copper layer of smog and glittering dust.

Giovanni's is packed tight, bare-armed strangers sticking to one another, clammy but happy, the cool interior deli populated by workers picking up an easy supper, picnics for the beach. The coffee-bar stools and narrow benches bordering the street are all taken, customers with the sun on their backs or reflecting in sun-glasses, ending their day or starting their night with some of the best coffee in the city.

As Mike Solarin ducks inside, a tall bar table at the end of the deck becomes free. He pushes past those standing, lays claim to the tiny circular plane, the single stool. He places his sunglasses on the table, leans out over the wooden barrier, looks down the street. He steps towards the bar, asks for a cold drink, is shown the big glass-doored fridge, told to help himself. He takes a red Grapetiser back to his table, screws it open, downs half; sees in his peripheral vision Gugu KwaDukuza on the street, waves. Her smile is very broad. She squeezes between the other customers. They embrace. He fetches her a drink, before they walk to the counters, wait in the queue chatting casually, pick plates, his carb-heavy, hers leafy and low-calorie. They carry them back to the table, clink glasses, eat.

After a few minutes, she says: 'The way you said, "I need to see you." It did not sound only like a nice supper.'

'No.'

She glances involuntarily around the café, onto the street. 'You want to ask me?'

He feels fraudulent suddenly, their casual friendliness stilted by tension.

'What do you think?' He lowers his voice although, above the happy cacophony, he surely cannot be heard. 'Two Islamic terrorists in a lorry in Long Street at eight fifty in the morning?'

'I think that neither I, nor my friends in the team, have seen anything to suggest that.'

'No?'

'No. But, then, that is probably because, two days ago, the usual teams are swapped over. Some new guys come in.'

'What do you mean, new guys?'

'Just a new team. One we do not know. In any case, this scene, it is not like anything we have worked before. Information not shared between teams. It is all fed into the system, but none of us know what it is.'

'What you said about the explosive?'

Her eyes flare. 'You have not repeated that?'

'No. What we say here is just between us. I will protect you.'

She smiles. 'I do not need you to protect me.'

'I mean, something is not right.'

'No, it is not right. I have studied what these extremists do, what materials they use, how they plan, operate. This is atypical. I think that it is not believable.'

'What in particular?'

'Two things. My friend who specializes in electronics. He tells me that they have found a receiver – what is left of it – and that it is almost certainly the means of detonation. This was not a suicide attack. This was detonated remotely, perhaps by a cellphone, maybe a transmitter of some kind.'

'Could it have been triggered accidentally?'

'Why would you ask that?'

'It was early in the morning. The street was busy, but not crowded. There are other more politically significant sites . . .'

'It is possible. I suppose that there are many signals travelling in the middle of a city.'

Solarin nods. 'What else?'

'You remember you asked me about the sticky gel you saw at the scene? I told you it was grapes. We found grape seeds, boiled pulp. Maybe three or four bunches, no more. Do you know that they can identify a variety from its seed? This was a grape called Souzão. That, my friend, is a Portuguese port grape. A cultivar, they call it, only grown in South Africa for port-style wines.' She glances around her again. 'So, seeing as how the van was taken from Oudtshoorn, I am thinking Calitzdorp.'

'Calitzdorp?'

'"The Port Capital of South Africa."'

'Ja?'

'Why would there be grape residue in the van if it had not stopped on its way from Oudtshoorn?'

'We were heading that way when they called us back.'

'When was that?'

'Yesterday. Maybe five p.m.'

'We delivered the report on the grapes to the supervisor. Maybe two p.m. That, as you conspiracy theorists might say, is a big coincidence.'

'Who have you spoken to about these grapes?'

'No one. We don't discuss what is in the reports. We, the technicians, we keep quiet, do our job, keeps our heads down. I know this is not how you are, Mlungisi.'

He smiles at the use of his proper name.

'No.'

'And you are going to challenge them?'

'Maybe. I was put with a white guy, Ray Black. He was not interested in his duties. I think he was talking to Colonel Juiles . . .' he shrugs '. . . to someone about where we were, what we were doing. He's not been stood down. Never showed at the debrief. I do not trust him.'

'But do not go risking your job. It will not bring back the people who died.'

'Don't you ask yourself, Gugu, why?'

'No. Never. That is not my job.'

'They call it Isis when we – you and me – know it is not. What are they hiding? That's the point. This is my job: to ask why.'

'Better I tell you before you saw it yourself, or someone texted you,' De Vries says, watching her body slump, hand shaking as she places the wine glass back on the table.

'Why?' Grace Bellingham says. 'Why would they do that?'

'We have a serial attacker – now a killer – and you are the best. They want to involve you in the investigation.'

'I told you,' Grace Bellingham states. 'No.'

'You told *me*. I didn't know they'd photographed us. How would I have any idea they'd have any interest? We didn't even

156

know what we had until today, and it was their bloody articles that confirmed it for us.' He stretches his arm out, but cannot quite reach her chair. 'I asked the editor to leave you out of it. I pleaded, Grace. They can attack me – they are attacking me – I'm used to it. But this bitch was having none of it.'

De Vries watches her breathing heavily through her mouth, head bowed.

'I haven't even seen this paper . . .'

'It's new. Low circulation, but the *Times* and the *Argus* will pick up on it.' He offers his hand across the cool metal table, but she ignores it. 'The city is in turmoil. The heat, the students' demonstrations, strikes, the bomb, for Christ's sake, and now this. This is what the media love. Ramp everything up, frighten everyone, find scapegoats. You got any idea what I'll face when I go in tomorrow?'

'Take you off the case?'

De Vries snorts. 'Never. They'll back the press, they'll make me dance, and if I don't find what I'm looking for, they'll get me out. It's always the same, Grace. It may be twenty-five years, but there's always a hundred facets to every struggle.'

Grace Bellingham looks around the crowded bar, more popular perhaps for its icy air-con than the claustrophobic metallic cacophony in the small basement room at the bottom of Loop Street.

'Tell them I'll help you.' She holds up a finger as De Vries sits up. 'I won't be seconded, I won't be employed by the SAPS. I'll talk to you, advise you, privately. That's as far as I'm prepared to go.'

'Thank you.'

'You come to my flat. We work. Nothing else. Any hope you had there is burned, my friend. You tell them that I'll provide a profile, advise. That's as far as it goes. No press, nothing official.'

De Vries nods.

She drains her glass, stands.

157

'I'm going now. If I find that any of this was your doing, I'll give them what I have on you. It may be old but, mark my words, they'll love it.'

De Vries is woken at seven a.m. by a summons to the top floor of his building and an interview with General Thulani, flanked by Colonel David Wertner of the Internal Investigation Bureau. After thirty years in the SAPS, he knows precisely how it will play out. For now, he will be backed and protected, but, if he fails, it will all be kept to indict him.

After a wretched night of craving sleep in his bedroom, where the temperature did not fall below thirty degrees, he is strangely calm and sanguine. He meets the scorn of David Wertner, who has long sought to discredit him, with a quietly defiant smile. He has been here before and, this time, he almost feels as if he doesn't care what they do to him. He lets the predictable warnings and repetitive aphorisms wash over him as he quietly calculates what must be achieved today. His mind is tired but clear. He does not counter what they say, does not fight. He agrees with their suggestions, accepts blame, reveals his agreement with Grace Bellingham for profiling services.

Finally, when he stands, Thulani studies him from his raised seat. 'I'm worried about you, Colonel.'

'Why is that, sir?'

Thulani glances at Wertner to his side. 'This morning, you almost seem like a rational human being.'

'Is this it, then?' Danie Malgas says. 'This the cream at the top of the bottle?' He is looking around the gloomy foyer to the Special Crimes building.

'It's no cooler in here than down your place.'

'Great way to save money, eh? Braai your workforce, take away their equipment, throw them into darkness. . .' He shuffles into the lift. 'As if it weren't dark enough already, out there.' He looks at De Vries. 'You should get out of the city, down to the beach.' He chuckles. 'Well, maybe check for the paparazzi first . . . But, you know, at least there's some breeze there. The wind off the water, it's actually cold, man.'

He follows him to his office, stands until De Vries has sat.

'Is it what we thought?' Malgas says. De Vries nods. 'You're too quiet, man. What's happening?'

'We've got a problem, Danie. This journalist, Ali Jelani – we haven't reached her yet, but we've talked to her editor – has information she shouldn't have. I need to know how she got it. Remember I asked you if your guys would keep quiet if I took over on Marie Garsten?'

'You think I'm leaking?'

'Not you. Not you, Danie, but one of your guys. Maybe?'

Malgas tips his head back, wipes sweat from his neck.

'I can't think of anyone. You know, no one said *fokkol* when the Marie Garsten docket went away. I told you, if they didn't see her, they didn't care, and if they did, they wanted to forget. Too much else. I mean, maybe now the press have it, someone might, if the money was good enough, but . . .'

'Keep an ear open.'

'*Ja*, sure . . . You get nothing from the samples?'

De Vries shakes his head.

'He's good. He's careful. He's staked out where he wants to take them, knows they can stay there, knows these are places he's not likely to be noticed. If there's more, I don't want to think what he'll do to these women.'

'You said the eyes . . .'

'Eyes, and with the first two assaults, he whispered something to them. "You shouldn't have been a mother" and "You left your kids alone" – something like that. Then we both find a chair facing the victim where she's been tied up, like he's watching her, speaking to her maybe.'

They sit silently a moment, then Malgas says: 'No one reads that new paper anyway, that *New Cape Gazette*.'

'Is it even for sale in Strand?'

Malgas tilts his head. 'I think they sold a few copies today, around the station.'

'Boosting their circulation. That'll make one Machiavellian woman very happy. We've had over fifty media requests already this morning. We didn't tell the public everything, so now they have us two ways. Builders' Holiday next, everyone flooding down from Gauteng, hot as horse shit straight out the arse, and this guy, somewhere out there.' He stands, opens his door. 'Come look at the boards. See if anything strikes you.' Malgas shuffles after him. 'You know what they say about a fresh eye . . .'

The three white Disa Park towers stand starkly against the dark backdrop of the Mountain's face, their cylindrical forms dwarfed by the incomprehensible mass beyond them. Looking up at the Mountain from the bay or Waterfront, they are all that interrupts the contoured plane of matt black rock. In the 1960s, the Murray and Roberts construction company exploited a loophole in the planning regulations, constructing their bases beneath the building line and developing up seventeen storeys. The Pepper Pots – the polite local nickname for them – seem lovely inside, mainly, their critics suggest, because at that moment you do not have to look at them.

Michelle Ricquarts buzzes De Vries into her block, is standing on the twelfth-floor landing as he arrives in the lift. She is dressed in a shortish white dress with bold flower prints, her hair up and back. Her apartment faces almost at right angles to the Mountain, so that one side of the view is just dark, overwhelming rock face; the other, the buildings and roads leading towards the city, with only a glimpse of sea in the docks beyond.

'Four more years on the bond.' She turns back to the window, smooths down her skirt. 'Think I'll make it?'

De Vries frowns. 'Make it?'

'Pay off the bond on here and I'm laughing, well, smiling. Just depends how long I can keep going at Ruby's.' She gestures for him to sit. 'You want a cool drink?'

When he shakes his head, she sits in a yellow velour armchair facing him, her back to the Mountain. De Vries sits forward.

'I wanted to meet you, to introduce myself as the officer who has taken over your case, and assure you that I, we, are doing everything within our power to find your attacker and make sure that he is put away for a long time.'

'Your sergeant yesterday, Sally. She was nice.'

'I'm sorry that the original inquiry fell short. My department was created to follow up these serious crimes and bring them to a conclusion.'

'I thought about that night again. I can't remember anything else. Anything I haven't said already.'

'I wanted to ask you one thing personally. In your statement you recalled that your attacker had whispered to you . . .'

'"You left your children alone."'

De Vries recoils. She has whispered the words, her voice deeper, accent stronger than her light Cape Town inflection.

'That's what he said to me. Like I said, if I was guessing, he was white, generic accent, not that thick. He said something under his

161

breath in the car when I was tied up in the back. A sentence or two, but I couldn't make out the words or his voice.'

'One or two attackers?'

'It felt like two on the street, but I'm sure there was only him in the car. I've thought about that a lot. Maybe it was only him on the corner of that street, and it's just pride makes me think that it took two men to bring me down.'

'When you got home, your children were safe?'

'I called them from the police station, told them not to answer the door, but nothing happened. I've worried, of course, so I take them to school, watch them walk into the building. I'm waiting there when they finish, but they're sixteen and thirteen now. You can't watch them all the time.'

'What happened to your husband?'

'Jerry? He got bored. Had a mid-life crisis at thirty-two. I don't know. He went. The money stopped pretty quickly, the calls to the girls after that. Now they don't even get a birthday card.'

'It wasn't him in the car?'

She smiles. 'I knew Jerry since I was fourteen. Got me pregnant before I was eighteen. That wasn't Jerry. If it had been, I'd have beaten the shit out of him. I don't do what I do because I want to.'

'And the guys at Ruby's Lounge, the regulars. No one there been paying you particular attention? You must have guys coming on to you. Anyone who took rejection badly?'

'Ja, ja and ja. You know what it's like? It becomes normal. You take no notice. I thought about it afterwards, sure. But I couldn't think of anyone. They're all still there, looking at me the same way. Nothing's changed.' She lights a cigarette. 'Do I get to ask you something now?'

'Certainly.'

'Is it true? You think this same guy went on to kill two women?'

De Vries appreciates the significance of the question, the understanding that she will realize now that she escaped not just rape and pain and misery, but death. He watches her suck on the slender white cylinder.

'We think so.'

She nods very slowly, exhales. Then she rests the cigarette in an ashtray and stands, gesturing at the view. 'At first I thought we'd made a mistake. I mean, it's cold, isn't it? The Mountain. But it's comforting too. It kind of wraps around us here, keeping us safe. My mother always said to me: "Wrap your home about you like a cloak." You can't trust a man, but four walls . . .'

He stands to face her. Against the black backdrop, she seems very bright.

'I'm pleased you've recovered reasonably, Ms Ricquarts, been able to continue with your life. I find some victims of crime – crimes far less serious than that against you – unable to carry on. I'm very pleased to see that.'

She smiles openly at him. 'The moment my husband left, I knew I had to be strong. Two daughters, living in a dangerous city. I'm still alive, but all those people who died in the bomb in town, and the two women after me . . . And, don't forget, I work as a stripper – and that has its moments. There are horrible things happening out there. We're all frightened but, for me, it just about falls into a day-to-day category I can cope with: an acceptable level of terror.'

'It doesn't matter what you have to do,' De Vries tells them. 'Trace her backwards from her email address. Get back to that condescending bitch, Van Reidel, whatever it takes, but find Ali Jelani.'

He strides to his office, slams the door.

Don February says to Sally Frazer, 'Perhaps tread carefully with Ms van Reidel. If we are seen to be too aggressive towards her and her newspaper, it might not look good.'

'You're becoming a politician, Don. You know how Vaughn hates them.'

'You are right but, working with him, one of us must show some tact.'

At five p.m., they gather for the six o'clock meeting. Ben Thwala reports that the sales representative at Nobulhe Estates, Greg Harrisson, was showing two families a house in The Glen on the afternoon that Hazel Calder was attacked, but has no alibi for the time Michelle Ricquarts was abducted. Sally Frazer tells the group that there has been no response from Ali Jelani by email, or any success tracing her current address. Penelope van Reidel's cellphone goes straight to voicemail and, so far, she has not called back.

'We want to talk to this Jelani woman,' De Vries says wearily. 'Tomorrow, Sally, can you co-ordinate all research on the children and families of the victims. On two occasions, this man has whispered to the women referring to motherhood and children – the only thing he said out loud – so we need to look into this. Anywhere their children could have intersected, going right back to their births.' He pushes himself upright from the table against which he has been leaning. 'Get some sleep. Prepare for the long days. I don't have to tell you. Right now, as we speak, he has probably chosen his next victim. We have to stop him.' He raises his eyes, nods at them.

Sally Frazer returns to her desk, sits, picks up her cellphone. The other officers gather belongings, begin to file out of the squad-room. Don February talks to two female officers who man the department at night. De Vries pulls his jacket from the back of his chair, checks the pocket for his cellphone, walks slowly towards the lifts. As he gets in, he sees another officer approaching, then checking himself, letting De Vries descend alone.

The early end to the working day at his office leads to more time spent in the agonizingly slow-moving traffic out of town. The duration and intensity of the rush hour has increased greatly in the last few years, and now even getting onto one of the three freeways out of town takes as long as the entire journey home in years past.

De Vries sits on Nelson Mandela Boulevard staring to his left at the docks, the cruise-liners glittering in the mixture of sea mist and smog. The season is under way: people are flocking to Cape Town from the UK, Germany, the north of the country. And there are people with bombs in the Cape; a man who seems to revel in the slow death of the women he abducts without being seen; rapists and thieves, robbers and muggers, pimps and pickpockets. He looks in his rear-view mirror at his city backed by Signal Hill, the pink in the sky starting early, enveloping the skyscrapers, the streets full of restaurants, bars and clubs, the Waterfront silhouetted against the dazzling pinky-white of Table Bay. Despite what he knows, he thinks it is beautiful.

PART 2

'Renting?'

'Sure.'

'You move quickly.'

Grace Bellingham smiles. 'I always did.'

'But here, out of town?'

'For the moment.'

She stands aside and De Vries walks into her apartment. The entrance hall and kitchen are both small and dark, but the living room opens out onto a terrace overlooking the southern slopes of the Mountain. He looks across towards Fernwood, an old estate, now developed with houses, where his friend John Marantz lives, but he cannot quite see his house. Marantz is an exile from the security services in the UK; he is the one man De Vries can talk to about everything. He reflects that they haven't spoken in many weeks. The sun is low, about to pass behind the crest; hazy sunbeams shoot from between the crevasses. The lush green of the slopes seems to defy the drought, the interminable heat.

'This is all right.'

'Only room in the place. My bedroom looks at downtown Claremont, but at least it has air-con.' She pulls a chair out from the table, gestures for him to sit. 'You eaten?'

'Sort of.'

'Sorry about the furniture. It was here already.'

'Got a fridge?'

'We can have a drink when we're done.'

She sits at the head of the table, looks up from the papers she has arranged in front of her.

'I want you to understand that I spent a lot of time soul-searching this morning. I know it's a mistake. I nearly called you. But I decided to do it for you, Vaughn, because you'd helped me out before and, although I'm not keeping count, this is returning a favour from a long time ago.'

'What favour?'

'You protected me when things went bad.'

'I don't remember.'

'It doesn't matter. Just know that I'm delicate. I've spent the last twenty years being strong, appearing strong, but that costs. It wears you down and I'm down now. So just remember that. Keep me out of it. I need that distance.'

'I will.'

In the silence, he hears her breathing.

'When I started reading these dockets,' she says, her voice clear, as if she has dismissed all that she has just said, 'I realized that I'm doing this for another, more important, reason. Everything we know that this man has done is a classic development of what people like to call a serial killer. He is escalating his action, and the violence that he shows towards his victims is increasing incrementally.' She shuffles papers. 'You must be a nightmare to work for, but I'll give you credit for one thing: you understand what's important.'

'I'll take any credit awarded.' He puffs out his chest and points at one side. 'Pin it here.'

'You write,' she continues, 'that Hazel Calder described seeing her attacker's hand shaking, that he appeared nervous. This is what

I would expect. This is a man who has decided that he will take action against women – or a certain category of women, whether normally recognized or created by himself – and, on this first occasion, or at least an early occasion, he is nervous, clumsy. This indicates a reticence to carry out what he has planned.'

'He was interrupted.'

'Yes, but the impression I gained from Hazel Calder's original statement, and then from your interview with her, is that he was moving slowly, deliberately. He was measuring what was going on, how he felt, what he could accomplish.'

'He intended to rape her, surely? That's why he tied her legs apart.'

'I'm sure he did. That is what he would have planned. But, if this was his first physical encounter with a victim, it may have turned out very differently from the way he had imagined it.' She produces another sheet. 'In her original report, she stated that she kept trying to talk to him the whole time because she felt that would humanize her. She said she didn't get many words out, but that she felt it was disturbing him.'

'Do you have any wine?'

She looks up at him, face serious, mouth set. 'This is work, Vaughn. I told you exactly what it would be and that's how it's going to happen. If we're done before I'm completely exhausted, we might have a glass of wine. If you want water, the tap's in the kitchen.' She slaps the page back on the pile. 'I want to keep going with this and then we may have time to discuss what we think we know and what we can learn from that.'

He sits back, rolls up his sleeves.

'He enters Hazel Calder's home when she is alone. This is easy. He abducts Michelle Ricquarts on an empty street, late at night. There is some risk in this action but, if he were to be challenged, he could always claim that she was propositioning him. He would likely be believed. He takes her to a shack near Milnerton Beach. This setting is industrial and utilitarian, so we cannot read anything into that location other than that he almost certainly knew it was abandoned and that he was very unlikely to be disturbed. The key element here is that he does not tie her up in a sexual position. He deposits her there and leaves. Why?'

'Can I ask a question?'

She nods.

'Have you made a report of this my team can see?'

'Of course.'

'I don't know the answer to your question.'

She smiles. 'I think it is because he is afraid that he has been followed. Possibly he wants time to prepare himself, anticipate what he is about to do. I have no doubt that the intent to rape, torture, kill was there. Thankfully, the victim escapes. There is something of interest there too. The victim escapes and he does nothing about it. As far as we know, he does not harbour anger towards her, frustration. If the reason for her being selected were deeply felt, I think we would see a change to his behaviour. Instead he starts planning his next attack.'

'But he's not picking them randomly?'

'No. Definitely not. He is selecting them but what I am saying is that it is not essential to his plans that he kills these early victims. Perhaps he feels that fear of rape, threat of death is a job adequately done, but – and be clear on this – that attitude will not last. He will increase the violence against his victims and he will kill them.'

'Is Michelle Ricquarts in danger?'

'I would say no, but I can't be absolutely certain. As I say, I think he will feel that she has been punished sufficiently, but he may plan to return to her at a later point.'

'There won't be a later point.'

172

'He abducts Marie Garsten in broad daylight, albeit in a hidden corner of a car park. The level of risk involved here is far greater, and this demonstrates the escalation of his desire. We don't know for how long he keeps her or what he does to her during the time of her incarceration, but the thing which bothers me – just as it did you, and Lieutenant Malgas in Strand – is the chair facing the victim. To me, this suggests that he is watching her suffer. If he speaks a few words to his first victims, I am sure that he has more to say to the latter two. He almost certainly asks them questions and, although we don't know, I suspect they are unlikely to be able to answer. The victim dies slowly, clearly in agony. Again, we do not know if he was there once or many times, but the fact that he posed the body on the fourth attack – on Bethany Miles – suggests to me that he returned to the victim throughout her incarceration.'

De Vries is nodding. Grace Bellingham is bringing together all the thoughts that have been unable to coalesce in his own mind.

'Bethany Miles is taken from a car park, with her child in the car, albeit asleep. That location at the garden centre, the nursery, is fraught with risk and danger. It tells me that he is becoming desperate, that once he has identified his next target, he is prepared to take ever-greater risks to obtain her.'

She pick up a tumbler of water, sips it, scowls. 'No ice.' She rises and moves to the kitchen. He hears her shaking the ice-box. When she returns, her water contains some slender shards. 'What happened to the weather while I was gone?'

'Getting hotter, but this year, I've never known anything like it.'

He watches her drink, studies the liquid as she swallows. He feels the slightest cooler breeze from the terrace, closes his eyes as it plays over his face.

'Bethany Miles reveals most – are you listening? – reveals most about his actions and completes a progression that indicates a mind which, though certainly predisposed to evil, for want of a better word, has suddenly been entirely released by the freedom of full-blown psychosis within his brain. Simply, unlike a normal human being, he sees nothing unusual, nothing wrong in what he does and, I think, he believes that he is providing a service.'

'What service?'

'The whispered comments, the rape – which, as you know, is nothing to do with sex and everything to do with power – the posing of the eyes and the howling mouth. Power, yes, but what this is really about is punishment.'

'For what reason?'

'We only have a little to go on. Hazel Calder and her husband chose to have children who were then, perhaps predictably, to suffer ill health and death at a young age.' She hesitates. 'There's one child still alive?' She takes a deep breath and lets it out very slowly, contemplating. 'Michelle Ricquarts? Did she mistreat her children? Is she shaming them by stripping? Or is leaving them every evening her crime? You need to find that out.'

'I appreciate this helps us to understand him better, but what do we know that helps us to catch him?'

'I'll precis because I know you don't really like "profiler's jargon". Is that what you called it?'

'Probably.'

'He is almost certainly white, between twenty-eight and forty-four, although I would say more likely towards the top end of that range. He is unmarried and lives either alone or with an elderly relative. There is another possibility, which I believe might fit this profile. It is possible that he has children of his own and that he is widowed or divorced. Normally, I would say that this is unlikely but, given his movements, and the fact that he almost certainly leaves the victims to do other things, it should be considered. A demanding job, perhaps.' She takes a deep breath. 'You've got me involved, and I don't know the answers and all the doubts are coming back. This is what I wanted to avoid.' She glances down at her notes once more, clears her throat. 'You can see the pattern of attacks on the map. I would think that Marie Garsten is an anomaly: something took him to Somerset West and a strong urge, probably a reaction to something he saw, made him choose her. The location where she was found did not require much prior knowledge – it was an abandoned building site – and, anyway, I think he was driven to kill her. So, his home location is likely to be within the parameters set by the three other attacks. Your people can work that out.'

She sips from her glass. 'And one more thing. As well as a home address, he may well have a second place he likes to spend time in. It could be an office, or a park, but more likely a den, some-where hidden, where he can think and plan.'

'How do we find that?'

'Until you have a real suspect, you probably don't.'

De Vries closes his eyes. He feels the tension in his face, tries to un-grit his teeth. In every case he pursues, it is his impotence that eats at him, his inability to set the running, to be forced to wait, in servitude, for luck or, worse, for his prey to act again, in the hope that he will gather the one sliver of evidence which might lead him to the right person.

'I would not rate him as being in a professional level of employ-ment,' she says, 'but something a little below that. He may own a small business, or be a manager of one. We know that he travels around the peninsula, but I suspect that he avoids interaction with groups of people, preferring individuals. This is a man who eschews being seen or socializing in a group, although he may have specific friends from whom he gains knowledge or experi-ence, even help. What else? He drives, he is strong, although I doubt that he is physically especially strong. He plans, carefully.'

'And he will attack again?'

'What I have learned is that, however close to a pattern these psychopaths follow, the next one may surprise you, but, yes, he will attack again and, when he has tortured and mutilated that victim, he will pick his next. Everything here suggests the classic pattern: he will kill and kill again until he is caught.'

De Vries stands up, walks out onto the terrace, stares up at the dark slopes, deep blue against a glowing indigo sky. Even here, in the bustling suburbia of Claremont, a cicada trills. From this terrace, he cannot see the City Bowl in its crab's embrace by the Mountain, but the yellow glow from it affords Devil's Peak a radiant halo.

He waits a moment, hoping that Grace Bellingham will join him, that perhaps he might put his arm around her shoulders. He turns, sees her bent over the table, her head resting on the highest stack of papers. He comes inside, touches her hair lightly with the palm of his hand, whispers goodnight.

The thermometer by De Vries's bed reads thirty-one degrees, despite his windows having been open all day, curtains drawn against the evening sun. He sits on his bed heavily, finds himself immersed in a mushroom cloud of fine dust. He coughs, stumbles to his feet and into his bathroom. He looks outside. Through the still, thin branches of the tree, he sees the tall, slender, beautiful black woman, lying almost flat on her mattress, the dog's paws on her belly, a mug of tea between her cupped hands. The television flickers, the tinny voices chatter. He feels shadows falling on him as the rectangular cubicle glimmers with bright pale-blue light.

On the leaves of the trees, on his burned-out lawn, on the yellowing shrubs and wilting flowers, he sees the dust: a landscape within hearing of a violent eruption. He plods back into the bedroom, pulls the sheet gently from his bed, and walks outside onto the sagging veranda, being careful to stay clear of the rotting balustrade, held up only by the giant tendril-like trunk of bougainvillaea. Holding his breath, he shakes the sheet gingerly, replaces it on his bed and lies atop it. Exhausted, he does not register the clay-like residue that has adhered to the sweat on the back of his hands and neck. His face is like a clay mask, pock-marked and old.

Cape Tribune

AL-QAEDA ATTACKS MOTHER CITY

Ministry of Justice spokespeople confirmed yesterday evening that the suspects behind the fatal bomb explosion in Long Street last week were allied with al-Qaeda West Africa. Despite no claim being made by the terrorist organization, Terrorist Squad officers have identified the remains of two men with known links to the terrorist cell, which has previously issued threats against what it regards as the decadent lifestyle of the so-called developed cities of South Africa.

ANC security sources said that since the Democratic Alliance took control of the Western Cape Province security provision has stagnated and that its citizens and tourists were now under direct threat.

'Under ANC governance, Cape Town experienced no serious external security threat in a dozen years, yet since the DA took over, the incidents in Cape Town have escalated to the extent that mass murder can be committed in the midst of the business and tourist areas of the city.'

The question all Capetonians must ask is this:

ARE WE SAFE TO ENJOY OUR CITY?

Cape Herald

AL-QAEDA IN CAPE TOWN

The Hawks, terrorist specialists and the SAPS have confirmed that the perpetrators of last week's Long Street bomb attack were allied to

Muslim extremist group al-Qaeda. The death toll now stands at 13, with more than 20 victims still in hospital, some in a serious condition, with doctors saying that a half-dozen more have less than a fifty per cent chance of surviving.

In the first press briefing of substance, Terrorist Squad officers say that they believe the two men, originally of Iraqi descent, left the radical al-Qaeda grouping, al-Mourabitoun, also known as al-Qaeda West Africa, as they felt that too little direct action was being planned, travelled down through the interior of Africa to Cape Town, where they planned and then executed with deadly force their suicide attack on the Mother City. Justice Department spokesmen claimed that analysts had been aware of the potential threat from al-Qaeda in southern Africa but that Democratic Alliance Party politicians had dismissed it as 'scare-mongering to damage the thriving economy of the Western Cape'.

How this attack will impact on tourism to Cape Town, both from within the country and from abroad, is yet to be understood, but DA administrators are now under scrutiny as to whether they have in place sufficient security to protect travellers to Cape Town.

New Cape Gazette

CITY ON FIRE

* Al-Qaeda strike at heart of Mother City – Muslim extremist link confirmed. 14 dead; many more 'not out of danger'.
* SAPS 'aware' but 'baffled' by serial killer stalking women with children. Two dead, two abducted. 'There may be others in the past and in the future.'
* Fires destroy forty dwellings. Three dead. Two parents and five children seriously injured. Police suspect arson.
* Students and unions demonstrate; marches close city streets. Heat claims one victim.
* Water restrictions now critical.

* DA administrators struggling to cope as tourists cancel visits and desert streets. Cape Town businesses threatened as city faces worst crisis of confidence since apartheid.

Sally Frazer swivels in her chair, rises to stand, faces the centre of the room, addresses De Vries.

'Before you ask, I don't know, and nor does anyone else, where Ali Jelani is.' She sits back down, beckons for De Vries to sit next to her. 'However, I did call both Mark Garsten and Luke Miles to ask them about their children and they both told me stories.'

'It's all about the children,' De Vries says, yawning, his hand reaching his mouth just as it is closing again.

'Yes, I think it is,' she says. 'Luke Miles told me that his son, Josh, had broken his leg when he was playing around the family car while Bethany Miles was driving. She was late collecting her daughter from an end-of-year event and, in effect, she had backed out of the driveway and driven over Josh when he was on the ground.'

De Vries raises his eyes to heaven.

'Some of us are good drivers,' Sally Frazer says. 'There was a crowd of people who gathered before the ambulance arrived. Apparently, some of them were pretty scathing about her.'

'What about Mark Garsten?'

'That was weird. He said that about ten days before she disappeared, she had come home from collecting the children from school, had pulled up at the traffic lights and the man in the car behind her got out and came to talk to her. There were people around and he was white, so she lowered her window. Apparently, he told her angrily that she should not be smoking in the car with children inside.'

'She give a description?'

'Not that the husband remembers, no,' Frazer says. 'He tried to help her dismiss it. He said that she was obviously pretty upset because she knew that he would be displeased to hear that she was smoking in the car, but she told him about it anyway. He said that she told him the man had been very threatening and it had unnerved her all the way home. She thought he might be following her, but she wasn't sure. Mark Garsten said that he went outside and checked the street, but he couldn't see anything.'

'This all ties in with what Dr Bellingham and I were discussing last night,' De Vries says. 'Yesterday evening.' He pauses, frowns, glances at his watch. 'It's seven forty-five a.m. Have you been home?'

'Briefly,' Frazer says. 'You said this is the moment that we have to stop him before he strikes again. When you say that, I can't sleep.'

He leans back in the cheap office chair, its front legs in the air, plastic back arching.

'Hazel Calder suffered from dwarfism, had three children, all affected. Two died in childhood. Michelle Ricquarts leaves her daughters alone while she goes out to strip – do we know anything else about them?'

Sally Frazer shakes her head, says: 'Marie Garsten smokes in the car with her children there and gets warned about it. By our man, you think? And Bethany Miles runs over her son's leg and breaks it.'

'Okay, let's go back a moment. Marie Garsten: where did this incident occur?'

'Just off Irene Avenue in Somerset West. I haven't spoken to Traffic yet, but even if there were cameras, it's been a month.'

'You ask the husband if she could describe the car?'

'I did, and he said she knew nothing about cars and didn't mention it.'

De Vries gets up, walks to the table where the squad-room

coffee jug sits next to the chipped, thick-rimmed crockery, flicks the empty glass container, turns back.

'We have a connection: children. Injured, deformed at birth, mistreated in some way. We know that he spends some time down towards Strand and Somerset West because he happened to see Marie Garsten and her children in their car. It's good, but how does it help us to catch him?'

Don February and Ben Thwala enter the squad-room in conversation, stopping when they see De Vries and Frazer at work.

'Any progress, sir?'

De Vries regards them. 'Thanks to Sally, some . . . Not enough.' He licks his lips. 'I'm going to make a quick call. When I come back, I want decent coffee for all of us, sweet things to eat, and the home address of Penelope van Reidel.' He opens his wallet, slaps an orange 200-rand note on the table. He looks up at Don and Ben Thwala. 'This is important police business, gentlemen. Get on it.'

Don February has icing sugar on his lips, making him resemble a minstrel from the New Year's Day parades, his eyes wide and shining. The strong coffee, pastries and doughnuts have imbued each of them with new energy.

'Security cameras on the private residences surrounding Rose's nursery: were they checked?'

Thwala swallows quickly. 'We asked, door-to-door, but private cameras usually do not retain footage.'

'What about those linked to a central computer, held by the security company?'

Thwala nods, still chewing. 'Sometimes, then, yes.'

'Just see what you can find.'

Don says: 'But we do not know who to look for or which road he would have taken.'

'No, but we know what car Bethany Miles was driving. He would have arrived a little before her or soon after. He couldn't afford to sit around in the car park attracting attention. More likely, he followed her. We might just pick up something . . .'

'It will be no more than flashes as they pass on the road. Most of the cameras only cover the gateways.'

'Don. This is what we have left. He's giving us nothing so we have to find it ourselves: a sliver, a glimpse. And you don't have to do it: this is why we second officers . . .'

Sally Frazer passes him a torn slip of paper. 'The Van Reidel address. Oranjezicht.'

De Vries tips back his head, taps the base of the little cardboard shot-cup of espresso, relishes the thickness of the residue as it hits his throat.

'Okay. I'm going to Oranjezicht. I've got a visitor coming. Don't engage with him. Put him in my office, offer him nothing, and tell him I'll be back soon. They'll call up from downstairs.'

Oranjezicht sits elevated above the City Bowl, adjoining the fashionable end of Kloof Street, bounded by the lower slopes of the Mountain. In Klipp Street, the fine Victorian villas remain as single dwellings, the old fruit trees contorted over century-old stucco walls. Even early in the morning, the sun seems to blaze almost horizontally over the tops of the skyscrapers, burning the wide roads and steep side-streets of the district. De Vries waits for two large domestic workers to wheeze their way up the pavement before opening his car door. Twelve Klipp Street is a soaring double-fronted villa, with dark stone steps leading to tall double doors, glazed with bevelled glass and ornate ironwork. He feels the sweat at his neck as he is merely climbing the staircase. In answer to the doorbell, a video monitor with speaker illuminates to his right and a strident male voice says: 'What do you want?'

De Vries holds up his ID. 'A word with Ms van Reidel.'

'You have an appointment?'

De Vries opens his mouth, but he hears her voice on the intercom.

'It's all right.'

Ahead of him, he sees a door open to a room off the long hallway. Penelope van Reidel dismisses a maid, who has appeared from the distance, with a flick of her wrist that is so much part of the lilting stride which propels her to the door. She swings it open.

'Colonel de Vries, before nine a.m.'

'We tried to contact you yesterday afternoon and yesterday evening . . .'

'Yesterday I was busy.'

'. . . but you did not respond.'

De Vries waits to be invited in, but she stands in the doorway, blankly mute, unmoving.

'Do you understand busy?'

'I'm busy, Ms van Reidel, trying to stop a man abduct, rape and then slowly kill another woman. I don't care about pleasantries, or playing games. I need to find Ali Jelani. It seems only you know her whereabouts.'

'I have no idea where Ali Jelani is.'

'She's providing you with copy.'

'It's filed electronically. She could do it from the other side of the world.'

'But she's not on the other side of the world. She's here in Cape Town, being fed information by a source with intimate knowledge of these crimes. Either that source is part of my team, in which case that officer is jeopardizing everything we are working for, or the source has knowledge of the scenes or the perpetrator. Do you understand how dangerous that is for Ali Jelani?'

'She is a brave and determined young woman.'

De Vries moderates his voice. 'There is nothing admirable about withholding vital information from the police, especially if doing so results in the unnecessary death of another victim.'

She studies him silently, then stands aside, allowing him to step over the threshold into the cool hallway. She closes the door, passes him, and walks to the room from which she first appeared. De Vries hears her heels against the polished yellow-wood floor.

'Just wait there.' She pulls the door behind her. It moves soundlessly, heavy and protective. The deep click of its closure reverberates down the broad hall with its antique furniture and fresh flowers, glowing wooden ceiling, gleaming, immaculate paint-work. He hears the muffled sound of domestic travail from within, the roar of the city behind him no more than stifled exclamation. He waits in the silence, understanding the power-play, the su-periority of her position. His breathing is shallow, but calm, yet he can feel the blood in his arteries right down to his fingers.

He sees the brass handle turn, the door reopen.

'Ali Jelani will speak only if certain conditions are met.'

'You spoke to her?'

'I am to judge the sincerity of your undertaking.'

'You told me you didn't know where she is.'

'I don't. She is contactable. I have done that for you.'

'What conditions?'

'She wants to meet casually, in a public venue of her choosing, with a senior female detective, plain-clothed, who has discretion. She wants assurance that she will not be taken to a police station, or prevented from continuing her work.'

'Agreed.'

'Agreed? Just like that?'

'Yes.'

'And I should believe you?'

De Vries smiles thinly. 'I understood that you were to "judge the sincerity of my undertaking".'

The corner of her mouth twitches minutely.

'You are good at what you do. I discovered that. Appallingly flawed, probably scarred. Unreconstructed, hereditarily racist, numbingly misogynist . . .'

'You should hear about my faults.'

'But you're not funny. Not at all.' She studies him, their eye-line plumb. 'I have your word that Ali Jelani will be left unmolested, that you agree to her terms?'

'You do.'

She stands utterly still, regarding him, then slowly raises her left hand, passes him a heavy handwritten card.

'The woman you send, what name will she use?'

'Sally.'

'Sally it is, then.'

'Is that it?'

'You have the venue, the time. For now, my trust. That's it.'

'Thank you.'

'It's like obituaries for famous people. I have two alternative front pages for you, De Vries. Which gets printed is entirely in your hands now.'

He bows to her. 'Better a headline than an obituary.'

Mike Solarin hears the chanting from several streets away, feet stamping on the hot tarmac, drums and tins beaten, the hoarse, amp-boosted cry leading the chorus. The cacophony hangs in the dry, still air like brake-lights in a time-lapse night-time cityscape.

He turns the corner, is taken aback to register the numbers

outside the Jumu'a Mosque of Cape Town. A core of perhaps a hundred protesters wave flags and placards, sing, chant and echo shouted phrases. The signs are either blatantly anti-Islamic or accuse Muslims of appeasing extremism. Some complain of new mosque construction in Cape Town. Beyond and around this group stand another two hundred, bedraggled, on the periphery. He studies their faces, sees them mouthing words, taking photographs, occasionally nodding in assent.

Solarin stops in the shade, leans against the cool stone façade of an old building just off Grey's Pass in the very centre of Cape Town, watches three Metro cops stand at the foot of the wide pink steps leading to the plain wooden doors beneath the pillared façade of the dignified, modest building. Their expressions tell of fatigue from the heat, assault on their senses, alarm at the increasing number of protesters, at the growing volume of the chants. Two men start screaming hysterically, leading an elderly woman to the foot of the steps. Her cries and wails draw more women around her. Each begins to cry, to moan, to yowl in mourning.

Solarin pulls himself away from the wall, the crying grating down his spine as he takes a wide arc around the demonstration. In the distance, mingling with the human sirens, he hears police response vehicles approaching, fears for what might happen. At the corner of the street, he circles within his step, glancing back at the scene, walks on. Out of sight, he stops, peers around the corner of the grey monolithic building, looks back at the gathering. Where he had been standing, another figure now waits, observing the scene. He wipes his eyes with the back of his hand, replaces his dark glasses, focuses. Beyond the blindingly bright white sunlight, in the comparative darkness of the shade, Ray Black stands, watching the scene.

Solarin laughs to himself. The man wears dark glasses too, the details of his expression indiscernible. He cannot truly see this, but he half observes, half imagines, that Ray Black is smiling, satisfied, his arms crossed in front of him.

'Sergeant Frazer.' De Vries is moving fast into the squad-room. 'Delightful as you already look, please find yourself a casual summer dress, adorn yourself appropriately, and get ready to go out for lunch.'

Several team members look up. He reaches her desk, says quietly, 'You're meeting our elusive journalist at twelve. I'll brief you on the way.'

'Me?'

'It's a girl thing, apparently. Our ears only.' He glances around him. 'Let the tongues wag.'

She says: 'Mr Stephen Jessel. He arrived about ten minutes ago.' De Vries looks towards his corner office, can see only the back of Jessel, upright in one of the chairs that face his desk. 'He's a bit of a whiner.'

'I hope you ignored him.'

'I did, but it is hot in there.'

'He only has a few minutes more. That's where I spend the rest of my career.' De Vries leans towards her. 'I was serious about the dress.' He looks at his watch. 'I think we should go at eleven fifteen.'

He straightens up, considers putting on his jacket, thinks better of it, moves to his office. As he swings open the door, Stephen Jessel rises.

'Did you turn off the air-conditioning in here?'

'No, Mr Jessel. This is how we live.' He moves around his desk, hangs his jacket on the other guest chair and slumps in his seat. 'Take your jacket off. This is a very informal meeting.'

He thinks that Jessel is wearing the same shirt and tie as he had been on his first visit to the Special Crimes Unit. He observes Jessel's shirt is already damp with perspiration, sticking to his chest, revealing pale, clammy skin beneath the thin material.

'Please may we come to the point, Colonel? I don't have the luxury of spare time in my day. This meeting inevitably compromises the next and so on throughout my schedule.' He lowers his voice. 'If you wish to discuss the man we discussed at our last meeting, I need to be reassured that the same terms of confidentiality are in place.'

'Totally.'

'And, other than his Christian name, it would be better if specific details were not discussed at this time.' He glances behind himself, through the glass partition onto the squad-room. 'Is there a more private room?'

'I just want to know a few very simple things.'

Jessel turns back around to face De Vries, feels in his briefcase and produces a clipboard, which he places on his lap.

'Very well.'

'When we last spoke, you – and then subsequently Leigh himself – told me that he did not leave his house often, and when he did, it was usually with some of his friends. Is that right?'

'Yes.'

'I asked you how you knew when he went out and you told me that he simply informed you. Do you have no other method of checking his movements?'

Jessel shifts in the sticky chair. 'Leigh Finnemore is not imprisoned. He is both a free man and the subject of surveillance and monitoring. He has lived in Plumbago Lane for almost a decade and there has never once been a complaint about him. Nor have I ever had cause to criticize the actions he has taken. Therefore he is free to move around as he wishes, but I know – it is known – that he rarely ventures outside.'

'Does he have use of a car?'

'There is a car in the garage there, yes. A Volkswagen Beetle. An old one. To begin with, Leigh ignored it, but now he sometimes washes it in the garage. I helped him get it serviced and fit to drive. I hoped that it would allow him a little more freedom. He occasionally takes it for a circuit down Camps Bay Drive, along Beach Road, up to Kloof Nek and back again. He says he feels that is far enough and he is happy to come home. It probably takes less than fifteen minutes. That is how he is.'

'Does he ever take anyone with him?'

'Not that he tells me.'

'And do you check his mileage?'

Jessel frowns, then laughs. 'No. Why would I?'

'To monitor how far he has driven.'

'Perhaps that is something I should do, but I haven't. If I did find that he travelled further afield, it would bring me pleasure. It would represent more self-confidence and a chance that he might be releasing himself from what is, these days, almost self-imposed solitude.'

'So no one monitors where he goes, or with who, or when?'

Jessel sighs. 'Not empirically. I discuss with him how he feels, what he's done, what he would like to do.' He fastens his pen under the clip at the top of the board and leans over it towards De Vries. 'If these questions are because you still suspect him of some involvement in the incident at the other end of Plumbago Lane, then I merely repeat what I told you last time. I have not seen any indication of aggressive or violent tendencies in Leigh.'

'But just entirely hypothetically,' De Vries says casually, 'if Leigh Finnemore wanted to go out at night – for whatever reason – stay out for an hour or two and come home, no one would know?'

'He would inform me.'

'He *should* inform you.'

'I have no reason to think that Leigh is withholding from me.'

De Vries smiles. 'But the answer to my question is no?'

'Out of context, and with no understanding of the subject or his history, I accept that the answer to your meaningless question is no.'

'That's what I thought.'

'Was that that man Jessel? The one who authorized the section eighteen on . . . Leigh Finnemore?' Henrik du Toit gestures that De Vries should follow him.

'I was on my way to you anyway, sir.'

'I'm sure you were, Vaughn.' They walk up the staircase in silence. 'What was he doing here?'

De Vries closes Du Toit's office door behind him.

'I just wanted to clarify some information.'

'And did you?'

'I did. Jessel confirmed what I already suspected. Despite what he told us last time, the impression he tried to give, Finnemore isn't surveyed or monitored. He's looked in on occasionally. He has use of a car and can go out when he wants, without letting anyone know, day or night. Before you say anything, I know his neighbours say they've scarcely seen him, but I've been in that street several times now and, first of all, I haven't seen any of his neighbours – not one, not once – and second, if he is going out late at night, those people are all asleep in their back rooms, escaping the wind. They'd see nothing.'

'You're painting him as a suspect?'

'He is a suspect. How can anyone who has murdered before not be a suspect?'

'He has killed before, perhaps accidentally. There is a difference.'

'There is, if you believe all that psychological mumbo-jumbo.'

Du Toit holds up his hands, a gesture to which he frequently finds himself resorting when listening to De Vries.

'These crimes are all linked to children,' De Vries says, 'to the treatment of children. You read Grace Bellingham's profile, sir?'

'I have, and I'm worried that you're calling me "sir".'

'Leigh Finnemore fits that profile like the proverbial glove.'

'All right. Just wait. What about this journalist woman?'

'Ali Jelani. We're going to talk to her shortly. At least, Sergeant Frazer is, woman to woman.'

'You found her.'

'It required some persuasion . . .'

There is a silence.

Du Toit says: 'Aren't you going to ask? Aren't you curious?'

'About what?'

'How you can be on the front page of a newspaper drawing criticism of the SAPS, this department, our unit, and there has been no thunder from above?'

'I was revelling in not knowing the answer to that mystery.'

'I told General Thulani that you had persuaded Dr Bellingham to assist us – and that was a coup, that you were making excellent progress in sorting out what was happening, and that you were working fourteen-to-sixteen-hour days and deserved some down time.'

'I'm grateful for your confidence.'

'Is it misplaced?'

'Well, you should know by now, Henrik. It's a gamble.'

'This is the coolest I've been since my summons to the top floor.'

She looks at De Vries, smiles. 'Air-con was recharged when it was serviced, two weeks ago. Eats petrol but, hey, best part of my day is in here.'

Sally Frazer turns her VW Golf onto the slip road off Nelson Mandela Boulevard down to Salt River, draws up at the queue to turn onto Main Road.

'You know what we want from Jelani,' De Vries says. 'What she knows, how she knows it. And, while you're at it, why she's being so elusive. Tell her that you need to be able to reach her if she prints any more articles. Gain her confidence.'

'I'm still SAPS.'

De Vries glances across at her. Her hair, so resolutely tied in the office, is loose over the collar of a pale blue summer dress. Bare legs show.

'Hard to believe.'

She turns onto Main Road, which runs from town all the way down to Muizenberg. Here, in Salt River and Woodstock, it is lined with factory shops and warehouses, the old businesses, which still just about keep a foothold along the main drag, and, increasingly, artisan coffee bars, restaurants and galleries. Even so, the street is full of people, there is noisy trading from stalls and markets, taxi-vans honking, produce transported by horse and cart, on scooters, atop the heads of stoical women.

She takes the Railway circle and heads for Observatory, a suburb that absorbs poor, artistic, student and hipster, every age, colour and religion. Half a kilometre from the designated meeting place, De Vries tells her to stop. He squints past her to a bar on the opposite side of the road.

'It says it has Wi-Fi, air-con, food, drink. This is my field-office.' He gets out of the car, leans back in through the passenger door. 'You know where I am. I know where you are. Don't let her take you anywhere without calling me. This Françoise place is over Station Road, *ja*?'

Frazer nods. 'I know it, sir.'

He ducks out, raises his voice against a passing truck. 'Good luck.'

'François/Françoise' is a bar and café, excavated from the shell of an old industrial building just off the main road. Its windows are dark and heavily barred but, within, fairy lights sparkle, Chinese lanterns glow and, beyond, green-tinged daylight suggests a leafy courtyard or garden.

Sally Frazer has walked past its door before, late at night, glancing momentarily towards discordant music, seeing cigarette tips glow in a fog of nicotine; she remembers that, at night, it is a venue for local bands. She turns sideways to slide through the narrow navy-blue metal door, finds the interior soothingly cool and devoid of glare. A gleaming brass coffee machine hisses at the end of the long dark turquoise-tiled bar, behind which a huge mirror reflects the ceiling-high display of fancy bottles, plastic street-stall toys and ceramic figurines, vintage signs and framed maps.

She walks past sparsely filled tables towards a wide opening onto a leafy courtyard, shaded by fig trees. She examines a bed of cannabis plants, their huge leaves sieving the sunlight, dappling it onto the cobbled ground. A sign states: 'Male Sativa Plants: Like Their Human Equivalents, Providing Little of Consequence'. She scans the half-dozen café tables, moves back inside.

In an alcove to her left, she sees a small African woman, head bowed, studying her. Sally Frazer determines to put the intonation of recognition into her voice.

'Ali . . . I'm Sally.'

The woman stands. Frazer moves past Jelani's outstretched hand, holds her shoulders, kisses her lightly on both cheeks. Ali Jelani shrinks from her, retakes her seat. Her eyes dart from side to side, her breathing accelerates.

'Are you okay?' Frazer asks. Staccato nodding. 'You wanted it casual. I thought we'd look like friends.'

'I do not consider you people my friends.'

'You want a drink?'

'Coffee. Black. They'll come.'

Frazer leans back, taking in the obstructed view to the

courtyard, her line of sight down the length of the bar. She catches one half of her face in a painted café mirror. With her hair let down, she scarcely recognizes herself.

'This is very private here. We can talk.'

'Maybe . . .'

A girl, probably a UCT student working her vacation, attends their table. Frazer orders for both of them. Ali Jelani continues to shake, eyes down but wide, her small fingers clenched.

'What's the matter, Ali?'

She looks around once more. 'You do not understand. All my life I have been afraid, ever since I was a child.'

'Afraid of what?'

Ali Jelani sniffs. 'Being trodden on, being ignored, being banished, being used . . .'

'Can we talk about your writing?'

'No. You can hear me first. I say what I want to say.'

Two young black girls, arm in arm, their heads immaculate and gleaming, walk past into the courtyard. Both are talking on cell-phones. Frazer watches Ali Jelani inspect them. Their coffee arrives. Jelani pulls her cup close to her, guards it with her hands.

'I come from Kenya. They call it a city, but it is only a town, called Eldoret. It is in the west. The Voortrekkers took it from my people in 1910, so I have come to take land here in South Africa, in the Cape.'

'All right . . .'

'Do you have any idea how hard it is for a girl to be educated where I come from? To study and learn? I did that. I volunteered and I wrote, and I gave the newspaper and magazine editors my work for nothing, and still they would not take it. Because I could not write as well as a man? No way . . .' She raises the cup to her lips, blows on the surface, sips gingerly. 'You have a husband?'

'Not yet.'

Ali Jelani laughs sadly. 'You have a choice! I was pregnant when I was seventeen, and though I begged him no, he made me pregnant again only a few months after my child was born. I gave him two girls and he wanted boys, so he left us and he told the town that I was cursed.'

Momentarily, she seems to have forgotten her fear. Her eyes never meet those of her interlocutor. They stare beyond her cup and saucer at the scratched wooden school desk that is their table, as if she is examining the markings in search of a lost story.

'So, despite my burden, I travel this continent to write and still it is hard for a woman, even when she is writing about women. I follow the African Union Mission to Somalia, spend six months volunteering in the Walalah Biylooley refugee camp, covering the struggle against female genital mutilation. I go to Ethiopia and Rwanda and Burundi. Last year, I travel to Syria to speak to the women who have been raped as an act of war, as a way for men to exert their strength, to impregnate women so that they might be damned for all their lives.'

Her voice is rising. The whites of her eyes seem to shine in the dim interior. Frazer raises her palms on the surface of the table.

Ali Jelani's nostrils flare, but she moderates her voice, leaning in towards her. 'No one would publish my work. Online only, in a country where the internet is still a rarity.'

'So you came here?'

'You are not listening to me. In your country, thirty-eight per cent of women have been raped. Men admit it, like it is a badge, a credit to them. Twenty-eight per cent of men admit it. Boast . . .'

'I know the figures, Ali,' Frazer says firmly. 'My colleagues and I deal with the aftermath of them every day. Believe me.'

'You know figures . . .' Ali Jelani sounds scornful, her thin fingers insect-like around the handle of her cup. She raises it, sips, sips again, says: 'You are not interested in what women must face here?'

Frazer speaks calmly: 'There is much to do, and many ways of achieving it. In our own ways, perhaps we are both achieving something. We must talk about your work for Penelope van Reidel at the *New Cape Gazette*.'

'That woman is whiter than alabaster. She has known nothing but wealth and privilege, but she is the first here, in the national press, to give me an opportunity. I grasp that opportunity. It is only a thin branch but I will make it bear fruit.'

'The stories about Hazel Calder and Michelle Ricquarts: how did you find them?'

'Work. Research. Labour.'

'But how?'

'I just told you.'

'Ms Jelani . . . Ali . . . These were two unpublished crimes in two different policing areas. We just need to understand how you made the connection between them, and then to Marie Garsten, who lived and was found fifty kilometres from here.'

'A good journalist has her sources.'

'You don't need to name your source but you can tell me: is it from the SAPS?' She lowers her voice on the final words as if speaking a taboo.

'It may be.'

'If you know something about who is committing these crimes, you must tell us.'

Jelani still stares downwards. Her eyes rise only to survey her surroundings, then lower again. Once they are beyond making any contact with Sally Frazer, she says:

'Do you know who is committing these crimes?'

'We are working very hard to find out. Why would you not speak to us?'

'There are many who want to silence me.'

Frazer turns towards the sound of voices. Four white women amble past them into the courtyard; two return and scrutinize the available tables indoors, then stand behind them, chattering, waiting for their friends to make a decision. She looks across the table at Ali Jelani. She cannot be more than thirty-five, perhaps younger, her small face fixed in its expression of toiling determination, jaw set, eyes constantly moving. Usually a person's face reveals as many secrets as words are spoken, but Frazer cannot see her eyes, or interpret veracity from her features, either frozen or animated, like a repeating tick.

The women move indoors towards the front of the bar.

'Who told you about the crime scene where Bethany Miles was found? You have to understand, whoever is giving you this information is either stealing from us – the police – compromising our investigation, breaking the law, or they have knowledge of the crimes because they were there.'

For the first time, Ali Jelani does not counter immediately, seeming to consider what is being said to her.

Frazer waits, then says: 'You must tell me. Whatever you think your source is giving you, whatever advantage you gain professionally, it is too high a price.'

Ali Jelani raises her head, speaking quietly and deliberately: 'There is always a price to be paid.'

Frazer leans towards her until their faces are almost touching. 'These women are stripped and bound and left alone in the dark without water for days. They are gagged and blindfolded, tortured and raped by a man who believes it is his right to punish them. He will not stop. Whoever is giving you your information must know more than we do. Help us.' She leans back, aware of her breath, of the heat in the alcove. She sees Ali Jelani's chest rise and fall; sees her struggle to wet the back of her throat; one hand gripping the index finger of the other. She waits until Jelani meets her eye. 'Whatever you think you can achieve with your writing, is any of that worth it if another woman is taken by a man, tortured and bound and murdered?'

197

Jelani looks down. Her small head seems to quiver.

'I write about African women, what they have to suffer.'

'You wouldn't help a white woman?'

'Don't lecture me on discrimination . . .' She trails off, the scorn in her voice desultory, her mind absorbed with other thoughts.

'Surely women must stand by women. What other chance do we have?'

Jelani shakes her head. 'You know nothing of the suffering of women on this continent.'

Frazer swallows her desire to argue, to fight her assertion, tells herself that she has only one role here. She drains her cup, looks around for a waitress.

Jelani reaches down to a small handbag woven from grass. She rights herself.

'You smoke?'

Frazer shakes her head.

'Please get me some cigarettes. Strong. They are behind the bar.'

Frazer stands, looks back at Ali Jelani, who has her bag on the table, a pen between her lips. She rounds the corner, asks the tall, smooth-skinned black guy behind the bar for cigarettes. As he turns back, smiling, she realizes that he is very beautiful, his face perfect, high cheekbones, broad eye sockets, his glowing complexion unblemished. She pays for the cigarettes, wonders whether he is the eponymous François, turns to their table, turns again, François/Françoise: perhaps he is both . . . She smiles to herself, glances back at her table. Ali Jelani is gone.

Frazer checks for Jelani's handbag, any sign that she might have slipped away to the bathroom, but there is nothing except a blank sheet of paper. She looks back down the length of the café, certain that Jelani did not pass behind her while she was at the bar. In the body language of her fellow customers, she takes in laughter and concentration, relaxation and boredom. She hurries to the lavatories, finds both sexes' facilities deserted, moves into the courtyard, scans the tables. In the far corner, behind one of the beds of sterile cannabis plants, she sees a door with a release bar. A fire-exit sign is hidden by one of the leaves. She stares at the table closest to her. A woman looks up.

'She went through there.'

'Just now?'

'*Ja*. One minute ago, sure.'

She pushes down on the release bar, drops her own bag on the ground to stop the door snapping shut and locking her out, finds herself in a narrow backstreet. The service entrances to the shops beyond line the far side, garages, fire-escape ladders and waste bins the other. She sees no sign of human life in either direction. She feels nauseous and angry, made foolish by a simple ruse.

She pulls the fire door open, retrieves her bag, returns to their table, sits. She sees the waitress and calls for the bill.

'The lady I was with . . . Has she been here before? Have you seen her?'

The girl shakes her head, turns away.

Frazer sees the sheet of paper in the waitress's hand, realizes that there is faint writing on the reverse.

'That paper.' The waitress turns. 'Can I have it back?' She takes it from the girl, waits until she has gone before turning it over. A single line is written in a faint, spidery hand. She feels her chest ache, bile rise. She slaps a hundred-rand note on the table, slides it under the brass ashtray. She starts to stride towards the door, out into the light, into what she finds is a blinding, stupefying sun, stumbles on the cracked pavement as she begins to run towards her car.

'Let me in!'

He sees light flutter in the peephole. He turns to the two uni-formed officers with him.

'Wait by the lift until I'm inside.' He watches them go. 'I'm alone, Grace.'

The door to Grace Bellingham's apartment opens abruptly. He enters, does not see her, hears the door slam behind him. She stands with her back to it.

'You call me, you tell me to lock the doors and windows, not to answer the front door. What danger? What danger am I in?' He comes towards her, but her stare stops him mid-stride. 'I want to know exactly what the nature of this threat is.'

'Come and sit down.'

'No, Vaughn. You're in my home. You made me do this for you and now you just do what I ask, or I swear I'll make you regret it.'

He sees that she has been crying, cheeks tear-stained. He walks over to the seating area by the wide windows.

'We tracked down this journalist, Ali Jelani. She took the photograph of us at the bar the other night, wrote the article, all the articles in the last six weeks. According to my sergeant who met her . . .'

'Your sergeant?'

'She wanted a woman – she'd only speak with a woman. I sent Sally Frazer. She's part of my core team. She's good. She says that before Jelani escaped and disappeared—'

'She lost her? This sergeant who's good?'

'—she got the impression that not only was she very afraid, but that she had had contact with our attacker, or someone close to him. She thought that she was making a breakthrough, but Jelani demanded cigarettes and used that opportunity to get away through the fire escape.'

'Jesus.'

'It happens.'

'But the warning?'

'On a sheet of paper, left by Jelani.'

'Show me.'

'It's being examined by our people in town. Jelani told a story about her background, but we don't know if any of it is true.'

She walks towards him. 'What did it say, Vaughn?'

'Your name. That he wanted to take you.'

She closes her eyes, the breath flowing from her body. She doubles over, pulls herself back up to face him.

'That's not good enough. I need the exact words.' De Vries hesitates. 'For Christ's sake, just tell me.'

'"He wants to take G. Bellingham soon."'

'The pronoun, not the name?'

'Your name?'

'His name.'

De Vries frowns. 'Just "he".'

'If he were a third party, she might use a name to distinguish between the killer and her contact. She's been in communication with him.' She shakes her head. 'Jesus, she could be working for him. You need to find out if she's been threatened, coerced, if her family has . . .' She walks around him towards the sitting area, her breathing fast and erratic. He follows her. 'He wants to take me. You're sure he used the word "take"?'

'*She* used it. It was her handwritten note.'

She is panting. He tries again to come close to her.

'Stay away. Just stay away. I begged you not to involve me. I've been back one week and this happens. Because of you. Because whatever you think of yourself, about your life, you don't really like being on your own, do you? You don't like sleeping alone and you don't like working alone, so you have to involve someone else, and I told you I didn't want it to be me . . .' She swallows tears, her hand pushing her hair from falling over her face. 'You have no idea what I went through in Virginia. They used me to reach this man, this monster of a man, and I was tired and broken and since then I can't sleep, can't work, can't think, and I let you, you . . . You make me do this.'

'I'll pay for a ticket. Get a flight. There's bound to be a seat tonight. Go to London, Amsterdam, Berlin. Get away from here. When I catch him and it's safe, come back, and I swear I'll never ask you anything again.'

'No.'

'No?'

'You don't run from these people. You run and they have power over you for ever. They know you run, so they find ways to follow you even if they're incarcerated, even if they're dead. You never stop running.'

'When we have him, he won't hurt you. You said yourself, these people are loners.'

'I didn't say that, and you know nothing about these men.'

'Then help me catch him.'

Her eyes flare. He sees her run the three steps towards him. She balls her fists and thumps them into his chest. The first blow against his heart winds him, shocks him; he stumbles, but she keeps pummelling him, over and over again, on his back, his neck, his head. He backs away, but she follows him until his back hits the wall and he has nowhere else to go.

'Help you catch him?' She is shouting, voice distorted by rage. 'Be my bait?' He tries to look up at her, but she punches him again. 'Yes, that's what men think women should be. That's what those cunts in America did to me. That's what they wanted, so they used me to get it.'

'I'm sorry, Grace . . .'

'You're sorry. You can't control your team, you can't control your witnesses and you sure as hell can't control him.'

She stumbles to the utilitarian sofa, falls onto it. De Vries waits where he is. They are both breathless; he feels tightness in his

202

chest, feels blackness descend on him. Even as he says the words, he knows he will not be believed.

'I can't undo this, but I can protect you.'

Her neck seems to give way, her head lolling onto the top of the backrest. She gasps to find a voice.

'Leave me alone.'

'I can't do that.'

She hauls her head up, sits forward, says quietly: 'I'm angry with you, but sure as hell I'm angrier with myself.' She punches the sofa. 'What have I become? I used to be strong.'

He moves across the room, kneels next to the sofa.

'I'm sorry, Grace.'

'Make me tea.'

'Tea?'

'Yes, a mug of tea. Two sugars. Then sit down over there while I think what to do. I need to think.'

He struggles up, moves to the front door, opens it. The two officers are by the lift as instructed. He beckons to them.

'Outside this door. Anyone approaches, draw your weapon.' He studies them. 'You understand that order?'

They confirm that they do. He closes the door, goes to the kitchen, turns back to her.

'Let me take you to my house. If he knows about you, he may know this address. The whole of upstairs can be locked down. I did it for Suzanne and the girls. No one can get in. You can rest.'

'Rest? You have no idea what this means.'

'It means I can look after you.'

She slumps lower into the sofa. 'It means I am already a prisoner.'

'Dr Bellingham has set up an office in my house. Three officers posted. She can lock herself in.'

Henrik du Toit seems to be staring at his mouth, watching the words emerge.

'If you are convinced that is the safest option.'

'I am.'

'I know how you feel about her, Vaughn. Are you certain you're making the right decisions for the right reasons?'

'As sure as I can be right now.'

'And this note? I've spoken to Sergeant Frazer. She says she felt she'd shifted this Jelani woman's view of what was happening, that the note is a genuine warning, based on what Jelani knows.'

'I think it is.'

'I want to ask you this: does Dr Bellingham fit the profile of the attacker's victims?'

'She's divorced, messily,' De Vries says. 'Her relationship with her children has been strained. Her biography is public knowledge online. Frazer's been researching what's in the public domain about her, says that in interviews Bellingham openly describes the effect of her work on her marriage, her family. If children are the link, there is reason to believe she could be targeted but, frankly, I think it's more likely that whoever the perpetrator is, he saw the picture of us in that *Cape Gazette* and thinks her involvement in the case makes her a target.'

'He thinks she can find him?'

'Possibly. And if the Jelani woman is working for the killer, even through a go-between, she could have given him Bellingham's history, her training and experience in the States.'

'Even if we believe that Jelani does have some form of contact with him,' Du Toit says, 'why would he tell her his target?'

'We don't know he didn't tell her who his previous two targets were.'

'Jelani had prior knowledge of his victims and told nobody?'

De Vries sighs. 'I don't know, sir. We know next to nothing

about Ali Jelani. The editor, Van Reidel, claims to know little about her. I think she started providing newsworthy copy and all scrutiny was abandoned in the name of a good story.'

'I hope you're wrong about that, Vaughn. It would be callous beyond belief.'

'I have long pondered the inhumanity of women towards women . . .'

'That's not funny. We need answers, and action, not attempts at glib wit.'

'We have two teams dedicated to working on this around the clock,' De Vries tells him, ignoring the criticism. 'I'll be briefing my team for the operation this evening.'

Du Toit shakes his head. 'Whatever it is had better work because I can tell you—'

'That you have had General Thulani and, no doubt, Pretoria on your back,' De Vries says wearily. 'Am I right?'

'You are. We're being scrutinized. As ever. I want every decision you make recorded and documented.'

'As ever.'

'How would he even know where Grace is now?'

'It's safest to assume that he does,' De Vries says. 'Or will.'

'And you think he'll risk trying to attack her?'

'Dr Bellingham's own profile suggests that he will take greater and greater risks. She knows these men, and she is afraid. That makes me afraid.'

'What makes you even think that this Jelani woman won't warn him?'

'Because if she is in contact with him or an informed third party, and she is as frightened as she claims, she won't risk letting him know that she has been speaking to us, let alone that she has shared his plans.'

'And we have no idea where Jelani is?'

'Not at the moment.'

'She's Kenyan?'

'She is not registered as a resident.'

Du Toit sits back. 'All right.'

'Have I answered all your questions, sir?'

He sighs. 'Frankly, Vaughn, I have no idea.'

As De Vries pulls off the street, waits while the gates slowly open inwards, he reflects that, in neighbouring houses, officers have taken up positions at various times in the past hours to monitor not only this road but the adjacent ones also. All vehicles and pedestrians will be photographed and recorded. The three officers left with Grace Bellingham have not shown themselves since originally taking their places. His entire team's presence is, he believes, concealed.

He edges into the driveway, parks to the side to provide a clear line of sight to his front door for the officers posted directly opposite. He gets out, takes four bags of shopping from the boot, walks to the entrance porch. The hard-wood door is heavy and solid, has protected him and his family for almost thirty years. He takes strength from it as he places his palm against the smooth surface and pushes it open. Inside, in the now unused formal dining room directly to the right of the entrance, an officer waits in the dimming evening light, pockmarked by the glimmering shadows of the branches of the two pepper trees. Until the front door is closed, De Vries does not acknowledge him. In the open-plan kitchen and living room, a second officer sits at the table, looking out on the scorched garden and half-empty pool.

De Vries sets the bags down in the kitchen, realizes that the space is airless and oppressive. The ceiling fan stopped weeks previously, still not mended.

'All well?'

'Yes, sir. No phone calls, no visitors. The builders left next door at seventeen fifteen. The couple you described on the balcony began moving their possessions inside and shut the sliding doors.'

'Good.'

'The school at the back there, sir? Dr Bellingham said she saw people in the grounds. We looked from the back windows and there were four men tending the cricket pitch. They left at . . .' he glances at the pad on the table '. . . sixteen forty.'

De Vries unlocks and opens the French windows onto the garden, looks up at the back wall of his property, to the tall eucalyptus trees on its far side, which line the boundary to the school playing fields. Not a leaf moves. It is silent. In the rectangle formed by his house and the perimeter wall, the last shards of sunlight reveal that the sultry air is thick with dust, filled with slow-moving, hovering insects. His throat tickles. He ducks back inside, runs the cold tap, pours himself water in his morning coffee mug. 'There'll be food soon. Only pies and pizzas. Has Dr Bellingham come downstairs?'

'No, sir. We took her a jug of water, later some ice from your freezer, and some tea.'

'If she comes down to eat, you can each take a few minutes' break. Otherwise, be alert for any sound or movement.'

The officer nods.

De Vries wants to shower, to change. His clothes stick to him and he can smell himself even amid the stale, acrid air. He turns away from the officer, leans over the kitchen sink, holding himself steady with tired arms, closes his eyes, sighs silently. He understands that there is only one good outcome from the night ahead: the capture of the killer. If nothing happens, his judgement will seem impaired, the threat to Grace Bellingham still active.

Yet he does not really believe that the man will come, struggles to reconcile Ali Jelani's motivation, both in the writing of her stories and in revealing the supposed nature of the threat. Until he understands that, he considers her an enigma of little use.

Mike Solarin reaches the café drenched with sweat, regretting that he has chosen to walk. Ever since the morning, he has been disturbed by the memory of Ray Black overseeing the demonstration outside the mosque, the unavoidable sensation that fear and loathing are fomenting in the city. He stands beneath the air-conditioning unit above the queue by the counter, feeling the perspiration thicken and cool on him, his head throbbing. As the temperature in the Cape rises, the mountain fires blaze, threatening property and life, so the atmosphere of dread intensifies, as if the skin of the city itself were alight, burning away, revealing the blood and bile within. He feels dizzy, nauseous, turns away to a table close to the back of the café, sits, tries to breathe slowly, deeply.

After a few minutes he feels better, sits up.. The door opens, and he waves, stands.

'Mike.'

They shake hands.

'Don.'

They smile. Neither is their birth name.

'I will get you coffee? A cool drink?'

'Shall we be very civilized?' Solarin says, affecting an English accent. 'Iced coffee?'

Don walks to the counter, orders two large iced coffees, pays at the till, returns to their table.

'You did not tell me that you were in town.'

'Posted here, attached to the Terrorist Squad. I was surprised myself. Think they drafted everybody in.'

'Quick work, Mike.'

Solarin frowns, glances around them. Jazz is playing quietly, a few other customers chatter or study laptops. None of the tables in their immediate vicinity is occupied.

'Maybe . . .'

Don February meets his eye. Solarin's expression seems blank, yet Don reads him.

'It is safe to talk here?'

'*Ja*. Better it is in public. Maybe I have a follower . . . You are my friend from university, from training. It is natural that you and me, we should meet up for a drink.'

The waitress brings them their coffees. They both admire her, both drink almost the entire contents of their glasses. They gesture to her for another round. Four pink tourists lumber in, loud and sweaty, rucksacks swinging against the counter, clipping the back of the head of a solitary newspaper reader. Don and Solarin talk about their lives in Cape Town and Pretoria, Don's wife, Solarin's now ex-girlfriend. More iced coffees arrive; the tourists take their drinks to go. The café reverts to its soothingly cool, low hum of recreational coffee-drinking.

'Imagine,' Solarin says quietly, 'if you were seconded to a team of officers investigating a major incident and, within a few hours of starting out, you are recalled because the matter is concluded, solved, and then you learn from a contact that the forensic evidence does not match up, that each element of the investigation is kept entirely separate from everyone but . . . I don't know who . . . someone. Imagine that you are on the road and it turns out that you have almost reached a location which might have been indicated by the forensic science and then, with your otherwise disinterested partner repeatedly, secretly, on his cellphone, you are recalled. How would you feel?'

'Like you feel,' Don says quietly.

'You are happy to be where you are. You maybe should keep your head down, but you think, Something is not right here, something which should not be left. A miscarriage of justice, a misappropriation of blame.'

'That is like my boss speaking.'

'Yes,' Solarin says quickly. 'That is what I thought. Colonel de Vries.'

'He is not doing so well just now. We have an investigation, which is . . . Well, you have seen the papers. It is not good.'

'I know. I hear what they say, but he has been effective in the past. You have confidence in him?'

'I do. It is tested, Mike, but I do.'

'Maybe I talk to him.'

Don smiles. 'I think he might see you as the next generation. But I do not know whether it is a good idea.'

'Why?'

'Because, you associate with him, it will not be good for you. I hear what people say. He is almost alone now. They think he is toxic.'

'But is that because he will not play political games? Because he wants the truth?'

'Partly, maybe . . .'

'That is how I want to be. That is how I am.'

'The politicians and the SAPS – they are so closely linked. You go against them, you may lose everything.'

'Maybe to win you have to risk everything.'

Don laughs. 'Oh, my God, Mike Solarin, the young black Vaughn de Vries.'

Solarin doesn't flinch. 'He has some time – in a week, even two – you call me. *Ja*, Don?'

'I will do that for you – but you just be careful, my friend. You may get what you want.'

Grace Bellingham comes downstairs to eat in the kitchen. She is quiet, drawn, her eyes nervous. She is not wearing make-up, her hair unbrushed. She wears a plain linen dress, pale against her tanned legs, which shine with perspiration. She does not make eye contact with the guards, does not acknowledge De Vries. Instead she walks to the French windows and stands at the threshold, her arms at forty-five degrees to her body, fingers wide. She catches no breeze. She lowers them, shoulders sagging, studies her surroundings. The walls of the garden are high, the gate down the side of the house to the street is locked and carries razor wire; the top of the wall by the neighbours' house is tipped with broken glass. When De Vries brings pies and a salad to the table, she sits at its end, granting her a view of both the internal entrance and the garden.

One officer eats on a tray, sitting in the adjoining living area. Another remains on the stairs, protecting the hallway, while the third showers, preparing for the long night ahead.

'Will you eat?'

She looks up at him.

'It passes the time.'

He sits with his back to the garden at right angles to her. He watches her slice the pie into four, place one slice on her plate and pull the salad towards her.

'What's your betting?' De Vries asks quietly. 'Will he come?'

'That rather depends on whether he has information, doesn't

it? On the one hand, does he know where I'm staying? On the other, has someone told him about this operation?'

'If the answers are yes, and no?'

'I don't believe that he would tell someone, even someone he believes he can control, who a victim would be. This is more likely a test of Jelani's loyalty than a genuine threat to me.'

'That's why you're calmer: you don't think this is real?'

She puts down her cutlery slowly. Everything she does has slowed. She says, deliberately:

'I am not calm. All I have to save me is my work. I have considered what he has done and what we know about him. My view is that he may want to scare me, perhaps dissuade me from aiding you. It wouldn't surprise me if something happens tonight to frighten me, but however great a risk he might be prepared to take, trying to abduct me defies logic, however desperate he may feel.'

'I hope he doesn't, but if he does, we are here.'

She smiles, picks up her knife and fork, positions a cherry tomato and a cube of feta cheese on the prongs.

'These men are cleverer than you think.'

De Vries's domestic worker winds the clock, but never adjusts it; its chimes are soothing but near worthless in providing a guide to time.

'What's that?'

He peers at his watch, back at Grace Bellingham. 'Twenty to one.'

They sit in the living area, an officer at the dining table, looking outside. He unlocks the double doors, hopes to feel coolness as he opens them wide. Air, a degree or two cooler than indoors, waits for him, intransigently refusing to drift in. Despite the small fan brought from De Vries's bedroom, the room is muggy, still; everyone is sweating. A cricket, probably in the bougainvillaea on the pergola outside, chirrups consistently, marking out the seconds, the minutes.

'Thank you for staying with me.'

'I'm not sleeping anyway.' He turns to her. 'But you should.'

Grace Bellingham twitches minutely. 'I won't, though.'

'It's hot. If I had time, I'd have worked on the pool . . . Not that we're allowed to refill them, with the drought restrictions. Anyway, you're safe enough here. You want anything?'

'Just water. Ice, if there's any.'

He pauses at the doorway, tilting his head to hear over the sound of the insects. He turns towards the kitchen, then back again, steps into the black garden, the outdoor lights inactive for the last two years. He turns to the officer at the table.

'Be on your guard.'

Grace Bellingham looks up. 'What's happening?'

He closes the doors, locks them. 'Probably nothing. Maybe an animal on the other side of the wall: a bird, squirrel. And there's smoke. Not braai. I'll get my torch.'

He goes into the hallway, calls upstairs:

'Be aware. I can smell smoke.'

De Vries fetches the torch from the hall table, returns to the kitchen, shines it around his garden. As the beam passes the back wall, it catches thick, billowing smoke. He refocuses his eyes, passes the beam over the area a second time. He is certain.

'Fire over the wall.' He turns to the officer. 'Get the fire crews out.' Then, to Grace Bellingham: 'This is it.'

Even as the officer calls, De Vries can see the fire now without a torch. The blaze is rising from the base of one of the eucalyptus trees, the fallen leaves and small branches piled up at their bases providing a natural accelerant. The dark smoke is orange-tinged as it rises above the wall. He sees the lower branches of the neighbouring trees ignite; the flames rise high and straight into the canopy. Through the narrow slits of window left open, he can hear the cracking and crackling, see the oils in the bark of the branches burst into flames. Tiny jets explode from them at right angles against black sky.

He speed-dials. 'You see it?'

'*Ja*, sir. Fire crews summoned. Do you want me to arrange your evacuation?' Don's voice is quiet and calm, unchanging.

'No. Not yet. That's what he wants. No one move. Maintain positions. Just send an officer to the front gates of the school – top of the road, fifty metres on the right. Whoever started that fire has to get out.'

He disconnects, looks back at the scene outside his home. Already the alarms on the neighbouring houses are sounding; at a certain point in their tone, they clash, and the discord hurts his ears. In front of him, four huge old trees are now ablaze, his garden brightly lit by the fast and almost constant flicker of flames, their sickly yellow reflecting dully and slowly on the surface of the thick green water of the pool. He can feel the heat even through the glass. A falling branch hits the windows, sits shattered, smouldering, on the pink brick paving around the pool. He is afraid now that the inferno will take hold of his property.

He looks behind him. Grace Bellingham stands, pressed to the back wall, seemingly mesmerized. He turns back, assesses the likelihood of the fire catching hold of his house, feels overcome by the smoke and dust and heat in the air. It is so still that the flames rise vertically; even the sparks just carry higher and higher into the sky. De Vries knows the danger of forest fires on the Mountain is very real. He forces himself to relax; the grip on his weapon loosened. Suddenly, there is a burst of shots, Grace Bellingham screams, slides to the floor. He falls, weapon out in front of him. In the garden nothing stirs but the tumbling, smoking boughs from the branches that overhang the pool. He hears the fire hiss as engulfed branches hit the surface, sees the steam rise from the mire. Over the wall that adjoins his neighbours' house, he sees the thatched roof on their pool house emitting thick dark smoke, the flash as it ignites, illuminating the garden and the room. The inferno fills his brain – flames blaze in his eyes even when they are turned inside, to the tiled floor of the living room. Finally, his mind processes the sound.

'Not gunshots.' He listens. In the distance, there are sirens. 'Not gunshots, Grace. Fireworks. Probably fireworks.'

He waits. Sirens. SAPS patrols.

'Grace?'

In his mind, the firestorm at the back of his house, panic and fear among his neighbours. At the front, chaos: residents, fire officers, uniforms, rubber-neckers. He does not know whether to take her out to the front, or remain where he is until they are either forced to evacuate or the scene is controlled.

'Grace?'

He looks around, sees her on the floor. He crawls to her.

'Are you okay?'

He hears her crying, sees her body shudder. 'Come here.'

He moves to her, takes her arm, pulls her to her knees. They crawl to the hallway, stand in the crook of the staircase.

'It's all right. The firemen are here. Fucking uniforms will be swarming all over the street. It's over. You said he'd try to frighten you, show you he knew where you were. He's done it.'

She is shaking, does not reject his arm around her shoulders, moves her hand into his.

Through the garden windows, he can see the flashing lights of a fire engine beyond the perimeter wall. The fire is high in the dwindling canopies now, burning itself out; the blackened skeletons of the eucalyptus trees glow and smoke. He sees water spray over his wall into his field of vision.

He pulls out his phone. 'Don. Keep everyone watching. He could come back. He could try something while people are on the street. Not likely, but let's keep this tight.'

'Yes, sir.'

'I'm staying here unless compelled to move.'

'Understood, sir.'

He rings off, feels Grace shaking under his arm. Her head is down, neck bent. There is no panic, no hysteria, but there is no fight left in her either; no energy, no life force. She feels limp and helpless. As the adrenalin, which has kept him alert, begins to diminish, he feels frustration and failure course through him. The killer came, and they didn't catch him, perhaps didn't even see him. The hall is haltingly floodlit by the flashing lights of the emergency services stationed outside his house; the armed officers still wait in his kitchen, his dining room, on the landing. Her hand feels cold, clammy. She has bent over so low that his arm no longer comforts her. He does not know what to do with his hands. He does not know what to do.

PART 3

DeVries sleeps fitfully, the smoke in his nostrils forcing him awake sporadically. He checks the garden from the upper-floor door to the veranda. In the bright dawn, beyond the wall, one fire engine waits silently, lights still flashing. The men are leaning against the vehicle, faces black – or blacker – holding cans of cold drinks.

He pads over the polished floorboards, listens at Grace Bellingham's door, thinks he hears her slow, consistent breathing. Just after eight a.m., the heat through his curtains drives him into his shower. Under a spray of feeble pressure, he lets the unheated water cool him, rinse off the thick sweat that, through the night, seems to have oozed, then dried, onto his body. His mind races through what he must do in the hours ahead, how he can look after Grace, re-energize the investigation, answer the accusations of aimlessness in his thinking. He dresses, knocks loudly on the guest-room door, trudges downstairs to the kitchen.

Outside, the water in his pool seems black from the charred debris on its surface. The paving is soaked from the hoses, the residue sludgy and grey. There are thin wisps of smoke or steam emanating from the thickest sections of the eucalyptus trunks. The air is heavy, dark with particulate, difficult to inhale without choking.

The doorbell rings. One of the three new guards calls, 'Brigadier du Toit, sir.'

De Vries hurries to his front door, opens it.

'Sir.'

Du Toit walks past him, through the hallway to the back of the house.

'Is this safe?'

'Safe enough. The fire crews are still around.'

'You didn't think to evacuate Dr Bellingham?'

'I did, and rejected the idea. The house remained the safest place for her to be. I think she has slept and I'll bring her into the office this morning.'

'Anyone see anything?'

'Not that they're saying, but we'll debrief. We have hours of surveillance to consider . . .'

'But no one beyond the perimeter wall there?' He nods outside.

'No. Since the wall is so high, I didn't post anyone that side. I felt he could not approach from that direction.'

'But he did.'

'He, or somebody else, nearly set the entire neighbourhood on fire, but there was no ingress from that point.'

'How is Dr Bellingham now? Does she feel safe?'

'I don't know. She wasn't convinced the threat to her was real.'

'Not real?' Du Toit gestures at the scalded garden.

'She felt, sir, that he was more likely to try to frighten her, possibly both of us. And he – or someone else – did.'

'And today?'

'Find Ali Jelani, work to identify the killer. He's clever. He's careful. But if that was him last night, he's taking greater risks, and that is how we'll catch him.'

Du Toit turns, paces the room. 'Your house all right?'

'Apparently. My neighbour's pool house burned down. The

guys out there confirmed last night that it was deliberate. The fire was started.'

Du Toit is looking into the kitchen, not at De Vries.

'I didn't tell you yesterday, wanted to keep you focused. They're thinking of sending a specialist unit from Pretoria.'

'How long do I have?'

'You're not surprised?'

'Not any more.'

'Perhaps today, possibly tomorrow. They're still working something up there, but they're keen to gain control, manage the press, take it from us.' Du Toit turns. 'You all right?'

'Yes.'

'No haughty indignation? No catalogue of justification?'

'I'll continue to strive to find this man,' De Vries says calmly. 'We have a profile, but we have virtually no evidence. I don't believe that anyone else, any other team, could have worked harder or more efficiently, but, sir, we will redouble our efforts.' Even as he says the words, he hears the weariness in his voice, questions how truly he believes his own defence.

Within thirty minutes of reaching Headquarters, De Vries has the back-up team, under the supervision of his unit's technical officer, Joey Morten, studying footage from two houses located on two different roads leading up to Rose's nursery. Despite it being more than ten days since Bethany Miles's abduction, both security companies are found to keep recordings for fourteen days and have released them. Neither camera is directed specifically at the streets, instead focused on monitoring who enters or exits the properties, but, with care, the cars passing the camera on the streets can be identified.

First, officers are charged with identifying Bethany Miles's metallic green Audi Q5. Then, working forwards from the sighting of the car, they must check for all vehicles that subsequently pass the two points in the direction of Rose's nursery until the time that the car, with the Miles' young daughter in the back, was discovered in the car park. Following this, others will track backwards, checking cars that arrived before Bethany Miles passed the point at which she was picked up on camera. All this information will be written up, allowing for comparisons with vehicles noted by the teams of officers around the scene last night.

Next, De Vries sends Ben Thwala and another officer to try to work out where the arsonist entered the school grounds the night before, and where a vehicle might have been parked.

Grace Bellingham descends to the basement to meet Harry Kleinman, with whom she had worked when she had been attached previously to the SAPS. They will, she claims, discuss the wounds found on the two murder victims, continue to search for clues in the killer's methodology.

Rejecting his suggestion to remain at home to rest, she had sat upright in the passenger seat on the way into the office, silent, staring forward blankly. He drove, uncertain whether to try to engage her in conversation or leave her. His own mind was so full, he stared ahead too, head spinning, his focus on the road faltering. As he turned from De Waal Drive to drop down into town, he caught the edge of a road island, jolting the car up at the back. His eyes opened wide, hands gripping the wheel.

'Sorry.'

She said nothing.

At nine forty a.m., De Vries receives a phone call that takes him out of his office and up to Vredehoek. This time, as he climbs the steps to Penelope van Reidel's grand villa, the front door is opened by a maid, dressed in black, with a frilly white apron. The editor stands in the hallway by the open door to her study.

'I am at a crucial stage of a murder investigation. This had better be significant information.'

'Significant, Colonel, and disturbing.' She ushers him into a grandiose book-lined room and invites him to sit down. She sits behind a broad antique desk.

'Ali Jelani told me that she was in danger,' she says, 'that she believed she was being followed. At her insistence, I agreed to call her every morning at eight. If she did not answer, I was to assume that she was in trouble. This morning, her phone is switched off.'

'Why didn't you tell me this before?'

'Because I left it to her to tell you. I assumed that she would explain this when you, or whoever you sent, met her.'

'You tried again?'

'Of course. I called the cellphone company; I have contacts and associations. They confirm that her phone is off. There's no signal registering.'

'When did you last speak to her?'

'She told me yesterday that she was working on another element of her story, that she would provide pictures.'

'What element?'

'She didn't specify. I understood, from what she said, it was a police operation.'

'Did she mention a name?'

'Dr Grace Bellingham.'

De Vries's stomach churns. An idea is already developing and, second by second, he believes it feels right.

'Where was Jelani last night?'

'I don't know.'

De Vries stares at her. 'Speculate.'

'On assignment?'

He gets up, walks slowly from her desk. He looks out to the panoramic view over the City Bowl, the skyscrapers silhouetted against the matt silver water in the Bay, the mountains of the peninsula on the horizon duck-egg blue against an even paler, cloudless shade. 'Ali Jelani may have been abducted by the killer.'

Van Reidel looks shocked. 'How can that be?'

'There was a police operation last night, which did concern Dr Bellingham, but she was not personally threatened.'

'So?'

'A fire was set . . .' He stops. 'You know this already?'

'About the operation? About the fire? Yes.'

'How?'

She smiles. 'I run a news organization. This is what we do.'

'Did you suspect that Ali Jelani had access to a contact close to the killer?'

'I assumed her information came from you, the SAPS.'

'Well, it didn't. We considered that she was either in direct contact with the killer or being used via a third party. Dr Bellingham speculated that he could have been testing Jelani by revealing Bellingham as a possible target. If that is the case, Ali Jelani failed her test spectacularly.'

'And now he has her?'

'Possibly.'

'That creates an entirely new angle . . .'

'New angle? For the story?'

'We helped you before. We can help you again.'

'Where did Ali Jelani say she would be last night?'

'You asked me that. I don't know.'

De Vries puts his hands on her desk, leans over it towards her. 'You said that she told you she would be submitting copy for your newspaper, including photographs. She told you the name, Grace Bellingham. Did she not tell you what her plan was?'

Penelope van Reidel shudders. Her strident, confident voice breaks minutely. 'She told me she expected something to happen last night, that she would be there. She would bring me the story.'

'She would be there?'

'Yes.'

'So you let her take that on alone?' De Vries asks.

'I had no choice. That's all she told me. I didn't know what she meant. She had worked alone before. She insisted on it. The story was hers. It remained her property until her copy was approved for the paper.'

'And it didn't really matter, did it, Ms van Reidel? Just so long as you got your story. Isn't that how it works?'

'Ali Jelani was not employed by this newspaper.'

'Why was that?' De Vries's voice rises. 'Was it so that if something happened to her you could deny responsibility for effective oversight?'

'No.'

'Or did you dangle the prospect of a full-time post in return for an explosive series of reports about this killer?'

'No.'

'Perhaps you suspected that she had contact with this man, and encouraged it, incentivized her to bring you everything. Was that how it worked?'

Now she sits back calmly, her hands on the armrests, her back straight.

'Ali Jelani,' she says quietly, 'came to me. I checked her story about the first two women: Hazel Calder and Michelle Ricquarts. Your SAPS press liaison officer confirmed that the information contained within the pieces was accurate. She made the connection. Her.'

'How long have you been calling to check on her?'

'Six weeks. Since she wrote the piece on Marie Garsten in Strand . . . She said then that she was worried she was being followed, possibly targeted. I suggested she contact the SAPS, but she dismissed the idea.'

'You obviously weren't very persuasive.'

'Jelani was a mystery. I took a punt on her because she seemed instinctively to have found something. You need people working for you who have a good nose, and an exhaustive mind. I have responsibility for scores of journalists.'

'But,' De Vries says, 'I bet she's the only one you called religiously every twenty-four hours, that you nurtured to bring you details, without questioning how she might be obtaining them. I guess it didn't matter. Everything and everyone is expendable, aren't they, in exchange for the story?' He stands. 'You live in a beautiful home, Ms van Reidel, but you're wading in shit. My shit. After a while, you're going to find you really don't like it. Keep calling Ali Jelani. You hear anything, anything at all, you tell me immediately.'

'What's happening?'

He is standing in a queue outside a coffee shop on Kloof Street, cellphone squashed against his right ear, his left forefinger pressed hard into his left. He wouldn't normally bother to wait, but this café serves the strongest, thickest coffee in Cape Town.

'Sergeant Thwala has located where someone could have entered the school grounds last night,' Don February says. 'A damaged area of the fence. He is going door-to-door asking about unfamiliar cars or persons in the area after midnight. The fire chief confirmed that petrol was used to start the fire, there was evidence of fireworks . . .'

226

'Hang on.' De Vries feels in his pocket for his wallet, his cell-phone jammed under his chin slowly slipping until he catches it, gets the cash, grasps the phone firmly in his hand. 'Go on.'

'He said that the fire would have taken hold instantly. There were piles of dry leaves and branches, which had been brushed up against the wall over several years by the ground staff.'

'All right. Cars around the nursery last week?'

'Still checking. They have to slow the recording almost to a stop before they can try to identify the vehicle make. Half the cars are white. Only Sergeant Morten seems to be able to identify specific makes and models.'

'You want coffee?'

'Yes.'

'I'll be back in ten minutes.' He faces the bored-looking barista. 'Two treble espressos.' He thinks what Don February drinks. 'And a cappuccino.'

Don February stands barely above him, even though De Vries is seated.

'Something is happening.' There is the slightest hint of excitement in Don's voice.

De Vries drops one empty espresso cup into a bin, passes him the cappuccino, flicks the lid off the second espresso, tips the contents down his throat.

'What?'

Don leads him across the squad-room towards Sally Frazer and Joey Morten.

'Ben Thwala called in to say that a couple in Killick Road, which is the other side of the playing fields, did see a car at around twelve thirty this morning when they arrived home after a party. A white Toyota Prius. The man remembers it because he says his children had been telling him that he must buy a hybrid car, like a Toyota Prius, and his wife had never seen one, so he pointed it out.'

'They see the driver?'

'No.'

De Vries shrugs. 'That could have been anybody.'

'Yes, but look at the picture here from the surveillance officers in the road that adjoins yours, sir.'

A black-and-white picture, obtained using a super low-light device, looking almost like an old-fashioned negative, is visible on the screen in front of them. The time code shows 00.55.

'Where is that?'

'Roma Grove. Parallel to your street. Outside numbers fourteen and sixteen.'

De Vries frowns. 'That's the top of the road by Rondebosch Common. There's a cut-through right there, between about sixteen and eighteen. You can walk through without going up to the main road. You get a plate?'

'Partial,' Joey Morten says. 'There are fewer than two hundred white Priuses in Greater Cape Town. We'll find it, but we're having problems with some of the computers.'

'Why?'

'I don't know. Possibly overheating.'

De Vries turns to Sally Frazer. 'Have you got the other team looking for a white Prius?'

She replies quietly, 'Usually it's better just to let them continue. You start mentioning a possible vehicle, people get careless with cars that aren't white, or don't look immediately like a Prius.'

De Vries addresses all of them:

'This could be a break. This could be our chance. Did no one see a woman on her own in my road last night? She could have been there one minute and gone the next.'

'Nothing in the surveillance reports. Are you asking about the journalist?'

'Ali Jelani is missing. Not answering her phone, despite arranging a specific time to be called. If she was there last night and so was our killer, she could have been taken.'

'Not Dr Bellingham?'

'Exactly.'

Don says quietly, 'Dr Bellingham is in your office, sir.'

De Vries looks up, sees that she is sitting in a chair with her back to the squad-room. He sees all his guests like this first – the backs of their heads.

'All right. Whatever it takes, let's identify this vehicle, see if we can link it again to other scenes.'

He turns towards his office, aware that, in his head, something has clicked, an understanding not yet quite appreciated, like a glimpse in peripheral vision. He enters his office, throws his jacket onto the adjoining chair. She turns around slowly, says:

'Ali Jelani is gone.'

'How did you know that?'

'She is?'

'She's missing, yes.'

'I thought more about last night. It was never about me. It was too ridiculous that he would tell anyone who he was going to take. I should have known. He manipulated Jelani and played me, and made fools of all of you. He wanted Jelani all along. He used her, then got her into the open – chasing the story, waiting for the picture – and, when the fire trucks and patrol cars arrived, and there were people on the street, all half asleep, shocked by the fire, fearing a conflagration that would consume their houses and possessions, he probably just walked up and took her.'

'We're tracing a suspicious car.'

She raises her eyebrows. 'I wasn't thinking straight. I'm sorry. I was selfish.'

'You were afraid.'

'Afraid of something that didn't exist. My perspective's shot. I told you, I'm spent, finished.'

'You're just tired.'

'I'm tired like you can't believe. I still missed the obvious.'

He looks out over the squad-room. 'You okay here? You want to go home?'

'I'll stay here. You go.' She indicates the sofa in the corner of his office. 'I may lie down.'

'Tell me when you want to eat.'

She doesn't answer. She gets up, sits on the sofa, lets her body fall onto the seat, adjusts a cushion under her head, curls her legs into herself.

He closes the door.

It strikes him as he hears the catch on the office door lock. He freezes. He hears the bustle of the squad-room, stares straight at the woodwork of the doorframe, sees nothing. He swallows, takes his phone, dials the number. It switches straight to voicemail. He pockets the phone, strides towards the other end of his floor. Through a missing blind, he sees Du Toit in his office, head over paperwork. He knocks, walks in; Du Toit has not moved his head.

'Henrik.'

'What?'

'I need your help.'

'That is your default position.' De Vries moves to his desk, thumps his hands on the surface. Du Toit raises his eyes. 'Good news?'

'Maybe yes, maybe no.'

Brigadier du Toit sits up, stretches his back, wipes his eyes. De Vries sees white residue at the corners of his mouth, wonders whether he has been asleep.

'What do you need?'

'The department that employs Stephen Jessel, controls the section eighteens and other restricted information. I need you to call them.'

'You need to speak to Leigh Finnemore?'

'No. I want you to ask them about Jessel, about his work record, where he operates and who his charges are.'

'Jessel?'

'We've identified a suspect car. Not confirmed yet, but around scenes. It's a Toyota Prius. I only know one person connected with this investigation who owns a white Toyota Prius. Stephen Jessel.'

Du Toit frowns. 'I don't understand. You think Finnemore has used this car?'

'No, Henrik. Forget Leigh Finnemore. I think that Stephen Jessel could be our man. He works with disturbed people who must be protected and from whom the public must be protected. He travels around. He has reason to be in different places at different times. We know for a fact that he has visited one of the sites in which a victim was found: Apostle Lodge. He admitted that he had driven to the house with Finnemore – to show him the neighbours on his street.' De Vries sees nothing resembling recognition or understanding in Du Toit's eyes. 'With respect, sir, can you call his department, find whoever is in charge and bring him here, along with Jessel's history and employment record? It needs to come from you, or even General Thulani. Immediately. Complete discretion, absolute secrecy. Jessel cannot be forewarned.'

Du Toit nods. 'If you're wrong?'

De Vries shrugs, exasperated. 'Then I'm wrong. For Christ's sake, sir. Ali Jelani is missing, presumed abducted. If that's the case, we have maybe two, three days to find her. That's if he doesn't take revenge on her betrayal immediately. Can you do this now?'

De Vries takes Don February and Sally Frazer aside.

'For the moment, us three only. I may be wrong.' He turns to Frazer. 'Find the licence plate for a Stephen Jessel. I don't know his home address, but it won't be far from town. See if it matches the partial you picked up from the surveillance.'

'Jessel is government?' Don asks.

'Government appointed. I don't know who runs his department. It doesn't matter.' He glances back at Frazer. 'He's the guy supervising our section eighteen, in Plumbago Lane. He owns a white Toyota Prius. Don, if it's a match, back-trace his home address and any other details on him. Keep it quiet just now.'

He stands up straight, watches the two officers move away to the relevant workstations. He sees Henrik du Toit stride towards him. Du Toit gestures to De Vries's office. He cuts him off.

'Dr Bellingham is resting, sir.'

They walk to the milky windows at the far side of the room.

'I spoke to the woman who runs the department. She says Jessel is on a sabbatical.'

'What?'

'You work ten years as a supervisor, you get a four-month sabbatical. He's taking it from the end of September this year until the end of January. She's biking over his papers.'

'September coincides with the first known attack – on Hazel Calder.' De Vries shakes his head. 'But why were we put through to him when we enquired about number one Plumbago Lane, Leigh Finnemore?'

'I asked that. It's a sabbatical, but it excludes section-eighteen charges. He remains on call for those. He has three. One went into hospital mid-September this year; attempted suicide. The other went back to Valkenburg Mental Hospital in August – at the request of Stephen Jessel.' De Vries nods. A pattern is forming, fitting the little information they have. 'The car?' Du Toit continues. 'You have any more on that?'

'We're doing it now. It's with February and Frazer only, until I'm sure.'

'We all met this Jessel. Did you sense anything in him?'

De Vries sighs. 'No, sir. I was more interested in his charge, a man who had killed before. I just found Jessel annoying, petty and obstructive.'

He sees Sally Frazer waving to him from the middle of the squad-room, reflects that any other officer would come over to him, but Frazer summons him. He smiles to himself, indicates to Du Toit to come with him. With Joey Morten and Ben Thwala, they form a group around one of the desks.

Frazer says: 'We have the final two digits of the registration plate. They match Stephen Jessel's car.'

'My God.'

She glances up at Du Toit, continues: 'We have a white Toyota Prius, only two digits of the registration mark identifiable, passing the camera on Southern Cross Road, just by the junction that leads to Rose's nursery. It is one minute, eleven seconds behind Bethany Miles in her Audi Q5.'

'Can you see who's driving?'

'No. It took Sergeant Morten here some time to confirm that it was a Prius and to unscramble the registration so that we got even that. It's the same final two digits.'

'They are unique to Stephen Jessel's Toyota Prius,' Morten says drily. 'It is enough to testify. But there's no detail. A good attorney could cast doubt over the enhancement technique I had to use.'

'To hell with the judges right now,' De Vries says. 'We have a rare car close to the scene of the fire, on the adjacent road to mine last night, and now following Bethany Miles. This is the car. We need to know who was driving it, but it's the car. How many vehicles were there between her and the Prius?'

'Two,' Morten says immediately. 'You'd need a wide tail down Southern Cross Drive. Long open straight.'

'Have you tried to reach Jessel?' Du Toit says.

'Straight to voicemail.' He turns to Don. 'You found his home address?'

'According to the records, he moved in August this year from a property near Milnerton to a place called "Two Feathers Estate".'

'Where the hell is that?'

'I am not certain, sir, but I think that it is one of the new developments off the N2 going into Somerset West.'

'Somerset West, Strand. He could have been house-hunting and found that abandoned building site . . .'

'And Michelle Ricquarts was taken to a shack on Milnerton Beach,' Frazer says.

'It's coming together,' De Vries says. 'Subject to consultation, sir, I think that we should consider releasing pictures of Stephen Jessel and Ali Jelani and hoping that someone, somewhere, has seen them.'

'Are we certain he has her?'

'Not certain, but it fits. Dr Bellingham reached the same conclusion that we did. Last night's fireworks, literally, were misdirection. He was there to take Jelani, not Bellingham.' He turns to Sally Frazer. 'You met Jelani, researched her background. Dig deeper. See what you can find, particularly what happened to her children. If we're right on the children connection, she will have done something to hers that provoked him.' He turns back to Du Toit. 'We need everything we have on Jessel.'

'I'll get back to his boss, see if we can't visit her or get her in. This is all good, but hold it here, between us, for one hour, see what else we can find. Then we'll make a decision on the press.'

'There isn't much,' Du Toit says. De Vries studies the man's collar, wet with sweat, top button fastened, tie tight at his neck, wonders if stoicism is implicit to his rank; reflects that, like him, Du Toit is old-school and that details matter. No wonder they are treated with suspicion by the new order. 'Either in the personnel files or from his boss: reliable, solitary, efficient. No one knew anything about his private life, but his boss thought he lived alone. The only real mystery is how he got appointed in the first place. In 2000, he was working pretty much as a low-grade office manager. Yet six months later, around the time of the transitional government, he was promoted to case officer. He's stayed there, moving up a couple of grades, ever since.'

'Nothing on his personal history?'

'No. His next of kin was noted as an aunt in London, UK. But there's nothing about his education, where – or even whether – he went to university, training, etc. It looks like a classic case of fraudulent assimilation. He simply became part of this semi-autonomous government department.'

'That's far from unique, especially around that time,' De Vries says. 'Records were being shredded, people were making their escape. It would have been easy for him to slip in and, once in, stay there . . . What about this sabbatical?'

'The woman is new there,' Du Toit says. 'She said she simply had no cause to look into Jessel. He was there, and his work was solid and reliable. In June last year, a few weeks after she was parachuted in, he approached her, explained that he had deferred his ten-year sabbatical and requested that he take it from late September onwards, since he was moving house. She told me he had leave owing over the years as well, and there was no reason to deny him.'

'His phone's still off. Warrant February is leading a team to his property on this new lifestyle estate, but I think we know he won't be there.'

'Where will he be?'

Du Toit's question hangs in the heavy, still air. They both turn to Grace Bellingham, who has sat silently in one of the two chairs against the side wall. She looks up at Du Toit.

'I'm not providing answers, Henrik.'

'It would be helpful if you could.'

She closes her eyes, a hand on her forehead.

'Suggestions?'

She sits up, wears a pat smile, says wearily: 'I suggest . . . that this man fits my profile pretty much exactly, except that he is a few years older than I would have anticipated. The fact that his next of kin is noted as an aunt in the UK suggests that his parents and siblings, if he had any, are either dead or not in contact with him. Obviously a broken home, a shattered upbringing are the first things you might consider when trying to find a motive for what seems to be a late-blossoming psychosis.'

'Thank you.'

'Furthermore, I suggest that this man is less likely to leave his victim this time, since he will want more value from the effort expended in capturing her. He will escalate his violent, sadistic behaviour towards her and, as a result, her life expectancy is shorter than those of his previous victims.' She stands up.

Du Toit rises also, followed by De Vries. 'Finally,' she says, her face blank, 'since I can't trust myself to function efficiently, I suggest that you don't rely on me to assist you any further.'

The Two Feathers Estate exists as an entity within a tall, double-layered steel fence. It is in its own territory amid the yellowed scrubland and burned-out grass of land reclaimed from the foothills of the low mountains that run alongside the southern coastal road. Cameras on poles taller than the fence watch the empty roads that meander around the half-built development.

The white render on the impressive gatehouse is already cracked, the surrounding landscaping dead or dying, the lawns yellow or brown, save for the emerald carpet outside a blindingly white show-home, flanked by poles bearing sagging flags.

Don February leads his three vehicles to Jessel's address, followed by two further security vehicles from the estate. The small rectangular house is on a close, each identical home facing others across a glorified roundabout. Only if you look high above the houses might you see hills or mountains, or nothing but empty blue sky above the distant coastline. Having surrounded the building, it is soon ascertained that no one is at home. The security team from the estate co-operate in opening the front door and disengaging the alarm. Don leads three officers inside.

He is struck first by the staleness of the air. Because of the demands of the alarm system, he is informed, no windows can be left open. The furniture is sparse and old-fashioned, positioned accurately and, where possible, symmetrically, as are items on shelves and counters. Everything is neat, but there is little of it. In the kitchen, the staleness becomes stench. He pulls open the waste bin, recoils. Flies rise, circling, unwilling to leave the gift of the black sack. He looks inside, withdraws packaging from a ready meal obtained from the supermarket, Pick and Pay; notes the date.

As he retraces his steps to the front door, he glances at three letters found in the mailbox, now bagged as evidence.

In the adjoining garage, there is no car, or any evidence that there has ever been one. Outside, in the backyard, there is no furniture, no braai, flowerbeds empty and dusty, a single staked tree in the right-hand corner, virtually leafless. The coastal breeze, which has travelled over industrial developments, local roads and the freeway, feels hotter than the ambient air. He takes out a cotton handkerchief, dabs his forehead.

He observes the search of the upstairs bedrooms, speaks further to the security personnel on site, rings the doorbell on the adjoining properties, but there is no answer. He asks several questions of the man calling himself the head of security, then leads his team out of the close, past other geometric arrangements of characterless houses, around the circle with the faltering borehole fountain, through the security gates back onto the local road, which leads to the N2 freeway into town.

De Vries stares at the foam bulb on the microphone stand; if he focuses on that, he can imagine there is no crowd of journalists, no brass watching him.

'We now want to speak with this man, Stephen Robert Jessel, whose home address is: number seventy-two Two Feathers Estate, Old Mansion Road, on the outskirts of Somerset West. We believe that he can help us in the search for the missing woman, Ali Jelani, a Kenyan journalist working freelance for the *New Cape Gazette*, who disappeared yesterday evening and who we believe may have been abducted by the same man responsible for two attacks and two murders on women in the Cape Town area over the past few months.'

De Vries looks at the expectant group of journalists, the two television cameras, two black men standing together at the back of the room, wearing un-creased suits and dry, fresh shirts.

'The contact details and photographs are in your packets. Please ensure that the numbers and email addresses are clearly displayed and transcribed correctly.'

As he sits down, voices are raised, hands waved. The press liaison officer, who stands to the side of the table behind which are seated De Vries, Henrik du Toit and Don February, points at the front row, calls out a name.

De Vries bows his head. He dislikes press conferences and public appeals, the reading of statements about, inevitably, an incomplete investigation but, most of all, he dreads the same questions from the same journalists, to which both he and they know he cannot give a straight answer. Instead, the clumsy verbal dance begins until they tire of its droning and repetitive rhythm. It is a pointless, depressing game, in an acidly humid, overcrowded room, late in the evening of a long, wearisome day.

He stands up, nods at Du Toit, walks from the room, hears the cacophony increase. He goes towards the small private custody area at the rear of the building, steps outside, lights the cigarette he has been palming for the previous minutes. It is damp, but he draws strongly, swallowing the thick, dark smoke.

'Don't do that.'

De Vries follows Henrik du Toit to his office, one weary dog trailing another.

'Close the door.' Du Toit sits. 'You can't do that, Vaughn. You can't just walk away. Don't sit down. Just stand there and listen. You made a breakthrough. There's a chance you've found our man, but I've told you before, you have to disseminate that success to the public. You have to reassure them that we have everything under control. You walk off like that, refuse to answer questions, what impression does it give?'

'That we're busy?'

'Did you see those two at the back? Pretoria. I told you they're watching us.' De Vries sighs. 'I know you don't care, Vaughn, but sometimes there are duties to be performed.'

'My duty is to catch Stephen Jessel and to find Ali Jelani. I can't do that if I'm wasting time with those people.'

'You may need those people to find Jessel. Warrant February tells me that he may not have been back to his home address for close on a week. We have no idea where he might have taken this woman, and, although it may be a novelty for car-buffs, this Toyota Prius just looks like any other white wedge on the roads, so the chances of anyone seeing it, let alone Jessel or Jelani, must be very small.'

De Vries nods. 'The public won't find them. I will.'

Du Toit sees assurance in De Vries's face, finds it fleetingly comforting.

'Why is Dr Bellingham so morose? She must realize that she is no longer a target for this man.'

'Dr Bellingham is tired, sir. Tired to the core. She has dealt with evil as a daily routine for twenty years and she has had enough. Although I'm not there quite yet, I sympathize.'

Du Toit shakes his head. 'None of us finds this work easy. Isn't that why we're here, fighting to try to bring these people down, with the experience we have? Because, frankly, we believe that others can't.'

'I wonder how long we'll keep thinking that.'

'For as long as we win, Vaughn. That's how long.'

De Vries snorts. 'Win? Have we ever done that? If we have, it's never felt like winning. Not once.'

None of the windows in the headquarters building opens. All are sealed to preserve the coolness occasionally granted by the air-conditioning system. De Vries has had the window behind his desk illicitly unsealed; he holds his hand out of the open window in his office, cigarette burning five storeys above the darkening downtown streets. Sally Frazer and Don February sip cool drinks, eat take-away sushi and sandwiches respectively.

'Nothing?'

'Not much,' Frazer says. 'The usual characters, a few Prius sightings, which we can try to follow up, but nothing on Jessel or Jelani.'

'What hurts,' De Vries says, 'is that we had them both. Jessel was here in my office and I didn't see it. I used to think that when I had a man in front of me I knew. Not any more. You were this close to Jelani. Now they're both gone.'

Frazer swallows, puts a folder on her lap.

'I have more on Jessel. He's forty-eight, only child, grew up in the Northern Suburbs. Lived in the Cape all his life. No record of education, matric or university. No criminal record. He has a bank account, which is in credit and always has been. He inherited the family home, used part of that money to buy this new property in Two Feathers Estate. Never been in debt.' She flips pages. 'Now it gets interesting.' She looks over to Don February, who is eating slowly, listening to her; De Vries is half out of the window. 'Can you hear me, sir?'

'Where did Dr Bellingham go?'

Don February covers his full mouth, says: 'She took a cab, sir. I went down with her, but she insisted. Said she was going home.'

PAUL MENDELSON

De Vries ducks back inside. 'Sorry, Sally.' He unscrews a two-litre bottle of still water, sloshes some down his throat, spills it on his shirt, sits heavily. He revolves his wrist to restart her report.

'Stephen Jessel's father was involved in a hit-and-run in 2004. He died in hospital five months later. The driver and car were never identified. Jessel's mother was alive until two years ago. In 2006, she was attacked in an underground car park in the early evening. She had hydrochloric acid thrown in her face. She lost the sight in both eyes, and suffered extensive scarring. There were no witnesses, no apparent motive. Her handbag was untouched.'

'No one thought about him? Stephen Jessel?'

'Bellville handled the investigation. I read the precis of the docket. Stephen Jessel was questioned, but was eliminated early on. He claimed that he was at work at the time of the attack, supervising one of his charges. His alibi was a respected doctor and a patient at Valkenburg Mental Hospital.'

'That place . . .'

'It gets interesting, sir. The patient who signed the witness statement is Leigh Finnemore.'

'Finnemore provided an alibi for Jessel in 2006?'

'Yes, and there is, as they say, more. The name of the doctor was Johannes Dyk.'

De Vries feels acid in his chest, his mouth dry.

'I knew that man. You remember, Don? Dyk was dying, but seven years earlier he had been advising the SAPS on the child-abduction case. He knew what had happened to those boys. He misled us, covered for a paedophile ring.' He grabs the water bottle again, tips it, gulps.

'Jessel's mother was hospitalized,' Frazer continues. 'Apparently her son visited her a few times early on, then wasn't seen again. I spoke to someone who remembers his mother. They contacted

242

him through work when his mother became terminally ill but no one remembers him coming to see her.'

De Vries switches on his old Anglepoise lamp. Outside, the sun has passed behind the Mountain and dusk has set in over the CBD. Already, in the street below, multicoloured lights are spilling from bars onto the dry, dusty pavements, strains of music drifting in the rising exhaust fumes past the open window.

'This isn't about children,' De Vries says. 'It's about parents. If Jessel was behind his parents' accidents then that was the beginning. Whatever they did to him, he got his revenge. It's what he's doing now, how he's choosing his victims.'

'I looked into Ali Jelani,' Don says, wiping his mouth with his handkerchief. 'She told Sally at their meeting that in Kenya she had two daughters and then her husband or partner left her. I cannot confirm this, but I did find an online article written by her last year where she describes leaving her children with friends and travelling to Syria. She said that she had planned to go for two weeks but had ended up staying for three months. She said that she felt bad leaving her children, who were seven and nine at the time, but when she saw the Syrian children she thought, My kids are lucky, they must just get on with it.'

'That sounds the kind of thing Stephen Jessel doesn't like.'

'Contacting Jelani online would have been easy,' Frazer says. 'Even though she was afraid, the information she was getting was too good. And when she learned that Dr Bellingham was the next target, she must have felt safe.'

De Vries sighs. 'Wherever he's taken her, he will have planned for it as carefully as he entrapped Jelani. We need to check for properties under the control of this section-eighteen department, an old family country home . . . I don't know. The places he chose previously were planned but, ultimately, opportunistic.' He frowns. 'He's moved into that estate. Check whether he looked at other properties in the area, whether there are unfinished developments, deserted buildings on land purchased by developers . . .' He flicks his wrist, but his watch is stuck to his skin. He twists it with his other hand. 'We all need to get some rest. Longest day of the year tomorrow. We're going to need every minute of it.'

'Why are you here?'

De Vries stands, again, in the dim, nylon-carpeted corridor, feeling the static electricity crackle around his shoes.

'I care about you, Grace. I need to know you're okay.'

The door opens. She is in her underwear, a wine glass in her right hand.

'Don't even think about it. This is extreme action in the face of an extreme climate.'

'What happened to the air-con?'

She walks away unsteadily towards the open doors to her balcony, points at a printed sheet on the kitchen table.

'System's overloading. One room at any time only. I'm cooling the bedroom.' He follows her onto the balcony. She is lying on a recliner, as if sunbathing in the gloom. He looks down over the railing, over the yellow-lit suburbs, back up to the view of the dark Mountain, Devil's Peak hiding the moon. Compared to the heat of her apartment, there is a little coolness in the night air, but no breeze. Days now without wind, without cloud: unheard of in Cape Town.

'Your profile was right. We discovered more about Jessel.'

'I'm not interested. I don't want to know. How I felt two nights ago, it reminded me of why I came home, why it's over for me. I can't hack it, and I don't want to.' She bends her head back to look at him. 'Don't you see them, Vaughn, when you close your eyes? Their ugly bloody-lipped mouths spewing all those lies, distortions . . . words to try to seduce you to their view of the world, to their sick, revolting, torturous, murderous desires.' She stares at him, studying his eyes, then relaxes her head again. 'I don't think you do, do you? I think you just fall asleep and wake up. They're not inside you.'

'No, they're not. I have the victims in my head. I have to represent them. I don't care about anyone else. If I can't, or I don't serve them well, that's who I see, and they judge me.'

She nods. 'I knew we were alike. Maybe not the same, but alike.'

'All the lights of the city, on the Cape Flats . . .' he looks up over the balcony '. . . the moon, the stars. That's what people look at: the brightness. We only see the dark. That's what we do. That's where we have to look . . .'

She empties her glass. 'The bottle's in the fridge. Fill me up and help yourself. In that order.'

He drops his jacket on the sofa, fills her glass and empties the bottle into a tumbler. There is barely ten centimetres.

'You want me to go get more?'

She reaches up, takes the glass, sips. 'There's red in the cupboard, but you're not staying.'

He pulls over the chair, sits next to her. She stares out at the night sky, glowing yellow from the streetlights around the other apartment blocks, turning black, the stars above them faint. He turns to study her. Her underwear is black and minimalist. Her head nods in time to some unknown rhythm. In the distance, he hears jazz, but it is not that to which her limbs minutely dance.

'Am I allowed to ask you one question?'

She shuts her eyes. 'That's your Colonel de Vries voice. Do you ever stop? If I say you can sleep with me tonight, lie in my fridge of a bedroom, will you just stop for one minute?' De Vries looks away from her. 'It's a serious offer. Fuck me and shut

245

up, or ask me and leave? What do you want, Vaughn? What do you really want?'

'Grace Bellingham believes that, if Ali Jelani represents his ultimate prize, Jessel will have somewhere ready for her, and that place will have a special, long-held meaning for him. We need to look back at his family history, find somewhere he used to go when he was happy – or where he escaped to when he was unhappy – before whatever went wrong with his parents happened. Old hotels, holiday cottages. We have to go back in time . . .'

'I thought,' Sally Frazer says, 'Dr Bellingham had removed herself from this investigation.'

De Vries glances away, feigning a yawn. 'We did a deal.' His cellphone rings. He looks at the display. There is no name, but it is a number he recognizes.

The Grand Daddy Hotel on Long Street is more chic than shabby, a bohemian boutique hotel, beloved by tourists and locals with a liking for the unusual. Inside, bar, restaurant and lounge are all theatrically decorated, burnished with copper, murals on the walls, wood panelling. Each bedroom is different, with contemporary South African artwork, interior design and craft on display. On its roof terrace, you can stay in sparkling bare aluminium Airstream trailers, each interior curated by a South Africa design maven. There are flowerbeds, pot plants and trees. Under canopies on a raised deck at its centre is the Pink Flamingo Rooftop Cinema, complete with vintage popcorn machine, rugs, a bar, picnic hampers. On Monday nights, guests and visitors settle down at dusk, watching the flickering screen until all is dark around them.

De Vries is hot and out of breath just from jogging the short painted staircase, which leads up to the roof. The heat seems to seep down it to meet him on the small landing, like a wave. The terrace, already baking in the mid-morning sun, appears deserted but for one member of staff at the rear, tidying chairs. He slowly rounds the first of the trailers, the sun's reflection momentarily blinding him. His eyes water. He blinks. Beyond the potted shrubs, by the wall and low railing overlooking Long Street, he sees the back of a straw-hatted figure. He approaches slowly, squinting. The figure turns.

'You were quick.'

De Vries stops, says quietly, 'You're an important man.'

Stephen Jessel smiles. 'It seems I am.'

'Why did you want to meet here?'

'It seemed a sensible rendezvous, convenient for whatever decision you make.'

De Vries stands still, just sheltered from the dazzling white light by the edge of one of the canopies protecting the seats in the cinema. Jessel is in the sunshine. He wears the same jacket, the same tie – possibly, De Vries thinks, the same shirt – as when they had met twice previously.

'What decision is there to make?'

'Whether to take me a few hundred metres across town – I'm sure you have officers on the stairs back there, maybe on the street – interrogate me, put me in a cell or let me leave this fine establishment, walk up the street, perhaps buy a cold drink, wander away.'

'Where is Ali Jelani?'

'Indeed, where is she?'

'I would like to talk with you, Stephen, but isn't it a little hot up here?'

'I like the sunshine . . . And I brought a hat.' He raises it, forms the same blank smile, replaces it, relaxes his mouth.

From below, there is a steady background hum of traffic, taxi-vans honking; occasionally music sails up on the urban thermals. Yet atop this building, in the stock-still air, there is a different measure of peace. De Vries tries to make his voice calm, yet, even to him, it sounds strident.

'What do you want?'

'Nothing.'

'Nothing?'

'It would have been easier just to carry on with my life peace-fully, but you made that rather difficult, didn't you? What was I to do? My face on the television, in all the newspapers. Obviously it was logical to meet you . . .'

De Vries finds Jessel's casual self-confidence annoying, wishes he could step forward, place handcuffs around the thin, hairy wrists, drag him down the stairs. He knows, that with Ali Jelani's life at stake, he cannot; realizes that were Jessel to climb the low wall and railing, he could be over the side before he could reach him. He has seen men jump before and, no matter what he thinks of them, for weeks afterwards, he cannot banish the sensation of falling. Nights are punctuated with jolting awake from vertiginous dreams, the feeling of vomit rising as blood drains from his head.

'I'd stay there, Colonel,' Jessel tells him. 'You're in the shade, and your current proximity feels about right. Don't you think?'

'Did you attack Marie Garsten and Bethany Miles?'

'If I had need of an attorney, he would tell me not to com-ment, but you seem to think that I did.'

'And Hazel Calder and Michelle Ricquarts?'

'Those poor women, whose names were, until I promoted them, unremarkable and unmemorable, suddenly flow off your tongue, like they're celebrities. I hope they're celebrated for what they truly are.'

'What is that?'

'At best, thoughtless, ignorant and cruel. More likely, each considered their circumstances carefully and chose to abuse.'

De Vries observes Jessel's stillness and composure, arms by his sides, the yawning concrete crevasse of Long Street ten storeys down behind him and, then, almost out of focus in De Vries's field of vision, the charmless façades of the office buildings on the other side of the street. Jessel seems to control not only this roof garden but the space around him, stretching into the blue sky, as far as the vertical sliver of Table Mountain just visible at the top of the street.

'The decision I must make?' De Vries says, trying to keep his voice even, to veil his impatience at being forced to agree to Jessel's arrangements. 'Why would I let you walk away?'

A broad smile now, reflected in his eyes.

'Ali Jelani has written a long and heartfelt article about the women I have made celebrated. It describes their abusive behaviour and how, in our thoughtless, uncaring society, such offences are tolerated and appeased, even when we are directly witness to them . . . People seem to believe they have a right to be parents, to breed at will. Some wish to buy themselves providers and carers for their old age, or they believe society expects it of them. Others want company in the house, or perhaps their religion tells them they cannot prevent the birth of one conceived through casual pleasure. Their abilities and suitability are not assessed. They are never checked. A woman produces a child so she – and usually the man – can do whatever she chooses with it.' He stares at De Vries. 'This article will be published or Ali Jelani will die. The article explains that if I am allowed to walk away, I will reveal where she is held. If I am incarcerated, she will die. The article states that it is your choice, De Vries. You decide whether she lives or dies. And I'm sure that there will be many voices to help you, many opinions in the media, on television, online. The whole country, perhaps the world, will join you in your dilemma.'

'What have you done to her?'

'Hidden her.'

'Deprived her of food, water?'

'Deprived, yes. There is also a pharmaceutical contribution, which ensures a consistent and inevitable deterioration. I prefer certainty.'

'What is it?'

'You keep asking questions, but there is only one question worth answering, and that is in your gift.'

'Why torture her? Why not publish her article and let her go?'

'You're doing it again, De Vries. The fact is, truth is revealed in the hours leading to death. A person is both physically and mentally weakened, but the lifeblood of hope spurs them to a remarkable candour, a sudden self-awareness wholly lacking hitherto.'

'So you torture them?'

Jessel frowns. 'I prepare them for revelation.'

In the distance, De Vries hears a helicopter. Beyond Jessel, he sees blue lights rising up the cream concrete sides of the office buildings.

'You can't walk away now, Mr Jessel. Perhaps later. I will have to discuss the terms of your deal with my superiors. But now . . .'

The thumping of the helicopter rotors grows closer. Suddenly its shadow darts across the terrace, its steel abdomen rising above the adjoining office block, its side emblazoned with SAPS markings. The canopies begin to sway, their concrete bases tipping. Chairs fall from the raised deck, plants bow and wave – even the trailers wobble. Jessel holds his hat, ducks his head. The helicopter passes them, the sun streaming through the blades, flickering on the curved mirrored trailers, like blinding interference. It rises and banks over the adjacent buildings.

Jessel shouts: 'You understand my terms?' De Vries nods, steps towards him. 'No cuffs. Take my arm and lead me, but no cuffs. Not here. Not on the street.'

De Vries grabs him, pulls him in shuffling steps around the obstructions towards the exit to the terrace, the engine noise reverberating in his head, the floor vibrating, his eyes watering, projecting white shadows on the inside of his eyelids, like an old monochrome movie, one frame at a time, with each long, gritty blink.

Sally Frazer says: 'Jessel's father was a pharmacist in Kenilworth where they lived. I have an address, but I'm not sure it's still there. I think that's where the new development is. I'm checking.'

De Vries turns away from Sally Frazer's desk, moves across the room.

'Anything come up on CCTV showing Jessel's car?'

Don February shakes his head. 'Most of the freeway cameras are just speed traps. I checked and no Toyota Prius has been captured in the last week.'

De Vries sees Henrik du Toit entering the squad-room. Du Toit catches his eye, heads for De Vries's office.

'Close the door.'

De Vries waits while Du Toit chooses to sit in a visitor's chair, then moves around the desk to take his own seat.

'The good news is that Pretoria are pleased. Obviously, they concur with General Thulani that there is to be no deal, but I think we knew that, didn't we?'

'That gives us, maybe, forty-eight hours to find Ali Jelani, assuming she's still alive. If you remember, Grace Bellingham suggested that he would be even more violent than the previous attacks.'

'You're not going to talk to him?'

'At some point, yes,' De Vries says. 'He can wait. First, he's enjoying being the centre of attention far too much so it may disturb him to be ignored. Second, he believes that Jelani is a bargaining chip, so he won't tell us where she is unless he's released, and, finally, we have better things to do.'

'You have to find Jelani,' Du Toit says. 'What other better things are there?'

'The article he claims Jelani wrote. We don't yet know to which newspapers he's offered it. Maybe all of them, but I'd bet pretty good money that the *New Cape Gazette* is top of his list, since Jelani has, to all intents and purposes, been writing for it.'

'I agree, but how should we be involved?'

'You don't want to try to stop them printing it?'

'We don't want them to print, but we won't ask. We can't be seen to be trying to influence what newspapers do or don't write.'

De Vries snorts. 'So, what is the point of our press conference, then?'

'To impart information to be disseminated to the public.'

'But it's what we want to tell them. It's not the truth. How is that not influencing what the press do and don't print?'

'Don't be naive, Vaughn. The press won't know what the truth is, or was, until later, and by then the story has moved on. If we were to ask this *New Cape Gazette* not to publish, and they told their readers, what would that look like?'

'I'm too naive to understand the distinction, sir. I'll take your word for it.'

'Whatever happens, it's bad. There's nothing good about it. You said he told you that you would be named?'

'It would be my decision, he said, whether Ali Jelani lives or dies.'

'Well, it isn't.'

De Vries laughs. 'No, sir.'

'Stephen Jessel will decide, and if he's psychotic, as Dr Bellingham predicted, then he will decide to let her die. Unless you can find her, of course.'

'Back to me. I understand.'

'So, your first action now?'

'Get in Penelope van Reidel. Find out what she really knows, whether she has this article.'

'Perhaps . . .' Du Toit twitches. 'Perhaps go to see her. It might be advisable to keep the press, and her especially, on side.'

'So, we pander to the fourth estate. I understand entirely, sir.'

'You don't, Vaughn. You never have. But, fortunately, I do. So, be guided.'

'Can I get on now?'

He stands, looks down at Du Toit, passes him as he lets himself out of his office.

'There can be no deal.'

They look at De Vries, awaiting more, but he says nothing.

'Can he not be made to believe that there is a deal and then, once he has revealed the whereabouts of the hostage, we can recapture him?'

De Vries turns to Ben Thwala.

'No.'

'Why not? I mean, in theory, sir?'

'Because the SAPS can't be seen to agree to this man's terms. Can you imagine how it would look if the TV cameras followed him walking out of here? We would have no guarantee that he would keep up his end of the bargain, or that we could catch him again. He may have planned some ingenious escape. So, the brass are right. He stays here and what happens to Jelani is down to us.'

Sally Frazer says: 'It was a house in Kenilworth. The family lived there for seventeen years, from when Stephen Jessel was three until he was twenty.'

'Where did they go then?'

'The parents went to a flat in Kenilworth, close by. There's no record of whether Stephen ever lived with them there, and I can't find anything about him at all between the ages of about nineteen and thirty, when he first started working the Section Designation Department, as a clerk.'

'No country house, weekend home?'

'No. I can't really tell, but there's no evidence to suggest that they were well off.'

'Relatives?'

'None that I can find. Not even the aunt in the UK who is noted as his next of kin. The address doesn't exist. The father was an only child, and I can't find birth records for the mother.'

De Vries turns to the circle of officers.

'If he's picked a random location, we're at the mercy of a witness, and he's proven very good at not being noticed. Dr Bellingham believes he'll have picked somewhere special for this victim. Special to him. He feels increased animosity towards her, not only because of her perceived abandonment of her children but because she betrayed him personally when he tested her.'

'We keep looking,' Frazer says.

'Don, talk to Brigadier du Toit about broadcasting an appeal for witnesses, but keep me out of it . . . And did you turn anything up at Jessel's house?'

'Nothing to suggest another location he has shown interest in. No, sir.'

'Right. Stick a couple of officers on the CCTV cameras. We spotted him last time. We might do again.' He turns back to his office, stops, calls to Don. 'I need to find the *New Cape Gazette* editor, Van Reidel. Find out where she is.'

'I have the article.'

Penelope van Reidel sits upright but relaxed at her desk in front of the stained-glass panel. De Vries notices that when he slouches in the chair opposite her a golden halo appears directly above her head; he assumes this has been designed.

'How was it delivered?'

'By email . . . and, before you ask, I've already had my IT team try to find out where it came from, but they say it's been tampered with just sufficiently to make it untraceable.'

'My people might be able to do more. I assume you're prepared to forward it in its entirety to us?'

'Perhaps.'

'Ms van Reidel . . .'

She holds up her hands. 'It was made very clear in the message that accompanied the article that it was not to be released or shown to anyone before the edition tomorrow morning.'

'I'm not interested in what a psychopath specifies, or in breaking some sadistic embargo. I want the material to study for clues. What you choose to do with it is entirely up to you.'

'Nonetheless . . .'

'Stephen Jessel is in a cell, but Ali Jelani is probably lying somewhere, bound to a chair, deprived of water and injected with a drug that will kill her if we do not find her. Even you, surely, cannot prioritize your front page over the life of a woman, one whose work you desired, encouraged and paid for?'

'Even I? Is that what you think of me?'

'That wasn't personal. It comes with your position. And I don't have time for feigned self-pity or, indeed, obtaining a court order, but if you won't co-operate with me, I will waste my time and that of my officers in getting a judge to sanction it – perhaps that is a detail your rival titles will wish to advertise – and then I will take the article and analyse the means by which it was sent to you, because that may prove vital to saving Ali Jelani's life.'

'You can take a breath now, Colonel.' She reaches inside her desk, pulls open a wide drawer, takes out a wide double-page lay-out and places it on her desk. 'This is the draft layout, which you may take with you. Leave the address you want my people to send the email to.'

De Vries stands, slaps a card on her desk. 'Good.'

'We have co-operated with you throughout.'

'Have you thought that, by printing the article this man has sent you, you are co-operating with him, rather than us?'

'He makes it clear that, if we do not print, Ali Jelani will die.'

'His hostage will die anyway if we don't find her, because he has no intention of telling us where she is, whatever anybody does or doesn't do. However, we have a free press in our new country, so you can do whatever you would like to do.'

'Indeed . . .' She stands also, proffers her hand across the broad desk. 'Colonel, when you read the article and you reach the part that concerns you, I want you to remember it wasn't personal. It comes with your position.'

The email is studied by Joey Morten and another officer expert in online activity. It has been sent using an encrypted private email address, unregistered and almost impossible to trace.

'Anyone can set up and use this type of account,' Morten says. 'I have one. Feels safer when you're sending any kind of private information. This one bounces it around a bit before forwarding it so that you can't identify where it came from.'

'Could the company?'

He looks at Sally Frazer. 'In theory, they must keep records of all data they carry, but in practice they won't co-operate because it would undermine their business. Probably take you years going through the courts.'

'Could we try asking them?'

Morten smiles. 'Sure, send them an email.'

'So I'm clear for the boss: we don't know when or where this was sent from, and we can't find out?'

'*Ja*. Definitely not within the timescale.'

'Can you run a cryptology program, or something like that?'

Morten and the other officer look at one another.

'What is that?'

'Something that looks for a message in the text. Is it possible that Jelani has given us a clue?'

Morten scratches his head hard. 'Sergeant Frazer, you've been watching way too much TV.'

'It could be worse, sir.'

De Vries looks up at Don February, then back down at the article layout, which has been blown up and is now spread across two desks.

'"I sat in front of Colonel de Vries and looked him in the eye and he knew nothing,"' De Vries reads. '"I met him a second time and then a third, and he was blind." It goes on. "Until I set my puppet journalist to work, the SAPS did not know there was any connection between the crimes. I had to tell them. They knew nothing. This is what you pay your taxes for. Ali Jelani was questioned by a female officer. They sat facing each other at a café, and when Jelani told her what I had instructed her to say, she disappeared while the officer's back was turned.'"

'The public will understand that these are his words. A murderer.'

'But they're true, Don. We had him and we had Jelani.'

'We did not know . . .'

'It doesn't matter. People will read what he claims about the women, about the victims.' He points at the spread. A photograph of each victim is displayed above the paragraphs describing the alleged treatment of their children. 'Apparently, Michelle Ricquarts's daughter wrote online that she wanted to become a stripper also. That's probably what triggered Jessel.'

Sally Frazer walks towards them.

De Vries swings around to her, expectant. 'Anything?'

'No, sir.'

General Thulani's office is verging on tepid, yet feels cool to Du Toit and De Vries. The man himself, tie off, his jacket on the back of his chair, is sweating, as are two fully uniformed senior officers from Central Division.

'I do not need to tell you,' Thulani begins, 'that when this article is published, there will be a firestorm. Expect the radio, the television, the worldwide web: all will be alight with indignation. We will be advised this and told the other. I have already instructed the brigadier here,' he indicates the man sitting on the far right of the semicircle in front of his desk, 'that his officers must expect reaction from the public. They must be prepared. And all of this on top of the explosion last week . . .'

'Long Street is fully reopened. We know who the perpetrators were. Terrorists.'

Thulani looks down at the brigadier.

'It may be open, but there are boarded-up businesses, closed bars and restaurants, damage to the buildings. The scarring tells the story and that is why the tourists are not so much in town. We hear that our city has more visitors than ever this year, and then there are these two events. It will only be bad news. Cape Town will be the centre of attention for all the wrong reasons.' He leans forward, pours himself a glass of water from a carafe, drinks half of it. Ice clinks. 'We are not here to reflect on the negative, gentlemen.' He turns to Du Toit. 'What can Central – and the other divisions – do to assist you?'

'We need witnesses. We need to find Jessel's white Toyota Prius, but, in all probability, it's hidden. Above all, we need a sighting, at some point, of Jessel in his car.'

One of the uniformed officers says: 'Can we ask all residents to make a check of garages, cellars, empty buildings?'

Thulani's heavy eyes fall on him.

'That can have undesirable side-effects. People's privacy is invaded, trespass is sanctioned. You risk their injury in trying to gain access to such buildings. And, as we have seen before, if you involve the public with more than their eyes, they all think they are police officers. It is the beginning of vigilantism.'

'We cannot even be certain that she is held within Greater Cape Town. He's operated before in the Strand and Somerset West areas, and he recently moved from Kenilworth to a new estate there. We've alerted the Somerset West teams.'

'You have nothing else?'

They all look to Du Toit, who resists the temptation to turn to De Vries.

'We have no definite information as to where he might have taken the hostage. His former and current address have been checked. Most pressingly, we believe that we have thirty-six hours, at most, to find her.'

'Why that timescale?'

Now, Du Toit does involve De Vries.

'Assuming that he treats her like his previous two victims, she'll have no water or food. He claims he uses a drug to speed up the effects of dehydration until vital organs fail. We don't know, but it would explain why the pathologists cannot pinpoint an exact reason for expiration.'

'This is very bad,' Thulani says.

'We have Jessel,' Du Toit says. 'We will question him this evening, but it is hard to imagine what will persuade him to give up where he has taken Ali Jelani.'

Thulani takes a black silk handkerchief from his trouser pocket, dabs his upper lip.

'We have no carrot and no stick. That is how we have to police in the twenty-first century.'

Du Toit glances to his left without moving his head; De Vries says nothing.

De Vries works in the squad-room with his team, studying everything that was found in Jessel's Somerset West home. Ben Thwala takes officers to the Kenilworth-Wynberg borders to visit Jessel's previous home and speak to the neighbours. De Vries wants to interview Jessel, but knows he will do better to wait: Jessel will give him nothing unless he has something to give him in return, even if it is one piece of information he is not expecting them to know. When the fans are directed away from them to stop papers being blown away, the heat settles in the open rectangle of the squad-room, the smell of body odour increases, pages stick to fingers, and the work rate slows. Don February buys every officer an ice cream; they all sit licking and sucking them for five minutes, in silence, breathing heavily . . .

The air smells of woodsmoke. Fire on the Mountain, maybe close, maybe many kilometres away. Looking up between Lion's Head and Signal Hill, the air is hazy-white, the Mountain about to turn from sun-bleached rock and grasses to deep purple shade as the sun sets on the Camps Bay side.

The squad-room on the opposite side of the building is deserted, dark and calm. Ahead, De Vries sees Du Toit's corner office, light showing through the heavy blinds with which he protects himself. He knows that, like him, Du Toit will work late, hoping that the volume of research eventually produces a break-through. As he approaches, he hears a second voice. He knocks, is called in, enters.

She does not turn her head, but he recognizes her immediately. 'Sir . . . Dr Bellingham.'

Du Toit waits for De Vries to sit.

'Dr Bellingham has come in at my personal request. She will not involve herself with the case further, or be present when Jessel is interviewed. It would not be appropriate for anyone else to know that she is making a contribution. Am I clear?'

'Yes.' He turns to Bellingham. 'Is Henrik on the same deal as me?'

'Deal?' Du Toit says.

'There's a reason,' she says sourly, 'that Vaughn is not renowned for his sense of humour.'

Du Toit frowns at her; De Vries smiles to himself.

'We were about to begin,' Du Toit continues.

'In fact, you had already asked me an important question: am I surprised by Jessel turning himself in?' She sits up. 'On the face of it, yes, since it seems likely that he could have made his escape if he had chosen to do so. However, he may have felt that escape was now impossible and that he could create as much publicity as possible for what he sees as his crusade by taking the action that he has.'

'Do you think he believes that we might release him?'

'With most psychopaths at this point in the offending cycle, I would say that their brains have become . . . focused, and that that focus is constantly narrowing: a corridor down which their next victim lies and which they must travel, making all preparations necessary, in order to get there. This, clearly, is something different.'

'He intends to let her die?' De Vries asks.

She turns to him. 'Possibly. Without becoming more involved than I am prepared to be, I can't say. It's conceivable that he'll reveal her whereabouts to demonstrate his mercy, to humiliate you and the SAPS, but, equally likely, he may already have killed her.'

'How likely is that?' Du Toit says.

'Guessing, trying to answer Vaughn's question without sufficient knowledge, I would say that ten per cent of the time he will save her, ten per cent of the time she's already dead. The most likely scenario is that he will refuse to give up the information and blame you for her death.'

'But he must know that, whatever he does, he'll never see the light of day again?'

'He may not see it that way, but I agree. Unless he has something else planned, his position is hopeless. For that reason, you can offer him nothing, so we all know how the scene will play out.'

'Unless we find her.'

'Unless you find her, yes.'

Du Toit has been sitting very still, very upright. His eyes meet De Vries's.

De Vries says, quietly, painfully: 'We don't have anything.'

She nods. 'He has demonstrated skill throughout his spree. He has taken increasing risk, but it has been weighed reasonably, interference has been judged effectively. I think it's most unlikely that you'll discover her whereabouts either from him in interview or through an error he has made.'

'I asked Dr Bellingham to consider any information that might guide us to where Ali Jelani could be being held.' Du Toit looks over to her expectantly.

Grace Bellingham sighs. 'There's not much here to go on. He's meticulous, intelligent, more reasoned than I would expect, but, despite all his cries that this is a crusade to highlight injustices he sees as having been meted out to undeserving children, this ultimately comes down to him. What happened in Stephen Jessel's life that might cause him to act the way he has?' She leans forward into the breeze afforded by the free-standing fan Du Toit has installed in his office. 'Sorry, but it's stifling.' She reaches for the small bottle of mineral water on the desk in front of her, gulps half of it, replaces it.

'Jessel's actions with his victims suggest the following. He binds them. This is for control, but it also suggests that he may also have been bound, or his movement restricted. It may not be as literal as that. He may simply have felt trapped – as most children do if they are abused. He either wants to, or actually does, rape them. This is control and power also, but it is likely to represent a sexual crisis in his own life. It's probably, but not definitely, from childhood and, with the history of his parents and their . . . how shall we say? . . . unexplained accidents, it seems that his first actions may have been revenge.'

'For what?' Du Toit says.

'For whatever event or set of events triggered this extreme distortion of the brain.'

'But why women? Did his mother abuse him?'

'Possibly. It would seem both parents may have been involved. However, I do have one theory. It revolves around the blinding of Bethany Miles. He knew that she would die – he may even have been present at her death – so why gouge out her eyes, and then pose them? There doesn't have to be a reason, of course. Profilers and psychiatrists waste many hours trying to decipher the meaning of every action and, sometimes, these actions have no meaning. They can be a deliberate attempt to mislead. They may be a hyper-sadistic act made on the spur of the moment when they are drunk with bloodlust. However, here, I wonder if Stephen Jessel is making a point about these women not watching, or watching over, their children.'

'Abuse leads to abuse,' De Vries says blankly. 'We see that repeatedly. I almost feel as if rationalizing the cause diminishes the act. Jessel committed evil crimes and we are lucky to have him behind bars.'

Bellingham turns to him. 'Your first point is banal but sadly true. I disagree with you entirely on your second point but commend you for describing his crimes as evil rather than the man himself.'

'I watch every word I say.'

'That,' Grace Bellingham says, 'will make a pleasant change.'

'Because describing sadistic, evil, ruthless killers as anything other than victims upsets too many liberals.'

'Thank you, then, for managing one sentence,' she says disagreeably.

'Do we,' Du Toit says loudly, 'have a basic theory as to what might inspire Jessel to his behaviour?'

'I think so,' Bellingham says, looking at Du Toit, angling her body away from De Vries. 'As I stated before, I think he had been using Ali Jelani as an unwitting ally for several weeks, and whether or not he planted the information about the supposed attack on me intentionally to test her or whether he did it because he assumed some trust or even understanding between them, Jelani betrayed him immediately. From the article, he had clearly followed her, knew her whereabouts, knew that she stayed within the sight of friends as much as possible. His plan to entrap her was complex, either by coincidence or design, and that suggests that, as a victim, she is important to him. Especially now, since it is her abduction that has led us to catch him.'

She leans forward, tips the water bottle into her mouth, drains it. 'He will almost certainly already have prepared a place for his next victim, whether he ever intended it to be me or not. It will be personal. It will link to his abuse or his escape from abuse. The family home, the home of family friends or relatives, a country home, perhaps even a guesthouse or rental. This goes back to the beginning.'

'He moved house a month ago,' De Vries says. 'We searched it. I've gone through everything myself this afternoon and there's nothing.'

'What about his previous house?'

'Thwala went there with a search team. They even tried some house-to-house. Just the usual. Quiet neighbour, kept to himself. No trouble, no music, no parties. No friends, as far as they could discover.'

'It's too recent anyway,' Grace Bellingham says. 'This all happened a long time ago.'

'So why now?'

'There is usually a catalyst or a trigger. These can be huge events, or so tiny as almost to be unnoticeable.'

'What is the difference,' Du Toit says, 'between a catalyst and a trigger?'

'You're right, Henrik. It's semantics. For me, a trigger is usually an event that occurs within the brain, stimulated by an act or

event that releases powerful memories and, with those, many pro-
found emotions. These flood the brain and begin the narrowing
process I described earlier. Again, for my own personal use, a
catalyst is most often a person – although on one occasion it was
a dog – who stimulates a sudden anger, either because they have
suffered in a similar way, or because something they say or do
simply clicks inside the other party and their route forward suddenly becomes clear. Sometimes this can be suicide, or attempted
suicide. More often, it is revenge.'

'Is it worth reviewing his parents' accidents?' Du Toit says.

'In as much as I suspect that he had a hand in them, yes. In terms
of discovering the whereabouts of Ali Jelani, no. They can wait.'

'What should I say or ask Jessel that might get him to make a
mistake, or reveal where Jelani is?'

She turns to De Vries. 'In truth, in twenty-four hours, nothing.
I spend months talking to these men, every day. You can ask him
about his childhood, but I doubt that he'll engage with you.
Although he appears doomed, he'll think that he holds all the
cards, that he has power over life and death. That is what people
with his state of mind crave.'

'Who should I take in with me? A male officer? A woman?'

'Definitely not a female officer. It is against women he harbours
such resentment and anger. Face him on your own. Do not pro-
voke him, threaten him, be sarcastic. In fact, just turn the usual De
Vries right off. Listen to what he says. Seem lightly impressed,
respect his craft, get him to tell his story. Just possibly, he will say
something that helps you to pinpoint where the first abuse
occurred. That could, conceivably, lead you to his hostage.'

'You won't come in with me?'

'Vaughn, Dr Bellingham made this quite clear . . .'

'No,' she says, turning to him. 'I've told you repeatedly. You
need to understand the difference between determination and

wanton blindness. I am spent. I can't do it, and I won't. I warned you that there is a price to be paid for dealing with men like Jessel. You are closer to the edge than you think.'

'I will do whatever I have to do to try to save Ali Jelani. That's all I can think about.'

'That,' Grace Bellingham says quietly, 'is exactly the point. Stephen Jessel will know that, and he will use it against you.'

'Stephen Jessel is in a cell, or shackled in my interview room. He won't be using anything against me.'

'You didn't believe me the first time I told you so I'll say it again,' she says intently, a forced calmness in her voice. 'These men influence, manipulate and attack from the grave, from inside prison, from within a sealed room. Ali Jelani may not be the only one still in danger.'

'Why are you both still here?' De Vries looks at the two tired officers, faces sallow in the fluorescent lights

'I'm not going home.' Sally Frazer says. 'Don is staying here too. We probably have less than a day.'

'We are thinking, sir,' Don says, 'unless you want one of us beside you, we would sit in the observation room, hear what Jessel has to say. If he references anybody or any location, we can immediately follow it up.'

'Good. I'll keep it short. If he won't talk, we'll leave him.'

'When will you begin?'

De Vries puts on his jacket. 'Now.'

The corridors are silent, the light dim and insipid, the air unmoving. He finds himself slowing as he reaches the custody desk, still uncertain what he will say or do. He nods to the custody officer, who opens the door to the interview room. He approaches the table behind which Stephen Jessel sits, upright but relaxed. He places plastic cups of water on the table, takes his seat.

Jessel stares at the cups. 'Why has yours got ice?'

De Vries silently swaps the cups over.

Jessel smiles. 'You doctored the one with ice?'

De Vries picks up the cup with ice, drinks from it, replaces it in front of Jessel.

'The cup is dirty now.'

'Take your choice, Mr Jessel. Ice, or no ice. They're both cold.'

Jessel reaches forward. 'It would be easier if I didn't have these cuffs on my wrists.'

'The protocol is to cuff you behind your back. I requested that you were cuffed in front of you so that you would be more comfortable. You can drink quite easily.'

Jessel picks up the cup, twists it, lifts it to his lips.

'This discussion is being recorded. Please confirm that you've refused to request an attorney or accept the offer of one being made available.'

'I have.'

De Vries mutters the verbal description of the interview, the personnel, the time. He looks up.

'Where is Ali Jelani? Everyone will know her story, why she was punished. You gain nothing by letting her die.'

'It is very hot in this room.'

'It is the same throughout the building.'

Jessel smiles. 'Ali Jelani? I suppose you are somewhat . . . pressed for time.'

'Do you disagree with my analysis?'

'I neither agree nor disagree. What time is it now? Did you say five past nine? Ali Jelani thinks she is strong, but I think she will be dead by morning.'

De Vries shivers. 'Did you trust her? Did she betray you agreeing to talk to us?'

'I have never trusted anyone since I was eight years old.'

'Why is that?'

'I'm sure that Dr Bellingham will already have speculated. Perhaps you have just come from a meeting with her. She probably told you what to ask and what to say. Am I right?' He stares at De Vries. 'I think I am.'

'I'm only interested in what you have to say, Mr Jessel. I don't listen to speculation.'

'She told you to humour me, appear interested in what I have to say, even if it doesn't help you in your quest?'

'I just want to know why. Why you would do what you've done, what you are continuing to do.'

'That isn't true. You just want me to tell you where the woman is.'

'I do want that. I also want to understand why you are doing this.'

'Why? You believe that I will spend the rest of my life in prison . . .'

De Vries takes a sip of his water.

'What happens in our childhood affects the rest of our lives. What happened to you?'

Jessel sighs. 'For my eighth birthday, my father bought me a Hornby H0/00-gauge model railway.' He is leaning back, speaking quietly. It sounds like a recitation. 'It was a two-track layout, complete with signals and control for up to four locomotives. The stations and streets and houses and shops each had tiny lights inside them. In the dark, the trains could travel through the night. We set it up together in the cellar of our house. It was my place. The place where my father and I could play together. When I was nine years old, my mother brought hot chocolate and cookies to us as a surprise. She saw what my father, her husband, was doing to me. I remember looking up at her. I was ashamed but I was also glad she could see, that it would stop. I understood from the look on her face that what was being done to me was wrong. I knew that. I could feel it, and what she told me by her look was that I was right. I hoped that the police would come and take my father away, that I would be left with her only. And, then, what happened? Nothing. She never spoke of it again, never returned to the cellar. When I was fourteen years old, I refused my father. He threatened me, but I threatened him more. It ended there for him. It ended there for her . . .'

He looks blankly at De Vries. 'I failed at school, had few friends, left home when I was sixteen. I worked in a hostel, and I lived there. No one hurt me. I got a job with the Section Designation Department. I knew that I would find people like myself there. When I listened to the case officers talk about them, I could hear the disdain in their voices, the mistrust, the visceral hatred. When the blacks took over from the whites, I made myself a case officer. Senior officers had left and they needed people to look after the mess. They wanted to believe I was who I said I was. They needed me, to supervise the damaged, dangerous few. And I met them.'

'Why did you attack Hazel Calder?'

'Didn't Dr Bellingham tell you not to interrupt me?'

'No.'

Jessel studies him, continues: 'The time had come.'

'To attack these women?'

'To sacrifice myself for the victims who have no one to represent them.'

De Vries frowns. Jessel's justification is as his own.

'Did you kill your parents?'

'They were unpunished.'

'That doesn't answer my question.'

'Words can be used to mean anything. What is the difference between yes and no?'

'The other women. Why did you take them? Why did you make them suffer?'

'Punishment.'

'For what purpose?'

Jessel bridles. His voice sounds petulant.

'What is the purpose of punishment? It is a deterrent. To warn others who might be tempted to err. I not only punished the guilty, I warned the rest of them. Naturally it must be well advertised. And I found two more women, guilty themselves, who would help me. It required no effort on my part. They begged me to let them help me. A newspaper editor starting a new title, in search of the exclusive, the story that would define her paper, and an ambitious Kenyan journalist, whose greed for success blinded her to all rationality and judgement—'

'Where is she? Where is Ali Jelani?'

Jessel slowly raises his wrists, places them on the table in front of him, meets De Vries's questioning stare.

'Waiting in the corridor of death.'

'Tell us where she is.'

'Release me. The bargain is simple. The public will not under-stand why you let her die. They will reason that, once she is safe, I can be recaptured.'

'So why offer us a deal you know we cannot accept?'

'So that you can fail.'

'No one cares about me. You claim to care for children, but you will make Ali Jelani's children motherless. How is that good for them?'

'She abandoned them. They will scarcely notice her passing.'

'You're wrong. Your father abused you and your mother

betrayed you, but the women you are taking are trying to be good parents. We all make mistakes.'

Jessel leans back, says quietly: 'You do.'

'What mistake, in your opinion, am I making now?'

'You will see.'

De Vries's tongue plays with his teeth. He feels time passing, cannot believe that anything is being gained by giving Jessel an audience.

'Time passes for all of us. For Ali Jelani. For you. For the guilty. Only when I no longer had to struggle for my own survival did I think about what I wanted to achieve. I read the papers, read the stories about women who harm their children, who abuse or abandon them. And then, just as I was about to begin, I read online about a woman called Ali Jelani. A woman who, in her desire to succeed for herself, left her two young children with people she'd barely known a month. It was perfect: she could be both accessory in – and victim of – my work.

'I told her I would attack Dr Bellingham and I waited to see what she would do with the information. Mrs Jelani was so frightened that she was being followed, when she looked around she could not even see the obvious. When she met a female police officer whom I recognized from my visit here last week, I knew that she had chosen her path. I followed her to your home street, decided to frighten you and Dr Bellingham a little and cause a distraction. Then, while you were all busy with the fire, I stopped just where she was waiting – where I had seen her hide herself so that she could record and photograph my capture – and took her. No one even heard her call out. Fire engines and police cars are like that – they provide perfect cover.' He leans forward. 'How is Dr Bellingham? Did she think that I had come to fetch her?'

'You could have set fire to the entire city.'

Jessel shrugs.

'You can be merciful. You can release Jelani.'

'You can release me.'

De Vries stands, the sound of his chair pushed back against the concrete floor jarring, shocking.

'There's nothing more to say.'

Don February and Sally Frazer are not in the observation suite. He walks to the squad-room, realizing that his clothes are soaked with sweat. A feverish shiver passes through his body. He thinks of Grace Bellingham and her warnings about the cost of inter-action with people such as Jessel. He feels diminished by his interview; feels weaker.

Three junior officers are still at work. Frazer and Don stand together in front of a trestle table, on which numerous larger documents and printouts are spread.

Sally Frazer turns to De Vries.

'His home was where the abuse took place, which he left as soon as he could. That's where Dr Bellingham said we should look, so that's what we're doing.'

'It's a building site.'

'It's a development. Completed in phases. Two are finished. I think the land where Stephen Jessel's house was located is part of that finished phase.'

'You think there's another building there? On that site?'

'I think he may have bought there. I rechecked what passed through his bank accounts. He paid three million for his Somerset West house, but we checked, and it cost two point three five.'

'Two Feathers in Somerset West and the Kenilworth develop-ment are projects of the same developers/estate agent,' Don says.

'So that's how he could hide the money?'

'It's a reasonable theory,' Sally Frazer says.

'We managed to get a plan of the new apartments,' Don says. 'I called a friend of mine who works in the Planning Department and he had the plans at home on his laptop.'

'I wonder what else he brings home from work.'

Don turns to De Vries. 'It was a work laptop . . . He emailed the plans for the original layout of dwellings, and the new development. We have tried comparing the two to pinpoint where Jessel's former home would have been, but it is not clear. Sally has asked Joey Morten to adjust the scale and superimpose one over the other. He is working now at home.'

De Vries feels charged as if, before they fail, he has one concrete chance.

'We need to go now. You'll stay here and co-ordinate, Sally? Don, come on. We can be guided once we're there.'

The pre-Christmas roads are quiet at ten p.m., but the journey still takes longer than De Vries anticipates because of an accident on Hospital Bend travelling towards the Southern Suburbs. He is uncertain how to get there the quickest, but settles for the local roads, driving along Camp Ground, past Palmyra Junction and towards what used to be called Lansdowne Road, but which is now called after an imam whose name he cannot remember.

Kenilworth is a sprawling suburb. Higher up on the hill was, and largely remains, smart: grand villas and mansions on large plots. Lower down, by the racecourse, the houses in the suburban streets are modest, many being redeveloped into apartments. Eventually finding Doncaster Road, then McKinley Road, De Vries slows to search for the show-home and sales office. Many of the nearby streetlights are out, the roads and pavements quiet. Following painted hoardings around the vast site, they finally stumble upon gates and, beyond, the show-home and sales office.

Don gets out of the car, peers through the gates. He turns to the keypad and intercom, presses a button low down.

'No one is answering.'

De Vries calls Sally Frazer, is told that the overnight caretaker is a Mr Chalbri. He will assist them, and as soon as she can identify the likely property, she will call back.

After less than thirty seconds the ornate iron gates part, and they drive in. The development is partly a building site, partly completed apartments. The road is covered with red mud, spilled gravel and sand. They stop by the show-home and site office, which are both dark. A plastic snowman stands incongruously on the healthy lawn, glowing greyly. They get out into the still heat, which smells of hot concrete and diesel fumes. Above them, two massive cranes stand sentinel, red lights at their apex slowly flashing in time. Two apartment blocks stand at right angles to one another; maybe one in ten windows is showing light. The place seems eerily deserted.

Around the corner, a dirty Chevrolet Spark appears, drives fast and stops hard. A small Indian man hurries out towards them. 'Colonel de Vries?'

They hold up their ID.

'Mr Chalbri?'

'Yes, yes. I speak to your lady colleague. She asks about a particular address, back from when there where big old houses here, but she does not know what it is yet.'

'Are there residents here?' De Vries asks.

'Yes. Maybe about thirty apartments in Lake View and Furlong Rise.'

'Do you know them? Can you get names?'

'I know most, yes. There is not security as such, you see. I am here to help residents and receive deliveries out of hours. The security men are over on the other side, guarding the tools and machines.'

'A single man,' De Vries says. 'Stephen Jessel.'

Mr Chalbri shakes his head. 'No, I do not know that name. Of course, I do not know everybody.'

'A white Toyota Prius?'

'Oh, yes, I have read about this. The man who takes the women?' He furrows his brow. 'You think he is here? His car? A white Prius. No . . . Maybe. There are white cars.'

De Vries looks around at the empty, muddy side-roads.

'Where do people keep them?'

'All underground car parking.'

'Take us there.'

'To where? The car park? Yes, please, but which block?'

De Vries looks at Don, who has his ear pushed against his cellphone.

'Sally says she thinks the Southerly block is positioned over where Armour Road used to be, where the Jessel family lived.'

'The Southerly block,' De Vries barks, turning on the spot, trying to decipher his position.

'Furlong Rise, over there.' Chalbri points to the further block, on ground raised slightly above where they are standing. 'You want to drive?'

De Vries is already walking. They follow him. Don stumbles as he continues to listen to Sally Frazer. He hangs up, trots to catch the other two.

'Sergeant Frazer says that when the plans are overlaid, there is no single apartment which occupies the land on which the Jessel family home lived. All the apartments are built at a different orientation.'

De Vries frowns. Inside, he feels that this grey, miserable place hides Ali Jelani.

Furlong Rise is squat, wider than it is tall, each front-facing apartment sharing long, curved balconies. De Vries wonders what they must see. Perhaps a glimpse of racecourse, more likely the warehouses and shopping malls, and probably the freeway. The building seems to grow in volume as they draw close. De Vries stops, waits for Chalbri to reach him.

'Is there a basement?'

'The car park only.'

'First floor, then.' He turns to Don. 'Can Frazer at least tell us which end it could be?'

'Eastern end.'

Chalbri points to the left-hand side of the building. Few windows are lit. They have still seen no other human beings.

'Is it always this quiet?'

'At night, yes. In the day, there are men on construction and people still making fixes to these blocks too. Next year, all these apartments will be full.'

De Vries looks up at what constitutes the first floor of apartments, sitting only three metres above ground level. He hesitates, rubs the sweat from the front of his neck in the V between his thumb and forefinger. The location feels right, but the apartments he is scrutinizing do not.

'We're looking for a cellar. A basement.' His voice sounds loud and strident in the still, concrete night.

Chalbri jumps. 'Yes. I do not know. You want to see the car park?'

De Vries starts walking. 'Yes. We need to look underground. Can we get in?'

'I have the key-card.' Chalbri overtakes him, hurries to the ramp, pushes the key card against a sensor and watches the barrier rise. Together, they trot down the ramp into complete darkness. Chalbri switches on a torch, which hangs on a string from a trouser belt loop. 'When the car enters,' he says, 'the lights come on. That is what should happen.'

De Vries looks round, sees that Don has a torch also.

'He could have left it here. The Prius. Safe as anywhere.'

They proceed to where the parking spaces start. There are maybe a dozen cars; none is a Toyota Prius. At the far end of the parking area, there is a dimly illuminated lift lobby behind sheet glass. They approach it. De Vries pulls the torch from Don, shines it either side of the lobby.

'What are those doors there?'

'Service rooms only. Plant rooms.'

'We can see inside those?'

'Yes,' Chalbri says, 'but there is no one inside. I check them all and relock them when I take over at seven p.m.'

'Are you sure?'

'Yes, sir. Every night, it is my first duty. In both buildings.'

'No other rooms down here?'

Chalbri is fiddling with the loaded key-chain.

'Maybe this way . . .' He enters the lift lobby and takes the door on the far right. 'This is the corridor to the stairs and the main starboard lobby.'

The corridor is lit only by grey LEDs. De Vries is already depressed by the soulless building. The working day would begin and end here, in the car park, in the narrow grey corridor. They reach a right-angled turn to the left. Chalbri stands by two sets of doors on his right.

'There are these rooms.'

'What are they?'

'I do not know, but I think that they are servants' quarters for the two big double-size apartments above. There may be stairs into the upper floor.'

De Vries knocks loudly on one door, then the next.

'Is anyone there?'

'I do not think so. The two big apartments are not lived in yet.'

De Vries looks down at Chalbri.

'Open them.'

'Open these doors? I do not know whether I can.' He looks down at the keys, squinting in the low light. 'In theory, I am supposed to have every key here.' De Vries feels a sudden pulse of adrenalin. Everything feels right: direct and uninterrupted access from the car park, an underground room. He looks at Chalbri sorting through what must be more than a hundred keys.

'This seems close,' Don says. 'And, if these are storage rooms, it would explain why Jessel apparently only paid half a million for it.'

'I know.' De Vries's hands are sweating, palms clammy.

Chalbri approaches the nearer door.

'Let me try this. The tag says . . . No.'

He fumbles again. Don can feel the frustration in De Vries's posture. The lights in the corridor extinguish. Chalbri stands rigid. Don illuminates the bunch of keys, and Chalbri continues searching, says:

'The lights go off when there is no movement. Make movement.'

De Vries takes a few steps backwards and forwards in the dark. He raises his arms and waves. The lights stay off. De Vries walks towards the sparkling bundle of keys. Chalbri places a key in the lock. All hear it turn.

'Stay here, sir,' De Vries says.

He takes Don's torch, pushes open the door. The movement of the light switches has no effect. The narrow corridor opens out to a small, low-ceilinged bedsit. The two doors off the corridor

279

open up to bathroom and, on the other side, the biggest room in the dwelling, the kitchen. De Vries enters each room, scans the floor, checks for further doors or cupboards, sees nothing but unfinished work, cheap fitted cupboards and basic furniture. He turns, retraces his steps.

'The other door?'

'I have the key,' Chalbri says, holding it up in the beam of his torch.

'This is closer to the road,' Don says, studying his cellphone. 'The Jessel home was on the road, on Armour Road.'

De Vries pushes ahead through the door, finds the same layout. This time the light switches produce wall lights in the corridor. He paces down it towards the bedsitting room, finds it empty; the bathroom – there is a shower curtain and two bottles of shower gel and shampoo; towels, a bathmat. He slams the door, opens the next to the kitchen. The lights come on and, on top of an island preparation table, he sees her. De Vries struggles to form words, his throat constricted.

'Here. Don, ambulance. Tell Chalbri not to come in.'

The body is spot-lit from the ceiling by a cluster of three halogen lights. She is naked, tied to the surface on her back. A huge kitchen knife sticks out of the surface where it has been stuck between her legs, the blade facing her flesh. There is blood between her legs, oozing off her face. Against the white-tiled floor, white Formica worktop, the white walls, the blood stands out so brightly, crudely scarlet. He walks towards her, concentrating on not gagging. He sees her face, one eye staring, the other socket empty and rust brown. He leans over her, gently prods her arm. It twitches.

'She's alive. Ambulance. Get Chalbri to open the gates, direct them here. Hurry.'

He looks back down at Ali Jelani. Her open eye blinks and flutters. He jumps back, then returns to the work surface, tries to dislodge the embedded knife but cannot. He whispers to her not to move, searches the kitchen for a knife, pats his pockets, finds his small school pocket knife, pulls out a blade, starts to saw through the first black cable tie. As he releases her arm; shaking, she brings it down by her side. He sees her left eye focus on him.

He says quietly, his voice breaking: 'Ali Jelani. You're safe.'

Tears form in her eye.

At the lift doors, Du Toit is waiting.

'What took you so long? They told me you'd come back ten minutes ago.'

'Do you mean to say congratulations, sir? Don and Sally Frazer brought it together. They deserve the credit.'

'Well done, Vaughn. Now what are you doing?' He waits until De Vries meets his eye.

'I'm talking to Jessel.'

De Vries starts to move away towards his squad-room. Du Toit follows.

Sally Frazer hurries to him. 'Is she all right?'

'The paramedic said her pulse was strong enough, but she's very weak. I'll visit the hospital later or first thing.'

'Colonel.' De Vries turns to Du Toit, who addresses Frazer: 'Take a couple of minutes somewhere else, please, Sergeant.' He watches her go, turns to De Vries.

'Leave Jessel alone.'

'I'm going to tell him we found her, that she's alive.'

'Why?'

'Because I want to. Jelani had her right eye gouged out. She must have bled for hours, left alone to die. Can you imagine that?'

'It serves no purpose.'

'It serves my purpose. Ali Jelani's right eye wasn't in the room.'

'Vaughn, stop it. You've beaten him. You picked up a serial assault-and-murder case late and there has been no other fatality. Take the win.'

'I am. I'm taking my prize. It'll be recorded. I won't compromise anything.'

Du Toit shakes his head. 'It won't feel like a prize in the morning.'

Jessel sits as he did before but, this time, his arms are behind his chair. De Vries walks to his own chair, undertakes the identification process, starts the interview. He looks up at Jessel, who speaks before him.

'You found her?'

De Vries twitches, says: 'We found her and she's alive. We found her at your old house, in the cellar. You were abused so you chose to abuse, terrorize, torture, murder others. You're out of here in the morning, and you can spend your time in Pollsmoor working out what sob story you're going to tell in court. If you make it there . . .'

'I can see that you are very pleased with yourself, Colonel de Vries.' Jessel is sitting forward now, the blank smile in place. 'Before you send me away, be certain you don't need me. Would be a shame to have to turn out again to fetch me.'

De Vries stands. 'No one wants you. Nobody needs you.' He leans towards Jessel. 'You took out Ali Jelani's eye. What did you do with it?'

'That is something neither she nor you will ever know . . . But it is with me always.'

Jessel smiles broadly. De Vries recoils from him, his smile, his breath, the image that, in De Vries's exhausted, blasted brain, he has conjured.

He pours again, fills the paper cups half full.

'I have a driver I can call,' Du Toit says. 'Don't drive home.'

'I never drive when I'm drunk, sir.'

'You said you'd go to the hospital. Leave it. She's not going anywhere and they won't tell you much anyway . . . I called Grace . . . Dr Bellingham. Phone's off. She helped us, Vaughn. She focused us on Jessel's past, where the first abuse occurred.'

'She did.'

'Was there . . . is there a problem between the two of you?'

'She offered me a Faustian deal, except this one had two options, both bad.'

'Well, it was worth it, this deal.'

'If you say so.'

They drink in silence, in the gloom, letting the lightest of night-time breezes drift through the open window, stir the heat with whirlpools of tepidity. Only when the sound of a roaring, swearing drunk in the street below reaches them does De Vries say: 'He sounds like I feel . . .'

'You think about it,' Du Toit says. 'He's taken five women, subdued them. He doesn't look capable.'

'You'd be surprised where the strength comes from to commit evil. I've seen it before.'

'I was thinking about Jessel when he came here regarding Leigh Finnemore, our section eighteen. You didn't like him from the start.'

'No.'

'He'll probably end up at Valkenburg.'

283

'Prison for life,' De Vries says. 'I don't care if he's sick. Don't care if he was abused, don't care if he claims he's lost his mind. He's capable of thought and, whatever he or they say, he knew what he was doing, and he knew that it was wrong. He admitted it. "I sacrifice myself for the victims." That's what he said. He wouldn't think that if he didn't know he was doing wrong. He gave himself away. So, no, I don't want him to receive help, don't want him to be able to tell his story. The death penalty increasingly seems appealing.'

'But it doesn't work, Vaughn.'

'Justice moves too slowly. There are too many opinions, too many apologists.' De Vries is banging his fist on the desk, but it makes little noise. 'Too many people afraid of infringing these people's human rights. It's black and white: guilty or not guilty, according to the evidence. You're guilty, you're gone.'

'Gone?'

'While we wait, while we obey the rules, they pass us, they overwhelm us. We have to deal with the consequences. You talked about winning, Henrik. Is that winning?'

They hear the sound of a vacuum cleaner, swing around, see a cleaner entering the squad-room. They watch him straighten up, take a long piece of lavatory paper from his trouser pockets, ball it, wipe his brow.

He dozes fitfully at his dining table. He has contemplated bed but, even with all the windows open onto the upper balcony, his room is hot, the air motionless. Downstairs is tangibly cooler and it keeps him there. The entire house smells of smoke, lodged in the curtains and carpets, cushions and sofas. He has dutifully drunk a pint glass of water, but still decides to open another bottle of red wine. Occasionally he loses consciousness while holding his glass, jolts awake, fearful that his wine has spilled. Each time his head bows, his chin hits his chest, he sees them: Hazel Calder, pulling her legs apart for him; Michelle Ricquarts scrabbling to escape the wooden beach-shack; Marie Garsten, grey like the raw concrete of the building-site cellar, raped and left to die . . . Half conscious, he is holding his breath. He splutters, but does not wake . . . Bethany Miles in the dark, damp emptiness of Apostle Lodge. He sees her black concave eyes, ants forming psychedelic patterns reflected and distorted on the chrome frame to which she is bound, her mouth twisted to a scream. He sees the metal bird on the roof, hears it cry. He sees the blank windows of the building, the blank eyes of Bethany Miles, the single eye of Ali Jelani, crying.

He wakes, mouth dry, neck sore. He sits up, slowly moves his open hand towards the glass, folds his fingers gently around the goblet, brings it to his mouth.

Dawn wakes him; treble-tinny music from outside stirs him. He lifts his head, opens gritty eyes, realizes that it must be the black couple who guard next door, out on the balcony. He wonders whether they woke him or whether for him now sleep is transitory. He is tired, but not hung-over. He is too drunk to be that. He views his charred, scarred garden, half-empty pool with its scalded wood and black ash surface, sees for the first time a distorted white plastic garden chair, melted by the fire. A gallery in Bree Street, he thinks, would pay for that. He showers while the coffee machine heats up. He makes two strong cups, downs them, fills his flask with two more measures and doubles the volume with brandy.

As he walks outside, he hears the music louder. He walks around the side of his house and looks up, seeing the balcony from the diagonal. The tall girl is dancing to music from, he thinks, the cellphone she has in her hand. She sways, she smiles, she raises her arms above her head. He turns away, envious that her joy can, seemingly, be accessed so easily, begrudging the joy itself.

He drives carefully to the hospital, fumbling in vain for his dark glasses, the morning sun burning his eyes, making them water. He feels wretched, dehydrated.

There is a disturbance in the waiting room, a physical fight. He is too tired to intervene, walks towards the wards. The only information he gleans is that Ali Jelani is out of danger. There are no doctors, no consultants to talk to him, only nurses, just as tired as he, but sober. It is enough.

He walks into the quiet car park, twists his wrist. It is seven ten a.m. He calls Grace Bellingham. Her phone is off. He sits at what he knows to be slow traffic lights from the hospital side-road onto Main Road. His head droops, although his breathing is fast. Grace Bellingham had told Henrik du Toit to call her anytime if there was news, yet her phone is off. He shivers, presses down on the accelerator, drifts left through the still red lights, speeds into the queue of traffic.

Her apartment is silent. He rings the bell, knocks repeatedly, calls through the letter box. A neighbour appears at his door to complain. De Vries badges him, avoids speaking, knowing that the words will not yet flow fluently. He doorsteps the building caretaker, demands that he gain access to Dr Bellingham's flat as a matter of life and death. He brooks no resistance, takes the spare key, sets off back to her floor, unlocks the door. Immediately, he hears the alarm bleeping a countdown. He stares at the keypad, realizes he does not know the disarming code. He turns away, strides into the living room, checks the bathroom, utility room and bedroom. Her bed is made. As he hurries to the exit, the alarm sounds. He feels his ears burn, slams the door, trots to the lift. In the entrance lobby, he meets the caretaker, slaps the keys into his cupped hands, leaves him amid the cacophony and inevitable dispute that will follow, runs to his car. His heart is beating hard. He feels pain in his left side, bile rising. He swallows it, starts the car, guns it away from the apartment block.

'Close the door.' Du Toit rises, walks around De Vries, shuts it. 'You're drunk, Vaughn. I thought we had an arrangement, an agreement—'

'I went to her flat. She's not there. No phone. She wanted to be informed what was happening.'

'Dr Bellingham could have gone anywhere.'

'She said she was going home. She's not there, the bed's made.'

'She may have wanted to sleep undisturbed and then, this morning, left early.'

'Listen to me,' De Vries says, sitting forward awkwardly in his chair. 'I've been drinking – and you started that last night, remember – and I haven't slept, but don't tell me what I know and don't know. Grace Bellingham hasn't been in her flat for at least twenty-four hours. I can smell that, Henrik. That's what I do. I detect.'

'So, what are you suggesting?'

'She's been taken.'

'Taken? Jessel has been in custody since we last saw Grace Bellingham.'

'Last night, when you told me not to, and I spoke to him, he said: "Be sure that you don't need me before you send me away." He said it like he knew I'd want to talk to him again. This is what Grace told me: these men can control things from within a cell.'

287

Du Toit sits back. 'I don't believe it. There'll be a simple explanation. She went to stay with a friend and her phone ran out of battery.'

'She claims she has no friends.'

'You claim that too. You take a comment like that with a pinch of salt.'

'Stop it. Stop trying to divert me. I'm telling you. She is missing. She could have been taken, and Jessel as much as warned me.'

'Very well. Send someone else over to her place to check it out. Get February or Frazer to pass the info on to Central and the other divisions. You need to sober up, get yourself together.'

'I'm perfectly together. This is what Jessel meant. I have to speak to him again. He'll offer us the same deal.'

'And we'll refuse it.'

'And we'll refuse it, but this time we have no clue, no idea where she might be, even who has taken her. And, if she's gone, we owe it to her. I talked her into this, to be involved, so I owe her.'

'Just be professional. Don't speak to Jessel. Do you hear me? Not yet. Not until I've thought.'

De Vries rocks in the chair, his eyes half closed.

'If it isn't him, we have no idea where she might be.'

Du Toit walks around his desk, puts his hand on De Vries's shoulder.

'We don't even know that she's gone.'

The face of a bear stares up at him from the surface of his cappuccino. Mike Solarin turns the cup to show Gugu KwaDukuza. She smiles, sips her red Grapetiser.

The Pretoria weather is hot but not stifling, still but breathable. There is drought here too, but it is well behind that being endured by the Cape. The city's trees, parks and green spaces still seem lush and refreshing. In the Magnolia Dell Park in Pretoria, families are picnicking, children play sports, dogs chase each other.

In the distance, Mike Solarin sees him. He nods at Gugu, stands, steps off the deck, and walks away from Huckleberry's Café. The man seems many years older now than when he had known him only ten previously, his short curly hair white. He holds a child's hand. She seems to pull him, like a tug a tanker, slowly trying to build up momentum. Nassor Mbwana was his mentor, a man who survived the Struggle, then took his place as a public figure within the SAPS, not for personal enrichment but for his country. He, Solarin believes, is the role model for this country, not the likes of Zuma or Malema. The older man sees Solarin, waves with his free hand.

'Mike . . . How are you, my friend?'

'Well, sir. Well.'

'This is Amara.'

Solarin puts his hand on the back of the child's head gently, but she does not look up, still tugs Mbwana's arm.

'We have an appointment with ice cream.'

Solarin falls into step with the old man and the child.

'I am sorry, sir, to disturb your time with your granddaughter.'

'That is all right. There is only so much to be said about ice cream. You are well? You are not in trouble?'

'No, sir. I merely wish to ask for your advice.'

'Well, that is what a mentor should offer.' He looks down at the child, sighs. 'But, first, there is a more pressing matter I must deal with.'

De Vries sits in his office, mind racing, his body still but for the jogging of his right leg. He has already sipped, then swigged, at his flask. He waits for Don February to return from Grace

Bellingham's flat; for Du Toit to talk to Joey Morten about tracing cellphones; for Sally Frazer to try to trace Bellingham's departure from their building the previous evening.

By eleven a.m., her now untraceable phone is still switched off. Grace Bellingham is recorded leaving the building at 21.47 hours the previous evening, walking to the right, and around the corner where, for several months, none of the CCTV cameras has been operational.

'No one saw Dr Bellingham last night at her apartment,' Don tells them, 'but she had only just moved in, and most other residents had not met her. It does not seem that she was there recently. We found her passport and some jewellery, as well as US dollars in cash.'

'Why didn't we drive her home?'

Du Toit turns to De Vries. 'I offered. She wanted to leave discreetly. Not round the back in a police vehicle.'

'You could have sent someone round the front looking like a cab.'

'I could, Colonel, but that was not what Dr Bellingham requested.' Du Toit's voice is tight. 'All right, we don't know that she is missing but we must accept that it is a possibility.' He looks at Don February. 'You've sent out alerts?'

'Yes, sir.'

Du Toit looks warily towards De Vries, considers not asking the question.

'What are you going to do?'

'Well, sir, if you've had time to think, talk with Jessel.'

'Is there really any point?'

'Probably not, but, by accident, he helped us to find Jelani. If Dr Bellingham is missing – if she has been taken – then Jessel knows. It will have been his plan. Maybe he will just gloat and grandstand, but maybe he will say something again to help us. I think I'm in the perfect state to act the stool pigeon.'

'Regrettably,' Du Toit says, 'I agree.'

They sit at the table on the edge of the deck with Gugu KwaDukuza, looking out across the park to where Amara is sitting cross-legged on the crisp, coarse grass, contentedly licking her ice cream. Solarin has spoken, documenting everything he has discovered during his part in the investigation and the evidence collected from other sources. He pauses only when a dog runs between their ankles, tail slapping their calves. Mbwana kicks it away. KwaDukuza explains her evidence, and Solarin concludes. Nassor Mbwana listens attentively, frown growing increasingly deep, until his broadly spaced eyebrows almost meet. When Solarin finishes, Mbwana sniffs, draws his hands together on the table, interlocking his fingers.

'Who have you spoken to of this?'

'Just you, sir.'

He nods. 'That, at least, is good.' He looks around him, glances down to Amara, who is stroking a Jack Russell terrier. 'Now that you have made lieutenant, Mike, you have to understand that men,' he looks across to KwaDukuza, 'and women, who are high up in public bodies in South Africa, have a wider responsibility than merely low-ranking officers serving in the SAPS, the Hawks, wherever it might be. Decisions must sometimes be made for reasons that, to be fair, the ordinary man in the street may not appreciate. You understand?'

'For what reason has it been decided that clear, coherent evidence should be ignored?'

Nassor Mbwana raises his hand. 'No, no, no. Do not say that. You have suspicions and doubts. There are unanswered questions, but there is no conspiracy here. The withholding and compart-mentalizing of information is for national security. It is so that those lowly workers seeking answers within their sphere are not provided with the entire picture. So that leaks may be contained and identified from the scope of the material released. This is all entirely natural . . .'

'But if the media pass on falsehoods . . .'

'The media will take anything and twist it.'

'But this is what we are telling them.'

'This is what is thought best to tell them.'

'I do not think—'

'That is right,' Mbwana interrupts, his quiet, steady voice rising. 'You should not think. Your duty is to adapt to your new role, to dedicate yourself, and to be as good as you can be. Do not be dis-tracted by politics or with challenging how things are done. You are too young yet to do that.' He takes a sip of tea, leans back, relaxes. 'They waited until I was sixty-three before they moved me to the very top floor, shared their secrets. They knew that then, only then, I was ready.'

'And are they secrets worth keeping?'

Mbwana's lips twitch. 'They are mainly very silly. But how a country is run, how it protects and controls its citizens. This is all complicated but, for society to flourish, it must be done.'

'So you do not think that I should speak to Colonel Juiles?'

'No. Definitely not. Leave it. Learn. Do not approach anyone. I have known you some years, Mike, since you first came to us. I don't want to have to repeat this conversation to anybody. I would not want any harm to come to you.'

'Harm?' Gugu KwaDukuza says unexpectedly, loudly. 'What harm, and from who?'

'Harm only to Mike's career,' Mbwana says smoothly.

'Is that what you meant?'

'There is danger, miss, in challenging that which you do not understand.'

'There is danger,' Solarin says firmly, 'in staying silent.'

'Trust me, Mike. One danger is greater than the other.'

KwaDukuza says: 'You talk of harm and danger . . .'

Solarin puts his hand on Gugu's arm, gives her a reassuring glance.

Mbwana is waving to Amara.

'I must go.' He stands, and Solarin and KwaDukuza mirror him. He turns to Solarin. 'Know your place in the scheme of things, and all will be well.' He bids both of them goodbye, walks slowly to the edge of the deck, steps down onto the grass. His hand is grabbed; the slow, uneven procession begins.

'He is not the gentle old man he pretends to be,' KwaDukuza says.

'No.' He looks down at her. She is breathing hard. He sits.

'I think he was threatening you, maybe us . . .'

'That was a very gentle piece of advice, Gugu. Nassor Mbwana documented the abuses of the police force during the Struggle and, afterwards, he became one of the new SAPS himself to see that the abuses of the past were not repeated in the new South Africa. He has had many fights, and he is still standing.'

'Maybe because he represses what he does not want to hear. He was telling you to be quiet, Mike. Telling you to shut up about what we know, or harm will come to you.'

'I think that it was more career advice.'

She pouts, says: 'You think what you think, and I will think what I think. It is time to forget what we know . . . What we think we know . . .'

Solarin wonders whether some have the capacity for that: to forget, to clear their minds and begin again, unknowing, innocent. For him, what is known cannot be unknown. He looks at her

293

face, set and drawn, smiles, offers her his hand. She either does not see it, or affects not to. He feels a barrier materialize between them. He withdraws his hand slowly, places it by his side, hanging free.

'You see, I was right,' Jessel says quietly. 'Fortunate I'm still here.'

De Vries has one glass of water in front of him. He leans forward, yawns broadly in front of Jessel.

'Sleepless nights, Colonel de Vries? More missing women? And drinking too . . . You're in a bit of a mess . . .'

'You say what you want to say,' De Vries says. 'Then the van will take you.'

'The van will take me and you will never see Dr Bellingham again.'

'I found Ali Jelani.'

Jessel laughs. 'You found Jelani because I told you where to find her. A child could have heard what I said and found Jelani. I hope you haven't taken credit for that.'

De Vries sips the water. 'Is that it?'

'Release me, or Bellingham dies. When she has expired, another woman will be taken. Maybe someone close to you, someone you value enough to make a deal. How far will I have to go?'

'About thirty kilometres to Pollsmoor,' De Vries says blankly. 'From there, I don't know the exact distance to Hell.'

Jessel shakes his head. 'You take me to that place, to Pollsmoor, and Bellingham dies instantly.'

De Vries stares at him through heavy dark eyes, scarcely open. For the first time, he senses a tiny quiver of stress in Jessel's voice, a momentary tension in the corner of his left eye.

'Not my decision,' he says. 'Procedure. The only way it could be stopped would be under extraordinary circumstances.'

'What might those be?'

'A current and revealing interview, in which the senior officer felt that crucial information in an investigation was imminent.'

'What information?'

'You know what information.'

Jessel opens his mouth, hesitates. 'I have no information for you.'

De Vries gets up. Twice Jessel has revealed minute indications that he is no longer in control, that he is beholden to whoever has taken Grace Bellingham. He watches him led away, realizes that he has just bet the life of the hostage on his reading of his prisoner.

Number one Plumbago Lane is surrounded by bleached grass, almost white. The shrubs are, in early summer, autumnal. The hottest afternoon sun blasts the houses in The Glen and those on the slopes of the Twelve Apostles down to Camps Bay. As he walks along the paving stones to the front door, he can feel the heat through the soles of his shoes. He rings once and, after a minute, a second time. Through the closed door, a deep voice says:

'We don't answer the door to strangers. You must make an appointment.'

'Colonel de Vries, Special Crimes. We have authority to speak with Mr Finnemore.'

A hesitation, then: 'I haven't received such authority.'

'His department released information to us and granted us access to Leigh Finnemore.'

The door opens. A broad Afrikaans man stands in the gap.

'Keep your voice down. This property and its inhabitant are subject to a section-eighteen order.'

'I'm aware of that. Let me in, please.'

The man stands firm, the door held by thick, strong fingers on big hands, studies him.

'You're the man who arrested Stephen Jessel, *ja*? He's discredited, hey? You need new authorization from the department head.'

'What's your name?'

'Rolf Viljoen.'

'Mr Viljoen,' De Vries's voice is low now. 'We have a situation where another woman may be at risk. Leigh Finnemore could have been one of the last people to see Stephen Jessel. They knew each other for a long time. I need to talk to him now.'

'I have to follow procedure. Just contact my boss, get the go-ahead and he's all yours.'

De Vries feels his teeth grind, hears the noise in his head. He closes his mouth, aware that his breath must stink.

'How long have you known Finnemore?'

'We rotate section eighteens sometimes. Gives us a new angle, check we're not missing anything. I know Leigh pretty well over the years.'

'You seen any tendency to violence?'

Viljoen shakes his head. De Vries glances at his watch, lets his shoulders fall.

'Rolf, the clock is ticking for me, maybe another hostage too. Give me five minutes now with him – you can be there – then I'll go get the permission.'

Rolf Viljoen's eyes dart from side to side. He frowns deeply. '*Ja*. You can come in.'

De Vries strides past Viljoen through to the kitchen. The back windows are open and he hears running water, steps out through the doors, sees Leigh Finnemore, naked but for a pair of black underpants, showering himself with the hosepipe. He turns to Viljoen.

'There's a level-three water-saving order in place. No hosepipes. Or are your clients exempt?'

'They are not clients and, yes, my department is exempt.'

Viljoen steps forward and reaches down to the tap on the back wall of the house, slowly turns it until the flow ceases.

Finnemore walks towards them, his long pale body freckled and glistening with water. He stands up close to De Vries, smiles broadly at him, smirks.

'Best way to cool off.'

'Safer than swimming . . .'

Finnemore frowns, tilts his head.

De Vries watches the water from his eyelashes, his nose, fall to the ground.

'Dry off. I want to talk to you.'

'Do you want tea?' The same smiling, slightly detached tone.

'No.'

Viljoen passes Finnemore a towel. He rubs his hair hard, making it stick out. He takes off his wet pants, drops them on the paving, walks into the kitchen and pulls on a T-shirt and shorts.

'What do you want to ask Leigh?' Viljoen says.

De Vries waits until Finnemore has sat at the table, then sits opposite him.

'Did you go out last night, Mr Finnemore?'

'No.'

'Not at all?'

'Not at all.'

'I can vouch for that,' Viljoen says. 'At least, between six and ten p.m. I was here.'

'Did you like Stephen Jessel?' He stares at Finnemore, sees almost no change to his blank countenance.

'He was strict with me, but fair. He explained what I had done,

297

what I needed to do, how I should try to make an independent life for myself.'

'Was he ever violent towards you?'

'Never.'

'Did he ever talk to you about violence? Against women, perhaps?'

'Colonel . . .' Viljoen's deep voice obscures Finnemore's denial, but De Vries scrutinizes him, watches the lips form the negative, sees the eyes freeze momentarily. 'I do not think that this is appropriate.'

De Vries nods gently, but his stare does not leave Finnemore. 'When did you last see Stephen?'

Leigh Finnemore's eyes redden.

'I don't understand. I don't know what you want. I liked Stephen and now he is evil. He has hurt women. I'm right, aren't I?' He looks up at Viljoen. 'I don't understand. I don't know what you want.'

'Enough now.' Viljoen puts his arm in front of De Vries, between him and Finnemore. 'I think you must do what we discussed.'

'And I will, Mr Viljoen. But it's a simple question. Just one simple question, for our inquiry. When did Leigh last see Steve Jessel?'

Finnemore sits rigidly. De Vries can see his breathing as his narrow chest rises and falls within the taut, still damp T-shirt. He senses a tension between Finnemore and Viljoen, waits silently. A long time passes before Viljoen says:

'This is why we have rules. You must go.'

De Vries rises, glances at both of them, walks towards the front door.

Viljoen unlocks it, opens it wide.

'You have to be careful with these people, Colonel. They are disturbed, disoriented, delicate.'

'He has a strange affliction indeed,' De Vries says. 'The inability to answer a simple question.'

He turns downhill at the junction, free-wheels the twisted road towards Camps Bay. At the traffic lights, he drifts right, meets the afternoon traffic on the main drag, white sand and cold blue sea beyond palm trees to his left, greasy, frenetic bars, restaurants, cafés and shops to his right. He pulls into a no-waiting zone, displays a parking badge on the dashboard, opens his door. The car horn startles him. He feels pins and needles in the palms of his hands, his throat dry. He closes his eyes, takes a breath, checks his mirror, waits until there is a gap in the traffic, pushes the door open again with his foot and struggles out. He crosses the road to the Indian restaurant, the quietest and coolest venue on the strip, walks deep into the room, into the dark, away from a few late diners on the pavement. He has sat down before a waiter has even approached him.

'Two tall lagers, lamb madras, pilau rice.'

'For two?'

'For me. Make it quick.'

He picks up his cellphone, speed-dials Don February. There is no news of Grace Bellingham, no evidence as to her whereabouts. Stephen Jessel has arrived at Pollsmoor Prison without any contact with the outside world. That will be denied him until further notice. He can hear from Don's voice that he is floundering, that there is nothing to go on, no leads, no clues. He hangs up, stares outside through, from where he sits, merely a wide-screen slit, sees the solid flow of tourists, the taxi-vans, the cars, the blue haze of pollution before the trunks of the palms, a sliver of sandy whiteness and blue water as high as the ceiling.

He looks for staff, waves at a waiter, then sees his beers

approach. He takes the first glass from the waiter's hand, downs half of it. He feels the cold envelop his mouth, his throat, the channel through the middle of him; he senses the tightness in his head ease, the thumping at his temples lessen.

He sits back, wonders about Leigh Finnemore, the alibi provided by Viljoen. The longer he contemplates, the more suspicious he is of Finnemore. He calls Don back.

'All known friends, associates, acquaintances of Stephen Jessel. Has he had contact with Pollsmoor Prison before? Did he visit anyone?' He hangs up, dials Du Toit's cellphone.

'I need authorization on Leigh Finnemore again. I spoke with him, but there's a new guy, Rolf Viljoen. He says we need to speak to his boss.'

'Why do we need to speak to Finnemore?'

'Sir, we do. Trust me. Finnemore knew Jessel better than anyone, probably spent the most time with him. I want to talk to him, maybe bring him in.' He hears nothing. 'Sir?'

'I'll make the call. Stay away from him until we have the permission.'

He hangs up, sits back from the scalding plate that is manhandled in front of him, smells the food arrive. He is almost too charged to eat. Almost.

De Vries spends the afternoon waiting to be brought information. When none materializes, he dozes, his stomach heavy and swollen. Henrik du Toit calls him to his office, tells him that the Section Designation office is prevaricating over providing access to Finnemore. He walks back to his office in a daze, his head subsumed with fear for Grace Bellingham, with guilt, with self-pity. By six p.m., most of the officers have left. Sally Frazer comes to his office to inform him that she needs to go home. He looks at her drawn face, stiff neck, wonders why anyone chooses to do this job. He follows her out, bustles all remaining officers home, suddenly craving solitude. When the squad-room is empty, he stands in the middle, his domain, finds himself emotional and drained, his hands by his sides, his head bowed. He stays there, as if underneath a shower, letting the responsibilities he has mis-carried rain down on him.

'Are you all right? Sir?'

He seems to wake up, sway, steady himself, his hand on an arm clothed in coarse fabric.

'You should sit. Do you need water?'

Don leads him to a chair by one of the workstations. He struggles to open his eyes, feels a plastic cup between his fingers. He lifts it, sips.

'Tired.'

'You have worked too long, sir. You must sleep.'

He looks up, confirms that it is Don February standing over him.

'Don't let Du Toit see me like this.' He holds up a hand dis-missively. 'Been drinking. So hot. Beer just seemed better than water.'

'I will be here for another one hour,' Don tells him. 'Then I must go or there will be big trouble from my wife. She will call you again.'

'We don't want that.'

'We have an invitation to dinner with neighbours she has been . . . What does she call it? Like a gardener?' He smiles broadly. 'Cultivating . . . for two years now. This is a big moment, socially. That is what she tells me.'

'Go,' De Vries says.

'I will stay with you just now.'

Don sits down at his desk, his back to De Vries.

'I have been looking at Leigh Finnemore, as you asked. It is not easy to find his history before the incident when he was ten years old.' Don types efficiently at the keyboard, uncertain if De Vries has heard him. 'I requested to have access to the beta-test site they are establishing with births, deaths, marriages all being recorded, transferred online. I think that they will keep it restricted, but maybe allow the public to access parts of it.' He scrolls through pages. 'I have this just now.' He stops, spins on his chair, sees De Vries bent over the desk, his breathing shallow, wheezing. Don gets up, walks over to him, leans down, checks his breathing. It is steady. De Vries exudes a musty, sour smell of alcohol from his clothes, his skin, his breath. Don recoils, turns back to his desk. A list of results for the search fills the screen. He runs his eye down the records, finds what he wants, clicks on the name.

After dark, De Vries sleepwalks to his office, falls onto the old sofa, which sits against the side wall, grabs a cushion and fashions it into a pillow. His dreams are filled with strident voices summoning him, hands pulling at his clothes, jostling him into a chair before a wide table, pushing him upstairs into the dock, separated by glass from the courtroom. One by one, they face him: his accusers. Failed responsibility, squandered opportunity, betrayed promises. Though weak, he stands tall, his dignity keeping him upright. He accepts each charge, feels the weight on him increase, feels the pressure grow.

He sees each of the victims of Stephen Jessel, each of their agonies, but Grace Bellingham's face is superimposed on each of their bodies: stunted and gnarled, sallow and rough, dusty and swollen, a disfigured face on a body encased in ants, like a bee swarm or a torso dipped in tar.

He wakes sobbing, scrabbling at the sofa, at his clothes. His wrists are raw; he realizes he must have been scratching them in his sleep.

His window is open. He can feel a breeze for the first time in days. Holding onto the chairs, he edges around his desk, sits heavily in his own seat, pulls it towards the window and breathes in deeply. His hair is matted to his forehead; there is blood on his cuffs from his wrists, yet he feels better. As consciousness returns, he feels an energy inside him, low but pervasive, which keeps his head aloft his neck, his brain running once more. He looks around his office, sees a fluorescent yellow square of paper on the floor by the sofa. He stands, feels his head spin, shuffles across his room to retrieve it. It is written in Don February's hand, presumably stuck somewhere, perhaps on himself, before he left for the evening. He squints at it, fumbles back to his chair, turns on the old Anglepoise lamp.

Finnemore mother (Julie/Julia) family name = Stahle
Architect in 1971 of Apostle Lodge = Anke Stahle – famous in Germany in 1980s. Related?
Servers down. Will check later. Don

He stares at it, his mind operating on some form of low-power mode. He stands, gingerly this time, exits his office and crosses the deserted squad-room to the water-cooler. It dispenses cold water to him, and he drinks three plastic cups before taking a fourth back to his office. It is eleven p.m. He has slept for almost four-and-a-half hours. His cellphone rings.

'It is Don.'

'Sorry, Don. Was out of it. This note . . .'

'I am calling to tell you . . . I left the dinner for a few minutes . . . because the internet was down in the office. Anke Stahle, who designed Apostle Lodge, lived there with her family for eight years. That is how her daughter, Julie, met her future husband, who lived at the other end of the street, across Camps Bay Road, at number one Plumbago Lane.'

'What?'

'Anke Stahle gave her daughter Apostle Lodge, maybe sold it to her, around the time she got married. Leigh Finnemore grew up in that house. That is where he killed his sister.'

De Vries's mind races. 'Why didn't we know?'

'Jessel must have removed it from the files and did not tell us.'

'Because he was protecting Finnemore.'

'Maybe, yes.'

'But it implicates him. That's where Jessel took Bethany Miles . . .' He feels a sudden stabbing pain in his chest, as if a knife is being driven into him. He gasps. 'I have to go.' He stabs at his phone, sees it drop onto the desk, spin. He doubles over in his chair, fighting for breath. He feels the pain dissipate, a fever run up through his ankles, to his groin, his stomach, his head. Dizziness envelops him, drenches him in sweat, leaves him. He looks up carefully, reaches for his water, sips, then gulps it down. Suddenly he knows . . . thinks he knows. He stumbles to his feet, snatches at his keys, half falls from his office.

At the top of Kloof Nek Road, he looks in his rear-view mirror, sees the city illuminated behind him, the moon on the horizon. As he crosses over the pass and drives down the other side, he feels a portentous shadow fall over him. The moon disappears from sight as he approaches the turning to Plumbago Lane. On the steep downhill road, he brakes, realizing that he is travelling too fast. He almost overshoots the left turn, his tyres screeching on the still-hot tarmac. He straightens his car, drops almost to a crawl, free-wheels towards the end of the street.

Beyond the gaping fall down to the garage area, Apostle Lodge is dark. The windows reflect only dull pinpricks of light from neighbouring houses, slivers of headlights from cars as they take the sharp turn right above them on Camps Bay Road. The bird cowl is still, silhouetted black against the indigo sky. He gets out of the car; crickets whine, cicadas chirp. He loves these noises but, here, they bear down on him. He cannot hear the cars on the road, or the music he suspects is drifting uphill from the Camps Bay strip. Then, to his left, up against the face of the Mountain, he hears the elongated, anguished cry of a bird of prey. It stirs him from his stupor.

He grabs the torch from the glove compartment, finds that it works, puts on the pair of winter gloves which are part of his kit kept in the boot. He approaches the raised walkway, traverses it gingerly, tacking from railing to railing, allowing the beam of the torch to light his way. The overhanging trees and sunken position of the house make it very dark, but also slightly cooler. It is quiet too: he is aware only of his own strained breathing. Ahead of him, police tape dangles from one side of the railing. He steps over it, tests the front door, finds it locked and unyielding. He moves along to the left of the building, around to the side door. Here, the insect noise is amplified, coming from the overgrown, dried-out gorge behind him. He checks both in and under the flowerpot where the keys had been left for Jessel to bring in Bethany Miles, but they have gone, correctly collected and sealed in evidence. Moving on to the back garden, he leans over a window and peers in as he did before. He braces himself for the shock of someone knocking on the window from inside but, this time, the house remains silent. He steps back, walks carefully down the crispy lawn until he is thirty metres from the house, looks back up. At the top of the Mountain, the cable-car station is dark, the light breeze smells of woodsmoke, perhaps from mountain fires a hundred kilometres away, the crickets in the dry riverbed to his right fill his ears with a cacophony of alien sound.

From the dying flowerbed, he pulls out a piece of rock the size of a tennis ball, stretches his fingers inside the gloves, assesses his strength, braces himself and marches up to the house. He angles his head away, swings at the window with the rock in his hand. The glass cracks, but holds. He turns again, and this time the impact bursts a hole in the thick dark pane. He pulls at the glass, levering it out of its frame, dropping the triangles onto the path outside. When he has cleared the base of the window, he leans in, scanning the perimeter of the full-width room with his torch, finds it empty. He hauls his leg over the frame, raises the other and jumps down. Apart from the chrome floor lamp, the furniture has been taken away. There are two dark patches of blood from where the chaise longue had stood, but the ants are gone. There are flies, but he cannot hear their buzzing over the interference of the night-time insects outside.

The house feels strange to him again, just as it did the night they found Bethany Miles, but he does not attempt to switch on the flickering fluorescent lights. It is cool, yet his face burns. He checks the back door from the inside, finds the anteroom door locked, with no key apparent. He retraces his steps to the entry corridor, occasionally startled by his own shadow distorted against the textured concrete walls. He climbs the stairs to the bedrooms, finds each empty, the air stale and old. In one of the bathrooms, he idly shines his torch into the toilet bowl and finds larvae hatching in water stained red with the blood of some creature brought to the birth site to provide food.

He turns back, descends the stairs, aware that he is clutching the banister rail to steady himself. He feels weak, propelled only by adrenalin and the sudden conviction he had felt back at his office when he had been overcome by the pain and emerged with new insight.

The front door is locked also but he turns the two heavy handles and hears the locks snap open. He leaves the door unlocked, turns right onto the staircase down to the garage. The steps are bare concrete and this part of the house is the coolest. At the bottom, he reaches the metal door that he believes opens out into the garage. He tries to slide the two heavy bolts, which lock the door from the inside, but they do not move. He puts the torch down by his feet, shining at the base of the door, leans against it, tries the bolt again. This time the bar shifts across. He pauses; listens. He repeats the process with the upper bolt. This time, he hears it. He grabs the handle and twists. It moves, but the door is locked also by a key. He puts his ear to the door. When he hears nothing, he thumps the metal, calls out. It is so faint that he might only be imagining it, but he believes that he hears a cry.

There is nothing else on the stairs, no sign of the key. He turns. Above him, he sees a shadowy beam of light pass in front of the door to the stairs. The shock chokes him. His hands, already sweating inside the gloves, seem weak, scarcely able to hold the torch. He extinguishes the beam, freezes, tries to control his frightened, uneven breathing. In the silence he hears not so much footsteps, for, on the concrete floor, there are none but the sounds of human movement. The door to the stairs moves slowly, as if held firmly by a hand. In the utter blackness, he slowly reaches for his weapon, realizes that, in gloves, he will be unable to hold it: his finger will not fit the trigger cage. He moderates his breath, slides the glove from his right hand, lets it fall, almost silently, to the floor. Above him, the door has been left ajar, the light, which he believes is from another torch, seems more distant, though still present.

He takes the first step upwards, feels the weakness in his legs, his energy dissipated by the fear that holds him in its vice. Here, there is no banister rail, no support. He holds his torch in his left hand, though he thinks he will be unable to illuminate it, his weapon in his bare right hand. He leans against the wall in the dark, pushing himself, hand on knee, up each individual hurdle. As he reaches the top, the light through the door intensifies. He senses rather than hears someone approach. The torch slips from his grasp, lands on the concrete with a metallic crack. He pushes his weight against the wall, steadies himself, now with both hands on his weapon, releases the safety.

The door above him opens. His voice box produces no warning, but for a strangled groan, his mouth gaping. The torch beam blinds him. He catches only the silhouette of the heavy figure before the door is slammed. He hears the lock turning. He launches himself up the final steps, beats on the wooden door, shouts, at first hoarsely, then more clearly.

'Open the door. It's De Vries. Colonel de Vries, SAPS.'

He bangs on the door again, listens, watches for the light in the sliver of opening beneath the plane of the door. Suddenly he sees the torch beam, brilliant and glaring on the floor under the door. The voice, loud and coarse, startles him.

'Who are you?'

'Colonel Vaughn de Vries. Open up.'

'You're armed?'

'Open the fucking door! Who is this?'

'Marten Cloete.'

'Open it!'

The lock is fumbled, the door swings open. De Vries does not lower his weapon, but stumbles over the threshold, pressing Cloete back down the corridor towards the front door.

'Drop the bat. Drop it.'

Cloete looks down at the baseball bat in his left hand, seems confused, lets it fall. It clatters on the hard floor.

'What are you doing here?' De Vries can hear the fear in his own voice.

'The window. I heard someone breaking the window round the back. Was it you?'

De Vries nods. '*Ja*. Why are you inside? Why didn't you call the cops?'

Cloete shrugs. 'I live next door. I keep an eye on things.'

'How did you get in?'

With his chin, Cloete points back inside the living area. 'Through the window.'

De Vries studies him. He scarcely trusts himself right now, but he recognizes a simple candour in the man, believes his story, believes his innocence.

'I need your help.'

'Sure.' Cloete lowers his hands.

'You have a crowbar? Something we can open a metal door with?'

'Why do you want—'

'Do you have it? Can you help? I'm not going to tell you why. Can you help?'

Cloete nods. '*Ja*. You want me to go get—'

'Yes. The front door is open. Go now.'

Cloete turns, trots the length of the hallway to the front door, lets himself out.

De Vries breathes fully for the first time in minutes, oxygen flooding his lungs. He wipes his face with his sleeve, fumbles his cellphone from his trouser pocket. Wet, shaking fingers scroll down the contact list. He rejects Don February, who lives twelve, fifteen kilometres away. He calls Ben Thwala, hears a sleepy voice trying to sound awake, alert.

'The keys to Apostle Lodge. Where are they?'

'Evidence, at HQ, sir.'

309

'I need them. All of them. Sorry to wake you, but I need them now. I may have found Bellingham.'

'You are there?'

'Yes. Now.'

'I can take my bike. ETA HQ maybe fifteen minutes, you in twenty-five.'

'Good. Be careful. All the keys. The garage remote. Everything.'

He hangs up.

He hears Cloete on the walkway, a grinding against the metal railing.

'Tony Vermeulen is out there now, watching me.'

'Forget him. Bring that down here.'

He flicks the switch at the top of the stairs, but no light comes on. He descends the staircase feeling his muscles burn, retrieves his torch, lights the door. When they are at the bottom, he holds up his hand.

'Wait.'

He presses his ear against the door once more but, with both of them breathing heavily, he cannot hear anything.

He reaches for the crowbar, realizes that Cloete probably has more strength than him, indicates the lock.

'Don't think it'll work, but try. I may have the key coming, I don't know.'

'You think there's someone in there?'

'Ja.'

'Is this the garage?'

'Ja. The other side.'

'Can you not open the garage?'

'No. Maybe. I don't know. Try the lock, Marten. Do it.'

He shines the torch at the lock, watches the big man try to insert the claw of the crowbar, sees that there is nowhere for it to find purchase. After a few moments, Cloete shakes his head.

'We tried. You need the key, man.'

De Vries gestures for him to go back up. He wants to call out, call to Grace Bellingham. His doubt stops him. He climbs the stairs once more.

'Go outside. We'll try the garage door. You think there's an override?'

He indicates that Cloete should take the lead, out of the front door, across the walkway, onto the street. Ahead of him, he sees Tony Vermeulen looking down at them.

'Get back in your house.'

'What's happening?'

'Get back in your house, sir. That's an order.'

The issuing of instruction calms him: the familiar reassures. He watches the man turn, amble slowly back, turning to study them. De Vries turns, bends his knees, begins to descend the steep track, leaning back into the gradient. At the bottom of the slope, in the parking area, he shines his torch around the heavy ridged-metal shutter to the garage. There is no sign of a handle or wheel. He tries to lever the door up, but it is locked down firmly. He pounds on the door with his fists, puts his ear to it, hears nothing.

'SAPS. Is anybody there?'

He hears that his voice lacks conviction. The call is half-hearted. He listens again, then stands straight, almost backs into Cloete. 'Okay, Marten, thanks for your help. You can go back home now.'

'No, it's fine, man. I can stay.'

He looks at Cloete, fears another pointless, stubborn verbal battle.

'We'll go up top and wait for my officer. You can't enter the house with us. May be a crime scene – you'll contaminate it.'

They clamber back up the gradient. De Vries walks as far as Cloete's low front wall, sits, pulls out his cigarettes.

'Were you here when the German family lived here, the previous owners?'

'*Ja*. They arrived thinking they had found Paradise, but it didn't last for them.'

'Why?'

'The wife hated the house. Said it felt haunted. There's some kind of protection on it. They couldn't change it. Spent a fortune on it and then it didn't feel like theirs, you know? I don't like it, man, I tell you, living next to it all this time. Something not right there.'

'And before the German family?'

'It was empty a long time. When we moved here, there was no one there.'

'You know about its history?'

Cloete shrugs. 'No.'

De Vries checks himself, aware that he might be about to break the confidentiality of the section-eighteen order regarding Leigh Finnemore.

'Architect was famous. German. Made a name for herself.'

Cloete seems uninterested. De Vries angles his body away from him, draws deeply on his cigarette. When he exhales, the smoke stays in front of him, unmoving. Under his open collar, he is sweating. His clothes adhere to him. His heart beats fast in his ribcage; he is aware of every pulsation. He takes a deep breath, wonders whether, when he listened at the inner door, he really did hear a cry, a moan.

Time passes slowly. Cloete stays silent. Tony Vermeulen appears at his porch sporadically, staring at them. A few other lights illuminate in other houses; curtains move; shutters inch open.

He hears the powerful motorbike decelerating down Camps Bay Drive, brake, turn into the street. Ben Thwala jumps off, retrieves packages from the sleek, glossy box at the back.

'Sorry to disturb your night, Ben.'

Thwala looks surprised at the use of his first name, follows De

Vries down the slope to the parking area, rips open the package, which contains the remote control, depresses the button. The door rises lazily, emitting the ear-splitting metallic screech. By the time it locks into place on the ceiling of the large garage, De Vries has scanned the empty room, heart sinking, doubting himself. He feels the energy inside him dissipate.

'I don't understand. I heard something through that door.'

He moves inside, flicks the light switch, but nothing happens, approaches the metal door at the back. It, too, is bolted top and bottom.

'There's no key for here?'

'I tried during the search. Tried every key here. None of them fitted. Back of the door is at the bottom of the stairs inside.'

De Vries steps away, frowns. He studies the ceiling of the garage, paces back to the door.

'Wait here a minute. Double-check the keys.'

He trudges back up the driveway, passes Marten Cloete, who is looking down on them silently, crosses the walkway and pauses at the front door. He leans over the railing, assessing the relative position of the garage door to the front door, counts the paces back to the internal staircase, descends. It strikes him then that the bolts in the garage seem redundant. You might have bolts on the inside to prevent anybody accessing the house from the garage – although the lock seems to do a convincing job already – but why would you have them in the garage? The paces from the front door to the stairs, minus the distance he travels as he descends, do not match the depth of the garage. He bangs again on the door with his fists, presses his ear against metal. In the utter silence of the house, in the dim stairwell, he is certain he hears a stifled cry, a muffled, high-pitched moan.

He trots up the stairs, his pelvis aching, legs weak, back outside. 'Give me your crowbar.'

Cloete hands it to him, wanders away. In the garage, Thwala has each set of keys laid out on the floor, testing them in turn.

'You heard me bang on the door?'

Thwala says: '*Ja*. In the distance. You were banging this door?'

'I don't think so. I think there's a space in there. This door isn't the back of the one inside. It's another door. There's a room in there, and I heard noises . . . The bolts: they don't make sense unless you want to make sure that both these doors can't be opened from the inside.' He hands Thwala the crowbar. 'We tried this inside. Try it here.' He points at the door. 'There's a ridge. You might be able to get it in.'

Ben Thwala struggles to find purchase, finds that it grips halfway up the side of the door, but the structure does not move.

'Try this.'

They turn, find Marten Cloete standing at the entrance to the garage with a sledgehammer.

'You can hit it with this. I brought metal-cutters too.'

De Vries walks over to him, receives the tools.

'Thanks. But you have to go back up. It's the rules. Wait at the top.'

Cloete turns reluctantly, trudges back up the slope. De Vries hands Thwala the sledgehammer, drops the metal-cutters, takes hold of the crowbar, still jammed in the frame.

'Just make sure you hit it and not me.'

Thwala lines it up, hits the crowbar. De Vries's fists jump off the handle. He shakes them. The crowbar stays in position. Thwala swings at it, hits full-on. The door buckles and swells slightly around the lock. Thwala hits it a further four times before the door cracks open, swings back hard on itself, hits the back wall of the garage.

De Vries retrieves the illuminated torch from the floor, points it into the dark gap ahead. He lights up perhaps four metres of empty space, enters, shines the beam to his right, onto a wooden door. He turns the handle, finds it locked.

'Get this open.'

Thwala returns with the crowbar. He inserts it into the wooden frame, jerks at it a couple of times until the wood splinters, hardware drops to the floor, the door opens. De Vries pulls it back, shines the torch into the area.

Ahead is a blank breeze-block wall. To the right, he sees Grace Bellingham.

'Jesus.'

He steps over to her, seeing, but blind to, her nakedness, withdraws the gag stuffed into her mouth, touches her face. She jumps, whimpers.

'Bring those cutters.'

He takes off his shirt, ties it around her torso. He looks up at the manacles around her wrists, holding her arms above her head. He looks down at her bound ankles. His heart is racing.

Ben Thwala comes in, focuses on the manacles, lines up the metal-cutters in the beam shone by De Vries.

'Be careful of her wrists.'

Thwala guides the jaws around the metal, checks that they will not cut into her flesh, edges his hands down to the furthest points of the arms, strains to pull them towards each other. The metal snaps. Grace Bellingham screams.

'You're all right. We'll have you out of here.' He stares into her eyes, both still in their sockets, sees blankness, as if she has shut herself down against the agony and terror.

Thwala moves to the other side, checks the position before breaking open the manacle. Bellingham's arms fall. She breaks at the waist, slumps into De Vries's arms. He holds her there, the torch squeezed downwards to light her ankles. The room is pitch black but for the partially obscured torch beam. It is cool, but smells of urine and concrete dust. He thinks, Blood, perhaps vermin. He hears the metal snap on the first, then the second ankle binding. His head throbs, mind spinning. When she is free, he takes her weight, waits for Thwala, and begins to half lift, half drag her from the tiny room, through the metal door, into the garage. De Vries takes back his shirt and ties it around her waist; Thwala pulls off his T-shirt and they manhandle it over her head, over her body. They take her up again, begin to walk outside, slowly climb the incline. As they reach the top, he sees a group of residents watching them from the street.

'Get back. I need sheets, blankets, water.'

They reach road level, stumble towards De Vries's car. He passes her to Thwala, unlocks the vehicle, opens the back door. They gently fit her into the seat. She leans backwards, panting now, but she does not keel over, her palms on the seat either side of her, like push-bike stabilizers.

'Water. Bring some cold water.'

The people stand away from them. De Vries leans against the side of his car, energy exhausted, hears Ben Thwala calling for an ambulance, for back-up. Water and a rug arrive, are left. De Vries hands her the big glass of water, holds it underneath for her as she shakily brings it to her lips, begins to drink.

When she has finished and lowers the glass, she opens her eyes, straining for each breath.

'Did he make you take anything? Inject anything? Grace, this is important.'

She shakes her head, mouths: 'No.'

'Did you see him?'

'No.' She forms the word, it struggles from her. 'He was strong.'

He reaches for her hand. She pulls it away. He asks:

'When did he take you?'

'Leaving you last night. Hit from behind.'

He kneels on the ground, leans inside the car. 'You're safe.'

'No.' She turns her head to face him, her eyes struggling to focus, each word separate, certain: 'I will never be safe.'

She turns away, stares ahead. He watches her tears fall, from two clenched eyes, her face distorted and convulsed with fear, with horror, with relief.

PART 4

'It's not open to debate.'

Henrik du Toit stands by De Vries's bed, glances out of the window across the road to the yellow parkland.

'Pretoria have sent someone in.'

'To close it down.'

'To handle the press, more than anything. They'll second our people, play it by the book, run through the motions and, if it falls in their lap, they'll catch him.'

'Is that good enough?'

Du Toit looks down at De Vries.

'It is if they say so, and they do. So let it go.'

'Let it go? I hate that hippie shit.'

Du Toit sits by the raised bed, picks at the grapes on De Vries's bedside table.

'Two weeks, Vaughn. You're exhausted, dehydrated, stressed. You don't even know yet if it's more serious. You leave here, sit at home, rest. After that you're back here for more tests on your heart, and only when the consultant gives me the all-clear do you come back. Be clear: that is how it's going to happen.'

'Someone, probably Leigh Finnemore, took Grace Bellingham and would have killed her. If it is him – whoever it is – they'll do it again.'

321

Du Toit holds up his hands. 'Calm down. Everyone on your team understands that. They'll be working with the officers from Pretoria. Forensics are all over that Apostle Lodge.'

'Finnemore. Search Finnemore's house. Someone has the key to those metal doors, to that cellar. Find them in his house and you have him. He lived there. It's his old house. That's why Jessel used it for Bethany Miles, why he used it for Grace . . .'

'He didn't use it. Someone else did.'

De Vries snorts. 'Believe me. He used it.'

'Warrant February has already suggested searching for those keys. We got clearance yesterday and the teams will take the place apart. You have to relax.'

De Vries grimaces as he tries to get more upright in the bed. 'Hard to relax when you're angry.'

'So stop being angry. It must wear you down.'

'Stop? Henrik, when I left the army, I thought about South Africa and all that was wrong with it and it made me angry, and I thought it's no use just being angry, I have to do something. That's why I joined the police. That's what keeps me doing what I do. Sometimes maybe it's right to be angry.'

'You saved two women's lives.'

'Two women.' He sounds exasperated. 'You talk about winning. You are surrounded by a million stinging ants and you tread on a few. Is that winning? That's what my life is, standing up for people after it's too late, making no difference.'

'It's something. Try to be more positive. Be nicer to people.'

'I don't like people.'

Du Toit sighs. 'Perhaps there's a course for it.'

'You already sent me to Interpersonal Dispute Resolution.'
'Did I?'

'I went twice, got sick of their shit and told them to fuck off.'

Du Toit smiles, stands. 'You're obviously feeling better. Grace

Bellingham was discharged this morning. Did they tell you?' De Vries shakes his head. 'She's leaving Cape Town, maybe the country. Didn't say when or where, but you can't blame her.'

'I blame myself.'

Du Toit walks to the door. 'I'll be checking on you, so don't leave your house. I may call in to see you if there are developments.'

'When do I get out of here?'

'The doctor said soon. Be patient. It's for your own good.'

'Why is it when people say that it's always because something bad is about to happen?'

The newspapers are dominated by the drought, the heat, and the fires that are sweeping across the Overberg, down onto the Cape Flats, towards Cape Town. The Mountain has been burning too, helicopters towing huge rubber sacks of water flying in and out of the Newlands Forest station.

By the fourth day at home, Christmas Eve, he is bored and frustrated. Henrik du Toit visits, bringing a hamper of healthy food with him; even the Christmas pudding is devoid of alcohol. De Vries tops up his glass with one hand, while pushing the empty bottle by his chair under it.

'Are you supposed to be drinking?'

'I think they said one bottle of good white wine per day.'

'A glass, perhaps . . .'

He shrugs. 'A glass, a bottle . . .'

'I don't know how you operate at all with what you drink.'

'It's *how* I operate, Henrik. It's fuel.'

'It's killing you.'

'Only a little faster than nature.'

'Someone been keeping you updated?'

'Don February's called me a couple of times. Remarkably, I'm actually doing what you told me.'

'If I believed you,' Du Toit says, '*that* would be remarkable.'

De Vries turns to him, attentive, smiling. 'Please tell me, sir, how is Pretoria's investigation progressing?'

Du Toit rolls his eyes. 'They spent three full days in Finnemore's house. No keys, no incriminating evidence whatsoever. They looked at his computer, searched every cupboard, took down panelling, partially dismantled the kitchen. Nothing. Apparently Finnemore has been placed in care over Christmas. He's depressed and suicidal.'

'I doubt that.'

'No matter what you think of him, he's clear for now. I spoke to the psychiatrist assigned to him. She says it's a classic reaction to the betrayal of trust by Stephen Jessel.'

'Textbook.'

'What?' Du Toit frowns.

'Textbook. Like the books on his shelves.'

'I know you don't think Leigh Finnemore is a victim, but he's shown no sign of causing anyone harm for the last twenty years. Instead, he's just a naive, repressed young man.'

De Vries stretches out on the sofa, his arms behind his head. 'That's what he wants us to believe.'

Du Toit shakes his head. 'Why?'

'Why? Because he was in and out of Valkenburg Mental Hospital at a time when we know, for a fact, that there were dangerous people there supposedly treating disturbed patients, and he associated with Stephen Jessel for twenty years. You think one killer doesn't recognize another?'

'Stephen Jessel deceived a lot people. I imagine Leigh Finnemore wasn't much of a challenge.'

De Vries smiles sourly. 'You always think the best of people,

Henrik. Isn't that very disappointing? Jessel said to me – out loud in interview – he went to that department, made himself a case officer because he wanted to meet disturbed people. People like him. He wanted to meet the child killers, the parent murderers, the sadists and perverts. And Finnemore is one of them, I'm telling you.'

'You can tell me all you like. There's no evidence. Believe me, your team tried.'

'Rolf Viljoen.'

'What about him?'

'You meet him?'

'No. Warrant February interviewed him, but he checks out, seems pretty normal.'

'I'll tell you what I've told Don. Anybody who comes into contact with Finnemore, watch them.'

'You've no business telling Warrant February anything. You're not involved . . .' He turns to De Vries. 'What are you doing tomorrow?'

'Tomorrow?'

'Christmas Day.'

'Is it?' He laughs without smiling, stares past Du Toit into his bleached front garden. 'Maybe talk with my daughters. Otherwise, it's always been just another day.'

'You want to come to us? We're staying in town because, with Pretoria here, I can't go anywhere.'

'No . . .Thanks . . . Alone . . . That's what I like.'

On Boxing Day, he wakes to hear a drill in the house next door. He has no idea what time it is, but he resents the disturbance. He swings out of bed, peers from the window towards the building site next to him. He can see nothing but a tiny stream of dust escaping from the narrow opening in the sliding doors. He watches the dust form a trail in the air, drifting towards him. He coughs.

At noon, Don February arrives. The pepper trees in the front garden are yellowing, their branches heavy with dusty pink fruit. The bougainvillaea flowers are brown and falling, the garden yellow, russet, unattended, coated with a fine layer of snowy dust. He finds De Vries sitting on his front stoep, a wine bottle in a Pyrex bowl of ice at his side, a book on his lap.

'I thought you might want some company,' he says. 'Just for an hour. I am on a short leash. My wife's family are staying.'

'You glad to escape?'

'A little, maybe.'

'Wine?'

'No, thank you.' Don sits on a wicker chair at right angles to him. 'I want to ask you something.'

De Vries rubs his eyes, folds over the page early in the book, places it on the tiled floor under his chair.

'First time I've been asked anything for a week. As long as it's not how I am. That's a *kak* question.'

'You remember my friend from university, Mike Solarin?'

'Yeah, the Nigerian guy . . .'

'Half Nigerian, yes. He was promoted and moved to the Major Crimes Unit out of Pretoria. He was appointed to the investigation into the bomb in Long Street.'

'The al-Qaeda attack?'

'Yes, and no. Mike and a colleague of his in Forensics found evidence that does not match that conclusion.'

'They report it?'

'That is what I am telling you. They were very careful. They took it to an officer who they felt they could trust. They said that when they told him, he was afraid, instructed them not to

326

continue. To go bury the evidence, get on with their other work. They were shocked, but they did as he said.'

'Probably wise, up there in Pretoria.'

'I have talked about you with Mike before. What I am here asking you, sir, is, will you meet with him?'

De Vries takes a deep breath. 'What good would that do?'

'I do not know, but I think that you might have similar ideas . . . and you did say that you were very bored.'

De Vries smiles. Don has developed a habit of retaining everything he hears and using the same words against witnesses and suspects, a technique people find discomfiting.

'Where is he?'

'In Pretoria. He says that he will fly down tomorrow if you agree.'

'I hate this time of year. You're supposed to have been happy and you realize that you haven't been and now you have to prepare to be happy again for New Year and this time you know you won't be – and when that's over, you're back at work, poorer and sadder and no wiser.' He looks at Don, who sits calmly, seemingly oblivious to his diatribe. 'Okay, Don. Why not? Tell him yes.'

Even before De Vries knocks on the door, he discerns that the apartment is empty. Each year that passes, he realizes that he knows more of what he will see behind a closed door. He waits, listens. Then he retraces his steps to the lift. When the doors open, the caretaker puts his hand over them to stop them closing.

'I saw you come in. She left last week.' He looks inquisitively at De Vries's unyielding face. 'You wanted Dr Bellingham?'

'Did she say where she was going?'

He shakes his head. 'Her belongings were taken by a storage company. The yellow and blue lorries.'

'I'm going down.'

'Get in. I only came up because I recognized you.' He stands away from the door, punches the button for the ground floor, lets De Vries step inside. The lift descends silently. The caretaker waits for De Vries to exit first.

'Hang on.' The caretaker pulls an envelope from his pocket and, without leaving the car, he stretches to hand it over. The doors close.

De Vries examines the envelope, his name and rank written in block capitals. The envelope has, he believes, been opened and resealed. He rips it open and withdraws a half-sheet of paper, handwritten.

You could have made a different decision.
You could have spared me.
I scratched his head. I guarded my hand. These are for you.
I won't testify. I won't come back. But, you will know.

Grace

He frowns, fumbles the inside of the crumpled paper. A small plastic packet falls to the ground. He picks it up, holds it to the light. It contains two hairs, a tiny quantity of dust, perhaps skin. He recalls Grace Bellingham in the back of his car, sitting with her hands on the seat, fingers held above the velour, refusing to hold his hand. He uncrumples the envelope, replaces the packet, stuffs it into his pocket, walks away. An old wound aches.

'You shouldn't believe everything you hear about me.'

'I don't, sir.'

De Vries smiles sourly. 'It's much worse.'

Mike Solarin laughs. His chuckle echoes from the cool tiled floor of the stoep. 'Maybe that's why I'm here.'

'Why are you here, Lieutenant?'

The late-afternoon sun burns them even through the branches of the bougainvillaea. The dappled light forces Solarin to keep on his dark glasses against the blinding pinprick beams. De Vries squints, slumps or rises in his chair to keep them from his face.

'What has Don February told you?'

'What does that matter?' De Vries says. 'You tell me.'

'He says I can trust you.'

'You can only trust me if I trust you. I don't know that yet.'

Solarin raises the can of lager.

'Thanks for this.'

De Vries nods, takes a sip of red wine.

'All right, kept short. Ask what you want later. Hawks, Terrorism Squad, media, the people: we are all told the Long Street bomb was the work of two disenchanted former al-Mourabitoun members, Iraqis. Suicide mission. The investigation is subdivided, each element kept separate from the next. Regular teams are suddenly replaced by new people. Only those at the very top get to see the full picture. But there's a problem. The timing and placement of the explosion seem suboptimal. One forensic team finds evidence of a receiver-detonator, another that the explosive is old South African Army ordnance, yet another that there was residue from grapes, a variety almost unique to a particular area between Oudtshoorn – where the lorry was stolen – and Cape Town. I'm sent there, then withdrawn before reaching it, just two hours after the grapes evidence is submitted. The officer I'm put with is in contact with our CO – I think tipping him off about our location. Then I see him again. He's either following me or overseeing a demonstration, which turns violent, outside the Jumu'a Mosque a few days later. I'm silenced by my CO, Colonel Brent Juiles. Then another old friend, a man from the time of the Struggle, I consider a mentor of mine: he basically threatens me to back off. Back in Pretoria, I'm put in charge of some data-retrieval shit, an office manager's job, but many weeks' work . . .'

He trails off, wonders whether, even with all his doubts spoken aloud, he is imagining something which is not there. He looks up at De Vries.

'Is that it, Lieutenant?'

'It?'

'*Ja*. Is that your case?'

Solarin feels a shiver of doubt, of fear, course down his back. He says quietly: 'Something is not right.'

De Vries leans forward, pours himself another full glass, replaces the bottle carefully on the tiled floor beneath the table, drinks slowly.

'Take off your glasses.'

'Sir?'

'Take off your glasses, Lieutenant.' Solarin pulls them away from his face, folds their arms, lays them on the table. 'Now, be clear with me. You have travelled, from Pretoria, to tell me this collection of almost random information, which, according to you, amounts to what? Suspicion?'

'Any one of them,' Solarin says. 'Any one alone would be reason to check the conclusion of the investigation, due diligence. Together, they pose too many unanswered questions for me to be able to ignore.' He sits forward, his voice rising, counting off his statements on his fingers. 'No one I know has seen evidence of these so-called al-Qaeda men; no one has acknowledged the detonating device; no one has identified where these men obtained their explosives and, if they did, who might then be working with them. Nothing is explained.'

De Vries is watching him, seemingly relaxed, cradling his wine glass on top of his stomach.

'So?'

'So,' Solarin says forcefully, 'so this could be anything. This could be a cover-up from the very top. When I am involved in a case, I do not finish until I am satisfied. I do not stop until I believe I have uncovered the truth. I do not care – because I believe that we don't have the luxury of caring – what happens to me, to my career. I want to do my job.' De Vries laughs. 'What? You think this is funny? You think I came here all this way for you to laugh at me?' De Vries laughs again. Solarin stands up. 'What?'

'Lieutenant, you are doomed to suffer a lonely career under intense scrutiny, mistrust, discrimination, mistreatment and danger to you and those around you.'

'You think I am wrong? You think I am some conspiracy theorist who belongs not in the SAPS but writing some crazy online blog read by no one? Yes? You will not help me?'

De Vries puts his glass on the table, gestures for Solarin to sit, leans towards him, his voice low and deliberate.

'I think you are right. I think you should be in the SAPS and, yes, I will definitely help you.'

The traffic is heavy only as far as the turn onto the N2, then increasingly lighter going against the earliest commuters, past the airport towards Somerset West and Sir Lowry's Pass, across the Overberg, out along the south coast of South Africa. De Vries sits back in the reclined seat, his eyes closed. When he is awake, he is aware of the velocity of the vehicle, the kilometres passing, the steady hum of a sophisticated modern car running at 120 k.p.h. or more.

When they pull into a garage, he gets out to stretch, walk off his fatigue, buy cool drinks, two hard-boiled eggs, two hot pies from the kiosk. Solarin pulls the car into some shaded parking, and they eat and drink with the doors open.

'Sorry. I don't sleep so well at night. Other times, no problem. Just not at night.'

'It's fine.'

'You want me to drive now?'

'Up to you. It's an easy car. You thought about what we will do?'

'I'm waiting for a call from a colleague of mine. He's going to find out what he can about the guys who cover Wingerdedorp. It'll be someone from Calitzdorp, but we won't get involved there.'

'Seems like less a town and more a main street with a bar, a shop and a few houses. Otherwise it's just the farms and vineyards.'

'But we don't know that it's right, what we're looking for?'

'No, but it is where almost all the Souzão vines in South Africa are planted. That makes it a strong favourite.'

De Vries nods. 'Let's keep going.'

They pass Mossel Bay, then the N2 becomes the Garden Route, travelling through the thin layer of lush and fertile ground between the mountain ranges and the Indian Ocean. The vistas broaden: the sky expands to fill their entire field of vision. The coastline comes into view, kilometre after kilometre of white sand lapped by light blue water, narrow lines of surf and turquoise swells waving gently landwards. The cabin is cool and quiet. De Vries admires Solarin's ability to sit with him in silence.

By noon, they have reached George. They stop again for petrol and a break, swap seats, and set off again for Oudtshoorn, aware from the digital readout of the temperature rising just short of forty degrees centigrade. Inland, the road is lined by endless fields of yellowing grass within wire fences, containing the country's greatest concentration of ostriches. The birds stand, bewildered, beneath rows of eucalyptus trees, looking out over their plateaus of dying grassland.

They drive through Oudtshoorn without stopping, turn onto the R62, the end of the route Solarin never got to travel on his previous expedition. They both understand that this is the way the stolen lorry will have travelled – if they are correct – on its way to Calitzdorp, then off the main road along dust tracks to Wingerdedorp. There are few places where it could have been witnessed other than by the oncoming traffic, and for them the twisting, scenic road would have been distraction enough.

Calitzdorp is little more than fifty kilometres from Oudtshoorn. The frequency of farm stalls and country cafés increases as they near the bustling country town, the proud sign boasting that it is the 'Port Capital of South Africa'. On the main street, two large coaches disgorge tourists to browse the quaint cafés, shops and copper-spired, verdigris-steepled Dutch Reformed Church.

'You been here before?'

De Vries laughs. '*Ja*. Ex-wife and I drove the R62 with our daughters, all the way. They were five and six, something like that. Children, winding roads, long journey. Both sick in the car. We spent the night here. You?'

'Never got that far.'

De Vries accelerates.

'Let's find out what they didn't want you to see . . .'

After detours, they find the road out to Wingerdedorp. Within half a kilometre, the tarmac runs out and the cabin is filled with the rattle of spitting grit from the dusty country tracks hitting the underside of the car. Behind them, a slow wake of dust drifts across the fields and an occasional vineyard, settles on the parched ochre ground. The road turns back on itself, runs parallel to the mountains in the distance, then turns towards them. Their way is now bordered on both sides by vineyards, lines of bright green amid broad swathes of deep red soil, diminishing into a simmering, shimmering heat haze.

Wingerdedorp is no more than a collection of buildings either side of the gravel road, ending in a nicely proportioned Cape Dutch house, which, before the hamlet was established, would have been a farmhouse. There are, on either side of the road, narrow tracks leading to discreetly signposted vineyards and estates. In a paddock to the left of the farmhouse, a single horse stands patiently under an ancient oak, flies buzzing its face, tail flicking.

'This is the town,' De Vries says. 'And that is its one horse.'

Solarin smiles.

'What do you want to do?'

'There's a bar, an inn, back there. You saw it? Die Druiwetros. That's pretty feeble: the bunch of grapes. These places are usually the centre of everything. I'm going to make my presence felt.'

'I can take the car?' Solarin asks.

'Yes.'

'There are workers' cottages back there. I can ask about the lorry. Whether there have been strangers in town . . .' He laughs at the cliché. 'What they've seen. Maybe they will talk to me.'

De Vries nods. 'You'll come back to the bar? There doesn't seem to be anywhere else to get a drink, something to eat. I'll stay there.'

He turns and drives back up the road, stopping outside Die Druiwetros. De Vries gets out of the car, feels the heat envelop him in what seems to be a scalding vacuum. Solarin swaps into the driver's seat.

'Good luck.'

De Vries watches the car move away, watches the dust drift

between the small dwellings, out into the fields and vineyards. There is one other car parked close to the bar. Otherwise, there is no one on the street, no sound of music or talking or machinery. He can almost hear the sun scalding the roofs, the trees, the grit on the track popping.

He steps towards the dark-green-painted wooden door, pushes it open, finds himself in a dark but cosy bar. At the back, a similar door opens onto a bare yard, shaded by vines, under which sit some assorted wooden chairs and rickety tables. One table is occupied by an elderly couple. They sit staring downwards, uncommunicative.

'*Welkom. Wat kan ek vir jou doen?*'

The man is deeply tanned, white beard and short white hair contrasting starkly with his lined skin. He stands behind his little bar, his smile strained. De Vries returns the greeting in Afrikaans, asks for a cold beer.

'What brings you to our *plaasdorpie?*'

'Police business.'

De Vries watches the man's hand quiver on the little tap above the trickling beer.

'*Ja?* Nothing happens in Wingerdedorp. Maybe one day I forget to change the barrel and there is no cold beer, and then I might get trouble, but the guys soon decide that brandy and Cokes are as good at the start of the evening as at the end.' He chuckles uneasily.

'I'm thinking more about visitors,' De Vries says calmly, watching the man place the beer on the bar. He picks up his glass, drinks half of it, nods. 'That's good.'

'It is good, isn't it?'

De Vries looks down at him. 'Visitors?'

'A few. Folks who love port. They go to Calitzdorp. They taste some wine. Then, maybe someone tells them, "This is mainly for

335

show. You want to visit the specialist farms. Drive twenty minutes to Wingerdedorp. There you can taste the wine we keep for ourselves . . .'" He gestures to the shelf of crudely labelled bottles behind him.

'You have rooms? If I want to stay a night?'

The barman frowns. 'Maybe, *ja*. You want tonight?'

'Maybe.'

De Vries drains his glass, gestures for a refill. The man places it under the tap, concentrates overly hard on the simple procedure.

'My name's De Vries. You the owner here?'

The man nods gravely, does not look up, murmurs, 'Japie van Rooyen.'

De Vries says nothing until the glass appears above the counter and is placed in front of him.

'Ten, twelve days before Christmas . . . Maybe thirteenth, fourteenth, fifteenth December. You see an old white lorry in town? Maybe going to one of the farms?'

'Lorries come and go all the time.'

'This isn't harvest time, Japie. An early nineties Nissan, with a white trailer?'

Van Rooyen's eyes dart up towards De Vries, then down again. He pouts, shakes his head.

De Vries forces himself to sound casual: 'The farmers: they come down here for a drink?'

'*Ja* . . . Most nights.'

'Good. What time?'

'Early. Maybe five p.m.'

'I can talk to them then.' He stares at Van Rooyen. 'I think you know what lorry I'm talking about. Driven by strangers. You know where it went?'

The bar is silent; the couple outside say nothing. There is no wind, no noise from the street, and even if there were, it would

not penetrate the thick stone walls and heavy wooden doors. If
there are birds and insects in the air, none stirs, all are quiet.

'Better not say . . .'

De Vries leans over the counter. 'Better to say, Japie. You don't
want trouble. I don't want trouble. Tell me.'

The old man shakes his head. De Vries thinks he looks para-
lysed, afraid of him, this stranger in his bar.

'All right . . . You serve food here?'

'*Ja*. Pies, cheese, sandwiches.'

'I'll come back in an hour. You'll have sandwiches and pies for
two of us, *ja*?'

Van Rooyen nods.

The main street is still deserted. De Vries finds a spot under a low,
wind-blown tree, where he can sit on a rock wall and watch in
both directions. He checks his phone, but there is no signal. He
feels light-headed but refreshed. The heat is intense and claustrophobic, but he wants to be on the street where he can be seen.
In the first half-hour that he waits, he sees not a single person,
nor any vehicle. A thin brown dog walks determinedly down the
length of the road, glancing at De Vries without breaking stride.
At the Cape Dutch house at the end, it jumps the low white wall
and disappears.

As the white vehicle emerges from the heat haze, he assumes
that it is Solarin, but the engine noise is wrong. The white bakkie
trundles past, the passenger staring at him. It turns onto a farm
track at the end, but De Vries hears it stop, its engine idling just
out of sight. Minutes elapse and then it reappears. This time, as it
passes, from under hooded eyes he sees the passenger lean across
the cabin, point his cellphone at him, presumably taking a photograph. The bakkie accelerates and disappears beyond the village.

De Vries smiles. Small-town inhabitants, suspicious of a stranger in town. Japie van Rooyen has silently, unknowingly, confirmed to him that they are in the right place. Now he will wait.

It is ten minutes more before Solarin appears in the Mercedes. De Vries is soaked with sweat, gasping for liquid once more. Solarin lowers the passenger window.

'You okay?'

'*Ja.* Come in and have a drink, something to eat.'

'Just now. You want to get in first?' He leans over and opens the passenger door. De Vries feels the cool air hit him as he sits down. Solarin passes him an unopened bottle of local mineral water. 'Got it from the camp kiosk. It's cool, not cold.'

De Vries tips it, drinks half without swallowing, almost chokes himself.

At the far end of the street, Solarin parks beneath an ancient eucalyptus tree, leaves the engine running to power the air-conditioning.

'They were here,' Solarin says.

De Vries turns to him. 'Who were here?'

'The lorry, two vans, strange cars. I went into the little township out there. Mainly domestics, handymen, a few farm workers. No electricity, no sanitation, just borehole water and that's it. No one wanted to talk, but I found an old woman, lived there last sixty years. Says she sleeps during the day and lives in the night. Cooler that way. Rest of the township thinks she's mad. Two in the morning, two weeks ago, she was washing outside. Suddenly she could see lights over at the Snyman farm.'

'Snyman?'

'Rudi Snyman. He owns the farm that backs onto the mountains. She wasn't sure it was at the farm itself but nearby, maybe at the mountainside. Said she could hear engine noise. People, she said, a group of people. Don't know whether we can believe everything, but she seemed genuine, and certain of what she saw. Then there was a lorry – couldn't say that it was ours, but like that – and two vans, went past on the track about four thirty a.m., before dawn.'

'The landlord of that bar.' De Vries says quietly. 'He knew what I was asking. Frightened, though. Think he called up his friends. Car came by, men inside fancied me, took a picture.' He laughs.

'That good?'

'*Ja*, that's good. News travels fast in a place like this. I want to see who comes out of hiding, who watches us, who threatens us . . .'

'Talk about threat: this woman said she was too old to be afraid, but on the way out, two of these guys get out of the car after the lorry and vans have gone by, come into the township, armed, brace this woman, push their guns into her body, anyone else awake, told them not to speak to anybody, that their lives depended on it.'

'Islamic terrorists?'

'No,' Mike Solarin says. 'Chinese.'

Their late lunch is simple but good: cheese and thick slices of white bread with creamy butter, two thick slices of meat pie with strongly flavoured meat jelly between the filling and the pastry. Solarin drinks one beer, then Coke; De Vries two more beers. The couple who had sat in the yard are gone. Van Rooyen serves them their drinks and a coloured girl brings their plates of food. Once again, the room is silent.

'You think they will come?' Solarin's voice is almost a whisper.

'They'll come, or we'll go. One way or the other.' De Vries chews a large mouthful of pie. When he has almost swallowed it, he says, 'You have any signal on your cell?'

Solarin produces it, glances at the display, shakes his head.

De Vries says, very quietly: 'You carrying your weapon?'

Solarin nods. 'The boot is locked. I checked the alarm when the car was delivered.'

'We may not have time to reach the big guns. Course, we may not need them. Just keep your ears open. They know the silence better than us.'

'You don't want to go to this Snyman farm?'

'Your lady friend ever see Chinese here before?'

Solarin laughs. 'Never. She said she only thought they were Chinese because she had been looking at old copies of *National Geographic*, and that's what they looked like.'

'So Snyman isn't who we really want. I'm waiting for the Chinaman.' He puts down his cutlery, wipes his mouth with the napkin, places it on the plate. Solarin looks up at him. De Vries meets his eye, says nothing. In the silence, they hear a phone somewhere in the building. It is answered on the first ring.

By six thirty p.m., two couples – one white, one coloured – have come into the bar. They all sit outside in the shaded yard. They seem local, take no notice of De Vries and Solarin.

They hear the phone again inside the building. A few moments later, Japie van Rooyen ambles over to them.

'Colonel de Vries? There's a phone call for you.'

A development is what he wanted, but this is unexpected.

'Who could know I was here?'

'You can come through to the hallway.' De Vries rises and follows Van Rooyen. 'You didn't tell me if you wanted a room . . . two rooms, tonight.'

'Depends.' He picks up the receiver. He has no idea who might be calling him. '*Ja*?'

'This is Colonel Wertner . . .' After the silence of the country-side, the quietly spoken Van Rooyen, the head of Internal Investigations' voice sounds even more aggressive and grating than it does in the city. 'Where are you?'

De Vries swallows, chokes a laugh. 'Evidently you know where I am, Wertner. What do you want?'

'You are to leave Wingerdedorp and return to Cape Town now. Bring Lieutenant Solarin with you. This order comes directly from Pretoria.'

'I bet it does . . .'

'Failure to comply will result in immediate suspension, and a full disciplinary inquiry. Make that clear also to Solarin.'

De Vries's mind whirs. Contact from his own department had not entered his mind; that someone in the SAPS might be involved was only just within his sphere of probability.

'Who in Pretoria?'

'Don't ask questions. Just comply with the order.'

'Listen, Wertner,' De Vries says, struggling to retain at least a spoken composure. 'Tell me what you know because, one way or another, this is going to have repercussions. Where in Pretoria does this come from?'

'That is not of concern to you.'

He takes a very deep breath, says quietly, slowly: 'It is of concern to me and, I promise you, it will be of concern to you.'

'Don't threaten me.'

De Vries faces the corner of the bar, pushes the receiver hard against his face, feels the slime on his skin, the throbbing in his temples. 'I'm not threatening you, you cunt. I'm deciding whether you're part of this or just some pig-stupid messenger. Where in Pretoria?'

He hears a faint hiss, distant machination, wonders whether it is the landline stretching across hundreds of kilometres of country-side, or Wertner's brain.

'Justice Ministry.'

'Thank you.'

'That changes nothing, De Vries. Get back here. Start now.'

'Do you know what I'm doing, Wertner?'

'No, and I don't want to. I've been authorized to make this one hundred per cent clear to you. It is a direct order and, if disobeyed, will result in the end of your career. Are you clear?'

'Quite clear.'

'Call me when you reach Cape Town, whatever the time. I will relay that information to Pretoria.' De Vries says nothing. 'Are you there, De Vries?'

'I'm just thinking . . .'

'Don't think. Obey. You know that at this moment I technically outrank you. Obey me, obey the ministry, obey Pretoria.'

De Vries lets his breath out very slowly, silently, says:

'Tell them we're on our way.'

They leave Die Druiwetros noisily, thank Japie van Rooyen vociferously, explain that they have been recalled, walk to their car. De Vries drives to the end of the main road, glances at the gates to the Snyman farm, turns and drives on, windows open, a radio talk show blaring amid a roar of interference.

Once they are past even the small rural township, De Vries turns off the radio, seals the windows. Even now, as the sun falls, the heat is stifling. He drives as far as Calitzdorp, where they stop at the garage, have the tank filled. Then De Vries drives to a quiet, tree-lined side-street, parks in a dark bay overhung with low branches. He opens the windows, switches off the engine.

'We have to decide what to do.'

They have already discussed the phone call, De Vries emphasizing the seriousness of the threat against them.

'I'm not going back until we know,' Solarin states.

'That's easy to say,' De Vries says, 'but you have to understand: this isn't an idle threat. You have a chance to make a difference in the SAPS. We have to decide if this is a battle worth fighting, worth risking what we have now.'

'You said Wertner is Internal Investigations. Why didn't your boss call?'

'Director du Toit is old school. If they involved him, he'd cause trouble subtly and for a long time. General Thulani doesn't much like being used as a go-between. I don't think either of them knows what this is, or whoever this is in Pretoria is aware they wouldn't touch it. That's why they went to Wertner.'

'He frighten you?'

'He frightens me for you. Me, I'm too old to worry about threats like that. It happens often now. This is the second time someone in Pretoria has taken exception to what I'm doing. If people tell me not to ask questions, it just makes me want to ask them even more.'

'I am not going back to Cape Town,' Solarin says. 'Not empty-handed a second time. If the Justice Ministry don't want us to investigate, they're covering something up.' He pauses. 'They're covering up the murder of fourteen innocent people, an attack on the Mother City. How, why, would they do that?'

'I don't know. But I'm telling you, if that is what they're doing, they won't leave us alone. Someone from Wingerdedorp has a direct contact with Pretoria. That worries me.'

'So we go in hard.'

De Vries laughs, his face deeply set in concentration. 'Maybe . . .'

'If it's what we think it is,' Solarin says quietly, 'if we break it, do it now, right now, no one can act against us.'

Dusk is settling on the town. Their shaded parking space is now dark, the trees obscuring the feeble streetlight and the moon. De Vries starts the engine.

'Problem, Lieutenant, is that in this country, the whistleblower still gets shot.'

They drive through Calitzdorp, coloured light bulbs on strings outside bars, glowing fluorescent-tube-lit signs promising the best ostrich and port wine, out onto the dark R62. Three kilometres from town, De Vries pulls over, extinguishes his headlights and waits. He watches in the rear-view mirror as Solarin stares ahead. Not one car passes them in the next three or four minutes.

'I turn here,' De Vries says, 'or I drive on?'

'No decision. Let's go.'

De Vries turns to study him. Solarin is the same age as Don February, but he seems younger, fitter, his skin darker, unblemished. Yet, in his expression, De Vries sees determination, fire, which he knows that once he possessed. He questions whether his own hunger for righteousness is waning: deep in his stomach, he feels that they should return to Cape Town. He narrows his eyes, squints at his country around him, fading in the dusk. If he drives home now, his heart may as well fail. He turns his head back to face the road ahead, relishes that Solarin says nothing, does not question him in these moments of silence.

From the sensation of blood coursing through his fingers, the adrenalin slowly adulterating his system, he knows that he has decided, knows that he will turn and drive to Wingerdedorp. He glances again at Solarin, his features set, waiting. He wonders whether there will ever be a time when he drives back to Cape Town, back home, or whether this is his life, to disobey, to challenge, to make his own path whatever the dangers.

He nods to himself, checks his mirrors, turns the wheel and crosses the main road onto the dirt track, which, according to their map, doubles back and rejoins the road to Wingerdedorp. He extinguishes even his side lights, drives at maybe 40 k.p.h., solely by the light of the expanded moon, which sits at forty-five degrees in the dark sky above the surrounding mountains. To their right, the Milky Way is spattered across the blackness. It seems that Wingerdedorp is located between the light of the stars and the beam of the moon, nestled in the blackness. For the first time that day, the cabin seems cool, although the car's glass is still warm.

By a stand of eucalyptus trees, he pulls the car over, exits the vehicle, opens the boot, covering the light with a plastic bag. He and Solarin unroll a hessian sheet to reveal a shotgun and a small, short, automatic machine gun. Solarin picks the latter, rests it in his arm, tests the catches.

'You ready to use that thing?' De Vries says.

Solarin turns to him, sees his face slick with sweat, grey in the moonlight.

'No point carrying if you're not.'

They get into the car, pull back onto the track, drive in silence until they meet the main gravel road. De Vries is about to turn towards the village when he sees headlights approaching. He backs away from the junction, and they wait. The bakkie does not slow, or seem to see them, as it roars by. He brings the car to the turn, makes it, begins to drive back towards Wingerdedorp.

There is no way to approach the drive to the Snyman farm without traversing the main street. Four of the six streetlights are out, illumination from the few houses that front onto the street is veiled by curtains, only a half-dozen cars and bakkies are parked outside Die Druiwetros. They drive slowly past the inn, on towards the Cape Dutch farmhouse at the end of the street. It, at least, is resolutely dark. De Vries turns right, stops at the gate. Solarin jumps out, finds no padlock, opens it, watches the car through it and re-latches it, before returning to the vehicle. The moon is now partially obscured by the mountains, and driving without lights has become more hazardous.

After two or three kilometres, they see dim light to the left of the road, pull up. Solarin produces a small pair of binoculars, struggles to find the lights amid the vast expanse of grey mountain and black sky, then takes time to fine-tune the focus and let his eyes adjust to the view.

'It's a squatter camp or settlement. Maybe half a dozen dwellings. Probably more than shacks. Small houses. *Ja* . . .'

'Farmworkers?'

'I'm guessing so, but . . .'

'But what?'

'Seems strange.' He lowers the binoculars.

'Why strange?' De Vries asks.

'Looks like new houses. Small, concrete. Electricity, TV, phonelines. Just seems out of place.'

'You want to go see?'

Solarin hesitates.

'Or we push on to this Snyman farm?'

'*Ja.*'

He pulls back onto the dry track, which has become more sand than gravel now, the wheels fighting for grip. A kilometre on, as they round the corner, ahead they see the main farmhouse. De Vries lowers his window, drives forward at a slow pace.

'Don't think they can see us . . . Don't think they can hear us.' He winds the window back up.

'Unless someone's told them we're coming.'

'Hopefully,' De Vries says, 'someone's told them we've gone home.'

The road begins to run more directly towards the mountains now, the moonlight obscured. It is so black, De Vries can no longer see his way, feels compelled to switch on his sidelights to proceed.

When they are three hundred metres from the farmhouse, the track widens into a lay-by containing two large piles of gravel, stacks of wooden crates. De Vries does a three-point turn, faces the car the way they have come, stops under a shrubby tree, turns off the engine.

They say nothing, get out, check their weapons and begin to walk fast, side by side, up the track towards the farmhouse, which is built in traditional Cape Dutch style, single-storey, with a long, low stoep running the broad width of the front, pink stone steps leading up to dark green double wooden doors, vines covering built-in pergolas over the stoep, dark wood-framed windows showing a dim light within. The crickets and cicadas are loud, but there is no breeze, no sound of voices or music or dogs.

When they are about fifty metres from the house, two strong Rhodesian ridgebacks appear, ears cocked, noses raised. They stand like stone ornaments at the foot of the stairs to the front door. The two men freeze. Solarin swivels his eyes towards De Vries. De Vries nods slowly, lays down the shotgun, begins to walk towards the house. Solarin sinks to the ground.

'Anybody at home?'

De Vries hears his own voice, dislikes the anxiety he hears in his call. The dogs snarl – a deep, low growl, their taut bodies soundboxes projecting the warning. De Vries's gaze is fixed on them, but they remain where they are. He slows his pace.

'Rudi Snyman?'

He sees a curtain move in the window to the right of the main doors. He takes one pace forward, waits, then another.

Suddenly the double doors open; harsh white light floods the steps. The dogs turn, rise, speed to the feet of the three men who walk out of the building. The first is short, squat; two taller men holding shotguns flank him.

'Who is this? What do you want?'

De Vries walks briskly towards them, ignoring the weapons. 'Rudi Snyman?'

'Stop where you are. This is private property.' His voice is high and nasal, thick with Afrikaans accent.

'*Ek kom net om met jou te praat,*' De Vries says – I have come only to speak with you.

The small man walks towards him, squinting in the dark to make out his face. The men behind him have raised their weapons, pointing at De Vries.

'I am Rudi Snyman,' the small man says, stopping a few metres from him. 'And I know who you are.'

'*Ja?*'

'You were ordered to go home, Colonel.'

'What were you ordered to do, Mr Snyman?'

Snyman's eyes flare. 'I am not ordered to do anything. This is my land, my property, and you will turn around and leave now.'

'I only want to talk.'

'I do not want to talk.'

'Where are the weapons?'

'My men are holding the weapons we have on the farm. They will not hesitate to use them if you refuse to stop trespassing.'

De Vries tries to interpret his response, reads it as an admission that there are, or were, other weapons, unacknowledged.

'Maybe call the SAPS. Have me thrown off your land, Mr Snyman.'

The small man steps towards him, his men following, their eyes trained down the barrels of the shotguns.

'I have authorization to take whatever action I want to protect my farm. From the *kaffirs*, from the Democratic fucking Alliance, from people like you.'

De Vries can feel his heart pounding, feels it shudder, the heat surround him, hemming him in, a straitjacket. He breathes, believes that, on the surface, he appears calm . . .

He raises his hands, steps forward. The men behind Snyman seem to focus on their prey, prepare to fire.

'You only have to speak with me.'

As the last word leaves his mouth, he sees Snyman's gaze change, his little head nod on the tanned, lizard-like neck. His men bound forward; a barrel is swung. He tries to duck, but it catches him above the right eye. He feels something in his head crack, pain stream into his right eye, feels himself falling. His ears are bombarded, subsumed by a deafening rattle. His torso meets the dusty ground, the side of his head hitting the red earth hard, eyes closed. Instinctively, he brings his hands to his head, covers his ears from what now sounds like screaming animals.

He forces his eyes open, sees blood in huge droplets atop the sandy grains of dirt spatter and disintegrate. He strains to push his head up, watches one of the armed men crumpling, wailing as he clutches his kneecap, his shotgun falling, barrel bouncing on the hard earth. He pulls his head up further, sees the look of terror on the other guard, gun lowered, then hears another burst of fire, and the same horrific screaming as he falls on top of his gun. He registers Snyman standing frozen, his mouth open, eyes bulging, lungs empty of breath. He hears shouted instruction from behind him, senses boots stamping across the undergrowth. He ducks his head, breathes, his lips thick with sand and dust and blood. He tests his body, feels movement in his arms and legs, the shock beginning to dissipate. He pushes all his weight onto his palms, flat against the hot soil, heaves himself up. Boots pass his head, hands reach down to pick up the two shotguns. He is on his knees now.

'Take them.'

He looks up at Solarin, sees his face taut, eyes wide, radiating utter focus. He struggles to his feet, using one of the guns as a crutch. Solarin passes him his stubby machine gun, pulls out his handgun. He pushes Snyman backwards, the little man struggling to keep upright. At the steps to the house, he falls, landing on the pink concrete, screaming and chattering, begging for mercy, all confidence sucked out of him, like a vacuum suddenly broken, his small hands curled and shaking in front of him. Solarin puts one foot on the step above him, leans down close over him, his weapon pressed into Snyman's face.

'Who came here? What did they take?'

Snyman's eyes bulge, the sound of whimpering and yowling from his men filling the silent, dark, sweltering air. He shakes his head fast, terrified.

'I'll kill your men, then I'll kill you. Tell me.'

'Can't.'

'You can.' He withdraws the barrel of the gun, then repositions it, harder, into the side of his head. 'Do it.'

'Two bakkies. Chinese. Guy called himself . . .' he struggles to find the words, to form the sounds '. . . Liu Xiang.'

'What did he want?'

'The cave.'

'What cave?'

'Didn't know. Cave in the mountain.'

Solarin pulls him up, the gun still pressed into him.

'Show me.'

Snyman is fighting for breath. 'Over there. Five, six Ks . . .'

'Then we'll take your car.'

Solarin looks around, studies De Vries. 'You all right, sir?' De Vries nods heavily, tries to ignore the blood on the ground, the crying of the two men still prostrate, convulsing. 'Can you check them for weapons, cellphones?'

De Vries feels light-headed, disoriented, the scene almost imagined. He stumbles to the first of the men, begins to check him over, recoils from the quantity of blood, retrieves a cellphone. Solarin pulls Snyman towards the bakkie parked to the side of the house. De Vries frisks the other man, awkwardly extracts a knife from the back pocket of his jeans, a cellphone from the front. Both men are quiet now, breathing heavily, pressing their hands against their spewing wounds. He pulls himself up, staggers across the dirt towards the bakkie where Solarin and Snyman wait, Solarin in the driver's seat, his weapon pointed at Snyman in the back. De Vries gets in next to Snyman, produces his own pistol.

'Guide us. Don't fuck us about.'

Solarin faces front, starts the vehicle, pulls away, turns onto the track Snyman has indicated.

'Tell us about these men.'

'They came in the middle of the night. The dogs heard them. We went out here and they were there . . .'

'Who?'

'The Chinese. There was a stand-off. I didn't know what was there. Still don't. Said they had stuff kept there from years back. There were seven, eight of them. They wanted access to the cave so we did a deal. That's all this is: a deal.'

'What deal?'

'Money. Secrecy. I promised them. They said if anyone found out, I'd be finished.'

'They were right.'

Snyman turns to De Vries, his little face white, quivering. His mouth moves, but nothing more emanates. There is silence as the car cuts between the end of the rows of vines and the scrubby outland of the farm, moving closer to the mountain outcrops that protrude into the land.

Snyman stares continually at De Vries, his eyes swivelling to register the car's position, then back onto the muzzle of the pistol so close to his face.

'There.' Snyman points with a finger in his lap. 'Up there.'

Solarin pulls the bakkie over, climbs out of the vehicle, looks up at the rock face, fewer than fifty metres away, gestures for Snyman to get out.

'You lead the way.'

De Vries gets out of the car gingerly, sees vines to their left, vine cuttings, dried-out grape bunches on the track where they are parked. Solarin pushes Snyman, who hobbles to a well-trodden but narrow, sandy path between spiky shrubs and low, almost leafless trees. The moonlight is dim now, occluded by the rock face, but Solarin has his torch lit, its beam leading the way along the path. Within two minutes, using steps constructed with rocks set into the ground, they have climbed towards the edge of the mountain, and Solarin can see the gaping mouth to the cave.

'What was there?'

'I don't know . . .' The words scarcely leave his lips. He coughs, chokes, swallows. 'Weapons, maybe. Explosives. I didn't know it was there. Owned this place forty years, never been here, but they knew, the Chinese.'

Standing by the face of the low mountain, the rock seems to exude heat, a strong smell of animal urine.

'What's there now?'

Snyman shakes his head, quivers. 'Don't know . . . Nothing . . . Baboons . . .'

'We're going in.'

Solarin meets De Vries's eye. De Vries nods slowly.

They enter the open overhang of the cave, the heat still not dissipating. From above, they hear a loud plaintive barking. It drags the breath from De Vries, makes his heart thump.

'Baboon.' Solarin says. 'Probably territorial. Unlikely to be any inside.'

The cave narrows at its back. A stained wooden door lies smashed and broken, pushed aside. De Vries sees animal scratches on its surface, deep and wide. Solarin points the torch ahead of him, pushes Snyman through the low, narrow opening. Inside the chamber, the smell of urine is replaced by an artificial, chemical smell of old ordnance, human sweat, the air still heavy, still hot, despite the location within the mountain. The room opens up to the right, the jagged wall lined with rusting metal staging and shelving. Solarin pushes Snyman against the far wall, instructs him not to move. Then he starts to examine the detritus remaining on the shelves: some paper wrappings, metal bindings, disintegrating boxes of ammunition.

He turns to Snyman, his voice strident, reverberating around the cave. 'What was here?'

Snyman cowers, shakes his head. 'Never came inside.'

'Yes you did – or you saw what they took.'

'Weapons . . . Maybe weapons.'

'I think I know what this is,' De Vries says. 'Secret stores, all over the country. National Party-sanctioned, maybe even supplied, for the Afrikaners, all through apartheid times. Allowed for local vigilantes in case of trouble. Plenty haven't been found or decommissioned.'

Solarin gathers what he can find, places it in the ammunition box that is least damaged. He shines the beam on the ground, finds ammunition there, a stick of some kind of old explosive propped up in the far corner. He reaches forward to retrieve it, then withdraws his hand, stands upright. He holds the torch in one hand,

353

photographs it with the other. Then he turns and, illuminating the chamber as best he can, he photographs the entire space.

De Vries waits by the entrance to the chamber, his gun still pointing at Snyman's torso, his senses slowly returning to normal, alert to what is happening within and also to what might be approaching outside.

Solarin pockets his cellphone, gathers the box under his arm, moves to the exit, stops in front of Snyman.

'They go anywhere else?'

Snyman shakes his head.

Solarin studies him, the torch beam making the little man's face seem very white and wrinkled.

'We're done.'

He makes for the exit to the chamber.

De Vries bars his way. 'Not yet. I'm not done with this man.' He hands Solarin his pistol, approaches Snyman. 'Who did you call?'

'Call?'

De Vries feels the frustration well inside him, as if his patience has utterly deserted him. He shouts in Snyman's face: 'Japie van Rooyen called you. You sent men to see who I was and then you called someone. Who was it?'

'A number I was told to call . . . if anyone came asking questions . . .'

'Give it to me.'

'On my cellphone.' Snyman pats his pockets. 'I don't have it. It must have fallen out.'

De Vries grabs him, feels his pockets, finds the slim phone, pulls it out and waves it in his face.

'You're a pathetic little shit, Snyman. You, the people on this phone, these Chinese. It's finished. The whole thing is done.'

He grabs the man's damp shirt, pulls it towards him, then pushes him back against the wall. He slides down the edge, ends up sitting, doubled over.

De Vries turns to Solarin. 'Now we're done.'

They turn, leaving the man in the dark. De Vries picks up the damaged wooden door – it is lighter than he expected – and pulls it across the opening.

Solarin takes a short heavy branch, props it against the door, smiles at De Vries grimly. They turn. Both start. Ahead of them, just outside the cave, is a huge baboon. It paces a few metres in each direction, turning its huge muscular body back and forth, its eyes never leaving them. De Vries and Solarin back up towards the cave wall. Solarin lowers the torch, reaches for his handgun.

'Don't shoot it,' De Vries says urgently. Solarin turns to him, frowning. 'Just don't. Fire to the side. It'll run.'

Ahead, the baboon is stationary, its thick arms bent, head low and facing them. Its eyes are fixed on them, its focus seemingly on the weapon. De Vries sees Solarin's hand shake as he squeezes the trigger. They slowly turn their faces away. Solarin fires. The explosion reverberates around the cave, shattering their ears. When they look up, the baboon is gone but, in the distance, they can hear barking, the sound of branches breaking, heavy bodies crashing through undergrowth, dislodged rocks tumbling, as the rest of the troop escape the noise.

The two men approach the mouth of the cave gingerly, looking from side to side, but there is no sign of animal life. They trek down the pathway to the bakkie. Solarin hands De Vries the box of evidence, starts the vehicle, begins to retrace their journey back towards the farmhouse.

'You know where you're going?'

'No.'

De Vries laughs, shouting above the noise of the straining engine.

'Why did you tell me not to shoot the animal?' Solarin asks.

'Seen baboon carcasses hanging up outside farms to frighten away the troop. Most horrific sight ever. Still have nightmares about it.'

Solarin shakes his head. 'You have many demons, Colonel.'

De Vries finds himself nodding, uncertain whether it is concurrence or just the motion of the vehicle on the rutted track. He squeezes his eyes shut, rubs them, feels the grit in their corners. He thinks aloud, murmurs:

'The Chinese take the arms, load up a lorry, blow it up in Long Street. Why?' Solarin shakes his head. 'Then the Justice Ministry does some deal with a slimy fucker like Snyman so nobody finds out. Stops your investigation, threatens us with our careers. What the fuck is happening?'

He gasps, suddenly aware that his body is aching, ears ringing. Now that the adrenalin is dwindling, the pain above his right eye is penetrating his skull. He touches the bloodied bruise, cries out as the bakkie jolts over a deep rut and his head hits the hard ceiling. Solarin does not let up speed, powering on towards the farmhouse, which appears, still dimly illuminated, to their right. As they turn towards their hire car, Solarin says: 'The men . . . They've gone. Get your gun.'

De Vries fumbles for his weapon, checks it, keeps it in his right hand as Solarin brakes hard next to the Mercedes. They transfer their weapons, the evidence they have found, into the boot.

'Where did they go?'

Solarin points to drag marks leading towards the steps to the house.

'Got themselves inside, probably managed to call for help. We need to go.' He turns back to the Mercedes. 'You happy I drive?' De Vries nods, takes the passenger seat. 'Keep a lookout. If they have associates, they may be waiting for us along the road, or in

Wingerdedorp. We have to get this out to other people or it's worth nothing. What we say is worth nothing.'

He starts the engine. They feel the cabin fill, first with warm air, then a cool breeze, becoming cold. The solid car surges effortlessly ahead along the gravel road towards the village. Halfway back, they see the beam of a torch at the roadside.

'Open your window,' De Vries says. 'Keep down.'

De Vries primes his handgun, points it past Solarin towards the right-hand side of the road. By the time they reach the point where they saw the light, it is dark. Solarin accelerates, De Vries focuses on any movement from the roadside, sees nothing. The car speeds by, jumping and jolting over the rough surface.

'Lookout maybe,' Solarin says.

'Could be. What are we doing about the gate?'

'Don't know. Felt solid. No way round it. Don't think we can ram it.'

They are approaching the short, straight section of road that leads to the gate and, beyond, to the end of the main street of Wingerdedorp. Solarin brakes hard.

'I need my weapon.' He reaches into the back of the car, retrieves his handgun. 'You think I need the automatic?'

'Let's just move.'

They drive on, see the gates, approach slowly. There are no lights, no apparent movement. Solarin lets the car idle, opens his window, leans out of the car, his gun primed. De Vries opens his door, jumps out, runs to the gate, opens the latch, hauls the gate open, stumbles back to the car, slams the door.

'Nothing. Let's go.'

Solarin pulls forward slowly, his headlights picking out the end of the main street, across the front of the old farmhouse, to the gate marking the boundary of another wine estate.

The collision is so sudden neither has time to register the unlit bakkie accelerate into the driver's side of their vehicle, the door bow, airbags explode. Solarin cries out, the windscreen cracks, then shatters, car skidding sideways towards the ditch at the side of the road. Solarin screams, grabs the wheel, angles it to the right, punches the accelerator. The car jolts away, swerves, skids, glass nuggets flying across the dashboard in a blast of hot night air. The Mercedes jerks across the road, Solarin fighting for control. De Vries grabs at deflating airbag material, pulls it away, shoves it out of his window.

'You all right?'

'*Ja*.' Solarin's answer is strangled, his jaw tight, teeth gritted.

De Vries looks behind them. A pair of full-beam headlights blinds him. He shouts above the sound of the road, the straining engine, the vehicle behind them.

'We got tyres?'

'Dunno.'

The rear windscreen suddenly shatters. The deafening explosion of the shots hits their throbbing ears only afterwards. Both duck, too late, instinct controlling their limbs. Solarin puts his weight onto his right foot, and the car accelerates still more, weaving up the main road, past the inn, out into the darkness of the Little Karoo. Behind, the lights still blind them, the vehicle maybe a hundred metres back, getting closer, yet shrouded in the thick dust. The speed of their vehicle seems visceral and alarmingly existent, the hot wind sucking the moisture from their mouths, from their eyes, slapping their faces through the open windscreen, the noise of the engine strident, the tyres spitting gravel and dust, popping and screeching.

As the road begins to turn and bend, the car seems to drift dangerously around the corners.

'Slow, Mike . . .'

He lets up on the accelerator, but the lights behind them catch them up until they can, once again, hear the older, louder engine thundering close behind them.

'Jesus. Back offside tyre . . . I'm losing control . . .'

De Vries stares at Solarin, sees his face contorted, fighting pain, knows that he will soon fail.

'Drive smoothly as you can.'

He lowers his window, checks that it is locked, leans out, turning away from the blast of night air. He can see nothing behind him, but for the headlights through the dust. His body is shaken about, seat belt around his shoulder, then around his neck. He feels pressure on his chest and ribs, fights the desire to fall back inside the vehicle and tend his wounds. He aims above and between the lights, fires off two rounds. The car behind brakes, the lights retreat.

'Breathing space, Mike. Keep going . . .'

Solarin does not reply. De Vries sees the headlights approaching again, regains his position, closes his left eye, fires four more shots, thinks that he hears glass breaking, knows immediately that the beams no longer follow them, but have veered off diagonally. Suddenly, there is nothing behind them but the dust and darkness illuminated red by the tail lights of their car. He pulls himself back inside the cabin, feels the car slow suddenly, looks across at Solarin, his body slumped over the wheel. He grabs the wheel, pulls the handbrake half on, grapples to punch his own foot between Solarin's legs, on the brake. The car swerves, leaves the road, thuds over a ditch. He stamps on the brake pedal once more, and the vehicle jolts to a stop.

De Vries pulls the handbrake full on, peers behind them through the broken rear window, clambers out of the car, around to the driver's side, releases Solarin's belt and pulls him clear of the cabin. Solarin screams. De Vries lays him on the ground. His body is heavy, slick with sweat, his breathing deep and laboured.

359

He murmurs something. De Vries bends down to his face, tilts his ear towards him.

'Ribs.'

He stands up, looks around them once more, sees nothing, hears nothing. If their pursuers went off the road, they must be a kilometre back. He squats down again.

'We can't wait here. Can you walk?'

Solarin tries to struggle to his feet, but seems unable to gain balance.

'We can't stay here. I'm going to lift you, help you around the car, get you inside. If we can get to Calitzdorp, we should be okay.' He leans down, grabs Solarin under his arms and pulls. The animal moan fills the silent night air, passes over the hidden vines into the distance. When he finally lowers him into the passenger seat, positions his legs in the footwell, he is exhausted, Solarin whimpering.

He surveys each of the wheels, finds three of the tyres intact, the fourth low but, he hopes, still usable. The bodywork and glass are a wreck, but the engine still runs smoothly. Before he squeezes back inside, he looks up at the sky, the Milky Way directly above him now, the blackness almost white.

The room is as he remembers it: oversized, high ceilinged, previously ornate, now Spartan. In the far corner, the broad desk sits at a diagonal. The man behind it seems small, insignificant.

'I hope, for the sake of your career, no one else knows about our meeting.'

The voice is a quiet tenor, clear and precise.

'No one.'

'How is your friend, John Marantz?'

Marantz is a former British security-services officer, whose wife

360

and daughter were kidnapped and murdered. He exiled himself to Cape Town and drank his way through five years of mourning with De Vries. Marantz had introduced him to this invisible man, with his contacts and encyclopedic knowledge of his country's workings.

'Don't see him so often now. He's rediscovered women.'

'If it keeps him out of trouble . . .'

Eric Basson raises his head, stands, shakes De Vries's hand. His own is strong; it determines every element of the greeting. He gestures for De Vries to sit.

'Your message was entirely predictable but, I confess, I had not expected it.'

'I have something for you.'

'Of course you do, and you want something from me.' Basson smiles. 'I understand our transaction, Colonel. Indeed, I have been speculating what it is that you might offer me.'

De Vries sits back, observes Basson across his desk. He has met him twice previously, when Basson's knowledge and contacts helped him to solve a complex political case and, arguably, save his life. He describes himself, De Vries remembers, as 'a conduit to the past' – an apartheid-era fixer for the then government, now working in some capacity both for, and as an observer of, the new administration.

'The Long Street bomb.'

Basson smiles. 'Ah, yes . . . Not your investigation. You, I assumed, were busy with Stephen Jessel.'

'I still am. That isn't over yet.'

'No?'

'No.'

'That is interesting. What do you wish to tell me?'

De Vries has questioned before whether Basson is a man with whom he should work, knows that he is already in debt to him, a man likely to demand repayment.

'Couple of weeks ago, on a farm near a tiny village called Wingerdedorp, twenty kilometres from Calitzdorp, a cache of old weapons and ordnance was taken by a group of Chinese men. Forensic evidence places the lorry that exploded in Long Street at that farm. The owner, who agreed some deal with them, told me that the leader's name was Liu Xiang . . .' He looks up at Basson. 'Why are you smiling? You know this man?'

Basson is nodding, the smile turning his thin lips minutely upwards.

'That explains much.'

'Who is Liu Xiang?'

Basson shrugs. 'Nobody knows. It is a very common name in China. A Van der Merwe, John Smith, John Doe. In fact, there may be more than one man operating under that name. Like the blacks in the past, that's the problem we're having with the Chinese just now: our eye isn't adjusted yet to distinguish between them.'

'But you've encountered that name before?'

'I have, and I will tell you about it – and it will interest you, but first, I will tell you what I did already know.' He sits up. De Vries recognizes the relish this man takes in his knowledge. 'Whatever happened in Long Street, it was not caused by the men the authorities and media claimed. Akram Ibrahim Jabouri, allegedly one of the suicide bombers, died in prison five weeks ago from, my source informs me, a combination of interrogation techniques and suicide. Abdu-Allah Baravan was arrested secretly over eight months ago and was being held in the Northern Cape. To my knowledge, he is still there. So I, and a few others well informed, we knew that what was being advertised was false. Your explanation makes perfect sense.'

'Why?'

'Because the moment I realized that this event was not what it purported to be, I suspected the influence of a particular individual, allied with the Justice Ministry and the SAPS, yet independent of oversight. A man working officially in some capacity, but unofficially in another role, to the benefit of the current administration.'

'The ANC?'

'For one small but influential element of the government, yes.'

'This man I dealt with before, Major Mabena. He instigated a state-sponsored killing for purely political ends . . .' He thinks back to a previous murder case where a potential donor to an opposition party was killed to stop her bankrolling a new political party. De Vries traced the action to Mabena, yet the controlling SAPS forces in Pretoria blocked any attempt to detain him.

'Colonel Mabena now. A man well liked in certain circles.'

'He organized the attack?'

'From what you tell me, from what I already knew, that seems likely. Liu Xiang is his man.' Basson adjusts his position. 'Let me make it clear to you, Colonel, since I believe your work has a tendency to make you insular. In the last two decades, the ANC and the Chinese have worked extensively together throughout our country. Deals, resulting in much mutual enrichment, have been signed. Our future, inexorably linked to China, has been planned in minute detail. All that might derail such all-consuming concepts is the loss of power by the ANC. They are losing control of municipal and local government, not just here in Cape Town but right along the south coast, even in Eastern Transvaal – which should be a heartland of ANC support. The Democratic Alliance is proving capable here, and Julius Malema's EFF may yet wrest control elsewhere. The government may do anything to try to keep control. Half a century of unwavering support from their people and, now, after twenty-two years of corruption, incompetence and in-fighting, their people are turning against them. So the ANC is striving to discredit the Democratic Alliance in provincial government: the removal of direct international flights to Cape Town by the state airline and others, a media war, the instigation of rioting and disorder and now, perhaps, the claim that Cape Town itself is unsafe . . . It's crude.'

'Fourteen dead, twenty still in hospital, for what?' De Vries stops himself, moderates his voice. 'Political capital? I wouldn't call that crude. I'd call it . . . despotic.'

'I try to keep emotion out of these matters.'

'Maybe you shouldn't. Maybe you should be angry.'

Eric Basson takes slow, shallow breaths. 'I've spent my entire life angry, Colonel de Vries. Just like you. Look at us now. All we can do is work. Our change is incremental, but it will be there.'

'You don't even seem surprised.'

'Conspiracy theorists believe that what they tell you is remarkable because of the magnitude of the deception. But what they describe is not amazing at all. Government agencies across the world engage in operations more incredible than the most imaginative conspiracy theorist can comprehend.' Basson narrows his eyes, sits back in his chair. 'I hope you have not come expecting me to disseminate this information?'

'No, but you might suggest how we can use it to eradicate Mabena and anyone who has ever used him.'

'You can't. Or you shouldn't. Expose what you know, but step back into the shadows. You're not a political animal, nor should you be. Stay anonymous, fighting for what you believe, out of the limelight.'

'Lately the light does not agree with me.'

'Then you and I have one more thing in common.'

'And how do I expose this story?'

Basson chuckles disbelievingly. 'Surely? Surely you have considered this.'

'I got back to Cape Town yesterday.' He touches his face. 'Think you can see it was a rough journey. Colleague of mine is worse off . . .' he chuckles, holding his ribs '. . . but at least we're doing better than the opposition.'

'But you have a slight problem with your own people?'

De Vries stares at him. 'A slight problem . . . I'm hiding. The SAPS want to arrest me and my colleague, probably for treason. Does that term still exist in our constitution?'

'Then let me assist you. I understand you have made some recent contacts in the newspaper world. Perhaps a new title, seeking exposure, would be interested in the story. And I think such a story could make a newspaper.'

'Or break it.'

'That option should not, perhaps, feature in your pitch. But, then, I am sure that you can think of an appropriately pioneering journalist, one who has recently found herself in the public eye, who might pursue it?'

'How do you know what you know?'

'Information has been my life, Colonel. I obtain it however I see fit, and use it to forward the cause I currently endorse.'

'An information mercenary?'

'If you will. Such a stance staves off disillusionment. For you, for your loyalty, what do you get? No matter how hard you fight, no matter how many battles you win, the war is already lost.'

'I don't believe that.'

'Of course not . . . But that doesn't alter the outcome.'

'The information on the Islamists. You have proof? I can use that?'

'I will think of a way that allows its use, that the evidence can be brought to you, or to your choice of journalist.'

'I may be in prison. I can rely on you?'

'You may.' Basson studies him. 'For a man kneeling on the gallows, you seem strangely unafraid.'

'Sanguine? Is that the word? If I cannot change the country I inhabit, maybe I should go . . .'

'Idealists in South Africa have to wait a long time. I don't see you as a patient man.'

'I'm not an idealist. I just believe in right and wrong. My definition.'

Basson smiles again. 'Stay away from politics, then. Stick to homicide. So much cleaner.' He stands, proffers his hand. De Vries takes it, meets his eye. 'I will do whatever I can to assist you in the coming time.'

'Thank you.'

'But don't forget,' Eric Basson says lightly, 'I *will* call on you one day.'

'That's something I never forget.'

De Vries walks away from the desk, many steps across the expansive, empty room, never turns back.

He sits at his long, empty kitchen table, stares down its length to his dark, scalded, vanishing garden. Everywhere he looks now in Cape Town, he sees plants and trees dying around him. Lawns are yellow or brown, pavements smell of urine, tarmac melts and distorts.

He rips the foil with the tip of the corkscrew, stabs the cork, twists and pulls. He hopes that Mike Solarin has done as he advised: disappeared for a few weeks, perhaps even gone home. He pours, stares down at the deep red wine. In the past weeks, he has been in too many confined spaces holding terrible secrets. He wants to rise and open his French windows to release himself from his cell, but he lacks the energy even to get up. There is a flash in his brain: he sees muzzles of guns, dark and hollow, pointed at his face; he sees Ali Jelani's bloody, empty eye socket, hears the tiny, helpless moan of life that startled him. He looks over to the darkened living area, puts the glass to his lips, drinks.

His doorbell rings. He studies the video answerphone, pushes the remote to open his gates, struggles up, hears the clock strike midnight as he walks towards his front door.

Henrik du Toit stands hunched as the door swings open. He pushes past De Vries, closes the door behind him.

'What have you done, Vaughn?'

De Vries feels dizzy, wide awake, but viciously tired.

'My duty.'

'No,' Du Toit snaps, spinning to face him. 'That you haven't. I told you: you want to survive, you obey orders, you toe the line, you keep your head down. What is it with you?'

De Vries walks past him, through the darkness, into his kitchen. 'I won't even tell you, Henrik. Then, if it all goes to shit, nothing will stick to you. You've trusted me before . . .' He leans unsteadily over the table, supporting himself with one hand, using the other to pour more wine.

'I told you to stay at home.'

De Vries shrugs. 'I did. I tidied the garden, cleaned the pool . . .'

'I came here. You'd paid a gardener to do it. I spoke to him. He told me. Why can't you let anything go?'

'Because that's what everybody else does. Someone has to take a stand.'

'Then let that someone not be you.'

'What have the Pretorian guard discovered about Grace Bellingham's abduction?'

Du Toit shakes his head. 'Not much. They interviewed Stephen Jessel in Pollsmoor. He was looking pretty beaten up – literally. Not at all co-operative.'

De Vries wonders when he will reveal Bellingham's unusable but possibly revealing sample. Potentially, it is collateral.

'They spoken to Leigh Finnemore?'

'I doubt they've been permitted to. He was taken away from his home while the searches were undertaken. Why are you obsessed with him?'

'Because everybody thinks he's a victim. They won't see what he really is. He links Apostle Lodge, Stephen Jessel, sadistic slow murder, probably with vengeance at its core.'

'Why couldn't you just have stayed at home?'

'Can't rest when I know something's wrong.'

'I can't protect you,' Du Toit says. 'Not this time. There's a nationwide warrant out for your arrest, and another officer's, a Hawks man, for God's sake, Solarin.'

'Then get out. Leave. You don't know where I am.'

'But they do,' Du Toit says. 'They'll come here.'

'Maybe.'

'What will you do?'

'Finish what I started.'

'Meaning?'

He straightens, rocks slightly, puts his hand on Du Toit's shoulder.

'To you, Henrik, there is no meaning.'

In his dreams, De Vries's mind replays his encounter with Stephen Jessel on the rooftop above Long Street. At some point, his form changes, like an image in a heat haze, a mirage, and he is then a short Chinese man holding an old-fashioned, oversized mobile phone. He bargains with De Vries, who rejects him, and then he pushes a button on the keypad and, below them, a little further up Long Street, a white lorry explodes, buildings shudder, glass shatters. Human screams and mechanical sirens mingle. De Vries feels sick, feels lost, feels responsible.

Rolf Viljoen stands at his threshold, barring any entry to Leigh Finnemore's house. De Vries steps from the scorching stone steps back onto the burned-out lawn.

'You can't keep coming here without an appointment. You will expose Leigh and that will be in direct contravention of the section-eighteen order.'

'Listen to me,' De Vries says, his stare fixed on the man. 'I have authorization from your office, complied with fully. I'm not asking for permission to interview a witness or a suspect. They make themselves available to me, or I arrest them.'

'You can't arrest a section eighteen.'

'Watch me. And watch yourself, Mr Viljoen, because I will arrest you for obstruction of a police investigation. You are here. Leigh Finnemore, I assume, is here. That is all I require.'

'But you didn't know I was present.'

'I do now.'

De Vries's head feels full and heavy, his stomach empty yet swollen. He wonders if he can retain his self-control. The sun on the back of his neck burns his skin; he has never experienced heat like this in Cape Town. He has lain in too long, too late; coffee has proven ineffectual. He looks around him; knows he has little time.

'Get out of my way, sir. Fetch Mr Finnemore and arrange for him to be interviewed by me. Do this now or I will take you both to my headquarters. You will both be charged, and you will both be imprisoned.'

Viljoen ponders, but accedes, standing aside. De Vries trots through to the back room, finds Leigh Finnemore sitting at the kitchen table. This time, there is no smile of greeting. He stares silently at De Vries who pulls a chair from under the table, sits facing Finnemore. He points to the end of the table.

'You sit there, Mr Viljoen.'

He produces two sealed packets from his pocket, puts on latex gloves, extracts, from the first one, a Perspex tube containing a cotton bud-like element, stands and moves towards Viljoen.

'Open your mouth, please, sir.'

Viljoen slides his chair back. 'What are you doing?'

'Procedure. We didn't take a DNA sample last time. We need it for the records.' Viljoen stands, stumbles backwards. De Vries looks at him, catches him glance at Finnemore. 'What's the problem, sir?'

'You. I work for Section Designation . . .'

'You could be the president, sir. We can still take DNA.'

'Not,' Finnemore says quietly, 'without an attorney.'

De Vries turns to Finnemore. The man's voice is different, strident and assured. Finnemore looks back at him, his eyes staring to the top left of the room, smiles nervously, giggles.

'What did you say, sir?'

Finnemore swallows, then sings, to a tune like a nursery rhyme, 'Not without an attorney . . .' Speaking normally. 'That's what Stephen told me.' The singing again: 'Not without an attorney.'

De Vries smiles at him sourly. 'Stephen isn't here but, if you prefer, we can all go down to the station, spend a bit of time there. I may have to put you in some cells as we're very busy but we'll probably get to you in a few hours, perhaps tomorrow . . .'

He studies Viljoen, observes his eye meet Finnemore's once more. Rolf Viljoen steps around his chair, sits down, opens his mouth. De Vries takes the sample, seals the tube and writes on it. Then he opens the second packet, proffers the bud at Finnemore, who stares at the tip as it approaches him, his eyes dark. He lets De Vries wipe the bud against the walls of his mouth. When De Vries removes it, Finnemore looks up at him, smiles mischievously. The tube is sealed, the label marked, the items replaced in his pocket.

'That was simple after all,' De Vries says, sitting back down. Neither man responds. Each seems uneasy.

'Is that it?'

He turns to Viljoen, stares at his eyes.

'No, sir. I told you. I've come to speak with your charge. I asked Leigh whether he'd ever been inside Apostle Lodge — the house at the other end of the street. Have *you* ever been inside that house?'

Viljoen's expression is set, but his breathing stalls. 'No.'

'Never?'

'No . . .' The single syllable struggles to escape from the held breath.

De Vries still stares at him, waits, watches his eyes, the pulse in his neck, the movement of his fingers interlocked with one another on the surface of the table. The silence intensifies. Viljoen's jaw locks tight.

'What do you want to ask me?' Finnemore says, his voice back to being light and musical, tone naive.

De Vries smiles, turns slowly to face him.

'You told me you had never been inside Apostle Lodge. But that isn't true, is it, Leigh?'

Finnemore regards him from his straight-backed height.

'You asked me whether I had been inside since I moved here. I told you no. That is the truth.'

'Your long-term memory isn't so bad after all.'

Finnemore sits rigid, static, says nothing.

'Your grandmother designed that house and built it. The start of a successful architectural career. You lived in Apostle Lodge as a child. You killed your sister in that house. When you came back to live here in Plumbago Lane, you told me that you and Stephen Jessel, a confessed multiple killer, went to see the house. What did you tell him about what went on in there?'

Finnemore does not move. De Vries looks over to Rolf Viljoen. 'Did you know that Mr Finnemore lived in Apostle Lodge, sir?'

Viljoen seems confused: he frowns, shakes his head.

De Vries smiles at him. 'I think you did.' He turns back to Leigh Finnemore. 'So, sir, you lived at Apostle Lodge, and when I came here to talk to you about another murder in that house, you said nothing. Why was that?'

'All my life,' Finnemore says quietly, 'for as long as I can remember, I have tried to forget what happened. Tried to understand why I did something I would never do. I'm ill. I know I'm ill, but I'm trying to get better . . .'

'That obviously works, usually?'

'What?'

'That story. Beautifully delivered, by the way. A little over-rehearsed, perhaps . . .' De Vries leans towards him over the table. 'But I didn't believe you when I first met you, and I don't believe you now.'

Finnemore remains sitting straight, his hands in his lap, his shoulders relaxed.

'What do you mean?'

'You knew exactly what you were doing twenty years ago, and you've parlayed this child-like act of yours into a very comfortable way of living, haven't you? And the man you spent so much time with, Stephen Jessel, he turns out to be a murderer too.'

He glances at Viljoen, but he sits dumbly, perplexed.

'He must have relished the idea of killing in the same house as you, Mr Finnemore. Did you discuss it? Did you consult you?'

Leigh Finnemore slowly brings his right hand up from his lap, scratches his right eyebrow, lowers his arm again. His eyes seem milky, dead. He looks in De Vries's direction, unfocused, silent.

'The keys to the doors of the anteroom between the garage and the internal staircase. No one ever found those. You had them, of course. Who did you give them to?'

Finnemore blinks languidly, his light eyelashes falling and rising almost in slow motion, his head still, breathing slow. It is as if he is falling into a trance. Rolf Viljoen gets up, moves to Finnemore, sits next to him, begins to rub his back and shoulders, starts whispering, then talking quietly, reassuring him, encouraging him to wake up, to move, to breathe. He glances at De Vries.

'You see what you've done? There's a reason this man needs protecting. He's vulnerable. You bully him, you can put him back months, years.' He raises his voice. 'This will be in my report, Colonel de Vries.'

De Vries rises, looks down at them both, certain now.

'And you, Mr Viljoen, will be in mine.'

'There are men here,' Don February says, 'looking for you.'

De Vries sighs. 'Tell them you called me, told me to come in. Don't say you haven't. They can check your cellphone.'

'You will be all right, sir?'

'Either yes, Don, or no.'

In the background, he can hear the bustle of his headquarters building: phones, fast footsteps on stone or marble, echoing. The signal seems to fade, then return strongly.

'What do I do?'

'What you always do when this happens. Keep your head down, stay in contact if it's safe. You got the package for Steve Ulton?'

'The envelope?'

'*Ja.*'

'Dr Ulton has it now.'

'I told him, so I'll tell you. Just you. Not anyone else. It's DNA from Dr Bellingham's assailant. She scratched his head, I think. Took it, preserved it. Useless in evidence now, but it could point the way.'

'You have a suspect?'

'Two. Leigh Finnemore, the section-eighteen guy at the other end of the road, and his new supervisor, Rolf Viljoen.'

'We combed that house for three days.'

'It won't be like that. Finnemore finds these men, controls them. When I get back, I'll find a way.'

'You are going somewhere?'

'Yes, Don, that's inevitable.'

'We could have met at Ben's Diner again,' Danie Malgas states. 'Had a decent piece of meat.'

De Vries laughs. The car's engine is idling, the air-conditioning fan stuttering, cabin hot and ripe. The backstreet is empty, sandy, blasted by the sun.

'Danie. You know how it is. Sometimes you don't want to be seen with someone.'

'I know,' Malgas says. 'That's why my wife always wants to do it in the dark.'

De Vries hands him the envelope.

'Hang on to it. If I don't come back, and you want to risk your pension, open it, come help me out.'

Malgas takes the fat envelope sombrely.

'What is it?'

'Just an account, evidence, of what's been going on. Someone pretty powerful in Pretoria is going to take me down. I need to know my friends have this, that they'll use it if I'm in trouble.'

'You know I will.'

'It could be just one guy and a room full of senior blind eyes. They may let him operate only while he's doing what they want him to – unofficially. If so, we may have enough to take him down, expose what this is . . .'

'What is?'

'You may never need to know. Or it could be an entire department with orders from the very top. In that case, I may just disappear.'

'Maybe that's what you should do, man. Disappear.'

'Maybe,' De Vries says, 'but that's not how I operate. Besides, I'm still working on our case.'

'A second killer?'

'Yes. And, if I'm right, a man who first killed when he was ten, who is now enabling others to kill also. Never been caught, always thought a victim.'

'Everybody is a victim now,' Malgas says.

'That's what we have to do: distinguish between the villain and the victim. Something not very fashionable.'

'Never been a problem for me.'

'Nor me,' De Vries says. 'Just everybody else.'

He sits in his car, his back aching, neck stiff. A feeling of resignation is overcoming the adrenalin that has driven him for the last forty-eight hours. He knows how quickly the depression will settle, the boredom begin to eat into him. To live for control and then to relinquish it. He shakes his head. He knows there is no other way. The back of his shirt is soaked, his groin damp, feet wrinkled, as if he has fallen asleep in the bath. He realizes that to leave his vehicle, even to buy a coffee, is to risk his liberty, but acknowledges that moment is approaching now. He closes his eyes against the bustling pavements, the busy streets, the corridor of buildings bearing down on him, seemingly converging at the horizon, trapping him, as he surely will be.

He runs through what he has done. The *New Cape Gazette*, Penelope van Reidel's surprise; Ali Jelani's weak, pitifully grateful interest. His envelopes of evidence, his reports, co-signed by Mike Solarin, the pictures, the hearsay from Eric Basson, which, if unsupported, will weaken their case, possibly fatally, all have been distributed to those whom he trusts, those whom he hopes will publish and opine and investigate. He has established safety protocols if they fail, or withdraw or recant, but even these, he fears, could be overcome.

Above all, he regrets that he still does not know whose DNA Grace Bellingham has trapped, although he suspects it will be that of Rolf Viljoen. All this time Leigh Finnemore has been present at the periphery of his vision. Finnemore knew Stephen Jessel for twenty years, perhaps Rolf Viljoen less well for half that time. He just cannot clarify who influences whom.

He glances at his watch, wonders where Mike Solarin is now. He hopes that he is among a multitude of anonymous others, unseen. To have him free provides hope that, if all else fails, there is one who can fight.

He looks up through his windscreen, then back in his mirror. He can see a group of suited men jogging up the hill towards him. He swings out of the car, stretches his shoulders, slams the door and locks the vehicle. Then he strides into the middle of Long Street, looking down at the newly laid tarmac, until he is standing in what would have been the epicentre of the explosion. Cars hoot, brake, cut each other up to avoid him, but he knows that he will not have to wait long. Already he can see two cars he recognizes as likely being unmarked SAPS cars. The men are less than one hundred metres from him, panting and sweating.

He glances around, sees two photographers on the left-hand pavement; on the balcony on the opposite side of the road, a video camera is pointed towards him. He turns to look back down the road, realizes that the cars have stopped moving, that he is suddenly alone in the street, cars beginning to back up down the hill as far as he can see. The heat on his neck is intense. The men in front of him spread out across the road, their handguns pointed at him. He raises his hands. A black car brakes behind them and the broad, bald skull of David Wertner emerges. He strides towards him, between the armed officers, the satisfied smile bursting from his pug-like features.

'I'm not even going to say it, De Vries.'

'Why not? You've waited a long time for this moment.'

Wertner leans forward, grabs De Vries's arm, turns it behind him, grabs the other wrist and cuffs him.

'You lived a charmed life, but it's over now. For good. You're on the next plane to Pretoria.'

De Vries opens his mouth, but decides that the man is not worth his breath. He walks, unresisting, with Wertner, towards the car. Two other officers flank him. He does not look at the passers-by, stationary now on the pavement, or his fellow officers, their heads turning to watch a senior officer taken down. As he turns to get into the rear of the vehicle, he resists just for a moment, looks up at the tip of the Mountain above the seemingly infinite point at the end of the street. The cable car is almost at the summit. The sun catches its revolving cabin, a ray of perfect white intensity shooting down Long Street, illuminating it for a split second, blinding him as his head is pushed inside the darkness.

EPILOGUE

Leigh Finnemore ties a bandanna over his hair, fastens the helmet. He looks at himself in the mirror: tall, slim, black Lycra, anonymous. He picks up the light sports bike, exits from the side door. He freewheels down the side of the house and onto the street. Within seconds, he is at the junction with Camps Bay Drive. He turns, drops down to the cross street below, which runs parallel with Plumbago Lane, speeds silently to the end, through a gap in the thicket of low trees. He dismounts, lays down his bike under an overhang of rock, begins to climb along and up the side of the rocky channel, which, in winter, carries water off the Mountain. The moon will be gone soon, but he does not need the light.

It takes him less than five minutes to reach his vantage point. He takes off his helmet and bandanna, sits at the place he has known his entire life. The rock allows him to take a seat and lean back, his head resting on a stone pillow. Above him, the only house visible is Apostle Lodge. It stands dark against the even deeper darkness of the Mountain. The insects squeal and buzz; the stars move in their apparent crescent around him. Time evaporates and envelops him. He never feels that he sleeps here, yet hours will pass. Perhaps, a meditation.

This night, the bird cowl twists slowly, gratingly, in the light breeze from the sea, an anguished cry, inanimate yet alive. He looks up at the Twelve Apostles, their peaks haloed by the dying moonlight, their troughs filled with spilling, perfectly white cloud.

His breathing calms. He turns back to Apostle Lodge. The view of his old home both frightens and reassures him. He thinks of his old bedroom, the cupboard that was his den, his exploration into the gorge beyond the garden, the feeling of freedom, of isolation, of control. Here, he made his decision to kill, planned how he would drown the girl; how it would be afterwards. But his life has become something more than he could have dreamed. The persona forced upon him protects and indemnifies him, allows him to take revenge unsuspected, influence and recruit, manipulate and control. He comprehends his power and the potential it bestows. He smiles to himself: it sits lightly on his shoulders.

ACKNOWLEDGEMENTS

I would like to thank Krystyna Green and Martin Fletcher, who have guided me and identified the means to hone my work into the finished product. My gratitude goes to Hazel Orme for her diligence in identifying imagined words, grammar and meanings – and for persuading me to correct them. I would also like to thank Rebecca Sheppard for patiently attending to my desire to lay out text in an unconventional way, and proof-readers who have spotted continuity irregularities and outright nonsense. Many thanks as well to my newly promoted SAPS advisor, Lieutenant Marianne Steyn. Finally, thank you to my much-cherished friends in Cape Town, who contributed ideas, comments, Afrikaans expressions and much local richness that might otherwise have eluded me, and to the composers of numerous disparate and un-noted web pages at which I have glanced and from which I have been inspired.